A WEAPON OF THE BOURGEOISIE

For all the victims of a past imperfect

Other books by David J Oldman

Looking for Ginger
A Voice from the Congo
On Wings of Death
Dusk at Dawn
The Unquiet Grave

A WEAPON OF THE BOURGEOISIE

DAVID J OLDMAN

Papaver Press

First published in this format 2017 by Papaver Press

ONE

Russia is in a <u>very bad state</u>; rotten, no food, only bread; oppression, injustice, misery among the workers and 90% discontented. I saw some very bad things, which made me mad to think that people like the Webbs (Sydney and Beatrice Webb) go there and come back, after having been led round by the nose and had enough to eat, and say that Russia is a paradise.

Letter from Gareth Jones to his parents in August 1930

1

Michael Standing was already dead when he made his last television appearance. I suppose some people may have welcomed the brief *frisson* that watching a dead man afforded although, to the possible chagrin of the morbidly curious, the news of his death did not become common knowledge until the following morning. Not that he would have attracted much of an audience in the general run of things; the fact that the programme had aired late on a Sunday evening and was — worse still — an arts programme would probably have limited the nature of its appeal to those with an interest in the subject under discussion; or, perhaps, to insomniacs. As it happens, I fall into both categories.

I heard the report of his death on the morning radio and, once over the shock, tuned into a television news channel and left it running to pick up anything fresh that might come in. Jealous of one of their own, the media had naturally made the story their lead item. Standing's wife had apparently discovered his body a little before midnight. She had been woken by a noise downstairs and, coming down, had found the front door wide open and her husband lying on the kitchen floor. Although the exact cause of death had not been disclosed, the circumstances implied that he had surprised an intruder.

The police were appealing for witnesses who might have seen Standing after he had left the television studios following the recording of his last programme, or had noticed anything out of the ordinary in the area in which he lived. Anyone with information was invited to come forward — a pleasant way of putting it, I have always thought, as if one might expect a glass of sherry while giving one's statement.

It was mid-morning when my sister, Olena, phoned. As a habitual late riser she had only just heard the news.

'Isn't it *awful*,' she said breathlessly, not making it sound awful at all. 'What are you going to do?'

'Me?' I said. 'Why should *I* do anything?'

'Well, you knew him. And he's got our stuff.'

'I didn't *know* him,' I said. 'We met a couple of times, that's all.'

'*Honestly!*' she said and I realized it was going to be one of those conversations, where emphasising words was going to take the place of saying what we really meant. I was use to abuse from my sister but her becoming suddenly proprietorial about *our* stuff was a new tack.

'Do you think his wife did it?' she asked.

'What do you mean, *did it*? They haven't said it was murder yet. For all we know he died of natural causes.'

She snorted down the phone. 'You haven't met her,' she said.

'And you have?'

'You know very well I have,' she said. 'I told you last summer.'

Her reply was quite off-hand but I still managed to detect a note triumph in her voice, betraying the fact that she was pleased to be able to point up my habitual inattention again.

'I swear you never listen to a word anyone tells you, Alex. No wonder you've grown into a lonely old bachelor.' Having caught me with that jab, she moved on quickly before I was able to respond. 'If you remember,' she said. 'I told you we were introduced at a gallery exhibition a few months ago. *He* wasn't there, of course.'

I wasn't sure what I was supposed to infer from Michael Standing's absence from one of Olena's tedious exercises in social preening, but to her the fact was now in some way obviously pertinent. What I *was* sure I was supposed to infer, from her remarks about my age, marital status and emotional well-being, was that she expected more effort on my part, to pull myself together and become an elder brother she didn't need to be ashamed of. But there was nothing new in this, and she was well aware that I didn't consider the elements of my life so widely disseminated that they needed pulling together. It was still too early in the morning for

Olena to mount a proper attack though, and this amounted to little more than the usual sparring. Hardly worth defending.

'Anyway,' I said, letting it pass, 'why would his wife do it? Assuming it was *done.*'

'Come *on!*' Olena said. 'You know, a man like that? He must have had women all over the place.'

She, of course, would have liked to have been one of them. Earlier in the year Standing had invited me to lunch following our first meeting and, when I was foolish enough to have told Olena, she had badgered me into letting her join us, wanting to concoct some elaborate plan to meet me 'accidentally' at the restaurant. I'd quashed that idea, although in the event, the prospect of her popping out on us from between the potted ferns like a predatory Stanley buttonholing an unsuspecting Livingstone had quite ruined my appetite. It was one reason I hadn't told her that Standing had been in touch again.

'I know nothing of the sort,' I told her. 'As far as I'm aware he was happily married.'

'A woman like that doesn't make people happy,' she announced authoritatively. 'There's something odd about her.'

'The only thing odd about her from your point of view,' I said, deciding to hit back after all, 'is that she still has a husband.'

She said, 'Bollocks,' and hung up, a reaction that while not wholly out of character, still left me with a feeling of irritation.

As I put the phone down I realized, of course, that I was wrong: Julia Standing no longer had a husband; he had been left for dead on her kitchen floor.

I was considering this and still looking at the phone when it rang again, startling me and knocking the thought out of my head. This time it was my former brother-in-law — Olena's ex-husband, that is, — Nicholas Maitland. I had always liked Nick and the divorce hadn't really changed much between us.

'You've heard about Michael Standing, I suppose,' he began.

After Standing's first approach, I had steered him in Nick's direction. Nick and I were cousins as well as brothers-in-law and shared not only a history and a grandmother but also a surname. What little that had survived of our grandmother's papers had come to me through my father, but I had thought there was a chance that something of interest to Standing might still be in the Maitland family's possession. Oddly enough, it turned out that Nick and

Standing had been contemporaries at Cambridge and was already acquainted.

'This morning,' I told him. 'Did you know him well?'

We had talked about this before but I thought some sort of expression of condolence might be in order.

'No,' Nick said. 'Until he got in touch a few months ago I don't suppose I'd seen him since Cambridge. As a matter of fact, he didn't even remember that we'd been at university together.' He paused before adding, 'They said he was on the TV last night. You watched, I suppose.'

'Yes.'

'Still having trouble sleeping then.'

Not wanting to go over familiar ground, I told him that I'd just spoken to Olena. He didn't show any curiosity about that so I said, 'I was wondering whether I ought to contact the police.'

'Why?' Nick asked. 'I can't imagine this has got anything to do with what he was working on.'

'You mean the Holodomor?' I said, a little nonplussed. 'Hardly.'

'The what?'

'Holodomor,' I said. 'It's the Ukrainian name for the famine.' I suppose I was a little surprised that Nick had not heard of the Holodomor, but then he had never shown much interest in that side of his family's background however tenuous the links. 'No,' I went on, 'I was wondering whether I should tell them I had an appointment with him on Saturday. We were supposed to lunch together but he never showed. I thought they might be interested.'

'I didn't know that,' Nick said. 'That he'd been in touch with you again, I mean. Anyway, isn't that just television crime dramas where they interview everyone the victim last spoke to?'

'Routine procedure, I think.'

'Well, you should know,' he said, taking his customary dig at what he supposed had been my background. 'From what I gather he came home late and disturbed an intruder. They'll probably be concentrating on that angle so I shouldn't think they'd be interested in you. Anyway, if he didn't turn up for your lunch you've got nothing to tell them, have you?'

'Except the fact that he didn't turn up,' I said. 'But you're probably right. He would have seen dozens of people in the last few days. Why would they want to talk to me?'

'Exactly.' He paused a second, then said, 'You've not got a guilty conscience, have you Alex?'

I laughed. 'And here I am without an alibi.'

'You can always say you were here.' For a moment there was one of those heavy, pregnant silences, lasting just long enough for me to wonder if he was serious. Then *he* laughed. 'I'm joking, of course.'

'Actually,' I said, 'I'm more concerned about getting my father's papers back. I was wondering if it might prove difficult ... now he's dead, I mean.'

Nick dismissed the thought. 'I don't see why there should be a problem. After all, they're yours so they're not going to get tied up in his estate or anything. Do you know where they are?'

'No idea.'

'Well, if there's anything I can do...'

I thanked him but said I didn't suppose there was. Then I asked after his father, my Uncle George, as I hadn't seen him since he had given up his City directorships and retired to the country.

'As a matter of fact,' Nick said, 'I'm going down this weekend. I've got to show my face in the constituency but I'll be staying with Dad. Why don't you come down with me if you've nothing else on?'

Nick was a Member of Parliament — one of the up-and-coming new breed, if you believed anything you ever heard concerning politicians — and had a rural constituency bordering the New Forest. Having been elected to represent the area, it was, unsurprisingly, where his father had chosen to retire.

It was a rare weekend I had anything on but I didn't want to admit that to Nick. To tell the truth, I had wanted to talk to George for months and, although Standing's murder had rather taken the wind out of my sails, I could see it would be an ideal opportunity. Besides, a change of scene rather appealed to me. I'd always got on well with George and his wife Jennifer — well, with George, anyway. My getting on with Jennifer was an entirely different matter. As it happened, back in the summer I had asked George if he still had any papers relating to his mother, Nastasiya, or to my father that had turned up in *his* father's papers. But I'd caught him in the process of moving out of his London house and the timing was inconvenient. Since I'd also given George's number to Standing, though, I was curious to know whether he'd been in touch.

I told Nick I'd like to go down with him as long as I wasn't going to inconvenience anyone and he said he'd pick me up at around five on Friday afternoon.

'And don't worry about the police,' he insisted, laughing. 'Just think of all those other historians who must have been itching to bump him off and take his place on the television.'

I put the phone down and decided that he was probably right. I'd get my papers back sooner or later. After all, they had no value except one of sentiment, and then — despite Olena's remark — only for me.

But if he was right about the family papers, Nick was wrong about the police.

2

Michael Standing had, I admit, caught me at something of a loose end. If he hadn't, perhaps I wouldn't have got involved. I might just have given him what he wanted and left it at that — no curiosity, no digging around. But then, ultimately, I suppose no answers. And I can't deny that it might have been better that way — at least without answers I would have kept my illusions. Or perhaps I should call them misconceptions. Whichever, that way I would have kept my peace of mind. But there are always trade-offs in any exchange and I suppose one can never tell what the chances of breaking even will be. When it comes down to it, it seems to me that getting to the truth must always be a gamble and, as in any gamble, one is attempting to beat the odds. Put like that, though, it suggests that we are little more than punters betting against the house — which naturally begs the question: who runs the house?

~

Dear Mr. Maitland,

I was most interested in the memoir of your father posted on The Foreign Few website and the fact that he was born in the Ukraine with the family name of Zaretsky. I am presently researching Ukrainian émigrés from the nineteen-thirties and wondered if your father might have held any papers — letters, photographs, diaries, that sort of thing — dating from that period which you might be kind enough to allow me sight of. Also, would you know if your family might in any way have been related to an Aleksander Zaretsky of Kharkov?

Regards, David Griffiths.

Dear Mr. Griffiths,

In answer to your enquiry concerning my father, Petro Zaretsky, am I right in thinking that your interest in Ukrainian émigrés lies with those who served in the RAF during WW2? Or are you researching émigrés who served in all of the Services? I'm afraid my familiarity is with the RAF only. However I do have some papers that belonged to my grandmother. She brought my father to this country in 1932 although her husband, my paternal grandfather, was never able to follow her. His name was Aleksander Zaretsky, but of course Zaretsky is not a particularly uncommon Ukrainian name and it's anyone's guess at the number of men called Aleksander. I do not know from exactly where he came. The last that was heard of my grandfather, I believe, was shortly after my grandmother's departure in 1932. The family has always assumed that he either died in the famine in the Ukraine, as did so many, or ended his days in one of Stalin's camps. My father never spoke much about his own origins and, for my part, I have to admit to not really having examined these particular papers that closely, most of them having been written in Russian (Ukrainian?). If you are able to give me some idea of your precise area of interest, however, I might be able to see if I have anything that might be relevant to your research.

Yours, Alex Maitland

Following the exchange of emails, it came as something of a surprise when I was contacted, not by David Griffiths, but by Michael Standing. He telephoned me one winter's Friday afternoon and, after some initial scepticism on my part as to with whom I was speaking, he said that he happened to be in the area and wondered if he might call upon me. Despite my doubts as to whether Standing ever just "happened" to be in any particular area and my surprise that he knew in which particular one I lived, I agreed and gave him directions.

Michael Standing, it hardly needs remarking, was an academic whose looks, voice, and particular brand of charm had made him a natural for television. As well as holding the chair in history at one of the Cambridge colleges, he was also a Senior Associate of Modern East European Studies at one or other of the prestigious American universities, positions that apparently hadn't precluded his finding time to make two very well received television history series in the UK. The purpose of his last appearance — on the evening of his death — was to offer (in the presence of the author) his opinion on a newly published history of the Russian Revolution. The early years of the Bolshevik Revolution were Standing's speciality and, as ever, he was charmingly erudite and objective, if unable to pass up the opportunity to plug his own work on the subject — a *quid pro quo* no doubt expected in those situations. Edward Maseryk, an historian of some repute in his own right, was also there to give his opinion — one in this case to which was added the piquancy of his being a Czech who had fled the 1968 Russian invasion — but an opinion which differed in several respects from Standing's own interpretation of the Revolution. It was unfortunate for the poor author of the book under discussion that their ensuing argument quite eclipsed both him and his ability to plug his own work.

My first reaction upon answering the door to Standing was that he was not as good looking in real life as he appeared on television. In the flesh his skin was a little more pockmarked and his hair a little thinner than they looked on screen. He was also wearing glasses, something that I did not remember from television. But then, it wasn't conventional good looks that marked him out as an historian and presenter. I had often thought there was something oddly casual about his appearance while watching him stride across an east European square or standing in front of one of those proto-brutalist architectural monstrosities the comrades had favoured. He'd more often be found in shabby Levis, checked shirt and crumpled jacket, than in a tailored suit; or scarfed and shod in a manner more suited to a trudge across a desert than for posing in front of some totemic Soviet statue or the baroque architecture of Prague or Budapest. He would have stuck out like a Dali limb, for instance, atop the mausoleum in Red Square attending a Mayday parade — for those who are old enough to remember them, that is. But no doubt had his director required him to do so he would have donned, like those grim old men use to, a heavy topcoat to fend off the icy Moscow wind. (They kept chairs up there for the less robust, apparently, and even a room with a bar, although despite such comforts Sverdlov, the first Bolshevik Head of State and tsar-killer, died in 1919 after catching a chill there. As, incidentally, did Klement Gottwald, the President of Soviet Czechoslovakia, after an interminable vigil attending Stalin's funeral. Probably not quite the manner of dying for the cause that either would have envisaged for themselves).

Poised as Standing was on my doorstep, despite the discrepancies in appearance, I found the charm that penetrated the camera all too real. He gave me a grin and apologised for any imposition. I, of course, said there was none and felt flattered by his interest, which, no doubt, was the intention. I asked him in and, when I enquired about David Griffiths, was told he was a post-graduate student doing research on Standing's behalf but that he had thought he might follow up this particular line of enquiry himself — if I had no objections.

Flattered, as I have said, I had none. But neither did I have any idea what possible interest my father's wartime service could hold for Michael Standing.

It was, I recall, a day in late February and there was just enough weak sunlight straining through the French windows to brighten the dining table that stood at one end of my lounge. I made a pot of tea and found a few biscuits that weren't so stale that they risked offending a television celebrity and set the tray on the table so we might enjoy the last of the afternoon light. We made small talk for a minute or two while I poured the tea. He held the cup in his hands as if grateful for the warmth.

His eyes, I noticed, were a particularly pale shade of blue and his gaze had a tendency to wander around the room, appraising as it went — looking perhaps for an historical context in which to place me. Given the state of the decor, if he found one he was polite enough not to mention it.

I was unaware back then, of course, of the attraction he held for my sister although his popularity among his female audience was no secret. And it wasn't just his looks. His first television series had not, as it happened, had any bearing on Bolshevik Russia but had ranged widely across those dark ages of Crusade and Christian conversion from the Baltic down to Turkey and it was his knack, even in the most inhospitable of territories, to make one wish that you were making the journey alongside him.

I asked if he had any plans for another series and he launched into a lecture on the possibilities of filming an account of the changing politics of Eastern Europe and the shifting balances of power in the region, which, by the time he had finished, I realized had not answered my question at all.

'I have been approached,' he confessed modestly, 'but there's nothing definite as yet. At present I'm researching Soviet-Ukrainian relations in the twenties and thirties.'

'Really?' I said, although before I could expand my platitudinous reply, he went on:

'Your father, I don't suppose he ever mentioned a foreigner he might have met while he was in the Ukraine, an American or Englishman, perhaps, by the name of Shostak? A shot in the dark, I know...'

'Shostak?' I said, not even needing to give it any thought. 'I can't say that I do. Of course, he was only a young boy when he left. Is that a Ukrainian name?'

Standing sipped at his tea. 'Ukrainian, yes, but not necessarily a proper name. That's why I asked. Shostak is the Russian or Ukrainian version of a nickname for someone who has a six-fingered hand. It's Shastak in Belorussian and Shóstak in Polish. It's supposedly derived from the szósty, a Polish coin, but actually its root is Jewish eastern Ashkenazic. Then again,' he said, 'it's some people's actual surname.'

'You seem to have taken a lot of trouble over it,' I observed.

'It's interesting,' he said, smiling tightly in that way some people have when they're reluctant to say more.

The whole notion struck me as peculiar.

'Odd that there are so many nicknames for that particular condition, isn't it?' I asked. 'Does it mean having six fingers is a common mutation in that region?'

His blue eyes widened a little. 'It just might,' he said and shrugged. 'Isolated communities. I remember there was a family of cats where I used to live in Dorset that had six claws on their front paws, although I've not come across it in humans before. I suppose it must happen, though. Then, as I say, it might also be a proper name and have nothing to do with extra fingers.'

'Sorry,' I said, 'but it means nothing to me.'

'What about the Black Sea Company?'

'No, I'm afraid not. What's that?'

'A trading company. No matter. Fred Beal?' he hazarded.

I shook my head.

'No matter,' he said again. He looked down at his hands for a moment as if compelled to count his own fingers. 'Perhaps you're familiar with the name, Gareth Jones, then?'

Having drawn a blank on his first queries, I gave him the courtesy of a moment's thought on Gareth Jones although I didn't really need to.

'I don't think so,' I finally answered judiciously. 'Who is he?'

'He was a Welsh journalist. He was on Lloyd George's staff in the late twenties. He went to Russia for the first time in nineteen-thirty.'

I suppose I must have been showing a modicum of interest because he explained:

'His mother had spent a few years there as a tutor and the stories she told him as a boy about the country inspired him to learn the language and travel there when he could. His mother had worked for the son of a Welsh industrialist who had actually founded a town in Russia — Hughesovka.'

He paused long enough to bite into one of the biscuits, dropping crumbs down the front of his sweater.

'The Russia Jones saw would have been a very different country from the one his mother remembered,' he went on, spraying fragments of biscuit as he spoke before decorously touching a knuckle to the side of his mouth as if that would solve the problem. 'He'd been up at Oxford and had done very well. Something of an intellectual. I don't know, but I suspect that like a lot of people in his circumstances he may have been predisposed to think well of the Marxist experiment.'

He raised his eyebrows as if he thought I might like to give my opinion of the experiment since the topic had been raised and, although I had one, I wasn't about to give it in front of a specialist like Standing. What I was chiefly thinking as he widened his eyes again, was that the paler skin at the corner of his eyes betrayed the fact that he was quite tanned and, given the time of year, he must have been abroad to catch the sun.

'You probably know,' he went on, 'that with foreign visitors and journalists the Bolshevik authorities took a lot of trouble to create a good impression. Jones was taken on a tour of one of their new State Farms — up-to-date machinery and buildings ... the kind of place guaranteed to receive a favourable response. Jones was his own man, though, and he wasn't fooled. He did his own travelling where he could and kept his eyes open. He saw the conditions for what they truly were. Even more unusual for a foreign visitor, he wasn't afraid to speak and write about what he found. Unlike those bloody fools from the Fabian society, Shaw and the Webbs, Stalin didn't blind him. He was more concerned with the people than with the Bolshevik bigwigs and their theories and ideology.'

One of Michael Standing's more likeable traits, I later came to appreciate, was that he spoke his mind in plain language. Beatrice and Sydney Webb, I suppose, have been fair game for years but George Bernard Shaw still has his adherents. Not many people even now would casually dismiss him as a fool; fewer still, I suspect, would have risked doing so to his face, although I wouldn't have put it past Standing.

'Jones wasn't impressed then,' I said.

'Not entirely, no. It didn't stop him going back, though, in nineteen-thirty-one when the American, Ivy Lee asked him.' He paused, perhaps wondering if I'd heard of Ivy Lee, but I must have looked as blank over this name as all the others. 'Lee was one of the founders of modern public relations and had all sorts of Wall Street connections. He was thinking of writing a book about Russia and had persuaded Jack Heinz — one of the baked bean family? — to go on a fact-finding tour for him. Heinz didn't speak the language, though, and Jones was just the kind of man they needed. The Bolsheviks, as you can imagine, weren't keen on their travelling independently and did their best to prevent them going anywhere unsupervised. What Stalin termed "dekulakization" had been underway for several years by then — finishing what Lenin had begun ten years earlier — and they'd also started on their programme of Collectivization. The result was chaos in the countryside. Riots and deportations and real hunger.' He gave me a grim smile. 'Even the Webbs might have been able to see that, but you never know... Anyway, Jones and Heinz managed to get down to the Ukraine. What they saw there appalled them.'

'The famine you mean?'

'Yes. Do you know much about it?'

'I've read a bit,' I said, 'although not as much as I should. My father never spoke about it even though he must have been old enough to remember what it was like before he left. Too traumatic, perhaps.'

'When was that, exactly?'

'When he left? Nineteen-thirty-two.'

'It got a lot worse after that.' Standing frowned, as if the memories were his own. 'Gareth Jones was there again in thirty-three and thirty-five. His last visit was at the behest of William Randolph Hearst.'

'The real Citizen Kane?' I said just to let him know that I did have the odd inconsequential fact at my fingertips.

He nodded and smiled. 'It must be galling to be remembered not for your life but for a parody of it.'

'More galling to be forgotten altogether,' I suggested.

'Possibly,' although he didn't sound convinced.

'Jones went back, then?'

'Yes. After his first visit he wrote several articles on the famine.' He gave a small helpless shrug. 'Needless to say his reports brought all of Stalin's apologists out of the woodwork, denying that it was anything worse than the unfortunate result of a bad harvest. How good or bad the harvest really was is still a matter of some dispute, although what isn't is the fact that Stalin, rather than feed the grain to the people, sold much of what there was overseas to help pay for his programme of Industrialization. There is also evidence that grain was withheld as a punishment for the Ukrainian nationalist agitation.'

I gestured at the pot and poured him some more tea. He glanced at me almost apologetically over the top of his spectacles as if he was afraid he might be boring me. 'But perhaps you know all this.'

'No, not at all,' I assured him. 'My father never really talked about his boyhood in the Ukraine and I'm sure he never mentioned Gareth Jones.'

'I doubt if he would have ever heard his name,' Standing said. 'Jones has been rather airbrushed from history. You have to understand that back in the thirties society was quite polarized over politics and before word of the worst repression got out there was a lot of western support for the Soviets and no shortage of people ready to come to their defence.' He grinned at me. 'Intellectuals and academics, perhaps, but no less sincere for all that. It was later, when Jones worked for Hearst, that the dirty tricks started.

'Strangely,' he said, edging closer on his chair, 'when his reports for Hearst appeared there were none of the usual denials. But when Hearst ran a story a little while later by an American named Thomas Walker about the famine with some accompanying photographs, one of Stalin's creatures, a man named Fischer, was almost immediately able to show that the photographs had been faked. Naturally, this not only discredited Hearst and Walker but Jones's earlier work as well.'

'A put up job, then,' I suggested.

'There is quite a bit of evidence pointing to the fact that Walker was a Russian stooge,' he said. 'So rather than it being Hearst trying to fake a story, it could well have been the Bolsheviks faking one they could easily discredit. And, by association, all of Jones's earlier stuff into the bargain.'

'Disinformation theory,' I offered.

Standing peered at me, wondering perhaps what I might know of disinformation theory.

'Conveniently for them,' he went on after a moment, 'when all this came out Jones was in China and in no position to defend himself. A few months later, he was dead, murdered by Chinese bandits.'

I pushed the biscuits towards him, beginning to wonder where this was all leading.

'There's no evidence, of course,' Standing said, taking another, 'but it has been suggested that his murder was arranged by Stalin's police.'

'This is all very interesting,' I interrupted once he had his mouth full, 'and forgive me if I seem a little dense, but I don't see that this has much to do with Ukrainian personnel in the RAF.'

He looked at me nonplussed. I gave him the gist of David Griffiths' email and my reply.

Standing pulled absently at one of his earlobes. 'And that's been the extent of your contact with David?'

'I'm afraid so.'

'Sorry, but David didn't go into detail with me. Or you either, apparently.'

'Apparently,' I echoed. 'So if this doesn't have anything to do with the RAF, how was it he got on to me? I don't understand.'

Standing finished his tea and placed the cup back on the saucer.

'What do you do for a living, Mr Maitland? If you don't mind my asking.'

It was the perennially awkward question, if one which I was practised at fending.

'I was a civil servant,' I said without elaborating. 'Retired now.'

'Oh? Well perhaps you might have some idea of the kind of work we do when we start researching a project like this.'

I might have reminded him that he hadn't exactly explained what the project he was working on was, but I let it pass.

'Paperwork,' he said. 'That's how it begins for me.' He made a circular motion by his ear. 'I have this vague concept in my head of how I want the thing to be and once that has some sort of form, I start looking for the material with which to construct it. I know the field, of course, so I've a head start, but it's the particulars I'm looking for. Once I have a general idea of what they are, it's time to begin ferreting around for the detail. Do you understand what I mean?'

I wasn't sure I did but I can nod persuasively.

'I'm not easy to live with at this stage,' he admitted with a boyish grin I suspected was part of his presenter's palette. 'My wife, Julia, takes the brunt, I'm afraid. I think I tend to get rather preoccupied and withdrawn. It's probably no better once we get down to chasing the details. That involves time and generally a lot of travelling.'

I tried to look sympathetic.

'You can't imagine the tedious nature of the documents we have to wade through. Foreign office reports, diplomatic traffic, committee memoranda ... all the records that get released years after most normal people have lost interest in them. Historians aren't normal people, of course.' He offered me a self-deprecatory smile I suspected might have worn thin on his wife years ago. 'But the real interest for me lies in the individuals. More personal accounts survive than you might think. We had a head start here, as there was a U.S. Commission on the Ukrainian famine that reported to Congress in nineteen eighty-eight. There was some very useful material there. Eyewitness accounts, that sort of thing. Then there are Jones's articles, naturally, and the journal that Jack Heinz kept. Jones also kept a diary although you can't imagine how bad his handwriting was and how long it's taken to decipher it.'

'Forgive me,' I interrupted. 'You're saying you're working on the Ukrainian famine, yes? But I'm afraid I still don't understand how this led David Griffiths to my father.'

'Cross-referencing, probably. Anyone whose name crops up more than once and who isn't one of the usual suspects is flagged-up. David would have done that sort of work in his spare time. It's almost like an antidote to the donkeywork one usually has to do.' He brightened. 'Of course, these days the Internet is a boon. What you read is quite likely to be unreliable but it's an outstanding way of making connections.'

Surprised, I said, 'You're saying Griffiths googled my father?'

Standing smiled apologetically. 'Your grandfather, actually.' He put a finger out and swivelled his empty cup around on its saucer. He looked at me sideways and I suddenly had the feeling he was about to broach a subject that he thought might be a little indelicate.

'Did your father tell you anything about the conditions in the Ukraine when he left?'

I opened my mouth to answer but found I didn't have one. My father's background and childhood were subjects on which he never spoke.

'As I said earlier,' I told him, 'he never liked to talk about it. Understandable, perhaps.'

Standing looked disappointed.

'Do you know where he lived before he left?'

'Kharkov,' I said, although I was by no means certain. 'It was the capital of the Ukraine then, wasn't it?'

'For a while it was, yes.' He was frowning and I assumed things had not turned out as well as he had hoped. 'The worst of the starvation was in the countryside. How old did you say he was when he came to England?'

'Twelve.'

Standing grunted with what I took to be an expression of dissatisfaction. But he seemed to make an effort to pull himself together and gave me a smile out of his television box of charm.

'David probably *did* google your grandfather — in a fashion. His name was Aleksander Zaretsky, wasn't it? You mentioned him in your article.'

'Not exactly,' I admitted reluctantly, not really wanting to disappoint him further, 'I said my father's original *name* was Zaretsky. In my email I think I suggested that it wasn't a particularly unusual Ukrainian name. I dare say there are hundreds of Aleksander Zaretskys.'

'Point taken,' he said. 'But in this instance the dates do fit.'

In retrospect, I really should have made my excuses then... I had the garden to dig, I was expecting company, Friday was my day for cleaning the toilets ... that sort of thing. Instead, like a fool, I asked:

'What dates?'

He pushed his spectacles back onto the bridge of his nose with a finger in a gesture I came to recognise prefigured a history lesson.

'Nineteen-nineteen to begin with,' he said. He leaned forward on his chair again, hunching his shoulders. 'Forgive me, but you have to understand the nature of the relationship between Russia and the Ukraine to fully appreciate why the famine happened. Apart from two or three brief periods over the previous four hundred years, the Ukraine had been part of the Russian Empire and was always regarded by them as such. In fact,' he said, 'it was known as "Little Russia". The Revolution changed nothing. Although Marxist philosophy maintained that there would be no nations or nationalities in a communist state and that everyone would be equal, it was a case of Russians being first among equals in a Russian revolution. The old notion that the Ukraine was an integral part of Russia merely bolstered the attitude that any sense of "nationhood" among the Ukrainians was *counter*-revolutionary. And you have to add to this the Bolshevik attitude towards the peasants — although here at least they were even-handed and as ruthlessly repressive towards the Russian peasant as they were to the Ukrainian. It was an ideological problem, you see.'

He absently raised and examined his empty teacup as if about to assess its value and I had the sudden impression that, even if I had picked him up bodily and sat him in a tub of ice-cold water, it still wouldn't have stopped him talking. He was into his subject and everything extraneous to it had been forgotten.

'Marxism, of course, is based upon the concept of class struggle and was devised to apply to an industrialized society. Their problem was that a peasantry defies classification in those terms. An agrarian working class is not a proletariat. The peasantry was made up of many different status levels. There were those who held several acres of land and employed others — the type who, in a town would be regarded as petty-bourgeois — those again who had a few acres which they worked on their own behalf, employing no one outside of their own family unit, and then there were others still who only had an acre or two that they tilled, hiring themselves out to augment their income. Then there were the landless peasants who worked for others and, at the bottom of the heap, the shiftless drunkards who neither held land nor worked at all if they could possibly avoid it. It was a custom for most of the above, at least as far as the Ukrainian peasant was concerned in particular, to hire out their labour in the towns for certain parts of the year as carpenters, builders and the like to make up their wage over the months when there was little to do on the land.'

I started to speak but Standing held up his hand. 'I'm getting to it,' he promised, 'but you do need to understand the background.'

I wasn't sure I *needed* to understand anything. I think I glanced surreptitiously at my watch, but I had no pressing appointments and no convincing excuses. And Standing was hitting his stride.

'Between the Bolshevik seizure of power in October nineteen-seventeen and the treaty of Brest-Litovsk in March nineteen-eighteen, the Ukraine for the most part found itself caught between Germany-Austria and Russia. An independent government, the RADA, had to evacuate Kiev in the face of an advancing Red Army and when they arrived the Bolsheviks took control. They were only there long enough to organize some grain seizures before the Germans advanced again and set up a puppet government. After Brest-Litovsk, they enjoyed a brief spell of self-determination but Lenin wasn't prepared to let them go and he sent the Red Army in again in nineteen-nineteen. Out of necessity, the Bolsheviks cobbled together a sort of proletarian peasantry to run the villages through councils, although in fact these consisted in reality of nothing more than a few of the poorest peasants shorn up by thousands of working class proletariat shipped out to the countryside from the towns. The real problem for Lenin was that the Bolsheviks never had more than a trickle of support among the peasantry. After all, what they wanted was to work their own land in their own way with a minimum of outside interference. Reasonable enough, you might think, but that sort of attitude ran directly counter to Bolshevik thinking.

'Of course,' he went on, 'these peasant councils didn't go down well with the vast majority of the population and there was a lot of violence. To make matters worse, given the nature of the men told to enforce Bolshevik rule, there was widespread drunkenness, arbitrary theft, beatings and executions ... all hugely counter-productive. Even Lenin eventually came to see it wasn't working and told his man in the Ukraine, the Ukrainian Cheka chief, Martin Ivanovich Lācis, to get rid of the disruptive elements.' He stopped abruptly and skewered me with a look. 'Do you know anything about Lācis?'

I felt distinctly like the classroom dunce although, given my past performance, I don't think he was expecting much.

'Sorry,' I said.

'Lenin told him to get Dzerzhinsky to help.'

'Ah,' I said, finally managing to get my name on the scoreboard. 'Felix Dzerzhinsky? Wasn't he the man who founded the Cheka, the forerunner of the KGB?'

22

I half-expected a sigh of relief.

'That's right,' Standing said, 'Cheka ... OGPU ... NKVD ... KGB... they all come down to the same thing. They're all acronyms for police oppression, all interchangeable and, ultimately, the most visible indication that the system wasn't working. The point being,' he said with a gesticulation that had QED written all over it, 'is that by the time you have to resort to the secret policeman, it's too late to go back.'

I felt I might have given him an argument about that, although first, of course, we would have had to agree on a definition of "secret policeman".

'Lācis...' Standing said. 'Well, he's better known as Latsis actually — Lācis is the Lithuanian version of his name Latsis— is the Russian. He was Lithuanian. Dzerzhinsky himself was Polish. A lot of Lenin's Chekists were non-Russian, a fact Stalin later came to find problematic.' The eyebrows came into play again and he gave me what passes for the pedant's apology. 'To be absolutely correct,' he said, 'Lācis was born Jānis Sudrabs, but nobody uses that name for him...'

Given the alternative passports I had locked away upstairs in my safe, I began to wonder whether Standing and I would have differed very much in our definition of a secret policeman after all.

'...well,' he went on imperturbably. 'Lācis used solid Party men to weed out the worst offenders. Although it has to be remembered that everything is relative — Lācis himself had an appalling track record and was even given to shooting dead in the street anyone he heard speaking Ukrainian, so if this is the kind of man you employ to moderate the actions of your controlling organs...' he tailed off and shrugged. 'Unfortunately it's a fact of life that being an exemplar in the field of severity and brutality is how people make their way in secret police organisations. As it happens, Stalin had him shot in the purges of the late thirties when he began clearing out the non-Russians.'

'Perhaps there is some kind of justice, then,' I observed.

He glanced at me morosely. 'I wouldn't go that far,' he said. 'Along with Lācis and the hundreds of other police agents Stalin disposed of, there were hundreds of *thousands* — millions probably — of innocent men, women and children that were shot, or starved, or deported. Lācis was a just a drop in an ocean.'

His eyes slid off me, looking elsewhere and he lapsed into silence. Perhaps it was the documentation of these atrocities that he had once examined, or the faces of the people themselves that he had somehow conjured and could now see.

I took advantage of the lull. 'But my grandfather,' I said. 'You still haven't told me where you got his name from to begin with.'

'I'm coming to that,' he promised. 'First, you obviously know who OGPU were?'

'Yes,' I said. 'The Soviet secret police. At least, in one of their guises.'

'In one of their guises,' he repeated. 'Lenin had set up the Cheka during the civil war when they were worried about spies and counter-insurgency and that sort of thing. The Okhrana, the old tsarist secret police, had been pretty hopeless by comparison. Although they had infiltrated various revolutionary groups, the revolutionaries had infiltrated *them* as well. It was difficult to say who was working for whom. A bit like *The Man Who Was Thursday*.'

'Chesterton's satire on revolutionary organisations?' I said, scoring my second point.

He seemed mildly surprised. 'I didn't think anyone read it anymore.'

'It was a long time ago,' I confessed. 'Not a lot of bite.'

He laughed, but not at my literary criticism. 'As a matter of fact, a few years ago someone thought they'd made a discovery when they turned up Stalin's Okhrana file and found he'd been in their pay. The surprise, of course, would have been to find that he hadn't been. After all, the best way to find out how much the opposition knows is to have a man on the inside, isn't it?'

I smiled innocently. 'I suppose it is.'

'Anyway, after the civil war the Cheka was allowed to run down. The Whites were finished and the foreign incursions had come to nothing and they'd just about crushed whatever was left of opposition within the movement. Economically, though, the state was in a mess. Grain production had dropped off a cliff and people were going hungry. The Bolsheviks were still widely unpopular in the countryside as they had had to resort to grain seizures in the same way as they had during the civil war. It caused a lot of unrest and several uprisings, particularly in the Ukraine. So Lenin ramped up the security again. First they were called the PGU, founded in nineteen-twenty-two, and then they became the OGPU.'

He paused and took a deep breath. I realized he had finally reached the point.

He looked at me seriously. 'Going through the files of that U.S. Commission report I mentioned, Zaretsky's name cropped up more than once. He was mentioned several times, in fact. The first time we came across him was as one of the men Lācis used to clean up the peasant councils.'

'Wait a minute,' I said. 'Are you trying to tell me that my grandfather was an OGPU man?'

He stopped and gave me the benefit of his sympathy.

'Yes,' he said, 'I'm afraid I am. Zaretsky was a Chekist.' He rubbed his hands together. 'So, what can you tell me about him?'

3

I have always thought of myself as a cautious man, although by which agent of the old dichotomy, nurture or nature, I couldn't say. Any praiseworthy attributes I may possess I have always readily claimed for myself as natural; any defects I have always blamed on my training. The one drawback of this defence has been my inability to submit any facts in evidence. Secrecy has always been paramount. A training that teaches you to lie, to practice subterfuge, to spy on your fellows and, ultimately, to betray those to whom one has become close, is hardly a defensible regime and therefore it is all the more galling when, having such a useful scapegoat to hand, I have never actually been able to use it in mitigation. Given all that, I suppose that it should have come as no surprise when one finds oneself on the receiving end.

Only it always does, of course.

The words I had exchanged with Michael Standing about justice and secret police organisations stayed with me long after he himself had gone. Both were a subject I knew something about although, as I say, I couldn't have told Standing that. I've always had some notion of the concept of justice, ill defined though it might have been, and that was probably why, once in the army, I applied for the Military Police. In the event it gave me no more than the opportunity to pull Nick's leg over the fact that he wasn't the first member of the Maitland family to become an MP, although at the time I had entertained the vague notion that it might be a good apprenticeship for a career in the civilian police force if I decided not to stay in the army. As it happens, after only a year or so as a redcap, I was co-opted into Military Intelligence. It was something for which I had an aptitude, I discovered, and when, as my first term of enlistment came close to expiring and I had to make a decision as to whether or not I stayed in, I was approached by a civilian who asked me what I planned to do after my service. It transpired he was from one of the Intelligence Services scouting for likely recruits and he persuaded me to go for an interview.

I had never thought of myself as a secret policeman *per se* — the very phrase simultaneously holds both connotations of repressive terror and farce — and I wanted neither to dispense the one, nor play the other. It never occurred to me that I was doing anything other than extending the same duty that I had been performing in the army. Once in the job I was given further training and mentoring, and almost before I knew it found myself in the field. But it was a different game to any I might have imagined and the concept of justice I found was like some hazy illuminated objective in an unclear future and very little to do with the job in hand.

My attitude to regular policemen was another matter. They were always to be avoided. This, given my background and earlier aspirations, sometimes left me with a vague sense of having a split personality, a psychological muzziness like a dull headache I could never shake. It is why, I suppose, that in their presence I often feel — and need to suppress — a sense of ambivalence, a mixture of fear and superiority. Nevertheless, they also fill me with curiosity as men on a path I never travelled, representatives of a tribe I never joined, and I like to observe them closely, looking perhaps for the kind of person I might have become.

~

It was on the Tuesday, two days after Standing's death that I received my first visit. I found two officers on my doorstep at an unconscionably early hour of the morning. By then the investigation was unquestionably one of murder, favouring the scenario of a "burglary gone wrong". But if the appeal for witnesses had brought forth any new leads they hadn't made it into the media. The police were keeping it to themselves.

26

There were two, as I say, a Detective Inspector and his sergeant and I say, "found them" because, early as it was, I wasn't in the house to answer the doorbell. At first light, awake and with no prospect of further sleep, I had got up and taken a walk in the nearby park. On my way home I bought another paper — another, that is, in addition to the one protruding from my letterbox behind the plain-clothed backs of the two men as they turned to watch me walk up the path.

'Mr Alexander Maitland?' the older of the two asked. He could not have been any more than in his mid-thirties but had already turned grey and sallow and either owned a blunt razor or was afflicted with a fast-growing beard.

I confessed to the identification and he took the trouble to observe that I was up early, managing to convey just enough suspicion in his north London accent to suggest I might have been trying to avoid them.

They introduced themselves as DI Bedford and Detective-sergeant Graham and displayed their warrant cards for verification. As we are always being urged to do, I took the trouble to examine the cards closely although this seemed to irritate Graham to judge from the restive way he shifted from foot to foot on the doorstep. Younger than Bedford, he also looked fitter and boasted more colour, suggestive of an hour already spent in the gym. He was dark-haired and wore it cropped short so that the shape of his skull was visible through the fuzz.

'It's about Michael Standing, I assume,' I said, unlocking the front door and holding it open for them.

'You've been expecting us?' Bedford asked, his manner betraying the fact I must have confirmed his earlier suspicion.

'Well,' I admitted, 'half-expecting you. I was supposed to lunch with Standing last Saturday and I can't think of any other reason why I should receive a visit from the police.'

'Supposed to lunch?'

'He never turned up.' I looked from one to the other. 'If you didn't know that, how did you get my name?'

Graham glanced at his colleague.

'David Griffiths, Mr Standing's research assistant gave us the names of people he had been in contact with recently,' he said.

'A long list, I should imagine.'

'Your name is also in Mr Standing's diary for last Saturday,' Bedford said.

'There you are then.'

'How well did you know Mr Standing?' Graham asked.

'Not well. We'd only met two or three times.'

We were in the living room, grouped untidily in front of the sofa. I told them that as I was about to make a pot of coffee they might as well sit down and have a cup. I excused myself and went into the kitchen. By the time I returned, Bedford was where I had left him but Graham had obviously taken a tour of the room and was at that moment bent towards the photographs on my mantelpiece.

'Is this you, sir?' he asked, pointing at a photograph of my father in his RAF uniform taken in 1944 and quite obviously of its time.

I looked at him askance. While it is true that facially I resemble my father, I am a much bigger man and I hoped Graham didn't think I was old enough to have appeared in that particular photo.

'My father,' I said and, always happy to brag on his behalf, added, 'He was a fighter-pilot in the war.'

'Really?' Graham said, moving on to a photograph from my army days taken at a formal regimental dinner. 'Military family?'

'Not really,' I said. 'My father left the RAF to join BEA. That's one of me when I was in the army. Military police,' I added to see what effect it might have.

Apparently none, Graham continued to look at the other photographs, reaching for one of Olena. 'And is this Mrs Maitland?'

'Yes,' I said, 'but not *my* wife.' I wondered if after two strikes I ought to be concerned for his clear-up rate. 'She's my sister. She married my cousin, Nicholas Maitland. He always joked that she only married him to avoid having to learn how to spell a new surname.'

Bedford smiled dutifully as Graham sat down on the sofa next to him. I poured the coffee and told them to help themselves to milk and sugar.

'Mr Standing's diary indicates he had a lunch appointment with you last Saturday,' Bedford said, 'but you say he never kept it?'

'Yes, that's right.'

'When was the appointment made?'

'Earlier in the week. His secretary rang me.'

'His secretary.'

Graham took out his notebook and scribbled something in it.

'You say you didn't know him well,' Bedford said. 'So may I ask why you were lunching with him?'

'Certainly. He was doing research on the Ukrainian famine of the nineteen-thirties.'

'And are you an authority on that, sir?' Graham asked.

'No, not at all,' I said. 'David Griffiths came up with my father's name while researching the subject for Standing. My father was born in the Ukraine, you see.'

Graham made another note in his book and I took the opportunity to ask, 'Was it a robbery? From what I've read they seem to think that he came home and found someone in the house.'

'They?' Bedford asked.

'Sorry. I suppose I mean "you",' which suddenly sounded very lame. 'The police.'

'We're keeping an open mind, sir,' Bedford said, 'but it does look as if he might have walked in on someone.' He stopped toying with his coffee cup and replaced it on the table. 'We know Mr Standing left the television studios at about ten that evening and his wife found him at eleven forty-five. He rarely drove himself in town and was in the habit of using public transport or taxis.'

'So you've got a gap of perhaps an hour and a half,' I said.

'You wouldn't have any idea where he might have been during that time?'

'None at all.'

'Did you get in touch with Mr Standing when he failed to make your lunch appointment?' Graham asked.

'I didn't have his number. He's ex-directory, of course.'

'Didn't you think it strange he missed the appointment without notifying you?'

'Rude, perhaps. Hardly strange.'

'So you'd not spoken to him since the initial contact?'

'As I said, we met a couple of times. We had lunch several months ago. Some time in early summer that must have been. Then he rang out of the blue and invited me up to a seminar in Cambridge in which he was speaking. That would have been around three months ago, in August. I went, listened to his paper and had lunch with him afterwards at his hotel. The Mill House, I think it was called.'

'We've spoken to Mr Griffiths. He said Standing visited you following up a line of research.'

'Yes, as I said.'

'Did you watch him on Sunday evening?'

'On the television? Yes.'

'I believe there was some kind of altercation, is that right?'

'With Edward Maseryk, you mean?' I was sceptical. 'Hardly an altercation. More of a disagreement.'

'What about?' Bedford asked.

'The Ukrainian famine, as it happens.'

'Oh?'

'Maseryk argued that Stalin was unaware of just how bad the famine was. Standing maintained starvation was a deliberate policy.'

'Is that all?'

Quite enough, I had thought at the time. But I didn't particularly want to elaborate. It had only been a discussion — albeit a heated one — and in front of cameras at that. Hardly secret. All the same, I couldn't help feeling that I was ratting on Maseryk.

'Standing more or less implied that Maseryk was an apologist for Stalin,' I told Bedford reluctantly.

He raised his eyebrows but didn't reply.

'Do you own a mobile phone?' Graham asked unexpectedly.

'Yes.'

'Your number, sir? We're checking Mr Standing's phone records.'

I recited my number. 'I've never used it to call Standing, though,' I said. 'When he called me he always used the landline.'

'That's what he did when he telephoned to invite you to lunch last week?'

'His secretary,' I said.

'What about Mrs Standing?'

'What about her?'

'How well do you know her?'

'I don't know her at all,' I said. 'We've never met.'

'So you've never been to their house in Kensington?'

'No.'

They suddenly stood up.

'I don't know if I've been of much help,' I said.

'We're just building up a picture of Mr Standing's movements at the moment. Everything helps.'

'Can you tell me how he died?' I asked. 'I don't believe it's been mentioned.'

They exchanged a glance and Graham said, 'He was hit over the head. More than once.'

'Nasty,' I said.

'There was quite a bit of blood,' Graham added unnecessarily.

I was still picturing the scene when they turned to leave.

'Thank you, Mr Maitland,' Bedford said. 'We'll probably want to speak with you again.'

After they had gone I experienced that odd feeling of discomfort that even the innocent can feel in the presence of the police. It persisted despite my conviction that I really shouldn't have been the sort of person likely to suffer from it.

I finished the pot of coffee and read the newspapers over breakfast. They were still reporting Standing's murder but in the face of a lack of new evidence were now resorting to street plans of the area near his house, illustrating the possible escape routes his assailant might have taken.

At 9.30am with Bedford and Graham still on my mind I put in a call to Charlie Hewson. Charlie and I had worked together for several years and if there was anything worth knowing on a given subject, Hewson could sniff it out.

'Alex,' he said, coming to the phone. 'How's the back?'

Since he had been standing next to me when I had received the injury but had escaped unscathed, I had always viewed his inevitable greeting as a case of, *There but for the grace of God...*

'Fine,' I said. 'I don't know why I retired. Look, Charlie. Can you do me a favour?'

~

There had been rain earlier and the roads were still glistening with reflected light from the traffic and the streetlamps. Some early Christmas decorations had already gone up giving the late November evening a festive air it didn't deserve. The temperature had dropped.

I found Charlie in the snug of the pub a short walk from the building in which we had both used to work. Charlie had moved on, though, across the river to those new, purpose-built offices that he complained still smelled of fresh paint and those unpleasant gasses cheap new carpet gives off. In contrast, the pub was a rather shabby place that never seemed to change no matter how long one had been away. Much like Charlie himself in that respect. He was sitting over the fire with his usual scotch when I arrived, fidgeting uncomfortably without the solace of his customary cigarette. In better weather we'd have sat out at one of the tables on the street to placate him, but that evening it was too cold with a fog beginning to drift up the river and I thought if I was going to have to listen to one of Charlie's monologues I wanted to do so in comfort. If you let him, he was liable to bore you rigid on the encroachment upon civil liberties that the smoking ban in public places represents, which is ironic in itself as his biggest complaint is reserved for the changes to British life that wider-spread civil liberties have brought. But Charlie was an inveterate malcontent and the smoking ban was just one among many *bête noires*, each of which he was always pleased to point out was proof — if further proof were ever needed — of the decline in English life under the onslaught of societal cancers like, among others, political correctness and multiculturalism. But I had long ago put all these down to character quirks which, given a cigarette, one would hardly notice in him.

Physically, he was nondescript and could have passed as a low-grade clerk beaten down by life, a kind of outline for an H.G. Wells' character of the sort Wells used in his social comedies. In some way it gave Charlie the aura of a man who had outlived his time. It wasn't until you knew him, though, that you found out that there was more to him that that.

I bought two more drinks at the bar and took the chair beside him. He watched me grimace as I sat down.

'It's fine, is it?' he said, voice heavy with irony.

I slid a scotch across the table towards him.

Surprisingly he didn't seem in the mood to complain about the iniquities of life and instead we caught up on the latest gossip before he asked, 'What's your interest in Standing? Professional?'

'Hardly,' I said. 'I'm retired, you know that.'

He looked morosely into his glass. 'I know that no one really knows anything at all,' he said.

I suppose I eyed him sardonically. It's what I always seemed to do with Charlie.

'Never mind the Socratic philosophy, Charlie.' I said, 'It doesn't suit you. I met Standing a couple of times, that's all. I had an appointment with him last Saturday but he never showed up.'

'The Ukrainian thing?'

'Yes.'

'Ah. Spoken to the police?'

'This morning.'

'And couldn't get anything out of them?'

'I didn't try.'

'Who interviewed you?'

'A DI named Bedford and a Sergeant Graham.'

Charlie opened his briefcase and took out a pink folder. He withdrew several sheets of paper and laid them deliberately on the table between our glasses.

'A contact of mine in Special Branch,' he said. 'I asked him to root out the details. Bedford's a bit dour. Won't scratch backs, apparently.'

He had hand-written the notes in his usual untidy script, hampered, no doubt, by the phone he would have had lodged between shoulder and ear.

'What about Graham?'

Charlie shrugged. 'It's not like our day, Alex. Sergeants barely register on the radar now.'

'Is there much that's not been released?'

'My contact says no. Standing was bludgeoned.' He looked up brightly. 'Odd word, *bludgeoned*. Something eighteenth-century-sounding about it.'

'Probably because it is,' I said.

'Could suggest either that the killer came prepared — i.e. it was premeditated — or it was spur of the moment.'

'Any weapon?'

'Not at the scene.' He pulled the sheets of paper towards him and looked through them quickly. 'A lot of blood apparently and some decent footprints.'

'Graham mentioned the blood,' I said.

'Well,' Charlie said, 'the rest is the usual — fingerprints, DNA.' He pushed the papers back towards me. 'It's all there, all I could get, anyway. If you can read my writing, that is.'

I folded the papers in four and tucked them away in my jacket pocket. 'I think I can probably still struggle through it, Charlie.'

He was pulling a face that indicated there might be something else.

'It's been suggested that the "intruder" might have been there for some while.'

'How do you mean?'

'Upstairs?'

'But wouldn't Standing's wife have...' I stopped as the penny dropped. 'You mean she was—'

'But notwithstanding,' Charlie punned and he grinned at me.

4

The most pertinent fact I knew about my grandfather, when it came down to it, was that I didn't know much about him at all.

Naturally, I had never known him and even my father had been a young boy when he had last seen him. And, as I have said, his early life was not a subject about which he ever spoke. Over the years he let slip the occasional fact but, if he had any memories of Aleksander Zaretsky, he never intentionally passed them on to me. Maybe he didn't actually know much. My grandmother, Nastasiya, would have known as much as there was to know, but how much she told my father I couldn't say. It might have been that, as a boy, he had had no curiosity and of course later, if he had developed one, it would have been too late. Nastasiya was dead, a victim of the Blitz.

I had an idea that my father had once said that Zaretsky was somewhat older than his mother was when they had married and that he was into his thirties when my father was born in 1920. That had been in Kharkov and so it seemed reasonable to assume that that was also where his father hailed from. I knew that, as a young man, Zaretsky had been active in the revolution of 1917. I had always assumed that by the time he sent his wife and child to England he had risen to be some sort of political functionary in the Ukrainian Soviet although at what level I had no idea. The fact that he might have been a member of the State police as Standing had maintained was a possibility I had never considered.

After David Griffiths had first contacted me, I had looked out what little material I had of my father's dating from the period. The bulk of his papers that I had retained after his death had concerned his service in the RAF, the rest had been a rag-bag of odds and ends, some of which I believe had belonged to my grandmother — among the few possessions of hers that had survived the bombing. I still kept them in the old biscuit tin in which I had found them after my father's death, and they had lain there undisturbed ever since.

I had spread them on the dining room table in front of Standing the day he had called.

There were two sets of Ukrainian identity papers, a few letters written in the Cyrillic alphabet my father had used when writing to his mother from boarding school — only one of which still had its envelope — a couple more later letters in English and two well-thumbed black and white photographs. There were some other miscellaneous papers, typed official-looking forms also in Cyrillic, which were a mystery to me. I didn't know if they were Ukrainian or Russian, not having the slightest grasp of the Cyrillic alphabet, or even, come to that, whether there was a difference between the two languages.

Standing picked up Nastasiya's identity papers and looked at the photograph. She was blonde, oval-faced and pretty.

'An attractive woman,' he said.

'Isn't she?' I agreed. 'I don't think she could have been much more than a girl there. I believe she was about seventeen when she married my grandfather.'

'Have you ever been to the Ukraine?'

He was sitting at the table looking at what I had laid in front of him.

'No,' I said from where I stood at his shoulder. 'I often wonder if my father would have liked the chance to go back. He never said he'd like to but then he didn't live long enough to see the thaw, of course.'

'You'll rarely see so many beautiful women in one place,' he said putting the identity papers back on the table.

I feared for a moment he was going to share a confidence with me about some tawdry sexual escapade, the kind that most third parties really wouldn't want to know about. But he didn't. His comment on Ukrainian women was apparently no more than just that. He picked up the other photographs and examined them.

Nastasiya was in both of them. The first, had it not been black and white, I had always thought would have been vibrant with the colour of the scene. I wasn't certain, but assumed, that it was a photo taken at her wedding. She was standing next to a man, arm linked through his, in a long dress with a rather elaborate head-dress obscuring half her face. What you could see of her face suggested that she was very young. The man, by contrast looked — by our standards, anyway — almost middle-aged. He was tall, quite thin with a pair of piercing eyes and a heavy moustache. I'd always seen a likeness to my father in him, but that might have been just because I had wanted to.

'Aleksander Zaretsky?' Standing asked.

'I've always assumed so,' I said. 'Although I suppose it could always have been her father. Unfortunately I never saw these photos until after my father died. I presume he would have known.'

Standing drew the photograph closer to his face and lifted his glasses. 'Too young, surely.' He took a look at the back but nothing was written on it.

'Did they still go in for elaborate weddings after the revolution?' I asked him.

He replaced the photograph carefully. 'Oh yes. In many ways it was a decade or more before much changed fundamentally for many of the rural population. They carried on much as they always had. It was Collectivization that changed their world.'

The second photograph was of Nastasiya and my father. He could not have been much more than eight or nine but in the intervening years she looked to have grown up considerably. Now a woman, she was holding her son's hand and was looking straight at the camera. Her chin was lifted and her hair, loose and hanging to her shoulders, gave the suggestion of blowing in some unseen wind. The girl she had been was gone and, although she displayed a look of confidence, there was also something about the almost grim set to her compressed lips that gave an impression of determination.

'And this is your father?' Standing said.

'Petro Zaretsky, as he was then.'

'From the Greek, *Petros*,' Standing said. 'A stone.'

'That was him,' I said. 'Bloody-minded and obstinate.'

'When did he change his name?'

'After it was obvious his father was never going to join them, Nastasiya married a man named Frederick Maitland. Petro became Peter, although I believe he kept the surname Zaretsky until he decided to join the RAF. Hitler and Stalin had signed a non-aggression pact and it was suggested that he'd get on better as plain Peter Maitland. I suppose he got used to it because after the war he never changed it back.'

'And Nastasiya Zaretsky was killed in an air raid, you say.'

'Yes, nineteen-forty, although she was Nastasiya Maitland by then, of course. To be honest, I'm not a hundred-percent sure she actually had my grandfather declared dead, or if she could have done for that matter. But she certainly married Frederick. I sat down next to him and picked up the photo of Petro and Nastasiya. 'My father never actually got on that well with his stepfather,' I said.

'Understandable under the circumstances, perhaps. Frederick and Nastasiya had a son, though; George, and my father always remained on good terms with his half-brother despite the age difference. Frederick was serving overseas when Nastasiya was killed. He married again near the end of the war and had several more little Maitlands. There's a lot of us around, you know, although strictly speaking, I'm not really one of them.'

I took a piece of paper from the table and wrote down George and Nick's phone numbers. I gave it to Standing and told him there was always a possibility that they might still have something of Nastasiya's or her husband, Frederick's that would interest him, assuming anything else had survived the Blitz.

'Nick is Nicholas Maitland,' I said, the MP? If you've heard of him.'

'Oh, it's *that* Nicholas Maitland,' Standing said. 'Of course.' He glanced around my rather shabby room again and I knew exactly what he was thinking. 'I wondered, but...'

Good manners prevented him from elaborating and instead he looked at me in a distracted way with a sort of half-frown creasing his forehead as if some new thought had suddenly wormed its way into his head. Then his mouth twitched into a half-smile and he picked up one the letters and opened it.

I said I doubted that they would be of much interest to him.

'They're mostly written in Cyrillic, from my father to his mother while he was away at school. Judging by the dates, they were written in the early years after they came to England. I've always assumed that the Ukrainian language was easier for them at first. There are a couple of later ones in English, but it's just the usual sort of correspondence between mother and son. I've not read them since I found them, actually.'

The single white envelope was now stained, creased and faded, the London address of my grandmother smudged where water had dampened the paper. Standing spread the letters out and glanced through one that had been written in English — from my father's last term at school — and then through another written after he had joined the RAF and was away at training. He pursed his lips, then dropped the letters back on the table.

'These other papers,' I said, pushing the typed forms towards him, 'I have no idea what they are about.'

He took one off the table, examined it and muttered, 'Interesting,' in a sort of non-committal way.

'Can you read Ukrainian?' I asked.

'Yes, I can as a matter of fact.'

'What are they?'

'Actually these are in Russian,' he said. 'Rail movement orders for grain shipments, apparently.'

'Oh,' I said, disappointed.

'No, not at all,' Standing replied picking up on my frustration. 'Actually it's just the sort of thing that's of interest.'

He spent a moment or two reading the movement orders and, while he was engaged, something else occurred to me. I went into the living room and took a small leather-bound notebook out of the desk drawer. I brought it back and handed it to Standing.

'What's this?'

'To be honest,' I said, 'I don't know.'

I had found it in a drawer at my father's house while helping Olena clear the place out after he had died. It hadn't been with the other items in the biscuit tin and so I didn't know if it was Nastasiya's or my father's. It was, as I said, bound in leather but showed none of the damage the other papers had sustained following the bombing. I had no idea what it was because the entries were written in Cyrillic except for several place names in English; confusingly, though, apart from cities like Kiev and Kharkov many were towns in parts of Europe other than the Ukraine.

'This belonged to your grandmother?' Standing asked.

'I've no idea,' I said. 'Given that it's mostly in the Cyrillic alphabet, I always assumed that it was given to my father with the other stuff of hers after it had been salvaged from the house when she was killed. Her husband was serving overseas at the time so I suppose anything of his that was salvaged my father returned to him — or his family. For some reason, though, my father didn't keep it with the letters and identity cards. I'd almost forgotten about it. All I can make out,' I added, 'are the place names written in English. I thought it might just be a diary of my father's or something to do with school lessons his mother had kept. Places they wanted to go together, perhaps? Although why the actual places are in English while the rest is Ukrainian I have no idea. For all I know, it could be a shopping list.'

'Certainly not that,' he said, taking my flippancy at face value. He squinted at the pencilled-in Cyrillic characters. 'I'm better at the printed language,' he admitted. 'You need a better eye than mine for hand-written Cyrillic. David — David Griffiths — is the linguist. I can't make much of it out. But I'd say it was Ukrainian rather than Russian.'

'There is a difference, then?'

'Oh yes. More pronounced in the oral tradition than in the written but they are distinct languages. The English entries are curious.'

He put the notebook on the table next to the other papers. 'If you're agreeable,' he said, 'I'll take these with me and get David to go through them. He'll transcribe the notebook for you, if you like. I'll leave the letters. There doesn't seem to be anything of relevance in them.'

'That's fine,' I agreed, 'as long as I can have everything back when you've finished.'

'Of course.' He reached for the coat he had brought with him. 'Why don't you make an inventory of what's here and I can give you a receipt. Then there can be no arguments.'

I made a list as he suggested which he receipted for me. I found an envelope for the papers on which I listed everything again, adding my name and address. When I finished, he put everything into the envelope and we exchanged self-satisfied smiles, confident we had guarded against every eventuality.

The one thing we hadn't guarded against, of course, was murder.

5

It was raining again by the time I got home from seeing Charlie Hewson. The house felt dank and I put the heating on and dried myself out then opened a bottle of wine. I sat at the kitchen table and unfolded the sheets of paper he had given me.

It took a minute or two to re-acquaint myself with Charlie's style, a mixture of abbreviations, capitalized words for emphasis, and half-finished sentences that seemed to expire mid-word as if written by a dying man.

The full autopsy report had apparently not yet been filed and Charlie's contact in Special Branch had had to make do with the preliminary medical findings. These suggested Standing had been killed by several blows to the back of the head by a blunt instrument although not a particularly heavy one. Splinters embedded in the skull suggested it had been made of wood. Time of death had been estimated at sometime between 10.30pm and 11.45pm when Standing's wife had called for an ambulance and the police. There seemed to be a little confusion pinning the time more exactly although Charlie's notes didn't say why. It seemed that the earlier time suggested that it might not have been the actual murder that had woken Julia Standing but the sound of the front door banging some time after the act had been committed.

I couldn't help thinking that finding him must have been a particularly unpleasant shock for Standing's wife. There had been — as Graham had said — a lot of blood. The spatter had been widespread. It was thought possible that Standing's assailant had been wearing gloves, as no bloodied fingerprints were found except for those of his wife who admitted she had touched the body in the hope that he might still be alive. As Charlie had said, no murder weapon had been discovered at the scene. The SOCOs — the scene of crime officers — had removed several items for forensic analysis including a file of papers found by the body, several other objects scattered around the floor which had probably been knocked down by Standing as he had fallen, and a bottle of wine and two glasses that had been on the kitchen worktop above the body. Charlie's contact had even noted the brand of wine — a Chilean Merlot from the Maipo region. Reading the fact made the hairs on the back of my neck bristle as I glanced across my kitchen table to the bottle of Chilean Maipo I had just opened.

My imagination screened an unpleasant scenario for a second until I managed to get a grip and tell myself that a decent bottle of Maipo could be found in any supermarket for less than ten pounds. That said, I made a mental note not to leave any bottles of Chilean red lying around in case Bedford decided to pay me another visit.

From the notes Charlie had managed to pull together it seemed that Julia Standing's statement to the police hadn't differed much from the version that had made it into the media: she had gone to bed early, a little after 10pm, knowing that her husband would be late. She hadn't planned to watch him on the television but had programmed the TV hard drive to record the show, as Michael usually liked to have a record of his appearances. She had read in bed for half-an-hour or so and didn't think she had been asleep long when she had been woken by a noise downstairs. She hadn't been able to say just what the noise she had heard was, but coming down

40

the stairs and seeing the front door open she assumed it had been the sound of the door banging that had woken her. Her immediate thought had been that Michael hadn't closed it properly behind him — the latch sometimes didn't shut properly — and after closing it she went into the kitchen where a light was on to see if he was there. That was when she had found him.

One of the officers had established that the front door needed to be closed quite firmly for the latch to engage. Also, in a routine examination of the rest of the house the bed in the Standings' bedroom had been found in an unmade state corroborating the fact that Julia Standing had been in it before she had called the emergency services.

There were some other details concerning a shoe print found in the blood on the kitchen tiles and further traces discovered in the hall leading to the front door but this area, being carpeted, did not readily show the print unless one was looking for it. It was thought unlikely that Julia Standing would have noticed them on first coming downstairs.

Other fingerprints had been found in the kitchen and Julia Standing and a cleaning woman who came in mornings had been printed so as to eliminate them.

I read through the pages again, really quite impressed by the comprehensive account Charlie had managed to obtain. His contact appeared to have one of his own close to the investigation. I didn't suppose for a minute that I was likely to come up with anything that the police hadn't (my training, after all, had been in a different area of expertise), but it seemed to me that the fact that there had been no hand or fingerprints found in the blood around Standing's body (excepting his wife's) did suggest at least the possibility that the assailant had worn gloves. This in turn suggested two things: either that he *was* a burglar who had come prepared not to leave his fingerprints behind, or that Standing's murder was premeditated and the murderer had come equally prepared not to leave prints. I wondered if the latter possibility had prompted the notion that Charlie had passed on, insinuating that Julia Standing might not have been alone when Michael had returned home. If it had, though, there was nothing else in what I had read to back it up.

I poured a second glass of the Maipo and put the bottle away, still thinking about Julia Standing and a possible lover. If they had been caught together, the other man, one presumed, was more likely to be naked than wearing gloves. If he *was* dressed — and shod, as the shoe print suggested — then it was possible that he was gloved. The weather (as far as I was able to recall) had been much the same as it was that evening, dank and chilly but hardly cold enough to warrant gloves. But I suppose one should never discount those who still clung to the old habit of always wearing gloves if attired for the street. If that was the case, though, I wondered who the police would be looking for — a burglar or an Edwardian dandy?

~

Having taken my papers with him, I had half-expected some sort of progress report from Standing. As it was I heard nothing from him at all. The whole business had piqued my interest, though, and I thought I might read up on the subject. My father's scant memories aside, my knowledge of the Ukraine consisted mostly of what I had learned through my work, and that of course Russian-orientated, although having spent most of my working life in the middle-east and Africa I soon discovered I was woefully ignorant.

Perhaps being half-Ukrainian myself it might seem surprising that I had never taken the trouble to learn anything of my own heritage. But I had always found the facts of my origin as a somewhat odd — even alien — concept, almost diametrically opposed to the sense of self that I had always nurtured. That, though, I put down to my father's attitude. From the moment he had joined the RAF I believe he had made a determined effort to turn himself into an Englishman through and through. On reflection, it was almost as if he had strangely mirrored those terrifying fanatics he had escaped as a boy by systematically rewriting his *own* history; not by pretending his Ukrainian past had not existed, but by leaving no trace of it behind. Perhaps that was just another way of reaching the same end. It was as if he had regarded himself as having no past at all until the day he joined the RAF as a nineteen year-old. That is why finding his early letters and the other papers among his belongings after his death had come as such a surprise to me. I still did not quite understand why he had kept them.

So, it was after Standing's first visit that I began learning about the country in which my father had been born. I still had those few letters he had written in Ukrainian that Standing had thought not worth bothering with and I had formed the idea of getting them translated myself. I mentioned the fact to Charlie Hewson over a drink one evening a week or two after I first met Standing, in the hope that he might be able to put me in the way of someone who worked in the department dealing with the newly emerged east European countries. Charlie, however, was less than enthusiastic.

'You know they don't like the staff freelancing,' he said. 'Particularly for people who've left the Service.'

I thought he was being uncharacteristically over-officious in applying the rules, particularly considering who was asking for the favour, and told him so.

'Come on, Charlie. It's not as if it's sensitive material. They're a schoolboy's letters to his mother, for God's sake. I'm not suggesting I set up my own network. All I need is someone who speaks Ukrainian.'

'I don't know why you don't enjoy your retirement,' he said. 'I'd have thought you would have had enough of that sort of thing. Why don't you take up bowls or something?'

'Enough of *what* sort of thing?'

'What about book collecting?' he suggested. 'All sorts of interesting fields in that.'

'I can't afford expensive hobbies,' I said. 'You'll find that out for yourself when they pension *you* off.'

'What about crime?'

'Studying it, or committing it to make ends meet?'

'Collecting,' he said. 'First editions of crime novels. I was reading this magazine—'

'Charlie...'

'All right, Alex,' he conceded finally, glancing at me sideways with what was almost a pitying look. 'If you're not going to drop it I'll have a word with one of the girls on the east European desk and see if she knows anyone who might be interested. I'll give her your mobile number.'

For once March had come in as the old adage decreed it should with two days of storms that lashed the streets and washed away the last of winter's litter. When it finally passed, the storm left behind a bright clear morning with an odd stillness to the air and just enough of a chill to remind me I was still alive.

I had been in the garden, clearing up after the storm when the mobile rang. The voice was female and strongly East European;

Russian, I would have said but I didn't have an ear for the Ukrainian accent then.

'Mr Alex Maitland?'

I told her I was.

'I have number for work in translating, yes? This is correct?'

I told her it was.

'Then I have question, please. Are you from Council or government office?'

I explained that I was a private individual.

'Retired,' I said.

'What is nature of letters?'

'I don't know. That's why I need them translated.'

'From who are they sent?'

I would have raised my eyebrows but there didn't seem much point on the phone.

'Does it matter?'

'It matters if I translate,' she said briskly, clipping her consonants and putting me in my place. 'If nature is technical.'

'No,' I assured her, 'Nature isn't technical. They're from my father to my grandmother.'

'Then why not your grandmother translate? Or your father?'

I told her that sadly they were both dead.

She said something that I did not catch about the Data Protection Act which, for some reason, I pictured her reading off a card. There followed some more questions, non-sequiturs thrown from a variety of directions. She asked where I was but when I offered to come to her she rejected the idea out of hand.

'No. I come to you. But not to house. You have park near, perhaps?'

I said I had and told her where it was.

'I call again when I reach park,' she said and broke the connection.

I stood looking at my phone for a moment, feeling an odd sense of familiarity with clandestine meetings in parks, although I couldn't help thinking that my working life had usually involved less secrecy than it appeared my caller wanted to indulge in. I decided I might as well walk down to the park, however, and drop in to the library, which lay on the other side, while I was waiting for her to call back. It occurred to me to call Charlie Hewson and warn him that I suspected the girl on the east European desk to whom he had passed my number was mixing with people of doubtful immigration status.

It was either that or the girl had some pretensions to undercover work and was planning on practising her tradecraft on me.

In the park, a pair of out-of-town geese had dropped in on the pond, enjoying what for them, I suppose, were the last days of their winter vacation in the south. A young mother with two toddlers in tow was trying to interest them in some bread but the kids weren't able to throw the crumbs any further than the greedy beaks of the resident ducks. Just past them was the old girl who could usually be found sitting on one of the benches, swathed beneath a woolly hat and several moth-eaten sweaters, her plimsolled feet hidden under a flock of pigeons eager to share her breakfast. I watched them for a few minutes then made my way to the east gate and the library. It was while I was examining what was on offer under modern European History that my phone rang again. I found a quiet corner behind Religion and Philosophy that could always be counted on to be empty and answered.

'I am in park,' she announced tersely. She asked what I was wearing then said, 'Please buy newspaper and sit on bench with paper under arm, yes?'

To humour her I agreed and rang off and went in search of a newsagent. Ten minutes later I was back in the park sitting on the old lady's bench.

I spotted my girl from some distance but she would have caught my attention even if I had not been looking for her. She walked straight past me on the bench, having first taken in my clothes and newspaper, then, fifty yards further on, turned with a display of overt nonchalance and retraced her steps. OGPU would have picked her up ten yards inside the park gates.

Tall and slim, she was dark-haired, wearing it cut longer at the sides than at the back in a kind of Mary Quant style that I could remember from years spent gazing with adolescent longing at magazine photos of fashion models. She wore round-toes shoes with chunky heels that I seemed to hear clicking on the tarmac path before she was even close enough to be audible. Her black winter coat was stylish but worn and she had turned up the collar against the March chill.

She sat down beside me and I turned to her and waited. She would have been pretty but for a sullen, pouting mouth that suggested it rarely found anything that pleased it. Her eyes, though, were grey and large and seemed to carry that *what-have-I-done?* look of the perennial victim. The combination, if not conventionally pretty, was appealingly attractive and I thought, as she returned my gaze, of how odd it was how different things in different women attract different men. Most of all she made me aware of how old I had got without noticing the fact.

'Mr Maitland?' she finally asked.

It was almost a whisper and I had to bend towards her to catch what she said.

Not only old, I thought, but hard of hearing as well.

'We spoke on the phone?' I said.

'I am Daryna. You have letters?'

I took out the one letter I had brought with me, the one with its envelope, and handed it to her. It was one of the early ones, all written in Ukrainian Cyrillic except for the address on the envelope.

'I have four altogether,' I said. She didn't reply so I asked, 'The friend who gave you my number, do you work with her?'

'We have social meetings only,' she said.

'Just a friend, then,' I said.

The grey eyes flicked in my direction briefly then down at the letter. Like the rest — except for the one written while my father was doing his RAF training — it had been written on the headed stationary of a small public school in the West Country, not top-flight but respectable. She turned the envelope over, extracted and unfolded the letter. Like the rest it had suffered some water damage that had smudged the blue ink, and the paper was worn, torn along the creases through handling as if it had been read many times. I looked down at the three pages of closely written gibberish while Daryna scanned through it quickly. Then she folded the letter back into its envelope.

'I translate for you,' she said, handing the letter to me.

'Good,' I said, 'thank you.'

'Twenty-five pounds,' she said.

'Each letter?' I asked, hardly keeping the surprise out of my voice and thinking one hundred pounds for four letters a bit on the steep side.

Her eyes widened momentarily and I sensed — belatedly — that she had meant twenty-five pounds for the four and that now she thought she had lost an opportunity. 'Fifty pounds for all,' she amended with commendable swiftness.

'All right,' I agreed. 'But I'd really rather not let them out of my possession.' She began frowning at this so I said, 'Do you need to take them home with you?'

'No,' she said abruptly. 'I translate, you write. I do not spell good English.'

'Fine,' I agreed. 'Where then? Your place? A café or pub? There's the library.'

'Crowded room not so good,' she decided. 'You have house?'

'About fifteen minutes from here.'

'We go to house.' She stood up. 'If wife does not care.'

'I'm not married,' I said.

'So that is deal, yes?'

'Yes,' I said.

'We go,' she commanded.

We got up and went. And as we went I couldn't help thinking: *not only old and hard of hearing, but not even a threat.*

'I am student of English,' Daryna announced at my door as if stating the fact was a precondition of her entering the house. 'I speak Ukrainian, Russian and Polish.'

Inside, I sat her in the lounge while I made a pot of coffee. When I came back with the tray she was at the far end of the room by my dining table — strewn, as usual, with books and the notes I had made of my initial research — looking through my papers.

'You have interest in Ukraine,' she declared, her tone falling midway between accusation and enquiry as she rolled her 'r's.

'My father was born there,' I explained. 'That makes me half-Ukrainian.'

'Your father's name, please?'

I made space on the table for the tray.

'Petro Zaretsky,' I said. 'His father's name was Aleksander and his mother was Nastasiya. From Kharkov, I believe.'

'I am from Kiev,' she said. 'I know no Zaretsky.'

'No conflict of interest then,' I joked.

She didn't smile. 'Conflict of interest? Explain please.'

'It was a joke,' I said. 'I was making conversation.'

'This is funny joke? I should laugh?'

'No,' I said, 'the joke was not funny.'

She began frowning, but before we got in any deeper I poured the coffee and told her of how my grandmother had brought my father to England in 1932.

'It was good time to leave,' Daryna said. 'Many died. Many.'

'You know about the famine, then,' I said.

'*Famine*? This word is new. What is meaning, please?'

'Starvation,' I said. 'Having no food. What you call the Holodomor,' I added, rather pleased with myself for being able to use a term I had only recently learned.

'Ah, yes,' she said, nodding solemnly, 'Holodomor. We learn this in school. It is *famine*? This was terrible crime.'

I was on the point of telling her about Michael Standing then thought how it might sound, as if I was trying to boast of an acquaintance in television. She had probably never heard of him anyway so I kept him to myself and drank coffee instead.

'You study famine?' Daryna asked.

'In a way,' I told her. 'I am interested because of my father. I am trying to find out more about his early life. I know so little about it.'

'He never spoke of famine?'

I could suddenly picture her introducing her new word at every available opportunity — *Take me to dinner, I am in famine ... I have to go to shops or I will have famine...*

'No,' I said. 'He left Ukraine when he was twelve but he never spoke about it.'

'And your grandmother also?'

'She died in the war. I never knew her.'

'But you have letters.'

'I have letters, although I doubt they will mention the Holodomor.'

'And your grandfather? Aleksander Zaretsky?'

'He never managed to follow her. He disappeared.'

'He died of famine,' she decided with conviction, an indisputable fact.

'Perhaps.'

We finished our coffee and I took out the letters.

'Pay in front, please,' Daryna said.

I felt a little affronted that she imagined I might renege on the deal and counted out two twenty-pound notes and a ten and laid them on the table. She took them then extended her hand for a formal handshake to seal the bargain. I shook it as solemnly as it was offered and sorted out the four letters by date and handed her the earliest. Of the two remaining letters, one had been written in my father's rather crabbed hand from school in still halting English and the other, far more fluent, had been sent from his RAF station. Both of these had still been addressed in Cyrillic, which Daryna had translated as 'darling Mother'. The first one in English from school was little more than a catalogue of daily activities; the second, a more enthusiastic description of his fellow RAF recruits and new surroundings. He had signed off the letters as 'your loving son, Petro'.

Daryna had opened the first of the four letters to translate and had flattened it on the tabletop. I drew my chair as close to hers as I could without appearing presumptuous, picked up a pencil and pulled a notebook towards me.

It proved a slow business. My father's hand-written English had never been the easiest to decipher, something I had always put down to his learning the Latin alphabet later than was generally usual, but it seemed as if his Ukrainian was equally execrable. The smudged ink did not help. Daryna struggled through each sentence, often finding that when she had at last decoded the Cyrillic word she was unsure of its meaning in English. This often resulted in our having to resort to a question and answer game full of gesticulation that resembled charades. After an hour I had written in the notebook: *Dearest Mother, Thank you for the cake which I ate in the dorm with the others boys. I hope you —*

In the end we settled on the method of Daryna writing out the Cyrillic alphabet on a sheet of paper so that, when she came across an illegible word, I was able to offer my opinion on the characters as well. By six o'clock that evening we had managed to translate only the first of my father's letters.

Reading through the translation when it was finished I was able to divine that he was getting on well at school although he still found the language difficult. He had made several friends and particularly enjoyed playing rugby football. In the summer he would play cricket although, as yet, he had not mastered the rules of the game. He had plenty to eat and the food was good. He didn't like the master who taught him English and once a week they had a church parade and the service was strange. As his mother had suggested he had not told his housemaster that he was an atheist but that he followed the Orthodox faith. He was unsure if the master thought any more of him because of it, though. All the boys wanted to know about the Bolsheviks. He sent her all his love and his regards to Mr Maitland.

By six poor Daryna looked quite exhausted. She made a show of looking at her watch and announced — in her fashion — that she had a prior appointment. We agreed she would return the following day. She reached for her handbag with obvious reluctance and offered to give me back the two twenty-pound notes.

I put my hand over hers. With uncharacteristic liberality that took even me by surprise, I said, 'Payment in advance,' almost immediately regretting the impulse to generosity. I tried to cover the fact with an unconvincing smile.

A look of relief flashed through the grey eyes and she snapped the bag shut, almost catching my fingers in the clasp. On the doorstep I waved her goodbye with the gravest of doubts as to whether I would ever see her again.

While I had not really expected the letters to advance my knowledge of my father's boyhood much, the one we had translated did throw up a couple of interesting points. It was dated March 14th 1934 and he would by then have been in England for around eighteen months if not longer. I knew he had been at school for much of this time and, from what he had once told me, was aware that the boarding school in Dorset was not the first he had attended. Knowing my father, I assumed that by the time he had written the letter he had achieved a decent grasp of spoken English at least, a better understanding, it seemed reasonable to suppose, than had Nastasiya herself (I had precluded the possibility that she already spoke the language before leaving the Ukraine). It therefore seemed logical to assume that he was writing in Ukrainian for his mother's benefit.

The second point of interest was the fact that Daryna had struggled over the name Maitland where my father had used it in reference to Frederick. It hadn't been until logic had suggested to me that it was a name and I had asked her to write my name in Cyrillic that it became obvious why it was so difficult. She puzzled over it for a while then did what my father had obviously done, that is transposing the Latin characters into their roughly equivalent Cyrillic characters. It seemed the logical thing to do if the name had no meaning that might be translated, like *Smith* or *Archer*. With Maitland, there was no underlying meaning, unless one broke it down phonetically and translated *Mate* and *land* and it didn't seem as if my father had attempted to do that, amalgamating the concept of partner and country into a new word. Or, for that matter, using *mate* in its sense of meaning friend (although I doubted that this particular piece of working-class familiarity had made its way into the English Public School system no matter how low down the register the Dorset establishment had been). And even Daryna had balked in the wildest of her gesticulations at trying to convey to me a

50

sense of sexually cohabiting earth. Just what any of this told me though — if indeed it told me anything — I wasn't sure. But it did make me wonder if Nastasiya had struggled over the name just as Daryna had or if the two of them had had occasion to write the name Maitland in Cyrillic before my father had left for school and had come to some sort of accommodation on how to represent it.

I suppose this might be seen as nit picking but what it did do was start me thinking about just when it had been that Nastasiya had first met Frederick Maitland. The only thing I could say with certainty was that at some point within the eighteen months after she had first come to England — and by the time my father had written the letter — Nastasiya had met Frederick and that also, despite spending most of his time in school, my father also knew him well enough to feel obliged to send his regards in a letter.

My father had referred to him as *Mr* Maitland which, by itself, didn't entirely preclude the chance of his mother having remarried but suggested not; how my father referred to Frederick after the marriage I didn't know, (*father* seemed unlikely). Of course, by the time I was around to notice what my father called him, long after Nastasiya's death, he never referred to him at all. Puzzling it over, I became aware how still very hazy I was about just when Frederick and Nastasiya had met and married. The one envelope I possessed was addressed to *Nastasiya Zaretsky* and it seemed reasonable enough to me that after just eighteen months in England my father and his mother would still be hoping that Aleksander would make it out of the Ukraine. Even if that was not the case and Nastasiya knew her husband was dead, I still couldn't help thinking it displayed a somewhat unseemly haste to remarry again so soon. But then, I wasn't a foreigner in a strange land with a dependent son and no visible means of support. What the fees per term for the Dorset school might have been I couldn't begin to guess but I was pretty sure that Nastasiya couldn't have met them. This alone suggested that Frederick was paying for my father's education by the date of the earliest letter and, judging by its content, that particular letter wasn't the earliest he had written from there. Perhaps it was just that my idea of unseemly was someone else's notion of pragmatism.

What I needed to do, I decided, was to check with George as to what he knew of the timeline, exactly when they were married and what documents he had that would verify this.

~

I must admit to being somewhat surprised when the doorbell rang after lunch the next day and I found Daryna on the step. She was wearing her same coat and a pair of black leather boots, scuffed at the toe and down at the heel. Tied loosely around her throat was a grey scarf that matched her eyes and in her gloved hand she clutched a faux-leather attaché case.

My surprise must have showed because she said, 'I have come to translate letters,' in case I had forgotten who she was.

Inside, she took off her coat. She was wearing the same woollen jacket and skirt she had worn the day before. She placed the attaché case on the table and took out a Russian Cyrillic-English dictionary.

'Ukrainian English dictionary is not possible,' she announced. 'Russian is close. Today it will be easier, yes.'

She motioned me to sit down and picked up the letters, which I had left, where we had finished with them the day before.

It crossed my mind to wonder where it was she was studying English if she was available in the afternoon on weekdays, and the notion deepened my suspicions about her immigration status. I was well aware that bogus English-language schools had long been an immigration scam, springing up at one premises as fast as they were closed down at another, the applicants for their courses entering the country on temporary visas before slipping into the crowd. The service designated to track down and deport them was hopelessly inadequate for the purpose — or perhaps I mean just hopelessly inadequate. Immigration, though, had never been my professional concern and, anyway, I was retired. Even so, I had always felt uncomfortable with the use of the term "economic migrant" — never mind "asylum seeker" — as one of denigration. If people didn't have the right to better their circumstances it seemed to me they had few rights worth having at all. I supposed, in essence, that that was what the Russian peasant who found himself under Bolshevik rule had tried and, in view of the fact that it had been barely more than two generations since they had escaped serfdom — in reality no more than another word for slavery — one could hardly blame them for consequently opposing a new oppressor who seemingly only wanted to exploit their labour just as ruthlessly as their predecessor had. To solve their problem in Russia and the Ukraine the Bolsheviks had resorted to murder. At least, with all our laws against unrestricted immigration no one had yet suggested we go that far.

But I thought it hardly politic to trouble Daryna with these considerations. She busied herself transcribing the second letter into legible Cyrillic into my notebook, then, with repeated references to the dictionary, into English. I sat and watched her for a while, apparently superfluous to the work in hand although quite taken with the frown of concentration that creased her brow and by the enticing way her tongue would protrude a little to lick her lower lip when troubled by a particularly knotty word. She looked up at me now and again even favoured me with the occasional smile from that sullen, disapproving mouth, but when I found myself smiling as well — not *at* her but *about* her — I thought it time I got up and absented myself to the kitchen.

'Tea?' I suggested.

'I would like tea very much,' she said.

She stopped work long enough to drink her tea and I took the opportunity to ask her a few questions; nothing that I thought might alarm her, merely the enquiries anyone might reasonably make of another.

She was twenty-eight years old and from a large family with two brothers and two sisters, she told me. She was the eldest. Her father was an engineer who worked for the Ukrainian railways and her mother was a chemist. They were all still in the Ukraine. She had been in England six months and liked it very much. She might stay, she said. Any further enquiries concerning her language school, however, or as to where she was living or what she did in her spare time were met either with generalisations or outright evasions. I didn't press her.

When she, in her turn, questioned me on what I had done for a living and about my family, I suddenly found myself being equally as evasive. And when she asked me outright why it was I was not married, I was unable to formulate a reply.

The old "never met the right girl" excuse seemed more evasive that ever, so I said instead:

'I was always abroad a lot with my work. That's hardly conducive to any relationship.' "Conducive" set her frowning again so I added, 'It's difficult when people are apart.'

'This is truth,' she agreed. 'And your work was always in other country?'

53

'Usually.' This time I had plumped for working in overseas development in the hope that it might sound boring enough to steer the questioning in other directions.

Although I saw no reason to tell Daryna, there *had* been the occasional liaison but none that had survived the periods of separation. As for anything serious in the way of inter-office or local connections, it had always been understood that these, for those tucked away in our peculiar niche, were frowned upon. We were, after all, grey self-effacing people — at times, I thought, barely corporeal in any meaningful sense at all — and for those who worked under even the shallowest of covers their supposed lives were never really anything more than a shell. In truth, there was often nothing of substance whatsoever.

I did feel like telling her how it had come as something of a surprise to find one day that, not only had I become suddenly middle-aged, but that I now also had to live the kind of life that once I only observed in others; that by then opportunities to meet people that once might have been thought of as so common that they could be blithely ignored, were now so disconcertingly rare and that if, like me, you were someone who suffered from a horror of lapses in judgement, you shrank from even these few opportunities in fear of lurching into disaster.

But I didn't, of course. To do so would have been to commit exactly one of those lapses I so feared.

Instead, I picked up her translation of the second letter and read my father's ramblings on school life as he thought fit to relate to his mother.

From references he made I could see that he was a regular correspondent and that the assumption that the letters I had must have been only a fraction of those he had written was correct. Either Nastasiya had destroyed the others (which begged the question as to why she had preserved these) or that they had been lost in the Blitz. Then it occurred to me that she probably wrote as frequently to him, and that these letters too were lost. Perhaps my father had discarded them after reading them, or at some point later had decided they were not worth keeping; so, as I sat with Daryna at my dining room table, I became aware that it was to only one half of a conversation to which I was listening, like eavesdropping on a private phone call. I had to fill in for myself the other voice as best I could.

Because of this there were many odd references of my father's that I did not understand. At that time I was unconcerned by this and thought that I would have plenty of opportunities later to puzzle over these allusions. In the meantime, I kept stumbling over Daryna's spelling and eccentric grammar. As she completed the second letter of that afternoon, I gingerly raised the subject.

'You are learning English?' I said to her at the risk of stating the obvious.

I imagine she thought I was labouring under a deficiency of memory because she said again:

'I am student of English.'

'Then may I,' I offered as tactfully as I could, 'show you where you have made a mistake?'

I half expected her to suggest where an old ingrate like me might shove my stained letters if I wasn't satisfied with the service she was providing. And, for a second, her grey eyes did flicker, but she would not have understood "ingrate", of course, and it might just have been apprehension I saw as if she was afraid I might want my money back. But she got over that soon enough and squared her slender shoulders and leaned across me toward the translation I was holding.

'I have made error?' she asked.

'*An* error,' I corrected, thinking if the thing was to be done it might as well be done properly. 'You mustn't forget the article.'

'What is article?'

I had to think about it for a moment. 'It's a word used with a noun,' I said. 'It specifies whether the noun is definite or indefinite.'

'Definite or indefinite? Please?'

I began to feel like a man who'd stepped into a quicksand.

'If the noun is not specific — indefinite — the article is "a" or "an". If it is specific — definite — then you use "the".' And I began pointing around the room. '*The* notebook ... *the* table ... *a* window...'

The brows knotted. 'Not *the* window?'

'I was speaking of windows in general,' I said, waist-deep and sinking fast.

Daryna pondered upon this, biting prettily at her lip.

'I have much to learn,' she said and her shoulders sagged a little as if I had punctured her self-esteem. Then she pulled her dictionary towards her and flicked quickly through the pages, a horrible jumble of what seemed to me a mix of Latin and Greek letters with mathematical symbols thrown in for good measure.

'I have *the* proposal,' she announced.

'*A* proposal,' I said. 'It is not a definite article.'

She wagged a dissenting finger at me. 'No, no, this is most definite proposal.'

I began to wonder just how far she was prepared to go to stay in England.

'I have to improve English. You have interest in Ukraine. You maybe like to learn language and Cyrillic writing?'

'I suppose so,' I replied cautiously.

'Then we teach each other, yes?'

She was sitting upright again, as composed as might befit a girl who has made a serious proposal.

'All right,' I agreed, failing to see the harm in that. And I mimicked her formal manner of the previous day and held out my hand to shake on it.

'No, no,' she said again, holding up the imperious finger. 'I have already knowledge of English language. You have no Ukrainian. It is right, I think, that you pay me small sum for this service. To put on proper footing as English say, yes?'

'How small a sum?'

She shrugged nonchalantly. 'Ten pounds for lesson?'

It did cross my mind briefly what use I might derive out of learning Ukrainian but then I saw her lick her lower lip with her tongue and I found myself agreeing.

'Ten pounds a lesson.'

She held her hand towards me and we shook formally.

'My name,' she said for the first time, as if confident now of her fiscal footing, 'is Daryna Marianenko.'

TWO

6

At the end of the week following Michael Standing's murder, Nick gave me a call to say he was on his way. Then, a second later, in one of those disconcerting moments that make you wonder if time has given some tectonic lurch, the doorbell rang. Walking to answer it, I had to convince myself that it couldn't really be Nick.

Nor was it. It was Daryna. She looked even further down in the mouth than normal and there was a puffiness around her eyes that told me she had been crying. She was hauling a battered suitcase behind her and was in through the door almost before I had time to get out of the way.

'I have problem,' she announced, 'and only come to you from absolute necessity.'

We had been giving each other lessons since the Spring, meeting usually at least once a week. Her grasp of English had improved considerably while I could be said to be still toiling on the Ukrainian equivalent of the nursery slopes. To save unnecessary damage to my ego, I had put this down to the difference in our ages and took what comfort I could from my ability as a teacher and the resultant expansion of her vocabulary. Indeed, I might just then have congratulated her on her use of the word 'absolute' although it didn't seem quite the right time.

As it happens I hadn't seen her for a fortnight and her mobile number had become unobtainable. I hadn't been particularly concerned since there had been similar periods of absence and despite our growing familiarity she still had told me so little of her personal circumstances that I had had no way except her mobile of contacting her. In another week I might have given Charlie a ring to see if the woman who had found her for me knew anything, but at that moment I was more concerned with my weekend away. I was pleased to see her again although my pleasure was tempered somewhat by the sight of the suitcase.

She wheeled the thing awkwardly through the hall and into my lounge then turned to face me. Her usual composure had been shaken. There was almost look of desperation in her eyes.

'I have nowhere to go,' she said, looking at me earnestly. 'I have been living with boyfriend but he turns into pig.'

We had made some progress in her use of the article before a noun but it seemed at times of stress bad habits reasserted themselves.

'Have you had an argument?'

'No. It is worse than this. I cannot tell you. It is too shaming.'

We had been tackling concepts expressed by the present participle and I had used humiliation and synonyms like shaming to demonstrate alternative nuances of meaning but had worried at the time that it might be getting too complicated for her. Listening to her use one of our concepts in context gave me inordinate pleasure and I smiled at her proudly.

She rounded on me sharply.

'You think is situation to laugh at?'

'No,' I said, mortified. 'I'm sorry. I'm sorry you have a problem with your boyfriend.'

'Pig!' she said.

'With your pig,' I corrected absently. 'But I'm about to go away for the weekend. My brother-in-law will be picking me up in a few minutes.'

'I only ask as friend,' she implored, on the verge of tears again. 'He cannot find me, please. Until I make arrangements otherwhere.'

'Elsewhere,' I said.

'Elsewhere,' she repeated, stamping her foot and closing her eyes in frustration. When she opened them she was looking at me pleadingly.

I gave in immediately. 'Of course,' I told her. 'Of course you can stay.'

She rushed at me, hugged me and kissed me on the cheek. 'You are *a* good man,' she said, accenting the indefinite article.

I put any thought out of my head of the definite article in that context and picked up her suitcase. I carried it upstairs. We were making the bed when the doorbell rang again. Daryna jumped nervously.

'That'll be Nick,' I said. 'I'll have to go.'

I hesitated. I wanted to be sure she would be safe yet didn't want to cancel my weekend in the country.

She sensed my reluctance and said, 'Go, Alex. I will be all right.'

'You know where everything is,' I told her. 'There's plenty of food. I'll give you a call.'

Nick pressed the bell again as I went down the stairs then the phone start ringing, as if Daryna had trailed a convention of campanologists in her wake. I stopped, caught between it and the door. I plumped for the door and opened it on Nick's expectant face. He said, 'Ready?' just as the answer phone clicked on behind me and a man's voice filled the hall in response to my curt invitation to leave a message.

'Mr Maitland? My name's Fielding. David Griffiths gave me your number. Could you ring me back?'

I backtracked to pick up, but by the time I reached the phone Fielding had given his number and rung off. I scribbled it down on a scrap of paper and thrust it into my pocket.

'Do you need to call him back?' Nick asked, looking at his watch.

'I'll do it later,' I said, grabbing the weekend bag I had already packed and left waiting at the foot of the stairs. 'Griffiths was Michael Standing's researcher. It's probably just a journalist looking for a new angle.'

But Nick wasn't listening. He was looking past me with raised eyebrows at Daryna on the stairs.

'I'll explain on the way,' I said quickly, reaching for my coat and closing the door behind us.

~

Nick had been accepted as a prospective Tory candidate for Parliament four or five years earlier, and they must have liked the look of him because when a safe seat came up in the south shortly afterwards they parachuted him in over the head of a local man. He'd got in, albeit with a reduced majority from the previous election, and promptly bought a property in the constituency to smooth the ruffled local feathers, spending as much time there as he could. This, in fact, was the straw that finally broke the back of his marriage to my sister. Although they'd done well to conceal the fact, things hadn't been too good for some time and the prospect of playing constituency wife to a politician was not how Olena had seen her future. They had waited for a decent interval after the by-election, like some sham period of mourning, and then quietly divorced. Olena kept the house in town and, besides the constituency house, Nick bought himself a flat somewhere close enough to Westminster to be on permanent beck and call to his new masters. Since being elected he had made rapid progress within the Party helped, of course, by the fact that money was not a consideration. His father, my Uncle George, had harboured political ambitions for Nick for some time and was quite prepared to finance the venture. He was so keen that, on his retirement, he had bought a property in the constituency as well, taking a sort of generational step backward in founding a dynasty.

When Nick had asked the morning after Standing's murder if I had any plans for the following weekend, I hadn't really had to think about it for long. I'd been meaning to catch up with George whom I hadn't seen since his retirement, and I decided the November rain I had been looking at for the past couple of weeks might look better through the windows of a country house. I had dug out my old canvas coat, which I thought might suit the country, a hat, gloves and scarf, and threw a sufficiency of other items into a bag to tide me over a weekend, then tossed a book on top to fill the idle moments.

Nick's black 3.1 BMW Roadster was parked at the kerb and while I was glad to see that becoming a shadow junior Minister hadn't rubbed off his more flamboyant edges I was a little apprehensive as to how my back would weather the drive.

Nick opened the boot to make room for my bag looking askance at the house and then at me.

'She's teaching me Ukrainian,' I said as I squeezed my bag into the boot. Then I opened the car door and squeezed myself into the passenger seat with almost as much difficulty.

'You old dog,' he said. 'I've heard a lot of euphemisms for it since I've been in the House, but that's a new one.'

'It's true,' I said. 'Her name's Daryna. I was looking for someone to translate those old letters of my father's and she suggested that in return for my improving her English she'd teach me Ukrainian.'

Nick grinned. '"Improving her English"? I'll have to use that one myself.'

'She just turned up on my doorstep,' I protested. 'She said she's had an argument with her boyfriend. I've got an idea it's more than that though. I think her visa's expired too.'

'Whoa,' Nick said. 'That's enough. I don't need to know any more. Think of the headlines: *MP's brother-in-law in love-nest with illegal immigrant.*'

'That would be something of a stretch even for the tabloids,' I said.

'You know what they're like.' Then, looking across at me, he suddenly said, 'You're not getting serious about her by any chance, are you Alex?'

'Don't be ridiculous,' I told him. 'It's all above board.'

I shifted my position and must have grimaced because he muttered:

'Stupid of me. I should have brought the Merc. I didn't give your back a second thought.'

'Forget it,' I told him. 'You'll get there twice as fast in this. Although may I take it that if you're still squeezing yourself into this thing you've not met anyone new you can take home to meet the parents yet?'

He grinned. 'Never underestimate the pulling power of a sports car. It must have been the same even back in your day.'

'My day? Bloody cheek,' I said.

'Actually,' he admitted, 'my mother scares off most of the girls I meet these days.'

'Don't you mean most of the girls you fancy these days?'

He chuckled to himself then took us west out of town towards the M4, following the signs for the south and the M3, weaving in and out of the Friday evening traffic with bursts of acceleration followed by minutes lost in jams. Sitting low to the ground, I found myself breathing in the diesel and gasoline fumes hanging like a ground mist at our level.

When we finally reached the motorway he floored the pedal, eyes flicking intermittently to his mirrors as we left the speed limit behind. We were free of the worst of the traffic before he brought up the subject of Michael Standing.

'Did you hear from the police at all?' he asked.

I felt a stab of apprehension at the thought of them turning up at the house again and finding Daryna there. I hadn't thought to warn her. But it had only been a couple of days since they'd spoken to me and I couldn't imagine they'd want to see me again so soon. I assumed they would have enough on their plate without chasing up tenuous leads like me. I told Nick about the interview I'd had then said:

'I daresay they're still looking for a burglar.'

'The press are giving it a bit of stick.'

And they were. Standing's death was still the lead in most of the papers, the tabloids at least, and looked to remain so until the next big story came along. If precedent was anything to go by, I feared lack of progress would soon translate into the police making a suspect of the nearest likely misfit available. It had become a depressingly familiar pattern over the years, which had resulted in long spells in prison for several unfortunate people until their cases had finally been quashed on appeal. Common sense, one would have assumed, would suggest that the worst abuses should be behind us with advances in DNA technology eliminating miscarriages of justice, but technology is only as good as those employed to use it and I was aware that careless handling — or wilful *mis*handling — of evidence and cross-contamination was an ever-present possibility. On the other hand, it often seemed to me that DNA evidence and other forensic techniques had taken on an aura of infallibility, one that risked eclipsing the possibility of sloppy procedure. The fact that some minute piece of lint could dictate whether or not a man would spend years in prison — or even if he were to continue living at all — was, when one came to think about it, the stuff of nightmares.

But it was an old hobbyhorse of mine that I had bored Nick with before, so instead of climbing back in that particular saddle, I said:

'What was Standing like when you knew him?'

'At Cambridge?' He sounded surprised I had asked. 'Well, I don't know that I did, really. Know him, I mean.' He grinned at me again. 'Had I an inkling he was going to be famous — well, what passes for famous these days — I might have cultivated him. But you know what it's like at university — a sea of new faces that come and go and what seems like friendship one day, a few years down the track, turns a face into a nagging memory you can't quite pin down.'

62

As it happens, I didn't know what it was like at university as Nick well knew, but thought I knew what he meant just the same.

'Rather like entering the Commons, I imagine,' I said.

'Yes,' he said, swinging out into the overtaking lane again, 'in a way. In the Commons, though, you know which side you're bread's buttered before you go in. At university it's all there to chose from and at the beginning you have no idea what's best for you.'

'Are we talking about girls again?' I asked.

Nick smiled, a little ruefully I thought. 'I never had that happy knack of meeting girls easily,' he said somewhat disingenuously. 'That's the one thing I do remember about Standing, as it happens. He always attracted the best looking girls even then.'

'Even then?' I said. 'When I spoke to Olena after it happened she assumed he played the field. Was he known for it? I must admit he never gave me that impression.'

'Well,' Nick said, 'you only met him a couple of times, didn't you? I'm only going on what I heard, although don't ask me where because I haven't the faintest idea. Probably Olena now you mention it.'

He asked after her but as I hadn't seen her for a while and had only spoken on the phone briefly I couldn't give him much information. For some reason, what I couldn't help thinking of was how Standing had been on the last occasion we had met. We were at his hotel after he'd given his talk at a seminar on semantics. He had been expecting his wife to join him for lunch and, when she hadn't, it would hardly have been an overstatement to say that he was distracted by the fact. To me he had given the appearance of a concerned husband.

Nick and I lapsed into silence for a few miles and we were past Southampton and cutting across the northern edge of the New Forest before we spoke again. A cold snap earlier in the month had hurried the seasonal leaf fall and now, the rain having cleared, under a gibbous moon the trees were stark against the November sky. The fields lay pallid and still, washed of colour like a monochrome photograph.

'So,' I said eventually, just to break the monotony of the BMW's guttural purr, 'how's your father taking to squirearchal life?'

'You'd think he'd been born to it,' Nick said. 'Wait and see.'

I didn't have long to wait. Somewhere west of Fordingbridge Nick swung the roadster onto a narrow side road and, after a mile, turned off between two large wrought-iron gates and down a long drive next to a Victorian lodge house. I knew George had bought himself a largish house and some land but my remark about the squirearchy was meant to be facetious. It was a reminder, as if I needed one, never to make judgements on too little information. The drive must have been half a mile or so in length and, after the first gentle bend, travelled through a thickly wooded rise. The moon slipped behind the overhanging canopy and the BMW's lights cut a tunnel through the trees like a borehole into a forested past. Nick slowed and shifted up a couple of gears.

'He's got deer here and they've a nasty habit of jumping out on you.'

At the top of the rise, the ground levelled and the trees dropped abruptly away. The lights of the roadster swept briefly across open grassland then down again as we dropped into a vale. On the further hillside the house stood under its illumination like a Regency mansion positioned with the precision of an Inigo Jones agrarian confection.

Perhaps I whistled — I'm prone to the odd cliché when surprised — because Nick laughed again.

'I know,' he said. 'A bit over the top, isn't it, but he said he's looking to the future.'

It occurred to me that it might have been a little late in George's life to be looking to the future and, although that was hardly the kind of remark to voice, Nick must have known which way my mind was running because he said:

'Not his. Mine. To be honest he's expecting big things of my political career and I'm not sure I can deliver. He's talking about a cabinet place after the next election and then, perhaps...' He didn't finish, as if putting it into words might tempt ill fortune.

Under that misshapen moon again, with a hanging ground mist that began to wisp in the headlights and obscure the house as we dropped into the valley bottom towards a stream and a stone bridge, I felt an impulse towards superstition myself.

'He thinks it's a suitably substantial country seat for a heavyweight member of the Party. So that's what I'm expected to become.'

I felt a pang of sympathy for Nick. Generally, such an emotion experienced on his behalf was usually connected with my sister, Olena, but perhaps for the first time I realized what expectations had been put upon him by his father.

Before he had gone into politics, after finishing his education, Nick had, naturally enough, gone into business. He had joined the family brokerage firm and discovered he had a facility for trading. After a spell at that, he had joined a bank. His father may have eased the way but he had by no means made it a foregone conclusion that Nick would climb the ladder on to the board. There were plenty of snakes, you might say, waiting to trip him up and grease his way down to the lower rungs again. But he made his way — and his own name — before deciding that politics was for the long run. After all, he might have sat back with a fistful of non-executive directorships and a steady income; he had the name and the connections and the City was full of that sort and no one would have thought the worse of him for it. Except Nick himself. And George.

Perhaps it was fortunate for Nick that he had put himself forward as a candidate for Parliament before the fact of being a banker — or former banker, for that matter — was tantamount to being a *persona non grata* in politics, not to mention among the general populace. I dare say if he had tried it today there wouldn't be a constituency selection committee in the land that would have looked twice at him. Not that he'd stayed in banking or trading long enough to have benefited from the kind of bonuses they were paying themselves towards the end of the bull market. In Nick's days as a trader his bonus would have been a Porsche, or, if he'd done particularly well, perhaps enough money to buy himself a small flat. Not to be sneezed at, you might think, and as a benefice it certainly added up in annual increments, but small beer by today's standards. Perhaps if he'd stuck it out he could have numbered himself today amongst the obscenely wealthy. Olena probably wouldn't have divorced him if that had been the case. But that wasn't what Nick was after. Or George.

And after all, when it came to obscene wealth George could be as lewd as the best of them. The Maitlands weren't short of cash. But long ago I'd come to understand that merely the acquisition of wealth wasn't the be-all and end-all for them. I speak, you understand, as an outsider. For them the maintenance of the fortune and what you did with it was what counted. Each Maitland (there was a network of family trusts although I wasn't a beneficiary of any of them) was expected to add to the pile, supervise it during their tenure, and then hand it on intact to the next generation.

George's father, Frederick, had founded the family fortune. Given the breach with *my* father, I had never known much about

Frederick's background beyond the fact that *his* father had been some sort of diplomat and that Frederick had been born somewhere in the middle-east during one of his diplomatic postings. Coming from an upper middle-class family, though, had given him a head start. He'd had his fingers in a myriad of pies as far as I understood, starting out when being a trader had meant ships and locomotives and a certain amount of physical effort and discomfort, not merely sitting in front of a computer screen. Although he had been my father's stepfather, at some point before or during the war they had ceased to get along and I had never had the opportunity of meeting him. The main consequence of the breach was that my father refused ever to benefit from Maitland money and had gone his own way. As an airline pilot, he had earned a decent salary, although for some reason money had never seemed plentiful. It might have been no more than relative appearances and, over the years, George, his younger half-brother, had on many occasions offered financial assistance. My father, though, had always turned him down. It was one of the reasons I had not gone to university. Towards the end, following my mother's long illness and after my father's own health had failed, extra money would have been useful, but while he was still able to make his own decisions he continued to refuse. Afterwards, when he was not, I refused on his behalf feeling it would have been a betrayal to accept the assistance he had spent the better part of a lifetime declining. He wouldn't, of course, take any money that came through Olena either. It was one of the reasons that, as soon as I was old enough to make my own decisions, I elected to make my own way as well. Olena, of course, thought me stupid. Perhaps I was. I just regarded it as being consistent. A bed for a couple of nights and a few decent meals, though, didn't seem to constitute a betrayal of my father's principals, so I had always been happy to accept George's hospitality for the odd weekend. Even then, though, there was always a voice in the back of my head that stopped me from making a habit of it.

Nick pulled the roadster to a stop in front of the house. Close to, it seemed even grander, rising up into the night under its yellow spotlights. George was atop a short flight of stone steps at the front door, grinning like an older — and more urbane — version of Nick. His hair appeared greyer in the unnatural light but he still looked younger than his sixty-odd years. He was a big, barrel-chested man who had kept himself in condition, broad and upright and carrying only enough excess weight to give him presence.

'I'll grab the bags,' Nick said, already halfway out the car. 'You say hello to Dad.'

Having stiffened up on the journey, I made an awkward business of getting out of the BMW and Nick was already at my side with our bags before I had gained the first step. George came down to greet us.

'It's time you got rid of that thing, Nick,' he said, 'if only for Alex's sake. How are you Alex?' He beamed at me and grabbed my hand. 'I don't see enough of you. I didn't see enough of your father in those last years and now I'm making the same mistake with you.'

I looked at him warily. 'Whose last years are you talking about now, George, yours or mine? I'm not looking to give up just yet and you look as though you'll go on forever.'

'You know what happens to businessmen when they retire,' Nick chipped in as he climbed past George with our bags. 'They fade fast and go out with a bang.'

'You hope,' George told him. Then to me, 'He's taken a fancy to this place and can't wait to get his hands on it.' He linked his arm in mine and we followed Nick up towards the entrance. 'Just drop your bags on the floor, Nick. Patterson will take them up to your rooms. You'll be wanting a drink.'

'My bag is the shabby one,' I told him unnecessarily. The holdall had followed me around the world to a variety of postings and showed the fact. I took off my coat and dropped it along with hat and gloves on top of the bag. I kept the scarf on, waiting until I had properly warmed up.

The entrance hall, from what I saw of it as George dragged me quickly through into a drawing room, was as grandly impressive as I might have supposed. The staircase was predictably wide and, although not stone, took a graceful curve towards the first floor with an ornamental carved oak balustrade that must have been the devil to clean. I was still craning my neck as we passed into a large room furnished with comfortable armchairs and occasional tables, pastel rugs and the kind of fine porcelain that owes its elegance to its simplicity. A great stone fireplace was the centrepiece and a log a man must have struggled to carry in lay burning on a bed of ash supported by a pair of iron dogs. Nick's mother, Jennifer, stood in front of the fire.

My aunt Jennifer was as elegant as the porcelain but there was nothing simple about her. She had been a real beauty in her youth, I could never help recalling, and had kept her looks as she had grown older. As far as I was aware, she had never resorted to artificial means to maintain her appearance and beyond makeup and perhaps hair colouring gave the impression that she put little effort into her grooming. Yet this very fact added a touch of austerity to her character, which, I suspected was designed to hold people at a distance.

She greeted Nick warmly though, holding his arms and reaching up as he stooped to give her a kiss. Then she turned to me and held out her hand. We had never kissed, not in the forty years I had known her.

'Alex,' she said in that husky tone of hers that always came as a surprise as it jarred with her air of reserve. 'How nice you were able to come.'

As I said, Jennifer was my aunt although in reality she was only four or five years older than I was. As a teenager, I had been more than a little in love with her. I had often wondered whether she had been aware of the fact and if that was why she had always kept me at arms-length. I had never been crass enough to declare myself nor, I hope, had ever trailed, moonstruck, behind her, but some people have an instinct for these things and I thought that perhaps she had realized and had decided never to encourage me. Or perhaps she had merely thought me pathetic, or just plain stupid. Unless she told you, one could never tell what Jennifer thought. She was a perpetual enigma as far as I was concerned.

Olena, of course, could have written a book about her ex-mother-in-law and would, given any excuse, try to deliver the audio version as well. Yet, even after years of listening to my sister on the subject, I was never any the wiser concerning Jennifer, nor ever learned Jennifer's opinion of me. The one thing I did know for certain was that Olena herself had never managed to plumb Jennifer's depths.

George was pouring drinks, an aged single malt — and not stinted, either — for us, and a dry sherry for Jennifer. She rarely took anything stronger and rarely more than one. We sat and exchanged the usual pleasantries for a few minutes until Jennifer had finished her sherry then excused herself on the pretext of making sure our rooms were ready. We stood as she left the room then sat down again — and, it has to be said, relaxed.

That evening we mostly talked politics. At least, George and Nick did most of the talking. I contributed the odd comment or two over an informal dinner, but politics — at least, present-day domestic politics — is not a subject I find interests me particularly. I have no affiliations; it was not something ostensibly encouraged during my time with the SIS; it was always assumed one was a "right-thinking" individual. Having served masters of differing ideological stamp, however, I have found, to be honest, that they're all much of a muchness. That in itself, I suppose, speaks of the soundness of our system.

After coffee back in the drawing room, Jennifer disappeared again. We had a couple more drinks but after a while I grew restless of the talk and stood. I warmed myself in front of the great fire and looked around the room. There were a good many photographs, framed and standing on most of the available surfaces where they did not interfere with the porcelain. By and large they were family and private, either informal or studio photos; George's collection of business photographs, him with politicians and other business colleagues, bigwigs and the occasional celebrity — rather the modern-day equivalent of a hunter's trophies, I had always thought — were absent. Collected together in a study somewhere for private delectation, I presumed. What remained was family.

I rather wanted to tour the room and look at them, curious, I suppose, to know if Olena had survived the divorce or had been purged and written out of Maitland history in a paraphrased domestic microcosm of Stalin's dictum: *no wife, no problem.* But somehow I thought the act of looking might appear too overt — at least, on my first visit — so I stifled a couple of yawns to lay the groundwork before, during a lapse in the conversation, announcing that I was tired and wondered if they'd mind if I went up to my room. George was solicitous and said he'd show me the way.

I said goodnight to Nick and walked beside George up the wide staircase. Near the landing he asked:

'How are you finding retirement, Alex? Are you managing?' I suspected the question had a financial facet that presaged an offer and so, to save us both embarrassment, wilfully misunderstood him.

'Oh,' I said, 'you know what they say, one wonders how one had time for work. I daresay it's the same with you.' But he didn't take the opportunity to tell me about himself as I had assumed he would and there was a small awkward silence between us for a moment.

'I wrote that small memoir of my father's RAF service, if you recall,' I said to fill the gap as he led me along a corridor. 'It wasn't long enough to warrant printing but I posted it on a website dedicated to foreigners who served in the RAF during the war.'

'I never thought of Peter as a foreigner,' he said, 'just as my big brother.' He smiled fondly. 'Although you could still catch a trace of his accent now and then, particularly when he lost his temper.'

I laughed. 'I remember that well,' I said.

'You'll have to show it to me,' George said. 'I'd like to read it.'

'I've been thinking of doing something longer, as a matter of fact. Well, try at least. I've been doing quite a lot of research over the last few months.'

We stopped and George opened a door and turned a light on in the room. He stood aside for me.

'Is that what that fellow Standing was helping you with? he asked me, stopping at the door. 'The one that was murdered?'

'He wasn't helping *me*,' I said. 'He was researching on his own account. But he gave me the idea to look into Dad's early life in the Ukraine. He seemed to think that Zaretsky — Nastasiya's first husband — might have played some part in the famine but I suspect he never told me all he found out. If Zaretsky was involved, I rather got the idea that it was not in a very creditable way so perhaps he was trying to save me from unpleasant news.'

'I've always wished I'd known my mother,' George confided, 'my real mother.' He stood at the door but did not come into the room. 'Of course, you know I was just a toddler when she died and I always thought of Elizabeth as my mother. But your father used to tell me about Nastasiya and she sounded quite a woman. It's difficult to believe that she'd have married your grandfather if he'd been capable of involvement in the kind of atrocities that were being committed back then.

'It would be nice to think so,' I agreed, 'but like the Chinese say, they were interesting times.'

'Well, I suppose we'll never know now.'

'Probably not,' I said.

'Sleep well, Alex. If there's anything you want... I'll see you in the morning.'

I closed the door and looked around the room. It was really more the size of a small apartment than a room and far grander than I was used to. A fire had been laid in the grate with a few logs stacked next to it. A large double bed occupied one corner but still left room for a writing desk and chair and an armchair by the fire. Another small stand at the foot of the bed held my bag. One or two things had been taken out and laid on the bed, but it looked as if the exercise had been abandoned halfway through, in disgust perhaps at the ragbag assortment of clothes I had bought with me. My toilet bag was no longer there, though, and I found a door to my right that opened onto an en-suite with bath and shower, all newly fitted by the look of it.

I finished unpacking, finding my hat and coat already hanging in a cupboard, but no scarf. I had taken it off downstairs after I had warmed up and left it on a chair. Tomorrow was soon enough to retrieve that, though, and I turned on the bedside lamp and switched off the overhead, then opened the drapes a few inches. The grounds were in darkness. The exterior lighting had been extinguished and the moon had set somewhere behind the trees. It was too dark to make out anything except a mass of shadow out across the lawns.

I closed the curtains and undressed. Emptying my pockets, I felt the scrap of paper on which I'd written the phone number of the man who had rung as I had left the house that afternoon. It was too late to call then so I scrawled *Fielding* above the number and left it on the writing desk where I'd find it in the morning. I cleaned my teeth in the bathroom then got into bed and opened the book I had brought with me, Robert Conquest's *The Harvest Of Sorrow*, an account of the Ukrainian famine. But it was not light reading, painting the picture it did of oppression and starvation, and after the alcohol I had drunk my eyes kept drifting over the same sentences.

The last thing I remembered before falling asleep was what George had said about Nastasiya and, although I had always known it, I think that that was the first time it really registered with me that, like myself, George too was half Ukrainian.

7

It had been shortly after Michael Standing had left me that first afternoon that I decided to investigate my father's early years. Left with just those letters in Ukrainian sitting on my dining room table I resolved, first to find someone who might be able to translate them for me and then to do some digging on my own account into what it was that had happened to my father that had so thoroughly decided him to reject his background. The difficulty of the task was not lost on me, but I had spent so much of my working life sifting information, making connections and following threads through a seeming clutter of unrelated facts, that I never really seriously considered that I might not be up to the job. I had made a career out of finding patterns in seemingly pattern-less facts — even discerning patterns in the fact that there *were* no patterns. But I had to admit that all this had been achieved with information at hand, of which the task of collecting had been left to other people. Now, I was proposing to start from scratch, in a field with which I was unfamiliar. After giving it some thought, I was at something of a loss as to where to begin.

That first evening I opened a bottle of Chilean Maipo and made myself a light supper so as not to feel guilty about solitary drinking. Then, having eaten, I turned on my laptop. Standing had mentioned several names during his visit, but I had not taken notes and most of them I had, by now, forgotten. I began with what I knew, though, and since Griffiths had apparently found me by Googling my father's real name, I typed in Zaretsky and hit the key. Most of the initial results concerned a pair of Israeli ice dancers who, though they had originated in Byelorussia, didn't seem to bear much relevance to my search. There was an Eli Zaretsky — an American professor of history who, oddly enough, wrote on Marxism and sociology and who had published much on the theoretical aspects of socialism — but even a second glass of wine failed to deaden the trepidation I felt at following his lines of thought. I passed him over for Victor Zaretsky, a Ukrainian who had actually painted a canvas depicting the famine; it was an interesting work but he was from Kyvov and I had always understood that my grandfather had come from Kharkov. I scanned down several more pages. There were quite a few contemporary entries (Zaretskys had made it to Facebook) and some genealogical sites concerning the Zaretsky name, which looked more promising. But I was daunted by the great number of leads it offered and reasoned that Griffiths must have run through these before he had actually come up with my modest memoir and name — which in fact *I* couldn't find, so just how he had managed to navigate his way to it I cannot say. It was entirely possible, of course, that he wasn't using Google but some other search engine more suited to academic research and that, unlike me, he was an adept in the mysteries of Boolean logic.

One name I did recall Standing having mentioned was Shostak, although a search in that direction was no more successful — an astronomer and an anthropologist being the most celebrated bearers of the name.

Giving up on what I knew, I began searching the websites dedicated to the Ukrainian Famine and found that there were far more than I could ever have imagined. A site celebrating Gareth Jones' short but eventful life proved a good place to start. His family, it transpired, had found his diaries, articles, and other material concerning his visits to the USSR all collected by his mother and kept under a bed at the family home. They were discovered following a burglary at the house where his elderly sister still lived. To the family's undying credit they had laboured to resurrect his all-but forgotten memory and restore him to his rightful place as the man who had alerted the West to the crimes committed in the Ukraine in the name of the Soviet state. I found, jumping from site to site, that the history of what had actually happened was still disputed (apologists for Stalin have lived on long after the death of the object of their veneration) but for the most part those who chose to play down the horrors of the Holodomor are obvious for what they are — unreconstructed hard-liners who still cling to a bankrupt ideology long after its corpse has decomposed. Perhaps that in itself is a clue to understanding their intransigence: to relinquish the cause to which they have dedicated their lives can only be to admit to a lifetime of self-delusion. Easier, one suspects, to keep the door locked and barred than to admit the facts.

It soon became apparent that discussion as to the causes of, and the responsibility for, the famine had resurfaced as soon as the Ukraine had unhitched herself from the Russian yoke. The event became a crucial element in the election and the "Orange Revolution" that followed. Many ethnic Russians lived in the Ukraine — the Black Sea Fleet had been based in the Crimea, for instance, around Sevastopol and the submarine pens in Balaklava — and many of the families and descendants of the sailors and shipyard workers still lived there and retained their Russian affinities. But fortunately this was a minefield I did not really have to enter; what I was interested in was documented fact, not political recrimination.

I played around for a while trying combinations of searches hoping vaguely to turn up something Standing and Griffiths had missed. He had asked about a foreigner — possibly English or

American — who my father might have met in the Ukraine. The site dedicated to Gareth Jones mentioned Jack Heinz and I followed the links, knowing, of course, that Standing would have already found as much as there was to find but telling myself that I was still learning. In the event, all I found was potted biographies of the Heinz family and company news that was big on beans (and associated varieties) but did not mention the Ukraine. Then I stumbled upon the story of Fred Beal, a young American, who I recalled Standing had mentioned and who, in 1929, had been a union activist involved in a strike in a textile mill in Gastonia, North Carolina. During a police raid on the union HQ a police chief was shot dead — exactly by whom was never established — which resulted in Beal and six others being convicted of conspiracy to murder. They promptly jumped bail and fled to Soviet Russia. According to a *Time Magazine* article dated October 1939, one of the fugitives became a professor in Russia (in exactly what field they didn't specify), three vanished (a local hazard, it seemed to me) and the remaining three returned to the US at various times, Beal to serve up to 20 years. I suppose what had caught Standing's eye was that, during his sojourn in Russia, Beal had found his way to the Ukraine — Kharkov, in fact, in 1931 — during the famine. What he saw had apparently shocked him sufficiently to turn him against the Communist system — at least as practised by the Russians. He had written a book, *Proletarian Journey*, detailing his disillusionment. As one US communist said to Beal at the time: 'The Russians should have shot you while they had you.'

Interesting though it was, I don't think it was what Standing had been looking for and therefore not what I was looking for, either. But, if Beal had got to the Ukraine, it seemed reasonable to suppose that one of the men he had jumped bail with might have as well. *Time Magazine* didn't provide any other names, although I supposed it should have been possible to track them down through reports of the trial for conspiracy to murder. I put that aside for the moment and tried a search for the Black Sea Company. After half-an-hour I hadn't found anything specific and doubted if I'd live long enough to follow every hit the search engine registered for the Black Sea. I gave up that line of enquiry, made a few notes, book marked all the sites I thought might repay visiting again and printed off some of the more relevant passages I found.

But once I had done that and looked over what I had, I realized that I needed some kind of anchor, a definitive place from which to start and to where I could always return, and that this had to be centred upon what I knew of my father's childhood.

Most of the papers I possessed belonging to my father — those relevant to any reconstruction of his past — dealt with his time in the RAF; anything dating from earlier years was scarce and somehow oddly disconnected. If one could draw a graph of a man's life as an ascending line (it could be *descending*, of course, which while strictly more accurate is a demonstration of pessimism that hardly suited an embarkation upon any enterprise) the documentation left of my father's life prior to the war would somehow, one feels, be marked by points a little off the graph. Anything else he had left behind was just an irrelevance.

He had lived much of his adult life in a semi in Chiswick. Olena and I had grown up there and our mother had died there of cancer at the age of sixty-one. He had muddled along for another fifteen years or so although the stuffing had been knocked out of him. When his own health had started to fail he went into hospital and from there into a nursing home. I was abroad at the time although I did what I could during my irregular visits home. His finances had taken a knock during my mother's illness and the nursing home fees did for the rest. He would not, as I have said, accept assistance from the Maitland family (which now, of course, included Olena) and so I helped where I could. The house should have been sold, naturally, but that always seemed to be a final acceptance — even if remaining an unspoken one — that he was never coming home again; a full stop employed rather than leaving the sentence unfinished. Thankfully, his last two months were spent in a hospice and I was able to take some leave to be on hand for the end. A week after the funeral Olena and I began the task of clearing the house.

It is an odd undertaking, one that hundreds of thousands of people have to go through, but odd nonetheless. For the vast majority of those who do it (people like George are an exception when I think of his clearing his London house) it will be an exercise in wading through banality. Shabby furniture and cheap mementoes are the norm; chipped crockery and faded photographs all the remaining evidence left to delineate a life. That is what I could not help thinking as we sorted through our parent's belongings (he had never got rid of any of our mother's things) and it struck me forcibly when we ended up dumping most of their possessions in refuse sacks destined for the tip. Even the things one would have thought of as saleable, or at least that might be welcomed by charity shops, turned out not to be sufficiently fire-rated, or too dated or beneath most people's expectations; they were valueless when all you want to do, anyway, is *give* the stuff away. So before long we were left with very little at all. The thought that this, in the end, is the sum of a person's life can be an infinitely depressing summation. But, of course, second-hand furniture and old photographs are not the sum of a life; a life is the accumulation of its friendships and memories that are left after it has been lived and, even if these things last no longer than a couple of generations, they still add up to more than stained dishes and tacky souvenirs.

Olena, in the event, wanted little for herself. She took a few photographs, our mother's jewellery, and some of her own childhood possessions that we found still lovingly arranged in her own room as if awaiting the child who can never return. One of these was Grigori, an old cloth doll with a wooden head dressed in a Cossack uniform. I had known him all my life and had, for some reason, always assumed that he had been Nastasiya's. My father had adopted him as a mascot for luck during the war and had always flown with Grigori in the cockpit of his Hurricane. He'd continued to carry the doll when he had started flying passenger aircraft after the war until Olena had been born, then she had inherited him. When she saw Grigori again she had picked him up with a squeal and put him in the box containing the few things she had elected to keep. The rest I was left with, dumped in the car to undergo a second winnowing in my own house. The family home, once cleared, was put on the market and within six weeks had been sold. And that was that.

What was left after the second purge (and the analogy has since not been lost on me even if undeserved) amounted to little more than a small case of papers, my father's medals and RAF memorabilia, and a couple of photo albums. Through these, one would have been forgiven for thinking that his life had started with his enlistment; from that fount, training, service, recreation, courtship, marriage and family, flowed like an unbending river. This was Peter Maitland. Of Petro Zaretsky there was no trace.

Except for those few papers of Nastasiya's I had found in a biscuit tin at the back of the top shelf of a wardrobe and the notebook discovered in a drawer. Someone less thorough than I am might have missed them altogether.

I have already itemized what I found and subsequently loaned to Michael Standing: the photographs and identity cards spoke for themselves; the letters and what Standing identified as rail movement orders were to me at the time a mystery in Cyrillic. So, *at the time*, I replaced them in their battered tin and found a new home for them in my own bedroom cupboard. The rest of my parents' bits and pieces I eventually sorted into piles and scattered, like ashes, around the house.

The odd man out had been the little leather-bound notebook written in Ukrainian. I recall puzzling over it at the time, even thinking that I might get a Cyrillic dictionary and attempt to work my way through it. But as Daryna subsequently discovered, Ukrainian/English dictionaries are not the kind of thing one finds in the local W.H.Smith so the impulse got deferred and eventually the notebook ended up in a drawer alongside other miscellaneous items and was forgotten.

When, shortly after my leave ended and I returned to work, I became subsumed in the business of countering the — then — embryonic but developing fundamentalist threat and within the year had become one of its peripheral victims. The following months of hospitalization, convalescence and recuperation were filled with other considerations, such as staying alive, getting back on my feet, and facing the fact of enforced idleness. After hospital I was more or less able to look after myself, despite unaccountable memory losses that seemed to lie in wait for me like potholes in the road of life. I had rented out my house while abroad and rather than evict the tenants or surrender myself to Olena's less than tender ministrations, I took up Charlie's offer to stay at his flat in Bermondsey. It was empty due to that fact that Charlie was back in Africa trying to get our operation up and running again following the attack, and because he disliked the thought of strangers ensconced among his personal possessions. He might have stored his gear and rented the place unfurnished, as I had often pointed out to him, but that was too much trouble for Charlie. I wasn't a stranger, of course, although I suspected the reason he had made the offer was more through a sense of guilt than one of generosity, my body having shielded his from the worst of the blast. I accepted nevertheless, had another couple of keys cut in case I mislaid his during one of my lapses in memory, and moved in until the tenants' lease on my own place expired. It was while I was at Charlie's that, due to what I was told would be permanent physical effects resulting from my injuries and the inevitable consequence of being stuck behind a London desk for the rest of my working life, I opted for early retirement. Taking it, I found, was pushing at an open door. After all, no one likes to see an example of their own professional failure shuffling around the office like a daily reminder.

Shortly after — I remember the particular evening — sitting in Charlie's flat, the problem of what I was going to do with the rest of my life loomed suddenly in front of me. It seemed a void so large (a mixed analogy, I know, but there it is) that the need to fill it became imperative and I resolved to begin (back-filling the void, you might say) by writing the memoir of my father. That, in turn, started me thinking about those few papers I had rescued when clearing his house, wondering if there was anything of use among them that might be of help. It was only when I finally got back into my own house, following the disinterment of those old papers, that I first began to consider how curious it was that nothing I found — Nastasiya's biscuit tin apart — predated 1939.

~

During the week following my initial meeting with Standing, a growing pile of printed material and a falling ink level testified to my assiduous search across the Web; even if I wasn't gathering much specific information, I was at least beginning to paint in the background to my father's first decade of life.

One or two things that Standing had alluded to struck me as particularly relevant: firstly, that if Aleksander Zaretsky had been a faithful Party man one assumes that the food shortages would not have affected him, or his immediate family directly. It is one of life's truisms, but of course one that springs from truth, that those in power never suffer the inconveniences endured by those over whom the power is wielded. If this had been the case, however, it seemed unlikely that the famine itself had motivated his desire to get Nastasiya and Petro out of the Ukraine. It made me wonder about her immediate family, as well. If they were Party members I assumed that they would not have been affected either, but one of the problems I had was that I did not know what kind of family Nastasiya had come from. If she had been of rural peasant stock they may well have become victims of starvation despite their political connections. I had discovered that, by 1931 or 1932, the better-off peasants had long been levelled by the Soviet system and if they had been unfortunate enough to have been designated as *Kulaks* they would, by that date, have either been deported or be dead, probably both unless Zaretsky had been able to save them. By their dress, in the photograph I had lent to Standing, I would have supposed that they *had* been peasants, but that didn't really offer any conclusive evidence.

Standing's second point was the suggestion that Zaretsky might have thrown in his lot with the nationalists. During the liquidation of the *Kulaks* and following the programme of Collectivization, resistance to the Bolsheviks had begun to spring up all over the country. It was why Stalin had sent in his OGPU men, to stiffen the Ukrainian Soviet's system of collecting the grain to fill the quotas that had been imposed upon them. Stalin's OGPU man in the Ukraine, I discovered, was Stanislas Redens, a member of the Alliluyev family and Stalin's own brother-in-law. Nepotism is a hardy plant that can survive under most ideologies, even if eventually Stalin did decide that Redens wasn't dealing firmly enough with what he regarded as recalcitrant peasants and had him replaced. It was after this that the hunger became a famine and a political tool to suppress dissent. If at this point Zaretsky had decided to break with the Party, it seemed to me that a desire on his part to get his family out of harm's way was quite understandable.

There was another possibility, though, which, after I had read much of the material I had gathered, I thought worth considering. This was that Zaretsky remained a Party man but did not agree with the methods being dictated by Moscow. It seemed to be a fact that even as late as 1932—33, Stalin was still obliged to tread carefully in what he did as there remained opposing views in the Politburo. He was not a dictator yet. He was the Party General Secretary and regarded as the leader, but it appears he always needed to take other members of the Politburo with him as regards policy. To his annoyance, after he had decided that he must come down hard on the Ukraine and the other grain producing regions if the Five-Year-Plan and Industrialization was to succeed, he found the Collectives did not produce the grain expected of them — the commodity that provided the currency to buy the machinery needed to modernize Russia. By then many of the Politburo members had begun to think they should ease up on the repression. There were many dissenters who were ready to argue with Stalin over the policies and Stalin could not, as yet, merely dispose of them. Killing *Kulaks*, counter-revolutionaries, revisionists, and those who could be included in that useful catchall, "wreckers", was one thing; to arrest fellow Bolsheviks and Politburo members needed more than suspicion and loathing — it needed evidence. Stalin had already had Riutin arrested in 1931 for organising an opposition to his policies, but the most he dared do to him was have him thrown off the Politburo. It wasn't until Stalin's own wife, Nadezhda, committed suicide and after Kirov was murdered that circumstances and Stalin's own disposition moved the system towards purges. It seemed to me a possibility that Zaretsky might have suddenly discovered that opinions which had once made him a member — however junior — of the ruling caste now, with a shift in the political wind, had turned into a liability, a threat, not only to his life but to that of his family's as well.

It was around this time, I suppose, that I thought to question anyone who might know something of my family's origins. George was the most obvious candidate for interrogation. It was true that he had been only a small child when Nastasiya had been killed, but he had known my father well as a boy and had been close to *his* father, Frederick, who must have known something of his first wife's history. It seemed only natural that Frederick would have told his first-born about his mother's and his older half-brother's early life. But, just then, George had been preoccupied with his move out of London and seemed more intent on his new future in the country and his son's political career than he did on delving into the past. At the time I thought it quite understandable and hadn't pressed the point.

Frederick's siblings were long dead but he had left another family courtesy of his second wife, Elizabeth — George's two half-sisters and another half-brother (apart from my father), all still living and all with families still orbiting the central nucleus of the Maitland fortune. They were mostly around my own age, if a little older, and I knew them with varying degrees of intimacy, meeting at weddings and funerals and now and then by chance. While the later generations probably knew little, and no doubt cared less, I thought it might be worth looking up George's half-siblings in case they had learned anything from Frederick or perhaps through Elizabeth. Nick and the rest of my cousins — first and second remove, and in reality

80

in name only — were really all too far removed from much chance of knowing anything that I did not.

When I had first embarked upon my research I had told Olena about it and how the unexpected appearance of Michael Standing had prompted it. She of course, as I had known she would, had wanted to know all about him and, although I had tried to question her about our father, she'd been too full of getting information out of *me* about Standing to answer any questions. To be honest, I doubted that Olena knew anymore than I did; I wouldn't have said that as a young girl she had been particularly close to our father and her marriage to Nick probably dropped the boom on any later paternal confidences. She had been closer to our mother, though, and a mother-daughter relationship is often a closed book to other members of the family. I freely admit I had no idea of what they might have talked about in the privacy of their own company, but if Olena had inherited her tendency of first eliciting, and then spilling, confidences from our mother I thought it worth the risk of it costing me an expensive lunch — or worse, dinner — and decided to try my luck and telephone her.

Then, out of the blue, Standing got in touch again and asked *me* to lunch — the lunch into which Olena had threatened to ingratiate herself — and I have to admit that this gave me the idea of using the engagement with him as bait. This time I thought the imminence of my second meeting with Standing might be more than she could resist and I was quite prepared to grill her, dangling the chance of an introduction in return for any small thing that she might have learned which I did not know. And having found out what I could, I was also quite prepared to renege on any deal involving introducing her to Standing — after all, taking her to lunch with him would, I knew, ruin any chance I might have of getting any further information out of *him*. The deception would not have troubled my conscience one whit; it was almost second nature to me and, besides, I was only too familiar with how much it was likely to cost me to eat in the kind of restaurant to which Olena had become accustomed.

To my surprise, though, she suggested that I lunch at her house instead of naming one of those expensive places at which she regularly lunched with the "girls". It was too hot, she complained, for traipsing about town. I was happy to accept, although teetering for a moment on the point of stipulating that it just be the two of us. For years she had been in the habit of trying to pair me off with some acquaintance of hers (it was never a good friend as I don't think Olena thought I was quite up to being matched with any *real* friend of hers), but in the end I didn't push my luck. Since my injury she had seemed to have given up on matchmaking, either sick of trying to find someone suitable or, more likely, having decided that a middle-aged man with a dodgy back was too far gone to inflict on even a mere acquaintance.

It was a Sunday morning in early May, I recall, during an unseasonably hot spell — although hardly too hot in town, I would have thought, for a woman accustomed to vacationing in the West Indies. The house was in Chelsea, hers and Nick's, courtesy of George's generosity, and after the divorce she had kept it. At the time I did wonder if Nick's acquiescence to this might have had more to do with his political career and a quiet divorce than generosity, but even then I wasn't sure if I wanted to know. Nick had moved out and bought himself a flat somewhere and the whole split had been admirably amicable.

In need of the exercise, I decided to walk from Lambeth. Passing along the Albert Embankment to Vauxhall Bridge, I saw the home of SIS rising like an off-centre step-pyramid and it put me in mind of Charlie Hewson to whom I'd not spoken since he'd put Daryna my way. I made a mental note to give him a call. The river looked sluggish and grey under the heat of an already oppressive morning. Across the river and along Grosvenor Road the traffic was Sunday-morning light and almost as sluggish as the Thames. I turned into Chelsea Bridge Road. Olena's house was one of a smart terrace that had avoided the disease of subdivision into flats (albeit up-market flats) which had afflicted many of its neighbours. I rang the bell and, to my great surprise, it wasn't Olena who opened the door. It was Nick.

8

The room was still dark when I awoke. I lay for a long while, trying to find a comfortable position and more sleep, before resignedly climbing out of bed and opening the heavy drapes. It was the first of the month and the days were on that gloomy slide towards the winter equinox. Too dark to see anything outside, I saw by the bedside clock that it was still only 6am. I showered and dressed and went downstairs through the silent house. I found the kitchen towards the rear, a big farmhouse affair with a new range and an acre or so of wooden worktops still leaving more than enough space for an island and a large refectory table long enough to seat a dozen people. There happened to be only two at that moment, Patterson and his wife, Nora. She was Irish, a short but sturdy woman with greying hair long enough to need pinning at the back of her head and always recalcitrant enough to leave a few strands falling untidily across her face. She was a good-natured woman, plain and a stranger to cosmetics, who had kept house for George and Jennifer in London for as long as I could remember. Her husband, only ever just "Patterson", was not as good-natured and had looked after the London garden and the cars and had come to that occupation after what had been a career in the ring. His face was a catalogue of every punch that had ever landed and one of his ears was a cauliflower that, once he had turned to gardening, might have graced a village show. He wasn't a man I had ever taken to and I was certain the sentiment was reciprocated. I'd heard tell of a son, too, a ne'er-do-well whose appearance was intermittent, dependent upon Her Majesty's Pleasure, but whom I'd yet to meet. I'd always assumed the genes had been passed by the father because Nora was gold. She got up from where she sat, nursing a cup across from her husband, and beamed at me.

'Mr Alex!' She came around the table and held out her arms. I stooped and kissed her and she wrapped me in a baby bear's embrace. 'I don't know when it was last I saw you,' she said. 'Now it's coffee you drink in the morning, that's right, isn't it? Black and no sugar.'

'It's been a while,' I admitted, 'but you're looking as well as ever.' I held out my hand to her husband who hadn't moved but who took it nevertheless with only the slightest suggestion of reluctance. 'You've got your work cut out here, haven't you?' I remarked to them both but only expecting a reply from Nora.

She poured me a mug of coffee from a pot that was still warming on the Aga and set it in front of me.

'It's bigger than we're used to, for sure,' Nora said, 'but Mr George has a full-time staff in the garden so Patterson only has to see to the cars, and there's a vegetable patch to keep him out from under my feet. I've got two local girls who come in to help me with the house.' She sat down beside me. 'But how's yourself? It's a real relief to see you back on your feet again.'

'It can't be that long, can it?'

'No, but if you don't mind me saying, you weren't really looking yourself the last time I saw you.'

We talked about the new house for a while until Patterson grunted something about having 'work to do' and got up and left. Then Nora asked:

'And how is Miss Olena? I do miss seeing her.'

'She's fine,' I assured her.

For some reason Olena had hit it off with Nora whilst her relations with Jennifer had been somewhat more problematic. I had always put it down to Nora's generosity of character and her willingness to overlook my sister's pretensions and wilder traits. But, to be honest, it was a subject about which I had always preferred to give little thought, as if, like Patterson and his genes, I had also inherited my father's prejudices.

I finished my coffee as Nora began to prepare a tray to take up to George and Jennifer, then went in search of my scarf. Dawn had not made much impression on the December morning and the drapes were still drawn in the drawing room. I turned on the lights. They were hung from a plain but rather elegant chandelier that the previous evening, along with the log fire and a smattering of table lamps, had lent the room an air of intimate warmth. Now it looked unnatural and unwelcoming in the harsh reality of morning. The fire had died, leaving no more than a charred log and a pile of grey ash. I found my scarf draped over the back of the chair in which I had been sitting the previous evening and, despite the fact that the central heating had warmed the room, I succumbed to the impulse to wrap the garment around my neck.

The house was quiet. A long case clock I had passed in the hall struck 7am. but there were no other sounds of movement so I took the opportunity to look at the photographs I had thought about the night before. Predictably, I suppose, Olena had more or less disappeared, the victim of an altered regime. Her wedding photos, usually so prominent, had, I presumed, been relegated to a storage box somewhere and the only trace I found of my sister was a shot taken in the garden of George's London house a couple of years earlier on the occasion of George and Jennifer's fortieth wedding anniversary. She was standing with Nick alongside his brother, Oliver, and sister, Georgia — known in the family as Kat — all flanking the happy couple. I was there too, orbiting on the periphery with the lesser Maitlands, no more than a head and shoulders between a pair of large summer-fête hats. I didn't look as if I was enjoying myself which was, upon reflection, a pity since within a couple of weeks of the photograph I had taken up the posting that had almost killed me and had spent most of the next six months in a London hospital, which hadn't given me much enjoyment at all.

On a dresser against the far wall I found a collection of older photographs. One or two showed George as a young man but the others were of his father, Frederick. One had been taken early in the war, the usual studio portrait taken of young men in pristine uniforms before being shipped off to do their duty, although in Frederick's case he didn't look particularly young as he must have been in his early thirties at least. "Shipped off" was apt, though, because Frederick had joined the Royal Navy, although a year or so into his service he had apparently transferred into the Commandos, a regime that I thought must have came hard to a body no longer in its first flush of youth. Behind this was a wedding photograph — Frederick's second wedding, that is, old black-and-white from 1944. George was there, still not much more that a toddler in short trousers and tousled hair standing in front of the bridesmaid, the sister of his new stepmother. My father was conspicuous by his absence. Perhaps he had been unable to get leave. Perhaps he had not.

Curious, I looked at all the other photographs on display to see if he featured anywhere. There were several more of Frederick in that perennial pose of his with one arm behind his back, like some back-to-front Napoleon, but my father was never with him. He was absent even from George and Jennifer's wedding pictures and I wondered if he had been there at all. I had no memory of the event myself although I was in my teens at the time. Frederick was there, ageing now but standing proudly in his usual pose by his son, Elizabeth at his side. Jennifer had been nineteen, I recalled, and seeing her in her wedding dress next to George suddenly brought back all those teenage longings I had struggled with and which, one would have hoped at this distance, might have been long buried. But perhaps that is what makes us human, being able to connect through memory with feelings that later one would be no longer be capable of experiencing.

I finally found my father on a small table by the French windows. He was with George and Jennifer and my mother,

85

Geraldine, on holiday by the coast. I knew where it was because it was the place that my parents had always holidayed, out on the Essex marshes where they could indulge their passion for dinghy sailing. He had bought an old wooden shack perched above the mudflats between the Crouch and the Thames estuaries and over the years had enlarged and modernized it. There was no electricity and water came from a standpipe and had to be heated on an old wood stove but they had loved the place and spent every spare minute they could there. George and Jennifer had often joined them for summer weekends after their marriage before George's business interests claimed the larger share of his attention, a happy foursome despite the age differences. As Olena and I grew up we had spent less time there — Olena, as a teenage girl, had come to hate the place — but our parents had still spent weekends there long after we had left home. The chalet had inevitably fallen into disrepair, particularly with the onset of Mother's illness when both time and money were in short supply. Always too proud to accept any kind of financial support even from me, I had finally persuaded him to sell the Essex place to a local boat-builder to help ends meet. I had never told him that the boat builder was acting on my behalf and that I had bought the chalet. He would have regarded it as charity, as the chalet would have come to Olena and me as an inheritance anyway, although by then I rather suspected that neglect would have eroded any residual value. I had thought of it as a way of helping out without it seeming like charity, even if the subterfuge had played upon my conscience. My father never found out and even asked me not to tell Olena about his selling the chalet, just in case, I suppose, it got back to George through Nick that he had been that desperate. He had his pride and would be beholden to no one, not even family. I never even spoke about it after he died although what difference that would have made I didn't know; Olena didn't care about the old chalet anyway as it was hardly the kind of place she'd now consider holidaying.

I didn't know when that particular photograph had been taken but it couldn't have been long after George and Jennifer's marriage because they all looked so startlingly young. They were windblown but happy and laughing at the camera. Even Jennifer looked as if she was enjoying herself. I wasn't there, needless to say.

I was holding the photograph when the door opened and George walked in.

'Good morning, Alex,' he said. 'Nora told me you were up and around.' He came towards me and put a hand on my shoulder as I replaced the photograph on the table. 'That was taken on the Essex marshes at the old chalet. Nineteen sixty-five, or six. Jennifer and I often drove down for weekends in those days. Your father taught me how to sail. Well, as much as I was ever capable of learning.'

'I don't remember that,' I said.

'You were probably in school. Jennifer and I hadn't been married long. No place for mooning teenagers.'

Despite myself I couldn't help blushing with embarrassment, a reaction I hadn't felt for years.

'Was it that obvious?' I asked.

'Only if you were a jealous husband,' he said.

I looked at him to see if he was serious but he only laughed.

'Good days,' he said.

'Before Nick and Olena were born.'

'Children change things.'

'I suppose they must,' I said.

'Whatever happened to the old place?'

I gave what I hoped was a wistful smile. 'Dad sold it when Mum got ill. It was in a pretty poor state by then, anyway,'

'Shame,' George said. He sighed then brightened, 'I always take a turn around the grounds first thing. I thought you might appreciate the exercise.'

I went back to my room for my coat and the boots I'd thought to bring and met George by the back door where a black Labrador and a golden retriever were bouncing excitably around his legs. I recognized the Labrador as Willard who was now getting on in years with a greying muzzle and thickening girth, but the retriever was new to me. He nuzzled against my hand as I bent to pet him.

'Dempsey,' George said. 'We got him when old Johnston passed on. I suppose I'm getting sentimental in my old age.'

A good few years earlier George had begun naming his dogs after the old heavyweight boxing champions of the world. It was typical of him that he had to begin and the beginning of gloved bouts and name the dogs after each successive champion.

'A couple more,' I said, 'and you know you'll have a dog called Schmeling, don't you? What's that to be, a schnauzer?'

George grabbed Dempsey's muzzle and gave it a shake. 'Oh, he'll have to be a German Shepherd, I think,' he said with a grin.

Light had finally seeped into the morning. The cloud cover was thin and the air had a sharp edge to it, almost whitening the grass beneath the ground-mist. Moisture hung from the trees, dripping like a steady rain. The dogs ran ahead of us along the worn red bricks of the old walled garden, cutting tracks through the dewy grass, Dempsey barking with excitement and putting up a pair of wood pigeons from a giant beech ahead of us.

'You were asking me about your father a few months back,' George said. 'If I had anything dating from before the war.'

It had been after Daryna had translated the letters and my father's schoolboy ramblings had put me in mind of Frederick. I thought George might remember something useful, or have something of Frederick's that had a bearing on Nastasiya's early days in England, but, as I have said, it had been a bad time to ask. George was presiding over Oliver's assumption of the reins of the investment firm, was backing out of his other City directorships and was in the process of buying his country estate. He had been as accommodating as he usually was but I could tell that he had his hands full and had not pressed the point. Now, however, he said:

'I went through all my father's papers before we left the London house. Most of it was rubbish I should have thrown out years ago but I found a few things that might interest you. Some photographs as well. Some of him and Nastasiya on their wedding day.'

I thought not for the first time how slightly odd it was that we both referred to her as Nastasiya. She was his mother and my grandmother, after all, but perhaps it was the fact that she had died before either of us had had the opportunity to know her that allowed us to think of her as a young woman. I tried to remember just how my father had referred to her and, with something approaching surprise, couldn't really remember his talking of her at all unless specifically questioned. I began to wonder if his differences with his stepfather, Frederick, had managed to reach back and taint even his relationship with his own mother.

'Yes,' I told George, 'I would be interested. It was good of you to take the trouble.'

'It wasn't any trouble, Alex. It's all in my study. You can go through it after breakfast if you like. Nick's got his constituency surgery and I've got a few things I have to do so you'll have the place to yourself. You can make copies of everything. There's a decent scanner and photographic printer and I've got some software on the computer if you want to try and clean them up.'

We left it like that and walked out across the back lawns towards the trees and he told me about the estate. A farm had come entailed with it and although it was tenanted, he had big plans for refurbishing the outbuildings and had developed an interest in rare breeds.

Coming out of the copse, we skirted a stubble field. Dempsey squeezed himself beneath the wire of the fence and put up three or four rooks that were feeding off the stubble. Out across the bare winter field the rest of the flock strutted and pecked, ignoring him.

'George,' I said, tackling a subject I had skirted many times but had never approached head on, 'what happened between my father and yours that estranged them so? Do you know?'

He bent down, picked up a stick and threw it for the dogs. Dempsey hurtled after it with Willard waggling in his wake.

'I don't think it was too much on my father's part to be honest, Alex. I don't want to blame your father, but I know mine did try to heal the rift on several occasions.'

'But what caused it?'

'I'm not sure it was any one thing. And I'm not even sure that my father knew. Peter never explained it to me, either. I suppose you asked him yourself?'

'I tried,' I admitted. 'But he never spoke about it at all. "We don't get on" and "It goes back a long way" were really all I ever got out of him. For a long time I thought it was because Frederick remarried after Nastasiya was killed, but I don't think it was that at all.'

George grunted with concurrence. 'I've always supposed that it went back to when Frederick married Nastasiya.'

He shrugged his heavy shoulders and tossed the stick a few feet along the path. Dempsey turned to him in disappointment giving Willard a rare opportunity to get to the stick first. She picked it up in her mouth and trotted on ahead of us, looking as though, now she had it, she wasn't going to relinquish the thing.

'You have to try and put yourself in Peter's shoes,' George said. 'He was just a young boy when he arrived here. Didn't speak the language and didn't know anyone except his mother. I suppose they must have been very close. Then she meets my father and perhaps he thinks he's been replaced in Nastasiya's affections. And on top of it all, he's sent away to a boarding school. I think I'd be a little aggrieved if it was me, wouldn't you?'

I said I supposed I would. But I didn't know if that was the whole of it. I *did* know that my father had actually enjoyed his school. He had made some friendships there that had lasted all his life. And, judging by the letters Daryna had translated for me, he hadn't sounded like a boy carrying an adolescent grudge. I wondered if the jealously had all been on my father's part. After all, wouldn't a stepson be a constant reminder of his wife's divided loyalties and of the man who had preceded him in her bed?

As if he had been reading my thoughts, George went on, 'I don't want to be crude but don't forget how old he was when Frederick came along. I suppose he was experiencing the same kind of sexual longings that every boy his age does. A stranger is allowed into his mother's bed, replacing the father who'd been left behind...' he didn't finish but I followed his reasoning.

'You're not going to get Freudian on me, are you George?' I said quickly, not wanting to pursue that particular line given my own teenage fantasies about George's wife.

'Well, you know that my father wasn't much more than a dozen or so years older than yours, don't you? Younger than Nastasiya, anyway. That couldn't have helped.'

Oddly enough I hadn't known. Or, more likely, had never given it any thought. As far as Maitland relative ages were concerned I had never considered any beyond Jennifer's and my own. But now that he mentioned it, there were oddities among us. Half-landings of age on the stairway of life, (excuse the metaphor but I had been up a while and hadn't eaten yet, you understand, and no doubt feeling light-headed). There was Frederick and my father; my father and George; George and myself; me and Nick... The half-points between generations seemed endless.

'I just think it was all such a shame, that's all,' I went on. 'You know he wasn't even going to attend Nick and Olena's wedding because Frederick would be there, don't you? If your father hadn't have died a couple of months before, he wouldn't have seen his own daughter get married.'

'Yes, I know,' George said. 'That's why he never came to my wedding. But it was all for the best in the end. My father really wasn't well by then. A full life but it had taken its toll.'

I muttered something suitable, and then he said suddenly:

'A word to the wise, Alex. Best not mention Olena in front of Jennifer. It's a bit of a touchy subject still. I would have thought by now that things might have settled down but...'

We had circled around, following the stream that Nick and I had crossed the evening before and had begun climbing across the grounds in front of the house.

By then we had tired out poor old Willard and I was ready to tackle breakfast.

Despite his years with Olena having infected him with a chronic case of late rising, Nick was already at the big table in the kitchen, an empty plate in front of him, coffee in one hand and a slice of toast in the other. Nora was at the sink, washing up, and Jennifer was floating between them, clearing away.

We said good morning and sat down, Nora bringing George a plate of eggs and bacon unasked and then doing the same for me. Jennifer poured us coffee.

Nick was wearing corduroy trousers and a roll-neck sweater. A waxed jacket hung on the chair behind him. I supposed he was hoping to appear to those constituents that turned up for his surgery like a countryman, much as they were themselves. The best politicians are chameleons, after all, blending into their background while predating upon it, but Nick's attire had a little too much of being fresh from the country outfitters about it to be convincing. He needed to slog through a few muddy ditches and get snagged on a few brambles for the impersonation to look authentic. I might have suggested as much but I suspected that Jennifer would have failed to see the humour in the remark.

'I've often wondered,' I said, 'what it is you get asked by your constituents at these surgeries. It's not all eccentrics with boundary disputes that turn on some old statutory lien, is it Nick?'

'I've had my share of those,' he admitted. 'But mostly it's people who've been short-changed by the system. By the time they come to me they've usually exhausted the customary channels and I'm office of last resort. Fortunately I've people on hand to deal with the details. All I'm expected to do is collar the Member who has departmental responsibility for the problem and make a nuisance of myself until something's done. Of course, I'm expected to handle the detail of my boss's problems, too. Smaller fleas *ad infinitum*,' he explained.

'It's like coming up through the ranks in any organisation,' George said. 'You've got to do the donkey work first before they consider you a player.'

'Tedious but true,' Nick agreed. 'Roll on the election. Until then I just have to keep my constituency Party sweet and brown-nose the Party bigwigs at Westminster.'

'Nick!' Jennifer scolded. 'I don't think there's any need for crudeness.'

'Mother dear,' he said, getting up and pulling on his Barbour, 'you have no comprehension of what crudeness is until you become involved in politics.'

'Then I don't think I'd care to become involved,' she said, giving him a farewell kiss on the cheek. 'And I'll thank you to leave it in Westminster.'

He shot me an amused look and waved us goodbye. 'I'll see you at lunch,' he said.

Jennifer had waited for George before breakfasting herself but ate only sparingly, a little dry toast and herbal tea. The regimen had done wonders for her figure but I'm not sure it had done a lot for her sociability. I could remember dinners years before, when my father had been alive, when we had all eaten too much, drunk too much wine, and argued good-naturedly over inconsequentialities. I hadn't seen a lot of her in the past decade, it was true, but she seemed to me to have withdrawn into herself, become more self-contained than she had used to be. I recalled when George had first brought her to meet my parents; the clichéd term "wild child" always occurred to me. It had been in the early to mid-sixties and young people were getting a taste of freedoms they had never enjoyed before. To my adolescent eyes — and, no doubt, imagination — Jennifer was everything a boy could have wanted: young, beautiful, adventurous, mischievous ... and she had corrupted George for a while as he had grown his hair long and had dressed in flares and Cuban heels and had smoked dope... He had somehow reasserted himself after marriage — as if waking up from an hallucination, I suppose. And Jennifer too — to her own family's relief — had lost some of her wildness. I couldn't understand it and used to watch her surreptitiously, looking for the girl who had once been there. I had become something of a tearaway myself in those years, as if wanting to make up for the taming of George and Jennifer, and I had been in danger of running off the rails. I often think it was the change in Jennifer that had finally prompted me to join the army, more as a way of getting away from what I imagined I had lost than through any sense of adventure or — God forbid — duty.

Now, though, I found myself considering everything I said before I said it when she was present, a self-censorship that left, if not a bad taste in the mouth, at least a feeling of discomfort, something I really didn't want to feel when I was with her. It occurred to me that even without George's warning I wouldn't have brought up Olena's name with her through my own sense of caution.

They were talking about some modification Jennifer wanted to make to the walled garden when George said unexpectedly:

'Alex was asking why Peter and my father didn't get on.'

Jennifer appeared as surprised as I must have and she looked across the table at me, holding my gaze for a moment in a way I don't think she had for years.

'Your father wasn't an easy man to get along with,' she said to George. 'Peter had his reasons, no doubt.'

'Alex knows that,' George replied. 'He wanted to know what they were.'

'What makes you think he confided in me? If he didn't tell Alex, he would hardly be likely to tell me, would he?'

'You were particularly close to Geraldine though, weren't you? And no doubt Peter told her everything.'

I listened to the exchange with the odd feeling that it wasn't meant to be any concern of mine. It wasn't that I felt they were talking about a subject I wasn't supposed to know about, more that George was enquiring on his own behalf, not mine. Curious perhaps, to know if his wife knew something that he did not.

Jennifer, though, chose not to answer him. At that moment Nora returned to the kitchen and Jennifer picked up our empty plates and ferried them to the sink for her, using them as a vehicle for her own evasiveness.

George scratched at his chin and I thought for a moment he was going to pursue the matter but instead suggested that, if I was ready, he'd show me the papers he had sorted for me in his study.

I stood up and followed him to the door, turning to thank Jennifer and Nora as I went.

Jennifer smiled fondly but I wasn't entirely sure if it was memory or me that was the object of her affection.

9

Although I had been surprised to find Nick at Olena's house that warm May day, I don't know why. The divorce had been amicable enough as far as I knew, but there are always currents in these affairs of which third parties are unaware and I assumed it had been so with my sister and her husband. It had all been over about eighteen months by then and had ended by mutual agreement. As marriages between people of their age and status generally founder over some transgression by the one or the other, I had supposed that above and beyond Olena's disenchantment with Nick's political career this had been the case between them. For once, though, Olena, the mistress of indiscretion, had not given me the details.

I am aware that I have not described Olena and may have given the impression that we did not get on. This isn't the case. I'd concede that we're not *that* close, but that has probably more to do with the fact that I have spent a lot of time overseas and because of the difference in our respective ages. I was already in my teens when she, a late baby, came along so we didn't exactly share a childhood. If there is any kind of lack of sympathy between us it is probably because I have failed to live up to her expectations. My defence is that they were set high when she married Nick and she never ceased raising the bar.

As a child she suffered from an excess of puppy fat about which I believe she agonized. This fell away as she passed through her teenage years and by seventeen she had been miraculously transformed into a tall and willowy and quite startlingly attractive girl. She is blonde with an oval face and almond eyes — Slavic with a hint of Tartary about them, our mother always used to say, although I always thought it was more her way of teasing our father over his origins rather than of complimenting Olena. She had turned, I now realize, into the epitome of those Ukrainian beauties upon whom Michael Standing had remarked, even if I always do expect her at some point to regress into a dumpy caricature of an old peasant woman, the kind that populate travelogues about rural Russia. But that needn't be the case; she was still in her early forties and money is a wonderful preservative that not only imparts the means but also the will to maintain the status quo. With still some way to go before middle age, Olena was as beautiful as ever with just the hint of a line or two around the eyes to give that impression of character, which I had always suspected she had lacked.

Her mouth was the only thing about her that reminded me of our mother and although I could sometimes divine in her traces of our father — those Slavic eyes, perhaps — most of all she reminded me of those photographs that remained of Nastasiya. Olena, I thought, was what Nastasiya would have looked like given modern dress and cosmetics. Given life.

We had eaten lunch out on the small terrace, screened from the sun by an awning and from the houses either side by trellises on which early blooming clematis and roses had intertwined. The surprisingly large landscaped garden ran down to a pool and the summerhouse where Olena kept her gym equipment and was at that moment being patrolled by Susie, Olena's tortoiseshell cat. We were finishing the third bottle of wine, courtesy of Nick who had trumped my somewhat proletarian Maipo with the product of a château with aristocratic pretensions. Usually unfussy about wine — he would happily drink anything — I had been impressed with his contribution and had abandoned mine to the kitchen. His were bottles, he later admitted, a friend had given him and he was often in the habit of taking another's contributions along to his next host. Helping myself liberally, I had already drunk too much and neither Nick nor Olena were exactly sober. I had been bemused all afternoon by their behaviour, it being oddly much as it had been when they had been courting. Perhaps I am old-fashioned, but I *did* expect a little more decorum from people so recently divorced — at least, after my share of the wine, I did — and Olena's habit of reaching across the table and laying a hand on Nick's arm whenever she had something to say to him, or running a hand across the back of his shoulders as she passed behind his chair, seemed particularly blatant. Nick, for his part, appeared to take it all in his stride and had even been playing up to her, looking more relaxed than usual having emerged from his politician's cocoon like a weekend chrysalis in slacks and a pale blue shirt.

His being there had put rather a crimp in my plan to dangle the prospect of meeting Michael Standing in front of Olena in return for something she might — once she had put her butterfly mind to it — remember. But just so the day was not a total loss I had tackled her again over lunch about anything she had been told of our father's boyhood. Unsurprisingly, she maintained that she didn't remember having been told anything. Teenage girls (and, I suppose, teenage boys for that matter) resemble religious theologians from the middleages in their confirmed belief that they are the centre of the universe and that every other body circles around them. As a young girl, therefore, any life of my father's before her birth had been so far beyond her comprehension that she had never enquired into it. Nastasiya, it goes without saying, was dead and forgotten, and had been nothing more than a name to her. It didn't surprise me that our father had never mentioned his youth to her — after all, *I* had taken the trouble to ask and had still been told next to nothing — but I thought our mother might have let something slip in some unguarded moment. Not according to Olena, though. Nor had George or Jennifer, her in-laws, ever said anything that I had not heard before. And, while she had met old Frederick on several occasions while courting Nick, he had been in bad health and she had never had the opportunity of holding any kind of conversation with him. To be honest, even if she had had the opportunity I can't imagine what on earth they might have found to talk about. All she said was that although she knew our father and Frederick never saw each other anymore, she had never given much thought as to why that was so, except that she didn't blame Dad as Frederick was a particularly unpleasant old man.

Nick hadn't been of much help either. In those days he had been more interested in cars and girls — Olena, mostly, post miraculous transformation. George, like our father, hadn't been keen on the match; only Jennifer and Geraldine, our mother, had seemed pleased by the turn of events.

'To be candid,' Nick admitted, once we had got on to the subject, 'I hadn't much liked Frederick, either. I saw him as an older version of my father only harder.'

Olena shuddered and a look of revulsion passed briefly across her face.

'He was a repulsive old man,' she said, taking Nick's dislike, I suppose, as carte blanche to go town on the poor defenceless old soul. 'After his stroke always drooling and yet you looked into his eyes and you could still see his mind working. And that hand—'

'Don't be ridiculous, darling,' Nick interrupted. 'He was just an old man, that's all. You thought anybody over thirty was repulsive then.'

She hit him playfully and ignored my raised my eyebrows following Nick's endearment.

He topped up my glass again and asked:

'What's prompted this sudden interest, anyway?'

I told him about Standing having visited me and having piqued my curiosity and that he'd been in touch again.

'The historian, you mean? Michael Standing?'

Olena began sitting up alertly and I noticed she took her hand off Nick's arm where it had been casually lying for the last minute or so. Despite the wine I had drunk I could hear alarm bells ringing somewhere.

'Yes,' I said to Nick. 'Hasn't he been in touch with you?'

Olena shot him a glance as if she suspected him of concealing information to which she had a right of access.

'Why would he get in touch with me?' he asked. 'I haven't seen him since Cambridge.'

'You knew him at Cambridge?' Olena demanded, wide-eyed.

He turned to her. 'Yes. Not well, but I knew him.'

'You never told me,' Olena pouted. Her hands were now firmly in her lap.

'Probably because I knew you'd never give me any peace until I got him over for dinner,' Nick said. 'Another trophy for the girls.'

Olena swung a petulant arm at him again, but habit must have warned him it was coming because he merely leaned a little further back in his chair out of her reach.

'I don't suppose he would have remembered you, anyway,' she said by way of consolation. 'You could hardly be contemporaries.'

'We were in the same year,' Nick said.

'But he's younger than you.'

'That's just make-up and the camera,' he said. 'We're actually the same age.' He leaned forward again and took a sip at his wine, looking over the glass at me. 'What makes you think he'd get in touch with me?'

'Because I gave him your telephone number, chiefly. And George's, come to that, just in case you still had any papers that might be of interest to him.'

'What on earth would we have to interest an historian?'

I told him then what Standing had told me; probably embellishing the nature of his research. 'He was trying to trace an Aleksander Zaretsky,' I finished.

'Why does that name sound familiar?' Olena asked.

'Because it was your grandfather's name,' I told her.

Nick said, 'What's he got to do with it?'

I could only shrug my shoulders. 'It's the way he works, apparently ... individual stories illustrating his arguments, or something like that... You had to be there. He was convincing enough at the time.'

Nick frowned and began to say that he still didn't understand, but Olena didn't let him finish.

'What's he like?' she interrupted. 'Does he look the same as he does on television?'

'Sort of,' I said. 'But bad skin. He wears glasses, too.'

'Oh.'

'I suppose it does makes him look more rugged, though,' I added, not wanting to disappoint her entirely and just in case I needed him for bait for future use.

'Well, that's not so bad,' she decided, obviously coming round to the prospect of him not looking exactly like a male model. 'I'm surprised he hasn't had cosmetic surgery, though.'

'He's an historian, not an actor, Nick said. 'I don't suppose he's the kind to run off to the surgeon every time he finds a blemish.'

'It was only a *mole*,' Olena insisted, quicker this time and slapping him on the arm, 'hardly a face-lift! Anyway, your looks are important in television. How many ugly presenters do you know?'

'Personally?' Nick asked, then reeled off a couple of names.

'They're political journalists,' she insisted. 'Their programmes are aimed at a different market.'

'An audience with brains,' Nick observed.

'That's a little unfair,' I protested.

'Well, I still think he's attractive.'

'So did the girls at university as I recall,' he said.

'You were probably just jealous,' Olena told him.

'No doubt you're right,' Nick replied resignedly. 'You usually are.'

'Actually,' Olena said smugly, 'I have met his wife.'

'Julia?' Nick said.

Olena shot him a glance and he responded with a look of wide-eyed innocence.

'Standing introduced us once,' he explained. 'They met at Cambridge.'

'She went to Cambridge as well?' I asked. 'What's she like?'

Olena affected a look of indifference.

'One of these peaches and cream women,' she said dismissively. 'You know, typical English rose... So *home counties*.'

Nick laughed. 'That's the Slav speaking,' he said.

She ignored him.

'I thought she was rather attractive, actually,' Nick added.

She stopped ignoring him. '*You* would.'

'You know her, then?' I asked Olena, stepping in like a referee.

'We've met once or twice,' she said. 'The usual sort of thing. I don't suppose we've exchanged more than two words.'

'Just as well,' Nick put in.

'But you've never met him,' I said, 'obviously.'

She glared at me, silently suggesting that any introduction was going to be up to me.

The conversation drifted away from Standing after that and I stopped drinking wine and took coffee instead. An hour or so later I said my goodbyes and walked a little unsteadily down the street towards the tube station. Nick was still there at the door with Olena when she waved me off.

~

She rang the following day, as I knew she would, to ask about Standing again and suggest that she might meet us for lunch. By now though, I thought the prospect of getting anything useful out of her to be practically nil so I told her that his wife would probably be with us and after that she seemed to cool to the idea of meeting us "unexpectedly". She said then that Nick had told her that Standing was rather "opinionated" and that she probably wouldn't care for him anyway. I said, I supposed that like any academic who held original views on his subject he would necessarily be opinionated but by then she had tired of the subject. We talked of the one or two other people we hadn't covered over lunch and eventually she got around to the subject of Jennifer. She would not have spoken in front of Nick about his mother, of course, but I was regarded as fair game as far as an audience went. So I listened for a while about how "frosty" Jennifer had been at their last meeting before I tired of it and gently reminded Olena of how good a friend Jennifer had been to our mother during her last months. This, thankfully, stemmed the flow long enough for me to get off the phone. I said goodbye, promising to let her know how the lunch with Standing went and whether he forced any unwanted opinions on me.

'Idiot,' she said and rang off.

Standing emailed me in the week and we met at a restaurant not far from the BBC television studios. He was already waiting when I arrived, sitting towards the back of the room. There were a dozen or so tables, some already occupied, but the maître d' insisted on escorting me to Standing's table with a show of unnecessary formality despite the fact that I could see Standing perfectly well from the door. The warm weather had not yet broken and it was a bright and airy place with midday light flooding in from the two large plate-glass windows, shaded by blinds from the sun. The decor was modernist with abstract art in reds and blacks on the walls and a marble-tiled floor with random veining that, I suppose, was meant to complement the tone. I prepared myself for a lunch of sharp-angled food and colourful drizzled sauces.

He was dressed in a rumpled khaki jacket and a pair of trousers that looked as if they hadn't seen an iron since the days they were warmed on stoves. I supposed being who he was he could get away with it. But I thought he looked tired, not quite a gaunt caricature of the man on television but older, so that when I first saw him it came as something of a shock. But that, perhaps, is the nature of being — to some degree — immortalized on film: the image is fixed in the memory and, unless the personality remains in the public eye, the last glimpse is the one that is remembered. It was hardly the case with myself, of course, I had seen him not much more than three months before, but he still appeared changed. Perhaps my memory of him had reverted to an image of his presenting one of his earlier series, or perhaps I am seeing him now in retrospect and finding something that was not there at all.

'I've been in Kiev,' he said, as if travel were an explanation of my unvoiced concern.

He had come that morning from a meeting about a new television series, he told me, but when I asked him about it he was obviously reluctant to say anything further and merely muttered, 'Early days...' I did wonder if it was professional caution or superstition on his part, but Standing didn't look to me to be a man who had much truck with superstition.

'How's the research going?' I tried instead.

He picked up the menu. 'Slow, to be honest,' he said, then broke off to order. He already knew what he wanted and suggested a bottle of wine while I made my choice. He asked for a particular Burgundy that wasn't on the list and the waiter returned a few minutes later with the bottle. He opened it and waited while Standing went through the ritual of taking the bouquet and tasting, then half-filled our glasses.

'It's rather good,' Standing said to me, sampling it again. 'They've not many bottles left.'

I drank some and found out why. It was far better than anything I was used to drinking and was glad it hadn't been on the wine list so that I didn't know what it cost.

'It's the detail. It's so difficult to pin down,' he suddenly said after the waiter had left.

'Oh?' I replied, trying to pick up the thread of the conversation.

He stared at me earnestly across the table and I could see that it was his skin that was drawn, old acne scars prominent on his chin.

'Yes. The thing that gives the whole ghastly business its human dimension.' He tapped a finger absently against the stem of his glass. 'You can state quite baldly that two ... three million people starved to death but what does that *mean* to us? Can anyone in a modern society possibly empathize with a peasant culture?'

I wondered if he was bringing the essence of his meeting with him from the studio, if he had got into his television character and was now involuntarily hauling all those peasant bones around with him in some empathetic sack on his back. Then I remembered what I had said to Nick about Standing's work over the weekend.

'You need individual stories,' I offered, 'real lives of real people to bring the horror to life,' thinking that if I hadn't been so befuddled at Olena's I might have made a better fist of explaining it to them.

It was, of course, his signature approach. Where other historians unfolded a great landscape of world events shaped by statesmen or social movements, Standing's approach was to get under the skin of individuals who had lived through the times. This was a method that worked well on television. The publications not linked to his television work might be academically drier, but for television Standing would home in on some person or family whose documentation had happened to survive, bring them to life in descriptive sketches and illustrate where possible with photographs or contemporary paintings — if not of the people selected, then people of their ilk who had suffered the same fate. It made for a documentary approach that tended to fix people and events more firmly in the viewer's mind. I had supposed it was why he had been chasing down Aleksander Zaretsky.

Our starters arrived but before he began eating he reached into his jacket pocket and took out a folded sheet of paper.

'David Griffiths found this the first trip we made to the Ukrainian archives,' he said. 'It was before I had even decided on the shape of the series and was just casting around for something to carry it. This caught his eye.' He pushed it across the table. 'It's a translation, of course,' he added.

I picked it up and unfolded it.

To Central Committee Ukrainian Soviet Comrade Chubar.
Copy to: Ukrainian Soviet Secretary Comrade Kosior.
DEPOSITION
Statement of Comrade Aleksander Grigorevich Zaretsky dated 4th June 1932 given to Kharkov Regional Committee of the All-Union Communist Party (Bolshevik).

Subject: Grain seizures from local Kolkhozes and surrounding villages as directed under Central Committee decree.

Following the failure to fill the quota required I was instructed to recruit a Buksyr brigade from village Soviets and Komsomol volunteers. I conducted a systematic search and seizure of all hoarded grain discovered in each village. We met with some resistance and an example was made of the worst of the kulak profiteers we encountered. I was instructed to deliver all grain so collected to a foreigner, Comrade Shostak, whose responsibility, I was told, was to supervise accurate measurement by weight in poods and to oversee its carriage to the central railways depot, Kharkov, for subsequent onward shipment. I rendered all assistance required to fulfil this task having first assured myself of Comrade Shostak's authorization.

Aware of penetration by anti-Soviet elements into some kolhkozes, I instructed that any grain found in kolhkozes, which had not fulfilled their quota was to be seized. Time and again I met with excuses that the harvest had been poor and grain, which had not been delivered had been reserved for feeding the kolhkoz workers and for seed grain for the following year. In accordance with Central Committee directives I brought them to the understanding that fulfilling their quotas was the first and only duty of the kolhkoz and failure to do so was to materially assist the class-enemies of the Revolution. To this end I again had to make an example of the more recalcitrant elements. The worst offenders in the villages were the kulaks who had avoided earlier purging or who had contrived to return to their former villages from exile. These elements were summarily shot. Middle peasants found guilty of hoarding grain were arrested and, in the most flagrant of cases, deported.

Now I have been told I am accused of a crime. Who are my accusers? Show them to me and I shall defend myself against their accusations. If I am guilty of anything it is in over-zealousness in following my duty to the Party.

Signed: Aleksander Zaretsky.

I looked up at Standing grimly and offered the paper back across the table.

'Is this the only mention of my grandfather you found in the files?'

He had started eating and he shook his head. 'That deposition was included in his OGPU file. There was quite a bit more concerning his arrest and statements given under questioning. We had been trawling through the files for that time to get an idea of the scope of arrests. Zaretsky's was just one of the files we came across.' He tapped his finger on the paper. 'It wasn't until we came back to it that we realized its importance.'

'What had he been arrested for? Arranging for his wife and son to leave the Ukraine?'

'No. There was no mention of his family.'

'Then what was the charge?'

'Disrupting grain collection.'

'How?'

'That's not clear,' Standing said. 'The charge was pretty much catchall at that time. He was denounced...' adding, as he looked down at his plate, '...by someone or other.'

'Why would someone do that?'

Standing merely shrugged. He looked back at me and dabbed at his mouth with his napkin.

'Any number of reasons. Personal grievance ... professional jealousy... It's still a sensitive subject. Names are often redacted. Given the circumstances and the Terror that followed and just how long ago this happened, there can't be any people left alive who had any involvement. But there still might be family members and, before names are released, the authorities like to be assured their own backs are covered. We'll get the information but it'll probably take a while.'

'Was he shot?' I asked.

'No. As a member of the Communist Party he was spared death but sentenced to deportation.' He drank some wine, adding laconically, 'Usually it amounted to the same thing. Up until this time being a Party member usually offered some form of protection. The worst you could expect would be expulsion and a period of exile, just long enough to make you see the ideological error of your ways. After the murder of Kirov everything changed. Stalin took the opportunity to rid himself of his enemies — and his perceived enemies, come to that. Little fry like your grandfather were usually shot out of hand. Much in the same way they had dealt with the opposition during the civil war and with the Kulaks after it.'

Our mains arrived. Standing picked up the piece of paper and folded it away in his pocket before dismantling a rack of lamb.

'In a way your grandfather was lucky,' he said. 'And he may well have survived. By the time of the German invasion it was all hands to the pump. If Zaretsky had been at all useful...'

He began to eat, immediately vandalising the work of art on his plate.

'What caught my eye about the deposition,' he said, through a mouthful of lamb, 'were the names of Chubar and Kosior. They were both top Ukrainian Party men. Chubar was a Ukrainian himself, a Ukrainian Politburo member, and head of the government. Kosior was a Pole and First Secretary of the Ukrainian Communist Party. When Stalin first started coming down hard on the Ukraine they had both protested about the severity of the quotas and the subsequent repression. When push came to shove, though, they fell in line like everyone else. But it may be that sending them a copy of Zaretsky's deposition was meant to be a reminder that their earlier opposition had not been forgotten, a warning that Stalin remembered they had tried to stop the grain seizures.' He raised his glass as if in an ironic toast. 'That was Stalin all over, playing mind games to wrong-foot everyone around him. He was a master at that.' He returned to his food, adding. 'In a way your grandfather may have been lucky being arrested when he was. Stalin was dissatisfied with the amount of grain the Ukraine was producing and the unrest. In January of thirty-three he sent Pavel Postyshev there. He'd been there back in the mid-twenties when Kaganovich was in charge — iron-arse, they called him. Postyshev had rooted out the Trotskyists and nationalists back then, this time he purged everyone who was reluctant to toe Stalin's line. His post was Second Secretary but in reality, being Stalin's man, he was the boss. He purged a hundred thousand or more, mostly shot, and stripped the region of what grain was left. That's when the famine really kicked in and he's regarded as bearing a large amount of the guilt for it. A couple of years later, though, when he saw the results, even he began to have second thoughts about the policy and said they'd gone too far. Stalin didn't forget that sort of disloyalty. He had Postyshev, Chubar and Kosior all shot in the same room one morning in January, nineteen-thirty-nine.'

I thought what a strange and terrifying world it must have been to live in, poised always on a knife-edge, waiting in the small hours of the morning for that knock on the door. Then that started me thinking about Aleksander Zaretsky, my grandfather, and one of the men who did the knocking, and wondered just how much my father had really known about him.

Standing picked up his glass and looked at me. He tapped at the paper in his breast pocket again.

'This was the key find, really. I knew I was looking for a particular foreign individual who was organising the grain shipments and I'd even come across the name Shostak before. It wasn't until this that we realized they were the same person.'

10

George's study was much as I had expected. Judging by the decor, it had recently been re-papered with an expensive-looking cloth, a dozen rolls of which would probably have paid my Community Charge for a year. There were a profusion of desk and table lamps to provide lighting although the morning had brightened sufficiently to infuse a milky sunlight into the room that lent the impression of it being under water. The desk I recognized from the London house, as big as a Roman triumphal arch and all polished mahogany and rosewood and ebony inlay and far too good to house some plastic-encased computer. That sat in one corner of the room on something more modest. The photographs I had missed in the drawing room were all present and correct but there was one I hadn't seen before of George with three other prosperous-looking men smiling smugly for the camera. One of them I recognized as the former US Secretary of State to the Treasury. Surprised by the circles in which he had obviously moved, I remarked upon the photo as George looked out the papers he had put aside for me.

'New York,' he said, matter-of-factly. 'The banking crisis, remember?'

I wasn't likely to forget. Carefully laid plans for financing my retirement had been wrecked in a matter of weeks.

'I wasn't a player,' he added, self-deprecatingly. 'They only took me along as window-dressing for the business community.'

'Still,' I said, hardly knowing what I *was* saying and impressed despite myself, 'your connections can't hurt Nick's career,' wondering as soon as it was out of my mouth whether it had sounded as crass to him as it did to me.

He cast me a glance that said it had taken a long time for me to learn the basic rules.

'It's like any walk of life, Alex. Who you know opens doors. But it's the Maitland name that'll help him most. Even if I say so myself, it's been a byword in the City for solidity and straight-dealing for seventy-five years.' Then he smiled wolfishly. 'Show me a politician who wouldn't kill for that?'

I'd known plenty of people besides politicians who would have killed for a lot less, but didn't say so. Instead, I said:

'I've never thought of Nick as the ruthless type. It's a murky world he's chosen.'

'Not as murky as the one you used to inhabit.'

I suppose I should have known that someone with George's connections would know all there was to know about anyone they cared to enquire into. Until then he had never alluded to my professional life and, on reflection, I should have realized that that was a suspicious fact of itself. Nick had always been fond of the pointed remark, as if probing something he had always suspected, but I suppose if George knew what I had been then Nick would have known as well and his comments were more in the way of a double bluff, as if he had enjoyed playing me at my own game. What struck me most however, given what George had just said about the Maitland name, and what I'd never before considered, was the distinct possibility that it had been my surname that had first flagged me up to the scouts.

Old habits die hard, though, and retired or not it wasn't something about which I was prepared to start talking.

'What I mean,' I said, as if I had not understood his allusion, 'is that he seems too good-natured for the cut-and-thrust of politics.'

'Don't let that fool you,' George said. 'There's steel at the core. It runs in the family.'

He turned on the computer and the printer, looked out some photographic paper and showed me the software for cleaning up photographs. Then he placed the folder he had taken out of a desk drawer next to them.

'Copy whatever you like,' he offered. 'I've an idea there are few things of Peter's here. You must take them, of course, but if you don't mind we'll go through them first.'

'It's good of you to take the trouble' I repeated.

'Family,' George said again, and left me to it.

I separated the contents of the folder into small piles. There were several photographs. They showed Frederick and Nastasiya at their wedding, first the couple, Frederick looking younger than I had ever seen him in a dark suit with lapels that betrayed the decade as the thirties, and Nastasiya in what must have been a light-coloured dress but not a wedding dress, hat, and carrying a bouquet of flowers. She was thinner than she had looked in the photographs I had given to Standing and not as girlish, but if she was older than Frederick, as George had remarked, it was not obvious as she stood on Frederick's left, smiling with her arm linked through his. He smiled, too, but it was more reserved and his eyes were not on the camera.

I still didn't know the date of their marriage and there was nothing written on the back of any of the photographs to help. The next photo was of the happy couple standing with a man and woman I presumed to be Frederick's parents. They were noticeably unsmiling and I wondered if perhaps they had disapproved of their son marrying a Ukrainian girl with a son in tow. There was a shot of a larger group, eight, or so, and this had been taken on the steps of some municipal building, suggesting a civil wedding. This might have explained why Frederick's mother looked rather displeased although as a widow Nastasiya could have married in a church again. Except, of course, according to Standing she wasn't a widow. But would she have known that? Whatever the circumstances, they seemed to have opted for a registry office. The group were a mixed bunch and apart from the newlyweds and a man standing on Frederick's right, thin and gauntly angular who might have been his best man and who had a vaguely familiar face, I recognized only one: my father. Aged perhaps thirteen and standing to the side of his mother, he was looking sternly at something out of shot to his right.

The last wedding photograph was a better one of him. He stood between Frederick and Nastasiya, his mother's left hand resting lightly on his shoulder. My father looked happy enough despite a rather bad haircut that had left a large tuft of hair sticking up like a single nascent horn. Behind his right shoulder Frederick stood in his customary pose, left arm behind him and his right at his side yet giving the impression that it needed to be grasping the lapel of his jacket in a schoolmasterly attitude. I recalled something Olena had said back in the summer and it began nagging at me and I remembered that she had described him as repulsive, actually shuddering at his memory. Looking at the photograph closely, I could see nothing that might have repelled beyond his pose, which might have suggested the makings of a strict stepfather. I wondered if our father had ever told Olena something that had coloured her memory of Frederick and worried at the possibility for a while, but in the end I was left with a feeling of a memory incomplete, something unfinished, that danced at the edges of my recollection but wouldn't come into focus. I made a mental note to talk to her when I got home to find out what it was. Then, not wanting to rely on a memory that obviously wasn't functioning too well, I scribbled Olena's and Frederick's name on a scrap of paper and added it to the pile.

The remaining photographs must have been taken later somewhere at the seaside. Peter was posing next to his mother who reclined in a deckchair. Another showed Nastasiya and her in-laws, any possible disappointments concerning the wedding apparently forgotten as they all looked happily, if a little windblown, towards the photographer. These, I assumed had been taken by Frederick as he was not present in any of the snaps. One character who was, I noticed, was Grigori, the Cossack doll, sitting on a rug next to Nastasiya. The last photo showed Peter, grinning broadly at the camera, still thin in his bathing trunks as if a surviving reminder of what he had managed to escape.

I scanned them into the computer and did my best to clean up the old images with the software tools. When they were as good as I thought I was going to get, I printed them off.

The papers in the folder, I found, were an odd assemblage of barely-linked material. A collection of school reports of my father's, dating from 1934-1935 showed, according to the remarks of his various masters, that he was doing well in most subjects if, understandably, behind his fellows in English. 'Working hard and improving', was the comment. His best subject was mathematics. There were several letters. One was from my father and addressed to Frederick at his overseas posting and dated January 5th 1941. In it my father told Frederick that Nastasiya had been killed in an air raid. There was a clinical detachment about the way he relayed the news that I found cold, but then I suppose that that was what living through a war and living with death constantly around you did for one's emotions. One bottled them up or else was overwhelmed. Having said that, though, I had to admit that my father was, on occasion, capable of coldness.

There were no other letters from him but, with his mother dead, perhaps there was no one to whom to write. If he wrote to Frederick at all, it seems that Frederick didn't keep the correspondence. The other letters were from Frederick to Nastasiya, posted early in the war while he was serving abroad. They were chatty, naturally saying little about where he was or what he was doing and mostly full of small endearments for her and suggesting that she leave London and stay with his sister Florence in the country. He always signed off by sending his love to Peter. If Nastasiya replied — as I assumed she would have done — the letters had not survived. It made me realize that I had seen nothing written in her own hand.

What remained were bank statements showing that my father had a bank account — although, at the age of eighteen, seemed to have no more than fifteen pounds to his name — some miscellaneous receipts and a very old birthday card to his mother. All of these as well as Frederick's letters and the school reports showed signs of damage. There was no marriage certificate.

I took a copy of everything despite doubting that George would want to keep anything besides the photographs and his father's letters, then packed the originals away in the folder and left them on the desk.

I was in the act of getting out of the chair when I unaccountably felt a sudden urge to take a prowl through George's computer files. I don't know what prompted it (well I do — it was a professional curiosity about other people's secrets — but what I mean was, I don't know why I should have felt that way towards George) and I managed to resist the impulse with little more than a momentary pause as I stood. As it happened, George opened the door just as I shut off the machine.

'Had a look?' he asked.

I smiled and felt like saying, 'No.' I told him that I had made copies of everything, adding that I wasn't sure if any of it was relevant to what I was after.

'There's no marriage certificate for Frederick and Nastasiya,' I said.

'Isn't there?' George replied. Then he frowned and said, 'Actually, I can't remember ever seeing one. How odd. Come to think of it, I don't know exactly when it was they married.' He grinned at me sardonically. 'If it wasn't for the photographs I might have wondered if they were ever married at all, what with her first husband disappearing like that.'

'I've never seen these wedding photographs before,' I said.

'Haven't you? They used to be somewhere in my father's house but perhaps you never went there. And, come to think of it, I don't think my stepmother was very keen on them being on show. She felt a bit ambivalent about Nastasiya, so she probably put them away just as soon as she decently could.'

'I'm surprised they survived the Blitz,' I said. 'All the other stuff shows signs of damage.'

'Some things survived the bombing,' he said, reminding me of the fact that he'd been one of them. 'The photos were copies my grandparents had. The snaps of your father, too. They were really quite fond of him, I think. Most of Frederick and Nastasiya's things were lost although my grandparents saved what they could.'

It occurred to me then that George's maternal grandparents had died somewhere in the Ukraine, but he hadn't meant them and I wondered if he ever gave them any consideration at all.

'My father was serving overseas at the time,' George said. 'Peter was with his squadron. I was told he came down a couple of days later to see if I was all right although I've got no memory of that time at all. My grandparents had me shipped out of London to my aunt Florence after that. I lived with her until my father married Elizabeth.' He opened the file and took out the photos. 'I'll keep these if you've copied them but really the rest of the stuff ought to be yours. Take it, please.'

'Your father's letters?' I said.

He shook his head. 'Why don't you keep it all together?'

When Nick returned from his constituency work we had a leisurely lunch before Nick and George cloistered themselves in the study — planning their strategy to get Nick into the cabinet should the Party win the next election, probably. I had wondered what Jennifer found to occupy herself now that she had been sequestered in the country and would have suggested some exercise but, after George and Nick left, I turned around and found she had disappeared as well. I poked my head into a couple of rooms and finding no evidence of her wondered if she was avoiding me. The memory of my adolescent infatuation kept popping into my head as it had not done for years and I began to feel uncomfortable at the thought of possibly making Jennifer feel uncomfortable. Left to my own devices, I decided that a long — albeit solitary — walk would probably be the best thing all round — the middle-aged man's equivalent of a cold shower.

I had seen an ordnance survey map in the kitchen so, to avoid the embarrassment of getting lost, I stuffed it into my coat pocket, laced my boots on again, took a walking stick from the collection by the front door and set out.

The milky sunlight that had illuminated George's study had faded beneath a thickening overcast. The wind had shifted to the north and beyond the tree-line a bank of cloud had begun to glower ominously.

Walking down the drive, I turned to look at the house and saw Jennifer at one of the upstairs windows. I raised a hand and waved but she gave no sign of having seen me. I turned again, oddly disconcerted, and after a while crossed the small stone bridge and the stream that Nick and I had driven over the previous evening. I stopped to look at the water running fast and clear over the pebble bed. For some reason, seeing Jennifer at the window reminded me of a day, years before, when coming home on leave from the army I had seen her standing at the window of my parent's Chiswick house as I walked up to the door.

It had been before I joined the redcaps and I must have been in my early twenties, filled out at last and fit from all the exercise I had been given. I believe I was more at ease with myself then than I had been since I was a boy and thought myself over my teenage fixation with my young aunt. But seeing her as I walked into the hall and dumped my kitbag on the floor brought all the old longings back to me. I was no longer the tongue-tied teenager I had been — bumptious instead, probably — and I greeted her and my mother like a young adventurer home from travelling the world, even if it had only been Germany. Jennifer had seemed surprised by the change in me — physical, I suppose — and I had been a little alarmed by the change I saw in her. She had had Nick by then, and probably Oliver, too, and the wild girl I had been so attracted to seemed sadly subdued and domesticated, like an animal penned into docility. George was not there but by then, of course, he had recovered from his brief brush with the counter-culture and was forging a career for himself in the City, still the same old George but sometimes now imbued with an inflated sense of self-importance that I couldn't help thinking the old Jennifer would have pricked with playful scorn.

My mother was cooking lunch and she told me to take Jennifer to the pub down the road for an hour so we went for a drink together and I found, disconcertingly, that time and the army had made no difference to the way I felt. But I was older by then and had learned how to hold a conversation with a woman and how to hide my natural emotions and we passed an enjoyable hour together and I saw that the old Jennifer was still there; she had just learned to hide her natural emotions as well. Recognising that fact gave me some sort of comfort as I walked her back to the house and lunch with my parents. Now, walking towards the gates at the top of the drive, I realized that I had forgotten all that and supposed that Jennifer would have forgotten it as well.

The gatehouse looked empty as I passed with no curtains at the windows or any signs of recent cultivation in the unkempt garden. Turning right along the narrow lane I walked by hedgerows sparse in winter with only a few flittering sparrows and robins for company.

After a couple of miles I came into the village, a small hamlet that consisted of little more than a handful of cottages clustered around a crossroads. What had once been a shop now displayed an old post-office sign above whitewashed glass and a boarded door. There seemed to be no pub around and fifty yards further down the road I found I had already walked out of the village. Bearing to my right again, I followed an even narrower track past a tractor's muddy tyre marks where they had churned up the entrance to a field. Another mile or so brought me to a gap in the hedge and a stile. The map suggested that I could follow a path along the edge of the fields and pass through a farmyard before swinging back towards the copse that George and I had walked through that morning. The afternoon had darkened and the cloud I had noticed earlier now said I'd see rain before I saw the house again. I had brought no umbrella, only optimism, so I clambered over the stile and quickened my pace along the edge of the field.

It occurred to me that only a few months before I would not have been physically capable of such a long walk. Now though, it was inactivity rather than exercise that reminded me of my back injury. Every *quid* had its *pro quo*, however, and despite the need for exercise I knew that I would undoubtedly pay later for over exerting myself. I toyed with this small paradox for a while, attempting to formulate some deterministic law of diminishing returns that would eventually leave me pushing myself relentlessly on, reluctant to stop and suffer the consequences. But it wasn't a theory I could trust to hold water and before long, picking my way around the increasing patches of quagmire, my mind began to drift back to the papers I had examined in George's study.

I considered the letter in which my father had told Frederick of Nastasiya's death and wondered if it had predated my father's rift with Frederick. As I have said, it seemed something of a detached communication but that did not necessarily point to the fact that the rift had already occurred. There were the good school reports and the photos taken at the seaside in which he appeared to be genuinely enjoying himself, and although it might have been a simplistic assumption on my part, it seemed to me that if anyone suffered from an unhappy home life it was reasonable to think that that disturbance would show up in his schoolwork. My father's disagreement with Frederick, therefore, most probably dated from after his schooldays and, possibly, after his mother's death. This, in itself, disqualified George's theory of sexual jealousy at having been replaced in his mother's affections.

Where that left me, though, I had no idea.

A cold rain began to fall as I negotiated the muddy farmyard and took a bearing on the copse. The afternoon had quickly dimmed to a premature dusk and a herd of Holstein cattle were kicking up a fuss after their second milking about the dinner service in their shed. The rain turned heavy and a few minutes later, passing through the copse, I startled something enough to send it crashing through the undergrowth, which in turn startled me enough to make me walk into the low branch of a tree. I stunned myself and cut my forehead. Blood mingled with rain and ran down my face, insinuating its way under my coat and shirt collar, dampening me inside as thoroughly as I was out. As I staggered around in the copse imagination began to transmute the pouring rain into flowing blood and, dazed by the blow, I momentarily thought myself back in Africa after the bomb-blast, lying on the office floor and wondering why, if the sprinkler system had not come on, I was feeling so wet. The office had had no sprinkler system and anyone who had been thinking logically at the time might have linked the dust and the masonry and the chaos to something a bit more serious than the malfunction of a non-existent system. But I wasn't thinking logically and didn't begin to do so for another twenty-four hours when the pain which, until that point had signally failed to make itself felt, began to kick in. By then Charlie Hewson had carried me through the rubble and down the stairs to the street — no mean feat given our relative sizes. From there, even for someone like me who appeared to be seeing everything through opaque glass, it became obvious that we had just suffered a major attack.

When I finally got back to the house I used the rear door, stripped off my wet jacket and took off my boots and only then noticed that there was, in fact, quite a bit of blood staining my shirt and jumper. I walked into the kitchen, looking for a mirror, and gave Jennifer a nasty surprise.

'Alex! What on earth have you done?'

'I walked into a tree,' I said.

'Sit down and let me bathe it.'

I did as I was told and she dampened some kitchen towel and wiped around the cut, holding the back of my neck with the cool fingers of her free hand.

'It's going to need stitching,' she said, told me to hold the towel against my forehead and rang for the doctor.

'Is it really necessary?' I asked as she was dialling. 'The rain probably stopped it clotting.'

By this time George had walked in, taken a look and prescribed a scotch. He must have kept a bottle handy in the kitchen because the medicine was in my hand in a trice and I drank it down without argument.

'You're soaked through,' Jennifer announced in the manner of a mother admonishing a wilful child who had been playing in the rain on purpose. 'Come upstairs and get out of those wet clothes.'

I did as I was told again, rather touched by her concern, and by the time the doctor arrived I was dry, in fresh clothes, and a little light-headed from the whisky. Light or not, though, the head had begun to throb.

I suffered the ministrations of the local doctor who, I suspect, had it been anyone other than the people in the Big House who had requested a home visit would have pointed them towards the nearest A&E ward. He swabbed the wound with antiseptic, extracted a sliver of bark, then stitched me up. I was ordered to bed until dinner. All in all, I couldn't help thinking that the treatment had been a lot more prompt than that I had received in East Africa.

It was dark in the room when I awoke and for a moment I was unable to get my bearings. Then the knock on the door came again and I realized that that was what had woken me. The door opened and I could see Jennifer silhouetted against the light from the hall.

'Are you awake?' she asked softly.

I struggled up in bed, feeling at a disadvantage lying prone while she was on her feet above me.

'What time is it?' I asked, then saw for myself from the bedside clock that it was 6.45pm. 'I'll get up,' I said, and reached for the bedside lamp.

'Leave it off,' she said and sat on the bed. 'How are you feeling?'

'It was only a bang on the head,' I said, 'and my own stupid fault. I disturbed something and wasn't looking where I was walking.'

She reached out for my hand and held it for a moment. Surprised, and unable to see her face in the dark, I said the first flippant thing that came into my head. 'It's not as bad as shrapnel in the back.'

'We all thought you were going to die,' she said.

'If I'd been in any condition to think,' I said, 'I probably would have thought the same.'

'Are you fully recovered?'

'More or less,' I told her, thinking it was all rather late for this kind of solicitude.

'Good. You need to take care of yourself.'

Then she was off the bed and at the door. She stood there a moment longer, still silhouetted so that I couldn't see her face, then she was gone.

I lay there for a while, trying to read more into what had just happened than there actually was, then got out of bed and took a shower, doing my best as I did to keep my bandaged head dry. I dressed and went downstairs to the drawing room. There had been a time when the family dressed for dinner although Nick had

115

reassured me that the move to the country had relaxed this convention. However, as I entered the drawing room I couldn't help noticing that all three had contrived to be smarter in appearance than I had managed. My clothes were rumpled and my general demeanour somewhat of a shambles and it struck me once more that, in truth, I didn't really belong to the Maitland family.

But they all seemed very concerned about my injury even if, as I glanced towards Jennifer, I saw there was nothing beyond that usual glassy exterior of hers to which I had become accustomed. Then another whisky put the memory of the oddity of the encounter in the bedroom out of my head and the four of us talked of other things until it was time for dinner. By then, I had nothing more than a slight muzzy headache to remind me that anything out of the ordinary had happened that afternoon.

It was later, over coffee, that George turned on the television to catch the evening news and we heard that the police had arrested a vagrant in connection with the murder of Michael Standing.

THREE

11

It must have been three months after our lunch together before I heard from Michael Standing again. It was early August and the good weather we'd had in May was little more than a memory. I was in the garden one evening dead-heading the borders following two days of rain that had made a mess of the display when I heard the telephone in the house ring. The answer phone wasn't on but Daryna was there as she had stayed for dinner after one of our lessons and, since I had my muddy boots on, I rather hoped she would answer it and save me the trouble. She never would, though, and, irritated by the interruption and half-expecting that by the time I had got my boots off and reached the thing the caller would have rung off, I trudged back to the house.

I frowned at Daryna as I passed her in the kitchen and said, 'You can answer the phone, you know.'

But she just shook her head at me and said, 'I do not like to. It is your telephone,' which I thought was a nonsensical thing to say.

Surprisingly it was still ringing when I picked up the receiver and it turned out to be Standing.

'Are you doing anything tomorrow?' he asked. 'I'm speaking at a seminar in Cambridge and wondered if you'd be interested.'

'I've no firm plans,' I told him, glancing involuntarily at Daryna who, despite it being *my* phone, had come to lean against the

117

kitchen doorframe to listen to the conversation. 'Nothing that can't wait, anyway. Have you got anything new on Zaretsky?'

'Only in the loosest sense,' he said, sounding evasive. 'But you might be interested. You did say your grandmother came to this country in nineteen-thirty-two, didn't you?'

For some reason I had the impression that he was flicking through notes as he spoke, to ensure he'd rung the right man.

'That's right.'

'I thought I'd touch base and it occurred to me the seminar might be of interest — if you've a mind to watch back-biting academics in their natural habitat, that is.'

'Sounds irresistible,' I said.

'Good. I'll leave your accreditation at the desk. It won't be hard to find each other — it's strictly minor-league stuff.'

He told me where the seminar was being held and I said I'd see him there.

I put the receiver down and turned to Daryna. She wouldn't answer the phone but she always seemed to want to I know to whom it was I talked. This was not a proprietorial thing on her part — our relationship hadn't got anywhere near the sort of footing where one might suggest that jealousy was a factor — but she invariably found some point in my end of the conversation about which to interrogate me — a colloquialism, or some commonplace greeting I had used, that interested her — although I wasn't always entirely convinced that these idiosyncrasies of language were the object of her questioning.

'That was Michael Standing,' I told her before she had the chance to ask. 'You remember that historian I told you about? The one who got me started on my interest in the Ukraine in the first place?'

'The man who is on television?'

'Yes. He's giving a lecture tomorrow and he wondered if I might like to attend.'

'This is about Ukraine and communist times?'

'I'm not sure, but probably.'

'I would very much like to hear this. To attend the lecture, yes? This is correct form?'

'Yes,' I said doubtfully, 'but he's leaving accreditation for me and—'

'*Accredation*,' she almost repeated, stumbling over the pronunciation. 'What is this, please?'

I began explaining how people attending that sort of thing were generally invited then, watching Daryna's face fall with disappointment, assured her that if she really wanted to come I was certain it would be all right and that I could mention Standing's name when we arrived, like some *open sesame*.

'But it'll be an early start,' I warned her. 'He's speaking in the morning and it'll probably take a couple of hours to get there. Can you be here by eight o'clock?'

She pouted at me and waited for me to relent on the time a little. When I didn't she said:

'Then I stay over the night. Will this be acceptable?'

'If you really want to,' I said, irrationally thinking more about how she had typically used the definitive article in the wrong place than the fact that it was the first time she had suggested she stay overnight. 'Do you have to call someone first?'

She glared at me. 'I make own decisions, Alex. I am not a child.' Then, perversely, she went back into the kitchen, made a call on her mobile and began an insistent, half-whispered conversation. To preclude any impulse to eavesdrop, I tidied up the dining room table where we had held our lesson earlier.

My Ukrainian had reached a point beyond which further progress was looking frustratingly unlikely. I had learned the Cyrillic alphabet and could read a few simple words aloud without any real grasp of pronunciation but suspected that any relevant OFFSTEAD report would have been generous if it awarded me primary school level. Daryna, with the best will in the world, was not a good teacher; she quickly grew impatient of my halting progress and displayed all the irritation of one who was born to the language and fails to understand why, if she learnt it so easily as a child, I had so much trouble mastering it as an adult.

I was coming to realize that she lacked empathy, that ability to put oneself in another person's shoes and see and feel through their eyes. She was egocentric, not in the manner of Olena which in her I had always regarded as an impulse towards selfishness, but in a more basic way that perceived everything in relation to herself, as if she was the one discreet particle in the universe while everyone else — and everything — formed some great amorphous mass that moved only in respect to her. Harsh? Perhaps it does give an impression of Daryna as a calculating user of people, someone whose natural first thought was always for herself, but I think it fairer to suggest that, from her own perspective, she must have felt alone and regarded herself as the only person who could be expected to assert her own worth. Then, of course, I've always suffered from an over-supply of empathy myself and, anyway, rather than it making her's an unattractive personality, I found this self-awareness somehow only added to her attraction.

Naturally, that had become a problem as I suspected it might be from that day in the park when I had first met her. I suppose it was her exoticness — although that is, perhaps, too strong a word. It was her quaint accent and odd manner of saying things that I was attracted to, as well as her physical appearance. Had she been English and had spoken with a Birmingham accent I probably wouldn't have given her a second glance. Then perhaps I would. There is no fool like an old fool, the saying goes, although, of course, there is: it is just that young fools are expected to be foolish whereas old fools are required to display a little more restraint. Not that I had made a fool of myself over Daryna: I had made no advances or ridiculous declarations, or even given an intimation that I might; I had just found myself watching for those telltale signs that betray the fact that any attraction was mutual, that any advance might be reciprocated. Nothing overt. One is always aware of the signs: the seeking out of the other's company, the lingering look caught by chance, the brief and unnecessary physical contact — the touch of a hand or the accidental brush as we passed... All these I had looked for and as yet had never unequivocally found. They were there and they weren't there. The problem, as I just said, was that I possessed empathy. I could see through Daryna's eyes and was able to look at myself and, to be honest, didn't much like what I saw. So we carried on as we always had, teaching each other our respective languages, sharing the occasional meal or excursion, growing increasingly more comfortable in each other's company ... and yet despite it, I still failed to learn anything more about her. She was as secretive as ever about her wider life, the one spent away from me, and all I was ever able to glean were those few small insights of character that sometimes our interaction provided. She had never, though, suggested she stay the night in my house before.

After she had finished her telephone conversation we spent the rest of the evening on a little more linguistic work before I put one of Standing's television programmes on, something I had recorded from a repeat some months earlier, so that Daryna could see just who it was she would be listening to the following day. It was a series he had made covering the birth of socialism in Europe, the

Leveller and Digger movements following the English Civil War, the proto-socialist movements that had grown out of the Enlightenment, the French Revolution and those of 1848, through Marx and Engels and the Anarchists up to the Russian revolution of 1905. The series had left off where Standing's true area of academic expertise began and I had always assumed that any following series would take up the story from this point on. But he had always been evasive about exactly what it was he was doing and I had often suspected that, even as far as my meagre contributions to his research went, he was always holding out on me, that he had discovered more than he was willing to disclose. I had found what he had told me about my grandfather to be bad enough yet, despite it, I was still hoping that when he had asked over the phone about Nastasiya, he had discovered more.

Daryna watched the programme intently, alternating a frown with a nod of understanding, and managing to keep pace. Now and again she turned to me for clarification of some point or other and, when it had finally finished, she gave a small grunt of comprehension and turned to me, ready, as I thought, to make some intelligent comment on what she had seen. A summation, perhaps, from her Ukrainian perspective. Instead she said:

'This Michael Standing... He is very attractive man.'

I looked at her and shook my head, wondering about the advisability of taking her anywhere near Standing at all.

I sorted out some bedding and asked which of the two spare rooms she preferred then, when it was time for bed, let her use the bathroom first while I busied myself doing nothing downstairs. When I heard the bedroom door close behind her I switched out the lights and went up.

She had washed out her underwear and left it hanging to dry in the bathroom on the towel rail. I cleaned my teeth and tried to look elsewhere. The house seemed unaccountably more quiet than it usually did and I called out 'goodnight' as I passed her door, jarring the silence. There was no response. In bed, in the dark, I thought I could hear her talking, that insistent whisper she had used on her mobile in the kitchen, but perhaps she was just saying her Orthodox prayers. Then I could hear nothing and for a long while lay, ears attuned to the silence and wide awake.

When I finally did sleep, I slept badly and it was only Daryna moving around in the early light before dawn that pulled me from a late slumber. Awake instantly, hearing sounds in a house I always had to myself, I lay on the bed for several minutes wondering what the hell I thought I was thinking of.

~

It was a pleasant enough drive once clear of London and one of those summer days made all the more pleasant by the prospect of a journey. For a change the sun was out, the air was warm and there was that smell of freshness that comes after rain.

We had left early after a breakfast of toast and coffee, a meal made awkward by a mutual embarrassment after I had walked into the bathroom and found Daryna dressed only in her newly dried underwear. She had been startled and I had been flustered and had backed out hastily with a blurted apology. Now, although she seemed to have recovered her composure as she sat beside me on the big front seat of the old Alvis, we didn't have much to say to each other. I had recovered my composure even if I hadn't quite erased the image I had of her in bra and panties ... of her pale skin and her smooth, tight stomach and full breasts beneath the worn and skimpy material of her underwear. If I dwell upon the scene it is because it wasn't until I swung the car onto the M25 that I found sufficient other distractions to claim my full attention.

Not the easiest vehicle to drive in heavy traffic, the Alvis was of 1940s vintage, roomy with leather seats and a wooden dashboard. Predating most modern accessories, it was comfortable but a bit of a tank to handle. My father had bought it second-hand in the 1950s and had lavished more care and attention on it than he had upon either Olena or myself. He had kept it on the road until the time came when he was too old to drive but still could not bring himself to part with it. It had been garaged for several years until, after his death, I decided the time had come to sell it, only to find that I couldn't bring myself to get rid of the thing, either. It's fuel consumption was an environmental disaster but it was older than I was and had survived long enough to become that automotive oddity, a vehicle that appreciates in value instead of declines.

Thankfully the traffic eased as I joined the M11 and we made good time to Cambridge. With more than an hour to spare we stopped for coffee and Daryna disappeared for ten minutes while I checked Standing's directions. Then I had difficulty finding somewhere to park and consequently we found ourselves running late by the time we finally arrived at the college. My heart sank as we followed the advertising board for the seminar and I saw that we would be attending a series of talks on *Semantics in Politics: an Historical Context*. I concluded that Standing's suggestion that I might find the seminar of interest was some kind of arcane joke and I couldn't help wondering what Daryna was going to make of a lecture that would most probably be incomprehensible to me let alone her. With her tugging at my arm I fought the impulse to turn around and go home and joined the queue of stragglers at the front desk where a girl on reception was dispensing seminar literature and instructions. I presented myself and when the girl looked at Daryna I introduced her as a Visiting Fellow in Medieval Cyrillic from the University of Kiev who had found herself unexpectedly available to attend the seminar. Daryna looked bemused and the girl behind the desk doubtful, but I mentioned Standing's name and was rewarded by a smile and a muttered, 'Of course,' as she gave me my name tag and then made one up for Daryna.

'Professor Marianenko,' I told her, and improvised some qualifications for our visiting fellow.

I pinned the tag to Daryna's jacket, fumbling as a picture of her in the bathroom that morning rose up before my eyes again like a genie evading the stopper in the bottle. Then I attached my own tag, becoming only too aware as we entered the hall that most of those around us — Daryna included — dribbled a plethora of letters after their tagged names while mine merely stated a bald and truncated: *Alex Maitland.*

Daryna grabbed my arm as we joined the crowd and whispered fiercely in my ear.

'What is "visiting fellow"? It is plain I am not "fellow". What do I do if I am asked questions, Alex? It is too bad of you. I think I do not want to stay.'

I patted her hand reassuringly, aware of the heads turned in her direction and the eyes reading our tags — tag in my case, at least; what they were looking at in Daryna, I could only guess.

'Don't worry,' I told her. 'If anyone wants to speak to you we'll say you understand a little English but don't speak much. You can say something in Ukrainian to me and I'll make it up from there.'

She pouted like a disgruntled child and tugged harder on my arm as if reining in a horse. 'This is not a funny joke,' she grumbled.

The venue was a college hall, looked eighteenth-century and boasted, I was pleased to note, a fine vaulted ceiling whose architectural points I would be able to inspect at my leisure should the talk become too onerous. The audience had begun taking their seats and the noise of scraping chairs was matched in volume only by bursts of static from a microphone being flicked by the finger of a man in the manner a sadistic schoolmaster might have employed upon a helpless pupil's ear. He was dressed in tweeds and looked as if he might have been less conspicuous at a country weekend shoot. He flicked his finger at the distasteful apparatus once more and said 'hello' into it as if expecting a reply. Finally satisfied it was working, he addressed those still on their feet in the tone I supposed he used on his students and seemed to make a particular example of Daryna and me, pointedly waiting until we had found chairs before bidding everyone attending a 'good morning'. As I sat down, I caught the man on my left peering at my nametag, checking rank first I presumed, before nodding a greeting. The man in tweeds formally welcomed everyone then began to outline the nature of the two lectures to be given before lunch, adding something that I missed as he turned away from the microphone towards Michael Standing whom I noticed for the first time was sitting alongside two other men and a woman at a table to one side of the lectern. Then he introduced him.

He stepped forward to a modest round of applause, juggled his notes at the lectern then looked over the top of his glasses out at the audience. He seemed to hold me momentarily with that unremitting gaze of his, as if he had already picked me out of the audience, then let his eyes drift over the rest of us before glancing briefly back over his shoulder at the panel sitting behind the table.

'I want to talk this morning,' he began, addressing some mid-point in the hall, 'about the Tyranny of Utopia.' He paused to let the statement sink in. 'What might seem on the face of it to be an oxymoron is, when applied to human society, an inescapable truth and one which more than any other paradigm illuminates the gulf between political theory and practical application.' He paused again and gave us the benefit of one of his boyish smiles. 'First, though, I will begin by establishing my parameters.'

'What does he say?' Daryna demanded loudly in my ear. 'I do not understand the words. What is utopia and oxy ... oxy...'

'Oxymoron,' I said.

'Oxymoron,' she repeated in her way. 'And paradigm...? And what is a *para* metre?'

The man beside me glared as I elbowed him while taking a pen from my pocket. I apologized and found one of the leaflets the girl at the desk had given us and handed it to Daryna.

'Take notes on what you don't follow,' I said. 'We'll talk about it afterwards.'

Daryna stared at the inadequate piece of paper and the man next to me said, 'Shush.'

To be honest, I didn't hold out a lot of hope of being able to follow much of what Standing was about to say myself and, if he was going to befuddle us with the complexities of academic language, Daryna would barely catch a word. But it occurred to me that at least we were in the fortunate position of being able to grill him later. In fact I was quite looking forward to listening to him explain in language Daryna could understand just what he had been talking about.

I had missed what he was saying about Orwellian *doublethink* and its derivative, *doublespeak*, and tried to catch up as a latecomer tardily took a seat near the front of the hall. The man turned around as he sat down and I saw it was Edward Maseryk. I recognized his face from the television where he often turned up as a talking head on the news, or any other programme that needed an item placed in its mid-European historical context. He wasn't in Standing's league as far as television celebrity went and I wondered if he was making some kind of point by being late for Standing's paper. Standing, to judge from the way he paused and waited for Maseryk to sit down before continuing, obviously thought so. I assumed that academic jealousies, once centred upon who was publishing what and which fellowship or chair they were angling for, may well have now moved into the field of television. Many, I didn't doubt, would profess that such celebrity was beneath them but there was more than the vulgarity of that kind of fame to consider — popular history shaped minds and attitudes and those who reached the largest audience had more chance of having their perspectives on historical events accepted than those who did not.

'On September the eleventh, nineteen-ninety,' Standing had begun again, 'George Bush, *père*, making his State of The Union speech to the joint houses of Congress, declared a "New World Order" in global politics. The context was the launch the previous month of Operation Desert Storm, aimed at expelling Saddam

Hussein from Kuwait in a conflict that was to become known confusingly as "The First Gulf War", a semantic oddity in itself as Saddam had spent the previous decade locked in a bloody conflict with Iran which, up to that time, had been known as "The Gulf War". President Bush had felt confident in applying the sobriquet, however, as this new Gulf War was a military action that was arguably only possible following the parting of the Iron Curtain. This barrier had divided the Eastern Bloc from the *Free* World — and I use the adjective loosely — for more than forty years, and its parting foreshadowed the collapse of the USSR into its component parts. Aside from the coincidence of the date of the speech which will have significance only for those students of conspiracy theory — a burgeoning field of research which I predict will have its own academic chair before too long...' he paused long enough to allow a ripple of amusement to sweep through the auditorium, '...the speech itself has since been regarded as a pivotal moment in US foreign relations. This of itself is beyond the scope of this talk. What does fall within our purview, however, is the term "New World Order". From the vantage point of twenty years hence we can see President Bush was mistaken — arguably a family trait — but perhaps mistaken only in his use of the word, "order". But many before him have used the term, or variations on its theme, and have been equally incorrect. Even so, George H. was not completely wrong. He had merely confused a beginning with an end. The death of Communism across its heartland was the conclusion, not the beginning, of "A New World Order". Although they themselves didn't use the term, seventy years earlier when the Bolsheviks seized power in Russia and instituted the world's first Marxist-Leninist state, they truly believed that they were establishing a "New World Order", the socialist utopia that Marx had foretold in *Kapital,* which would be the final stage of human social development. How far wrong they were can be measured by the brutality they chose to employ in order to construct and maintain their version of this Utopia.'

The man sitting beside me grunted but whether in agreement or in exception I couldn't say. I stole a glance at Daryna but her eyes were fixed on Standing.

'Utopian visionaries are almost always the children of either religious theology or political theory. Rarely does the military strategist attempt to construct Utopia. Soldiers are a far too practical a breed, which is perhaps why most military dictatorships degenerate into brutal banalities. Even the destiny-struck Napoleon Bonaparte refrained from any pretence that, firstly his consulship and then his empire, was striving towards any Utopian dream; this, it ought to be said, in contrast to the *patrié* of virtuous citizens that the Committee of Public Safety had been working towards, and quite distinct from the linguistic forms the latter had employed to that end. The Bolsheviks, for their part, married the quasi-religion of Marxist philosophy to the political theory of Lenin—'

Now the man beside me did take exception and I half-expected him to raise an arm and shout, 'Point of order,' but Standing was barrelling along and probably wouldn't have stopped for an interjection from Vladimir Illych himself:

'—sure in the knowledge that Utopia was within their grasp — and it might be useful to remember here that Lenin himself was an admirer of Robespierre and the Terror. According to Marxist theory, of course, all that was required of them was a period in which they were to act as facilitators — the Dictatorship of the Proletariat, that is — to ensure that the necessary preconditions were in place for Utopia to spring up, like a mushroom after the Bolshevik reign — and here I use a deliberate homonym...'

Another ripple moved through the hall among those quick enough follow Standing's allusion, but he wasn't inclined to wait for anyone.

'The State would wither ... crime would disappear ... those fitted to do the most demeaning of jobs — which generally means those most unfitted to do anything else — would do them out of an overflowing generosity of heart and with, presumably, a smile on their collective face. Nonsense, of course. And nonsense that Lenin quickly realized was the case — assuming he hadn't already known before the Revolution that it was. Marx, it turned out, while living off the droppings from Engels' table, was trying to feed everybody else pie in the sky. To establish the Marxist-Leninist Utopia it was clear that first Lenin, and then those who had inherited — or perhaps I should say squabbled over — his mantle, would have to roll up their sleeves and *build* Utopia. After all, Marx could not have been *wrong*, that was Revisionism and the Party had rid itself of that particular heresy. No, Marx wasn't wrong, it was *they* who had misread the conditions. After all, Marx, while developing his political theories, had had Germany, an industrialized state, in mind, not an agrarian state like Russia. If Communism was to flower to its full Marxist potential, the Bolsheviks argued, first Russia — or rather, what had become a union of soviet socialist republics — would have to industrialize and this, with the time-scale the Bolsheviks were working to, was problematic. It would inevitably mean blood.

'This was not a problem. For those who abrogate to themselves a divine right to mould human social development, a certain distance from the fundamental clay is required. There is a *natural* distance born into these potters of human existence in that they are, by and large, sociopaths, men — and some women, it has to be said — psychologically apart from the general run of humanity in that they are not bound by such impulses as sympathy and empathy.'

The man beside me was getting restive and I noticed had started to take his own notes, glancing up at Standing and grunting as he wrote, a choleric colour rising in his face.

'Shush,' I said to him.

'It is true,' Standing said, 'that to accomplish their work they need willing accomplices — after all, there is a limit to the number of times one finger can pull a trigger...' He shrugged philosophically. 'And then their are the graves to dig...'

There was a little uncomfortable laughter. Standing watched us until he appeared to feel we had squirmed in our seats long enough.

'So, these movers and shakers, moulders and breakers, invariably employ a tool that has the power to direct a host of fingers on a multitude of triggers. And that tool is language.'

There seemed to me to be an almost perceptible sigh in his audience in relief that he had at last married his talk to his brief, and that we had not all been gathered under false pretences to listen to another Standing diatribe on the deficiencies of Communism. My neighbour, however, seemed to have had enough. He rose noisily to his feet, looked pointedly at the lectern and pushed past me without apology. I took the opportunity to catch his trailing — and no doubt Marxist — ankle with the toe of my shoe and he gave a satisfying yelp as he passed. Standing waited until the man had gained the aisle before continuing.

'This language is one of denigration and denial, of dismissal and ultimately of destruction. In recent history the Bosnian Serbs used it against their Moslem neighbours; the Hutus against the Tutsis in Rwanda. The Nazis employed language to deny a human existence to the Jews and the Gypsies and, before them, the Bolsheviks employed semantics to winnow from their new utopia anyone who either opposed them or simply did not fit their approved Marxist-

Leninist model. The mechanics of their Procrustean manner of trimming all those awkward bits that couldn't be accommodated within the Bolshevik template are beyond the scope of this morning's address, but an example or two of their methods might be instructive.

'Lenin himself, an old bourgeois at heart, had always held an abiding contempt for the peasant, as did many of his associates. The "working classes" were a concept to them rather than a living reality. Few of the Bolsheviks themselves had ever actually worked for a living, as we might understand the term, most being from bourgeois backgrounds or even from the lesser Russian nobility — Polish nobility in the case of Felix Dzerzhinsky. Rather than resort to honest labour, as at least Engels to his credit had done, they had provided a model for many later political movements by indulging in criminal acts like robbing banks to fund themselves while all the time rationalizing this behaviour as "revolutionary action" against a societal model they refused to recognize and wished to destroy. The leading Bolsheviks regarded themselves as intellectuals. Even Stalin thought of himself as an intellectual and, since the one job outside of revolutionary politics he ever held down was that of a weatherman in Tiflis, in Georgia, perhaps he had a point. It was certainly more than most of his contemporaries had achieved. But he certainly couldn't be regarded as "working-class" and perhaps the only real peasant among them was old Kalinin, who held the post of President for so long that finally a grateful Stalin decided to retire him and have him shot.'

There was a laugh or two and rather more general coughing and restlessness and Standing paused long enough to look around the hall once more, almost as if trying to judge whether or not it was worth his continuing in this vein. It seemed there was a weariness in that honeyed voice of his as he continued.

'But to return to my point, which is the language the Bolsheviks used to distance themselves from the object of their endeavours. For them there were no "fellow men"; these wallowed within the Marxist term, "the masses", a suitably amorphous blob of humanity which, by its very connotation, suggested a subject ripe for moulding. Within this mass, people were subdivided into classes — not a very revolutionary idea, I grant you, until you begin to examine its application.

'Despite all the obvious signs to the contrary, the peasantry were not regarded as "working class", not to be thought of as members of the proletariat. They did not exactly fit the Marxist template, being one forged for an industrialized society, and as such were therefore subject to Procrustean trimming—'

Daryna had filled her leaflet, I noticed, with a mixture of scribbled Ukrainian and English and was finding it difficult to make more room. She turned the paper around, her tongue licking along her lips as the pen moved. That done, she looked back up at Standing as if ready for the next indigestible gobbit.

'—they were subdivided,' Standing was continuing, 'into three further classes: the rich peasants, the middle peasants and the poor peasants. This, of course, left little room for shadings — one either fitted the model or one simply didn't exist. The rich peasants — and to be regarded as rich you needed only to own a couple of horses, or a piece of land, or employ another man occasionally — the rich peasants were, in Bolshevik terminology within an agrarian landscape, plainly and irretrievable bourgeois. What put them beyond the pale (an interesting term in itself given its history) was that these peasants had ambitions to better themselves. They wished to work on their own account — to own the land they worked, sell the surplus they produced and ameliorate the burden of their labour. In short, they wished to be masters of their own destiny. All this, naturally, was anathema to Bolshevik ideology. So, as a class, the rich peasant would have to be destroyed. To this end they would first have to be separated, as a class, from their fellow peasants and then denigrated to the degree that would shine a light of *natural justice* upon their fate. Those whom the gods first denigrate may they later destroy.

'To facilitate this they were termed "Kulaks". Kulak in Russian means "fist". This was a double blessing in that it might be applied to the alleged kulak habit of oppressively hammering the less industrious peasant whom they occasionally employed and to his equally alleged habit of squeezing them dry through the lending of money.

'This use of language was, of course, no new phenomenon. Socialists had softened themselves up for decades by adopting the language of the dialectic and other Marxist phraseology, those terms we have come to love that trip off the tongue like the "metamorphosis of commodities" and "relative surplus-value" and, perhaps my own favourite and a concept old Karl could never have dreamt would become dear to so many hearts, "commodity fetishism".' He stopped a moment to favour the hall with an ironical smile. 'But what *was* a new phenomenon was that, following the end of the nineteen-fourteen-eighteen war and the consequent Russian civil war, the Bolsheviks upon seizing power found, rather scarily, that they had to put what they had been talking about for years into practice. And when they tried they unsurprisingly found that the peasantry and a majority of the urban working class did not readily want to volunteer their lives to be structured along Marxist lines. This hardly mattered. Lenin knew at least as early as nineteen-eighteen that a Marxist state would have to be *imposed* — his Hanging Order of that year issued against rich peasants is eloquent testimony to that fact.

'And so, then, we are faced with the reality of the Bolshevik utopia; from the outset it was a paradise that had to be imposed regardless of the desires of those it was to be imposed upon. This is the heart of the problem with any Utopia. If human nature was such that we were, as a collective species, capable of engineering such a construct, the concept of Utopia would not in fact exist. It would not need to exist. In fact, it is clear that, *to* exist, it must do so — can *only* do so — in opposition.'

He stopped, took a long sad look at us and inhaled deeply.

'The Bolsheviks had no love of the working classes — the proletariat. All they had was a loathing for the exploiting classes. As their grip on power tightened so did their need to expand the section of society they saw as the exploiters. It has been said that great literature can never come out of a contempt for humanity. By the same token, Utopia cannot be founded upon an absence of love. Hate makes for a poisonous foundation.'

He gave a curt nod and picked his papers off the lectern. For a moment or two there was a surprised silence until a smattering of applause rippled around the hall. Standing retreated to the table with the other panellists, tossing his notes aside with the air of a man who has decided he was not going to need them again. The man in tweeds approached the microphone once more and thanked Standing for stepping into the breach.

I wondered if I had missed something and looked through the literature I had been given. There was nothing about Standing in it so I took the leaflet I had given Daryna back. She was looking about the hall in her disgruntled fashion as if the morning had not lived up to expectations. The programme was covered with her scribbling and it was only with difficulty that I could see that the scheduled speakers for that morning did not include Michael Standing. A man named Hervey was supposed to have given a talk entitled: *Egyptian Demotic and its Transitions Under Pharaonic Hegemony.* I was almost sorry I had missed it. I noticed that Edward Maseryk was due to speak that afternoon but next up was Professor Colin Stansfield, Associate Fellow in socio-economics at the University of East Anglia whose subject was to be *The Foundations of Monetary Exchange & its Influence on Language.*

The man in tweeds was introducing him and, as he approached the lectern, I stifled a yawn and wondered if I dare risk closing my eyes.

Within a minute or two it became clear that Stansfield's mode of address fell somewhere near phenobarbitone on the scale of sedatives and was delivered in a droning monotone that any hypnotist might have envied. After manfully following his argument for half-a-dozen sentences I decided that closing my eyes wouldn't hurt for a few moments, seeing as I hadn't slept well, and I stretched my legs in front of me as best I could and folded my arms across my chest. My last thought, I recall, was to wonder what had prompted Standing to step into the breach left by the absent Hervey.

12

It was an insistent tapping on my shoulder that woke me.

I opened my eyes to find Daryna's exasperated face looking into mine and the recalcitrant Marxist whose ankle I had clipped towering over me. He had obviously reclaimed his seat from the aisle at the other end of the row while I was catching up on my sleep but now chose to exit again on my side.

'You are sleeping,' Daryna complained. 'It is too bad, Alex.'

'Excuse *me*,' he said.

I muttered something about people who couldn't make up their minds and tried to gather my wits. The auditorium was emptying with an alacrity that suggested it must be lunchtime. I got out of the yo-yo's way then tagged on behind him with Daryna in my wake. We left the hall through a side door into a room less ornate where a makeshift bar had been erected. Through the crowd, I caught sight of Standing. He was talking to Maseryk and, to judge by the expression on his face, was not particularly interested in the other end of the conversation. He saw me and waved me over. As I joined them, Standing put an ostentatious arm across my shoulders.

'Maitland,' he said. 'I'd like you to meet Edward Maseryk. Edward's an old friend. He's an historian, too.'

It was an introduction pitched to make Maseryk sound like an also-ran. Closer to, without the benefit of studio lighting and make-up I could see he was a little older than Standing. His hair, greying around the temples, lent him an air of distinction and the malicious thought crossed my mind that the colour might not be natural. The rest of his crop was dark and tended to bristle rather than flow and was perched atop a face that boasted a long and prominent nose that gave him the look of a Pointer with its hackles up. He turned his steel-grey eyes on me, making me feel for a second like a small game bird hiding in the shrubbery, then he smiled and extended his hand and the dog impersonation vanished.

'I prefer Edvard,' he said, as I shook his hand, 'as Michael well knows.' His smile included Standing so I supposed he was used to the ribbing.

'Sorry, Ed*vard*,' Standing said, accenting the second syllable. 'I don't want to undermine your Czech credentials.'

'Now how could you do that, Michael? I was born there.' He laughed easily and released my hand.

I could find no discernible trace of his mid-European descent in his impeccable English accent even though I was listening for it, and I was reminded of my father who, by contrast, carried his like the faintest of birthmarks all his life. I recalled how Standing had once describe Maseryk as a professional Czech, and a man still clinging to the belief that Dubcek could have made a more liberal form of communism work. I was about to remark that I had seen him on television when I realized that both men had lost interest in me and had turned towards Daryna who was hovering at my shoulder.

'I'm sorry,' I said, moving aside. 'This is Daryna Marianenko.'

But they had noted her nametag, given her their names and shaken her hand before I had time to complete my sentence. For a second there was one of those pregnant silences as they both turned to me for a fuller explanation and I saw I would have to back up Daryna's fictional credentials or admit to the fraud and suffer the consequent embarrassment. I said:

'Professor Marianenko is from the Ukraine,' and began to explain, 'Her English is—'

'My English is better now, thank you Alex,' Daryna interrupted, turning to them both with the kind of winning smile I hardly ever saw brighten her face. Standing said something in either Ukrainian or Russian that I had no hope of following, catching only 'Kiev' and something I imagined was 'visiting' but might equally have meant washing detergent.

Maseryk listened intently and chipped in but I got the distinct impression that his grasp of the language was not quite as good as Standing's.

Daryna replied then turned to me, as did both Standing and Maseryk. I looked innocently back at them while they apparently expected me to say something. As I had no idea what, I simply smiled and said:

'I'm still learning the language.'

'We are all students,' Maseryk said expansively.

He asked if I had enjoyed Standing's address. I could tell by the nascent smirk on his lips that the question was pointed but not necessarily in my direction.

'I did,' I replied, a little more forcibly than I had intended but trying to wipe the smirk off his face, 'but then I have a interest in the subject.'

'Oh,' he retorted condescendingly, 'might I ask what that is? Language as a political tool, or perhaps history as one?'

'Tools are manufactured articles,' Standing said. 'You're not proposing we travel the Soviet route and manufacture history are you, Edvard?'

Maseryk arched his rather fine eyebrows but refused to take the bait.

'Not always manufactured, my dear Michael. Do not chimpanzees use sticks as tools to extract termites from their mounds?'

Out of the corner of my eye I could see Daryna looking at me and I knew she had chimpanzees on her mind. Before I could explain, Standing replied:

'But that was not the stick's original purpose. The chimpanzee has subverted its purpose.'

'An interpretation of the stick, wouldn't you say?'

'History is facts,' Standing said. 'Interpretation carries the interpreter's bias.'

'Family,' I chipped in, just in case they had forgotten we were there. 'My father's family was in the Ukraine—'

'Why is it?' Standing interrupted abruptly, 'that we always talk shop at these affairs? You'd think by now we'd all be sick to death of the subject.'

'But it's all we have, surely?' Maseryk replied, not altogether seriously.

'Well,' Standing said, 'I for one have other interests.'

'Television does broaden one's horizons,' Maseryk allowed, and he winked at Daryna.

'That's travel, Edvard,' Standing said. 'You ought to try going somewhere other than the Czech Republic.'

Maseryk looked at Daryna, then said to me, 'If all the ladies are as lovely in the Ukraine as Professor Marianenko, I shall certainly consider making other travel arrangements.'

Standing glanced heavenward but Daryna smiled sweetly at Maseryk.

'Don't let Edvard's looks fool you, Professor,' Standing said to Daryna. 'He has quite a reputation for the ladies.'

I thought the remark was rather insulting but Maseryk ignored the slight and said, 'And speaking of lovely ladies, how is Julia? Not languishing at home, I hope?'

Standing scowled at him and made a point of looking at his watch.

'Actually,' he said, 'I'm supposed to meet her for lunch. You don't mind, do you Maitland? We can talk over that matter I mentioned on the phone. And Professor Marianenko, of course.'

Maseryk gave a small philosophical shrug to acknowledge that the invitation had not extended to him. 'I still have a little work to do on my paper,' he said, adding in a voice full of irony for my benefit, 'We who still have our reputations to make have to work that little bit harder, you understand.' He shook hands with us again, holding on to Daryna's a little longer than necessary as he expressed the hope they would meet again.

'Look,' Standing said after Maseryk had left, 'I've arranged lunch somewhere else. All you'll get here in the vac is limp salad and a baked potato since they've contracted out the catering. And there's no rush, there's nobody else worth listening to this afternoon.'

'I thought Maseryk was speaking,' I said.

'So he is,' said Standing.

He led us out back through the hall and under an arch into a quadrangle, ignoring the few faces that turned his way as we passed.

'You drove up, I take it,' he said. 'I came by train so we'll use your car unless you prefer a taxi?'

'No,' I said, 'not at all.'

When we got back to where I had parked the Alvis he stopped in surprise.

'What is it?' he asked.

'It belonged to my father.' I began to explain, assuming he was an enthusiast. But I soon saw from his face that he wasn't; he was merely expecting something a little more modern.

He opened the front door for Daryna then climbed in the back. He began looking for seat belts that weren't fitted.

'I suppose an air bag is too much to ask?' he said.

'Air bag?' Daryna repeated. 'What is this?'

I left it for Standing to explain as I negotiated the Alvis back onto the road. They fell to speaking Russian again and I listened with half an ear until there was a gap in the conversation.

'I meant it when I said I enjoyed your paper,' I told him.

He leaned forward and rested his arms on the back of the front seat. In the mirror I saw a sardonic smile playing at the corners of his mouth.

'Kind of you to say so although it was hardly apposite. Not what they were expecting, at any rate.'

'Linguistics in politics? A bit tenuous, perhaps.'

'Not my field,' he said. 'Go straight on and right at the first lights.' He waved vaguely through the large windscreen. 'Any port in a storm, though, and it was the best I could cobble together at short notice. Hervey's down with laryngitis and had to cancel.'

'I saw you weren't on the programme,' I said. The road we were on was taking us out of Cambridge. He waved me straight on at an approaching roundabout. 'They were fortunate you were able to step in, I would have thought.'

He laughed. 'I doubt if they think so. Second left,' he added. 'To be honest, I only accepted to put Maseryk's nose out of joint.'

'You speak to break Professor Maseryk's nose?' Daryna enquired, turning around to look at him.

'It's a colloquialism,' I said. 'Idiomatic language. Remember, we talked about this? "To put someone's nose out of joint" means to upset them.'

'So you now have requirement to apologise to Professor Maseryk?' she asked Standing.

'Not in this case, I think,' he said.

We had turned into an avenue of large houses set back in their own grounds, half-screened for the most part by stands of beech and chestnut.

'There on the left,' Standing said, 'the sign for the Mill House Hotel. Let's just say it's professional rivalry. We take a different perspective on some points of twentieth-century history. His parents brought him out of Czechoslovakia in sixty-eight — the Prague Spring? He was only a small child and is as British as you or I am, but he believes having been born under a communist regime gives him some insight denied the rest of us. The way he carries on you'd think he'd have preferred it if his parents had left him behind in Prague.'

I pulled up outside the Mill House Hotel, a gabled late-Victorian redbrick building with elaborately carved barge-boards that looked as unlike a mill as any structure I'd ever seen. Standing climbed out of the Alvis and held the door for Daryna before leading us up the steps to the entrance.

At the reception desk Standing asked a thin young man if his wife had arrived. She hadn't so Standing suggested a drink while we wait. We followed him into a bar that gave on to the dining room. It was furnished with faded plush seats and matching drapes of another age, its jaded grandeur not helped by the shafts of sunlight streaming in through a pair of open doors. Outside was a flagstone terrace with a stone balustrade. The terrace looked onto a lawn that sloped towards a stream. We took a table near the door where we could admire the view while a waiter hovered waiting for our order.

Standing asked for a pint of the local bitter, observing that talking made him thirsty, and despite having to drive I joined him, feeling dry not through talk but from sleeping through Stansfield's paper.

Daryna asked for a soft drink then said, 'You excuse me, please,' and disappeared down a corridor following the signs for the toilets.

'You know she's not from Kiev university,' Standing said to me when she had gone.

I smiled apologetically. 'That was my idea, I'm afraid. After you rang yesterday she said she'd like to come. It was the first thing I could think of when we got to reception.'

'It's just I happen to know some of the faculty,' he said.

'Were you speaking Russian?'

'Yes. Her's is very good.'

'I met her originally when I wanted those letters of my father's translated. If you remember them?'

'Of course. Anything of interest?'

'Only what you'd expect,' I said. I glanced through the open door and caught sight of Daryna on the edge of the terrace on her mobile again. She turned as I watched and saw me looking at her. She smiled in her grim way and put the phone away, coming back into the bar.

'I remember I tell a friend we would meet,' she explained, sitting down again. 'I telephone to cancel arrangements.'

'We can be back by mid-afternoon,' I offered, 'if you want.'

'You do not stay to listen to Professor Maseryk?' Daryna asked.

'What's his topic?' I asked Standing.

'Nineteenth-century idioms within Marxist dialectic,' he said.

'Tough choice,' I said. 'Is he one?'

'One what?'

'A Marxist.'

Standing laughed humourlessly. 'So he'd like you to believe. But it's only a pose. He's one of these latter-day pseudo-Marxist historians who thinks that biting the hand that feeds them affords them some sort of moral objectivity. On the one hand he criticises the West for interfering in the affairs of sovereign states and on the other berates it for not going to Dubcek's aid in sixty-eight. He's fortunate, of course, that the Czech government didn't have the opportunity to prove that communism with a human face would work. The fact that Communists were voted out the first chance anyone in the Eastern Bloc got and that none of those who have crept back in since proposes a system that bears any resemblance to communism, *per se,* puts a bit of a crimp in his argument. Then there's the fact that the only thing remaining Communist about China is that the Party have retained absolute political control and you begin to see that none of it adds up to what the old boy had in mind at all.'

'*Crimp* I do not know,' Daryna said, 'also not why someone bites hand that feeds, but you are all very lucky, I think, in ability to discuss this in academic way and not live under communistic system, yes?'

'You're absolutely right, of course,' Standing agreed, giving her his winning smile. 'We have had the luxury of making careers out of dissecting and examining a largely defunct political system without ever having to suffer the horrors it generated. That's what chiefly irritates me about men like Maseryk. They use semantics to mask the human face.'

The waiter came in from the dining room and asked if we'd like to order. Standing took another look towards the door — for his wife presumably — then said we would. I saw Daryna blanch at the prices and caught her eye and with a sinking feeling discreetly indicated I would pay. Standing was still deliberating over the menu and so, unfettered, Daryna adroitly ordered a filet mignon. Standing restricted himself to a salad.

'Big breakfast,' he said by way of explanation. 'Up early working on my bloody lecture.'

I asked for a salad as well, to ease the pressure on my wallet. Standing suggested wine. I declined, gesturing towards my pint and said I was driving. Daryna said she would like a little and so he settled for a bottle of Pinot Noir at a price that might have paid her rent for the week. Perhaps he saw the look on my face because, as the waiter left, he said:

'The seminar is paying my expenses.'

I must have muttered something facetious about Oxbridge and privileges because Standing took rather an exception to it.

'As a matter of fact,' Standing said, 'I came here on a scholarship. 'The first in my family to go to university as it happens.'

I felt abashed. 'I didn't mean—' I began.

'And as far as privilege goes,' he interrupted, 'it was *your* family's scholarship,'.

'*My* family?'

'The Maitlands.' He raised a corrective hand. 'Sorry,' he amended, 'as you've pointed out, not strictly *your* family. Your cousin's grandfather, Frederick Maitland.'

'That's the first I've heard of it,' I said.

'Oh? Weren't you aware he endowed the college with a scholarship in political science? I'm surprised you didn't know.'

So was I. I knew George wasn't in the habit of boasting about his charitable giving unless the propaganda would prove economically advantageous to some business venture of his, but the endowment of a scholarship to Cambridge was another matter. And it had been Frederick.

'The meaning of *political* science, please?' Daryna asked Standing.

He turned those clear blue eyes on her.

'The study of political organisations and institutions with particular regard to governments,' he said, as if reading it off a prompt card behind her shoulder.

'And this political science is your ... your...'

'Within an historical perspective,' he explained.

'I have further question on talk this morning,' she announced resuming her usual imperious manner.

Standing grinned at her. 'I'm gratified I managed to interest you.'

'It still seems like a lot of trouble to go to just to annoy Maseryk,' I said.

He transferred what was left of his grin to me. 'It was more than that,' he admitted. He finished his beer and sat back in his chair. 'I know academics have a reputation for indulging their petty jealousies but it wasn't only that. Let's just say I like to remind them of their past.'

'Who, and in what respect?'

'Burgess, Maclean and Philby?'

'The Cambridge spy ring.'

'The very same.'

Daryna looked at us, from one to the other.

'What is this spy ring?'

Standing was watching me with amusement and I could see he was waiting for me to explain. I leaned towards her and told her how the men Standing had mentioned had all been Cambridge students in the 1930s and were recruited as agents for Soviet Russia; how Burgess and Maclean had been uncovered in the early 1950s and had fled to Russia and that Philby joined them a dozen years later. What I didn't tell her was that Philby had worked for SIS and, although he was long gone by the time I had joined the Service, his ghost still haunted the corridors and that the rumours about who

140

else had been in the ring still rattled down the halls after it. The wash that had followed in his wake had finally settled in the last decades of the century even if it hadn't quite stilled.

When I had finished, Standing asked:

'Do you remember I asked you if you had ever heard of the Black Sea Company?'

'Yes, I remember,' I said. 'But you didn't tell me what it was.'

'It was a company that traded out of several Black Sea ports in the years between the wars. I've not been able to find out much about it, to be honest, but I do know it had representatives in Odessa and Sevastopol.'

'Did it trade with the Bolsheviks?'

'I presume so. But, as I said, information is sketchy.' He glanced at Daryna. 'The point is, I believe the company was in part a cover operation for the relaying of information.'

'On what was happening in Soviet Russia?'

'Ostensibly,' Standing said pointedly, 'but not exclusively.'

'Ah,' I said.

He smiled at me knowingly.

'Can I infer you believe it might have been connected to the Cambridge spies?'

Standing shrugged. 'It was too early for Burgess, Maclean and Philby.'

We looked at each other across the table and I saw that his answer wasn't an answer at all but just another question. Unconsciously I had already reverted to speaking in that guarded way I always used when talking to an outsider about company business, a manner that some of the more paranoid officers I had worked with even adopted with each other. But I was out of it and saw no reason to shy away from the subject anymore.

'You think there were others?'

'We know there were others,' he said. 'After all, someone recruited the Cambridge ring. More than one tutor came under suspicion, for instance.'

'And you like to remind Cambridge of the fact?'

'I first came here in the late eighties just as the curtain came down.'

'The iron curtain,' I explained for Daryna's benefit. She had been uncharacteristically quiet and I didn't want her to feel excluded from the conversation. But I should have known better because she obviously didn't feel anything of the sort.

141

'This I know, Alex,' she said sharply. 'I am not baby. I was born behind this curtain.'

Standing regarded us for a moment with amusement again, his head cocked slightly to one side. When he saw the spat was over he said:

'They had unmasked Anthony Blunt a couple of years after Philby defected although, in their wisdom, MI5 had decided not to have him prosecuted. When Margaret Thatcher finally had to come clean about him all the rumours started again, of course.'

I waited for Daryna to ask who MI5 were but the reference must to have eluded her. At the time I didn't give it any thought, being more interested in Standing's attitude to Blunt having escaped prosecution. The reason from MI5's perspective — those who ran counter-espionage and who dealt with Blunt directly — was that an offer of immunity was far more likely to uncover the extent of Soviet penetration than the judicial revenge of a prosecution would. In the event it might have been argued that the exchange favoured Blunt — some lesser fry were exposed but no really big fish and Blunt was able to keep his anonymity and his reputation. For those who needed it, some sort of biblical satisfaction was finally derived when, several years later, his treachery was exposed and he attracted almost universal odium. It was a time of his life when he was least able to deal with it and when he died he was a broken old man.

'Being here at the time the wall came down,' Standing was saying, 'I thought I sensed a certain feeling of disquiet among some members of the faculty.' He smiled a little wistfully. 'Believe it or not I was quite an earnest young student in those days. It wasn't all beer and girls. Perhaps it went over the head of most of the other students, but I was studying the subject and stuff had already started leaking out of the Eastern Bloc's police files and it was the first inkling I got that there might still be more to come out concerning Cambridge.'

'Perhaps not so surprising,' I said. 'The initial investigation had been unsatisfactory although Hollis had been under suspicion for some time—'

'Not proven,' Standing put in.

'—although he was an Oxford man, of course.'

Standing raised an eyebrow.

'Peter Wright's book, *Spycatcher*,' I explained. 'I got hold of a copy after that kerfuffle in the Australian courts.'

There had been half a dozen copies circulating in the office, in fact, and we'd all read it trying to catch up on what we should have known in the first place.

'There was a lot of mud,' I said. 'Your dons were probably more concerned with their colleges' reputation rather than any new allegations.'

'Certain mud needs to stick,' he said. 'It seemed to me at the time that the spy ring was looked on as more of an academic argument between two opposing legitimate points of view rather than as the dirty business it really was.'

I drank some more beer. It was going down very well and I was beginning to wish I had had the foresight to take the train like Standing.

'You're preaching to the converted here,' I told him.

'Don't get me wrong,' he said. 'I fully understand the argument that in the early and mid-thirties the Soviet system seemed the one bulwark left against fascism. The pro-German sentiment in this country among the aristocracy and the upper-middle classes — the Establishment — can't be over-stated. Not only was fascism seen as a system of government equal to the task of eliminating left-wing politics and preserving the status quo — that is the privileges of the privileged classes — it also appealed to their bigotry and their racial prejudices. For any young intellectual, or thinking member of the working class looking for a just society, it was no contest. A visit to any European country would be enough to convince any open-minded individual that fascism was a ruthless and, at base, an unjust ideology — left-wing skulls were being cracked in just about every city on the Continent. On the other hand, the iniquities of Bolshevik Russia were a far better kept secret. For every Gareth Jones who worked to uncover the truth, there were a dozen starry-eyed nincompoops who were only too happy to have the wool pulled over their eyes.'

Daryna began getting restive and what sort of animal she imagined a nincompoop under a sheep's fleece to be I could only guess. But I reached out and laid a hand on hers to forestall any questions. In the event she pulled her hand away sharply at the contact, but it served to put her off any irrelevant enquiry.

'But surely,' I said, recovering from Daryna's reaction, 'that argument ceased to hold after the non-aggression pact with Hitler?'

'Certainly,' Standing agreed, 'and by then most of those who had flirted with communism earlier in the decade had relented. And you

143

have to understand that before nineteen-thirty-one or two there was very little political involvement at this or any other university in Britain. It was a very brief flowering of left-wing sentiment for most, and those that the Spanish Civil War didn't disillusion soon had other preoccupations by nineteen-thirty-nine. Even then, though, the consideration must have been — is one, by simple dint of one's birth, obliged to go against one's conscience? Or, as Orwell put it, of my country right or wrong? But that's an old argument. What interested me are those few committed individuals who were recruited before nineteen-thirty-one. They obviously had a distinct bearing on Philby and his friends and remained embedded even after the Cambridge ring was unmasked. Blunt was older, don't forget. Did he know them? Were these earlier recruits the people involved in the Black Sea Company?'

I supposed Standing was thinking of the elusive Shostak who'd been in the Ukraine in the early 1930s and who he believed, no doubt, had been involved in the Black Sea Company while Philby, Burgess and Maclean were still debating in undergraduate societies over the pros and cons of communism. The deposition he had shown me last time we had met had demonstrated there was some connection between Shostak and my grandfather, which was why he had traced me in the first place, but, to be honest, the deposition and what it had revealed about Aleksander Zaretsky had taken the shine off of my enquiries. I was beginning to think that perhaps knowing something of the kind of man his father was, was what had made my father repudiate his past and was the reason he never discussed the subject.

I was also thinking about how this fact had thrown into even sharper relief my own views of those clever young men who Standing had referred to and who had flirted with communism in the 1930s and had later abandoned the cause. It was these men, of course, who twenty years later sat at the heart of the Establishment and who, when the scandal of the Cambridge spies began to unfold, did nothing — or worse, were obstructive — towards the investigation into how deep the Soviet penetration had gone. Their attitude had been a mixture of unwillingness to believe that members of the ruling elite could betray their country (after all they were *gentlemen, our kind,* and the idea was unthinkable) and total funk at the prospect that *their* connection to the traitors and *their* old allegiances might come to light. I had known some of these individuals — the last dregs had been my superiors and masters —

and the very thought of their duplicity and incompetence had made my blood boil once I had learned of it and never ceased to do the same each time I thought of it.

It was coming to the boil again, that minute, which is why, I suppose, I never really noticed that Standing was starting to look agitated. He kept casting glances towards the door and finally said:

'My wife, Julia, was supposed to be joining us. I'd have thought she might have been here by now. Excuse me, would you? I'll go and see if she's left a message.'

He went off to reception. Daryna watched him go then turned to me.

'Spy ring,' she said. 'You know more of this?'

It was, as I have just outlined, a pertinent question, having been one area of the curriculum for those joining the Service in which instruction had been conspicuous by its absence. A sharp contrast to the discovery made, once in, where one found it hanging around in the shadows like the spectre at the wedding. Or perhaps that should be funeral. One assumes things are different now. Time heals all wounds, so they say, or maybe it's more a case that one learns to sublimate old pain. As is perhaps obvious, I had never quite been able to do so, and neither had others for the depth of the treachery was never exposed until the odd whistleblower or two had become so sickened by the hypocrisy that they found they could keep quiet no longer. Or was it no more than a case of old men looking to supplement their pensions with some decent book sales? (Wright, for instance, needed to replace his pension which had been stopped over a technicality in the face of a "gentleman's agreement" — a small betrayal by comparison but indicative of the culture). Whatever the motives had been, the civil servants and ministers had still kept their ostrich heads stuck in the sand and their feathered arses in the air in the vain hope that if they ignored their own incompetence and duplicity the whole problem would go away. It didn't, of course, and when Wright, for one, left the service and published his memoirs, rather than admit to their own failings they preferred to drag him into a foreign court and make the country a laughing-stock than consider prosecuting those that had been guilty of the original treachery. Perhaps, as they maintained, there wasn't enough evidence to support a prosecution but sometimes it seemed, and as I often suspected, it all depended upon whether or not you happened to be a member of the "club".

'Just a little,' I said eventually to Daryna, keeping the rest bottled. 'It all came out a long time ago.'

She was peering at me with an odd expression on her face while I was still pondering the old question as to whether it *had* all come out. After all, we are ever only told just how much those in control want us to know. It was like being in the Service and labouring under the old "need to know" rule for, even as an insider, I was always more aware of what I did *not* know rather than how much I actually did. The consequence of that was, the more one found out, the more one became aware of what a deeply paranoid organisation an intelligence service really is. Perhaps that is an axiom that borders upon becoming a truism. The fact that the very nature of creating an intelligence service presupposes that we suspect there exist dangers of which we are unaware, and what better definition of paranoia is there than that?

Standing returned, frowning at me in a disconcerting way, and sat down again.

'Nothing from your wife?' I asked.

'No.'

Then the waiter came up and told us our lunch was ready to be served so we finished our drinks and filed into the dining room.

Sitting at the table, Daryna placed the paper on which she had made her notes beside her plate and began questioning Standing. They conversed in a mixture of English and Russian that left me with the impression of a conversation that a censor had redacted, leaving my imagination to fill in the gaps. All the while, though, I noticed Standing appeared distracted. He glanced towards the door once or twice as if still expecting his wife and feeling guilty for having started lunch without her. To my mild surprise he was extremely patient with the persistent Daryna and at one point began fishing in his pockets, producing the crumpled notes of his lecture and giving them to her.

During the brief period of peace her examination of the notes afforded, I reminded Standing of his phone call. 'You said you had something to tell me.'

'Did I?' he asked, as if I had caught him by surprise.

'"In the loosest sense," were your words.'

'Well,' he admitted, 'we're still going through all the stuff we brought back from Kiev.'

Daryna's ears immediately pricked up. 'You have been to Kiev?'

'A few weeks ago.'

'What about the notebook?' I asked before he became side-tracked. 'Have you translated that yet?'

'Notebook?' Daryna repeated.

'The little leather one?' I reminded Standing.

'Oh, yes, that. Actually David's still struggling to decipher it. The handwriting...' he grimaced.

'Not as bad as Jones's, I would have thought.' I had seen an example of his on the website dedicated to him.

'What is this notebook?' Daryna asked again.

'Just one of the things I gave to Michael,' I told her. 'If I'd known I was going to run into you, you could have had a crack at translating it.' Although given how long it had taken her to decipher the letters I was glad in retrospect that she hadn't.

'I'm not sure it's of any importance,' Standing said, 'but I'll hang on to it if I may... You never know.'

Daryna's eyes flicked towards Standing and I wondered if she had picked up the note of evasion in his voice. I had interviewed too many men over too many years not to recognize a half-truth when I heard one. That Daryna might have recognized it too was a surprise, but perhaps she was in the habit of keeping the company of liars.

'When you are finished,' she said to Standing, forcing her pout into a smile as false as a pensioner's teeth, 'perhaps I can see notebook? It will be good for my English to translate and good for Alex to read in original Ukrainian. It is Ukrainian, yes?'

'Yes,' Standing said. 'When David's finished I'll let you have it back by all means.'

'Does it shed any more light on Zaretsky's career in the OGPU?' I asked a little sarcastically.

'No,' he said, apparently not noticing. 'But it is a bit of a curiosity.'

'Oh?' I asked, 'in what way,' and for a moment I thought he looked quite discomforted, like a man who wanted to say more but didn't quite feel as if he ought to.

13

When the arrival of the Sunday papers that morning was announced by a heavy thud at George's front door, I couldn't help remembering what Michael Standing had suggested about my grandfather over that lunch in Cambridge.

The knock on the door is the traditional precursor of arrest and interrogation and I suppose its anticipation had frozen countless of hearts over the years. Given how I had spent my professional career, I wonder now that I seldom attempted to put myself into the shoes of the recipient. But empathy for the opposition, or even those individuals one uses, is a dangerous emotion for one who is steeped in the righteousness of the cause.

The previous evening, I had kept one eye on the news but little fresh had been forthcoming concerning the man arrested for Standing's murder. According to the bulletins, he had been known in the area and was being held for questioning, and that was all. The Sunday papers offered a variety of embellishments upon the known facts, but had already gone to press by the time the news of an arrest had broken. In the absence of that, they relied on theory for copy. One imaginative journalist, having posited a link between Standing's murder and some supposed work-in-hand, suggested that he had been the victim of a KGB assassination. The hypothesis rested (a lucky shot in the dark or inside information?) upon Standing's recent examination of old police files and even posited his research into the Ukrainian famine as a possible motive. The supposition was that he had uncovered new facts that would have proved embarrassing to the Russian government. It seemed a little far-fetched to me as guilt for the Holodomor had been apportioned years ago, and mostly in Stalin's favour, and any new revelations would necessarily involve people now long dead. It seemed utterly fanciful to me to suggest a link and I couldn't imagine anyone other than conspiracy theorists who would be likely to put any credence in that sort of reasoning. I assumed that they, along with the author of the feature, were now somewhat miffed by the arrest of some vagrant since it provided a new plughole down which their supposition could disappear. But then, given a wilder imagination, even that seemingly contradictory fact could be cunningly woven into the kind of organic conspiracy that often flowers around an odd circumstance like Standing's murder.

I remarked upon the theory to George and Nick over breakfast on Sunday morning.

'There you are, Alex,' Nick replied over his teacup. He had put away his countryman's outfit and was back in slacks and a sweater. 'They'll be giving you radioactive coffee next if you don't drop your research.'

'Or is it still stabbing with poisoned umbrellas?' George asked, stabbing the knife he had just used to spread marmalade over a piece of toast in my direction.

Nick considered the suggestion with mock-seriousness. 'Just what is the favoured method of assassination in espionage circles these days, Alex?'

I gave him the withering look I reserved as the standard response to such baiting although, as usual, Nick remained resolutely un-withered and merely laughed into his plate of poached eggs.

We let the subject drop and spent a lazy morning pretending we were comfortable doing nothing. Jennifer insisted on re-dressing my cut head and unwound the bandage to reveal nothing beyond some dried blood and a puckering of skin around the stitches. They gave me a feeling of tightness where they pulled at the skin above my eyebrow.

'Don't forget to make an appointment to get them taken out,' she reminded me.

'Yes matron,' I said, and she surprised me by giving the undamaged side of my head a playful push, which I couldn't help but think was progress of some sort.

'There's not much of a bruise,' she said, replacing the bandage with some lint and sticking plaster.

'I've never bruised much,' I said. 'Thick-headed, I suppose.'

'Like your father,' George remarked pointedly, having come up on us unheard.

I felt Jennifer stiffen.

'Peter was not "thick-headed" as you put it, George,' she said coldly. 'He was a proud man, that's all.'

I wondered if the conversation we had had the previous day had continued in my absence but then George caught my eye and raised his eyebrows in a good-humoured way and no more was said.

We took another walk before lunch, Jennifer joining us this time but not Nick who could never have been described as a walker (another characteristic he shared with Olena). We didn't go far and said little to one another beyond responses to George's voiced plans for the estate.

Over lunch I was reminded again that George kept a decent cellar and it occurred to me that Standing would have appreciated the Burgundy that he opened to accompany the meal. Nick restricted himself to a single glass as he was driving and wanted to get back to London before it was dark. With no such reservations I helped George finish the bottle. Any resultant headache I was prepared to put down to the blow to my head. George offered to open a second but there are limits to self-delusion and I shook the same already noticeably lighter head at him.

'Not for me,' I said. 'Retirement's enough to addle the brain without helping the process along.'

'Good man,' George said. 'I've seen too many spend their days watching the clock until it was time for the first drink. You've got to keep the brain active. Develop new interests.'

'Alex has,' Nick said, giving me a wink. 'I saw her when I picked him up.'

Jennifer looked enquiringly at me as if about to ask what he meant, but not wanting to get into a conversation about Daryna I recalled something Standing had told me when I'd attended his seminar, and said to George quickly:

'I didn't know Frederick had endowed a Cambridge scholarship.'

George glanced at Nick as if giving him the opportunity to answer. Nick seemed unconcerned and George said, 'Didn't you? The Maitland scholarship has been around for years.'

'Michael Standing told me he was a recipient.'

'I never knew that,' Jennifer said.

George shrugged. 'Is there any reason you should have, dear?'

'But we always go to the annual lunch you give for the Maitland scholars. I don't recall ever seeing him there.'

'Perhaps he never attended,' George said.

'How long ago was it, Alex?' she asked. 'Did he ever say?'

'It would have been nineteen-eighty-eight,' Nick said. 'That's how I met him, actually. We went up the same year. Standing heard there was a Maitland at the College and he asked me if I had anything to do with the scholarship. He said he wanted to thank the family.'

'That was thoughtful,' Jennifer observed.

'What was it that prompted Frederick to endow the scholarship in the first place?' I asked George.

He looked abstractedly at the roast beef on his plate before slicing off a sliver. 'To be truthful, I'm not sure,' he said before popping it in his mouth. 'Perhaps because he was grateful for the education he had received?'

'But that wasn't through a scholarship, surely?'

'No, his father was in the Diplomatic Service. Very Establishment.' He smiled facetiously. 'I sometimes think the family's slipped down the social ladder a rung or two since those days.'

'Don't be a snob, George,' Jennifer said.

Even if the remark was facetious, I couldn't help wondering, glancing from George to Nick, if he wasn't — albeit unconsciously — making a reference to Nastasiya's dilution of the Maitland bloodline. His half-siblings and their families, issued through his stepmother Elizabeth, were pure (speaking from the standpoint of an English snob, that is) and it occurred to me for the first time that there might be some sort of residual feeling of envy for those of Frederick's second family lurking in George. Nevertheless, he was accepted as head of the Maitland clan although I now began to suspect that that might have been due more to George's driving ambition than the simple fact of being the first-born.

But the whole subject made me even more aware of how little I knew about Frederick's origins. All I did know, in fact, was gossip and reminiscences picked up over the years from other members of the family.

'Where did he serve?' I asked.

'My grandfather?' George chewed for a moment. 'India, middle-east... My father was born in Tehran.'

'Iran?'

'Persia, as it was then. He negotiated some of the first oil concessions.'

'The foundation of the family fortune,' Nick put in sarcastically. George threw him a disapproving look.

'I thought Frederick was given the credit for that,' I said.

'The oil interests were only a sideline as far as Frederick's father was concerned,' George said. 'The diplomatic service was his thing. A bit of an odd bird, by all accounts. Liked to dress up like the natives. It was Frederick who made his connections in the oil business work for him.'

'I don't suppose,' I said, 'you've heard of a concern called the Black Sea Company by any chance?'

George pursed his lips, thinking. 'Rings no bells,' he said. 'Nick?'

Nick shook his head.

'Why do you ask?'

'It was something Michael Standing asked me about, that's all. He'd picked up some sort of reference to it in the business he was looking into but wasn't able to find out much, apparently.'

'Well, I'm pretty sure I've never heard of it,' George said again. 'I can ask around if you like. What sort of company was it?'

'Commodity trading, Standing told me. Went out of business at the start of the war.'

'I've always found it surprising,' Jennifer said, 'that Frederick founded the Maitland scholarship. Elizabeth told me once that she couldn't ever remember his going back to Cambridge at all after the war.'

'He went to Cambridge University as well then?' I asked. 'As a student, I mean.'

'Of course he did, Alex,' she said. 'That's why Nick followed in his footsteps.'

'George?'

He smiled at me ruefully. 'I was always a bit of a duffer in the academic stakes,' he said. 'You know that.'

Whether he believed it or not I wasn't sure. Even if he did I still found it curious that Frederick hadn't pushed him towards a university education. In the event he had gone straight from school into the business.

After coffee Nick decided he needed to call by his constituency house to pick up some papers before we headed back to London.

I excused myself and went to my room to pack my bag before returning to thank George and Jennifer for their hospitality. George grabbed my hand and insisted I come down whenever I cared to; Jennifer smiled glassily at me after kissing Nick goodbye. I turned back to wave as we drove away but they had both gone inside.

Nick's constituency house was a modest enough retreat, a detached, three-bedroom early twentieth-century building that would have resonated with the sort of rural voter to whom he appealed. Owning it, I supposed he could appear sufficiently man-of-the-people to those who might otherwise be intimidated by his family's wealth. The house gave no impression of being lived in though, except that in walking around while Nick collected his papers, I thought I detected the evidence of a woman's occasional presence. It was nothing obvious like cosmetics in the bathroom or clothes in a cupboard (I admit to having looked), more the sense of a residue left behind, a faint aromatic trace in the air. It crossed my mind that Olena might have been there with him — it would hardly have been comfortable for her to stay at George and Jennifer's following the divorce, after all, and, given how they had acted together at lunch back in the summer, I suspected that the normally stultifying ripples that follow any divorce hadn't quite reached every corner of their particular relationship. I couldn't help thinking that Olena, had she ever stayed at the house, would have left more of herself behind than the trace I found though — evidence casually discarded, perhaps, in the manner of an animal laying her scent trail to deter rivals. But I supposed that, if he had brought a woman to the house, even someone like Nick who was at best in no more than the corner of the public eye would still have to be a little circumspect in his behaviour. No one could expect him to live like a monk — except the puritans in the Party, perhaps, and I suspected there were precious few of those at Westminster. But politics is a dirty business and I didn't doubt that those who look to manipulate public opinion wouldn't have hesitated for a moment to jump on any perceived misdemeanours if they thought they could turn it to their advantage.

I might have enjoyed ribbing him about my suspicions in much the same way as he had ribbed me about my work, except that would have left me open to a counter-attack concerning Daryna's presence in my house. As it was, apart from his remark over lunch, he had been oddly reticent about her and I really didn't swallow the implication that her immigration status could be any sort of issue for him — certainly not one that would even stop him asking me about her. Still, I wasn't complaining; Daryna was not a subject I particularly wanted to talk to Nick about. I had tried to call her over the weekend two or three times and found — unsurprisingly — that she wasn't answering my phone. Her own number was still unobtainable so I wasn't sure whether she was still at the house. I tried again from Nick's constituency house while he was making a couple of calls himself, only to hear my own disembodied voice telling me that no one was home and to leave a message. I was about to leave one to let her know I was on my way back when Nick, having finished his calls, walked in on me. I smiled and turned my phone off.

'Ready?' I asked.

He collected his papers and we left, locking the door on that faint trace of femininity. We climbed back into the BMW. A pale December sun hung low in the afternoon sky washing the forest in watercolours of muddy green and brown. The trees looked spent already with their bare-boned boughs and branches, frozen still as if braced against the winter to come. It was the kind of landscape that encouraged introspection and it never took much for my thoughts to wander off down paths once trodden and now half-forgotten. I began thinking of times in my late teens when Olena was just a toddler and Nick had been not much older and George and Jennifer had spent time with my parents. I had felt like something of an odd (but not quite yet) man out, a callow gangling youth awkwardly attached to two couples each with a small child in tow. No one made me feel that way but adolescence is a strange time of change when one fits neither with a past one is too eager to renounce, nor with a future one can't apprehend.

I was back there, experiencing all that odd sense of displacement again when I realized Nick was talking to me.

'Christmas,' he was saying, not for the first time apparently.

'Sorry,' I mumbled. 'I was miles away.'

'I asked what plans you've made for Christmas.'

Whenever I had been in England I had always spent it with Nick and Olena — and usually with the rest of the Maitland clan — but the divorce had changed all that and the previous Christmas I had spent a desultory day alone with Olena, listening to her complaints about the family into which she had once been so keen to marry. Fortunately, this year she had announced her intention to go abroad with a friend over the holiday and with some relief I had looked forward to spending the day alone.

'Well you know Mum and Dad will be expecting you to come down,' Nick said. 'Just because Olena and I aren't together any more doesn't change anything.'

But of course it changed everything and I started to make excuses that even a gullible man wouldn't have swallowed.

We were somewhere near Micheldever and my mobile phone began to ring rescuing me from further dissimulation. I muttered an apology and, expecting it to be Daryna, pulled the phone out of my pocket. It was Charlie Hewson.

'Where are you?' he asked.

'On my way back home,' I said. 'What's up?'

'Can you talk?'

'Better not,' I said.

'Call me when you get back, then.' He gave me a number I didn't recognize — Charlie was always switching mobiles — then cut the connection. I keyed in the number, turned off the phone and put it back in my pocket.

'Everything all right?' Nick asked.

'Just a friend,' I said. 'I'll call him back when I get home.'

I started talking about George's plans for his estate to forestall any further mention of Christmas, or of anything else meaningful for that matter, and that filled the time until we hit the traffic south of London.

Nick dropped me outside my house. The lights were off. If Nick was still curious about Daryna, he kept it to himself. I pulled my bag out of the BMW's boot and said my goodbyes, promising to have a drink soon. I waved him off before letting myself into the house.

I don't know what it was, a sixth sense, paranoia or just a working life spent in a milieu of distrust, but I immediately felt as if something was wrong. I shut the door behind me quietly and stood in the dark hall, holding my breath and listening for something that wasn't there. The red light on the answer-phone was flashing like an insistent alarm. I waited a moment, then put the bag down and made my way into the lounge. It was then I realized what had felt so wrong. The air was fresh and chilled. The central heating was on but the house felt cold.

I switched on the light. The French windows into the garden were open and the glass in one had been smashed. Shards lay on the carpet inside the room. All the papers that were usually crowded untidily over the dining room table were spread across the floor.

I turned around and took the stairs two at a time.

Daryna's bed was neatly made, the way we had left it on Friday. I looked for signs of her having been there but there were none. I went across the hall to my bedroom. It had been turned inside out. I checked the small safe, anchored at the foot of my cupboard, and found that someone had tried to jemmy the door. It had remained intact, though, and when I opened it the contents were still inside.

Downstairs again, I shut my French windows and closed the curtains. It was then, when I turned around and looked at the dining room table again that I realized my laptop had gone. I spent the next thirty seconds cursing before calling the number Charlie had given me.

'I'm home,' I said. 'Someone's turned the place over.'

'Really?' he asked in a tone that sounded as if he found the fact no more than mildly diverting.

Irritated, I said, 'Yes, Charlie, really.'

'Give me half-an-hour.'

'I was going to call the police,' I said.

'I don't think I'd do that quite yet if I were you, old man,' he said and rang off.

I checked through the rest of the house to see if anything else was missing then went into the back garden and pulled some old sheets of boarding out of my shed and did what I could to secure the French windows. It began to rain before I finished. I locked the doors and started to pick up the shards of glass littering my now damp carpet. I hauled out the vacuum cleaner for any pieces I might have missed and gathered up my papers. I was squaring them back on the dining room table when Charlie arrived.

'Good God! What happened to you?' he said as I opened the door.

'What?'

He pointed to sticking plaster on my head. 'I thought you said you just got back.'

'I did. I banged my head on a tree on Saturday.'

'I thought you'd been mugged.'

'I have,' I said. 'In absentia.'

'What have they taken?' he asked, walking in.

'My laptop. Nothing else as far as I can see.'

'Cash? Jewellery?'

'What little bit of cash I keep in the house was in the safe. They tried to force it but didn't manage to get it open. If you recall, I don't go in for jewellery.'

'Just a common burglary, then,' he said.

I was thinking of Standing and *his* not-so-common burglar but didn't say anything.

'There is something else,' I admitted.

He gave me that look of his that suggested there was *always* something else.

I told him about Daryna and that I had left her at the house on Friday evening.

'Is this the Ukrainian doxy you found?'

I winced at "doxy" and said, 'You found.'

I knew what he was thinking. What did I expect if I was in the habit of leaving someone I knew next to nothing about in the house?

'You found her for me,' I reminded him.

'I didn't propose you have her as a house guest,' he said. 'I didn't propose you *have* her at all.'

'It's nothing like that,' I insisted. 'It was just for a couple of days. She was having boyfriend trouble.'

'Don't they all.'

'Anyway, why would she break the door from the outside?'

'To make it look like a break-in.'

'Not very bright if she's the only suspect.'

'Whoever suggested that petty thieves are bright? Having said that, though,' he added, 'she seems to have pulled the wool over your eyes.'

'Come on, Charlie. Credit the girl with enough sense to look the house over and see there's nothing worth stealing before she smashes it up. She's been here often enough.'

Charlie raised a prurient eyebrow.

'Even the laptop is obsolete,' I said, ignoring the implication. 'She wouldn't get anything for it so it doesn't make any sense for it to have been her.'

He sniffed, cornered by logic, and looked around him. 'You're probably right,' he accepted. 'But if it wasn't her, where is she?'

That's what I had been asking myself ever since I had opened the front door.

'Perhaps she left before it happened.'

I had phoned her twice from George's house, then again earlier that afternoon from Nick's. She had not answered on any occasion. I walked into the hall. The light was still flashing on the answer-phone. I pressed the button and heard myself ask Daryna to pick up if she was there or to call me back. Then there were two more beeps to indicate other calls with no message left.

Charlie was standing in the doorway, watching.

That's the message I left Saturday evening. The one I made earlier on Friday evening has been erased,' I said.

'And the calls with no message?'

'One was me. I rang from Nick's house to let her know I was on my way back.'

'But you didn't tell her,' he said.

'Nick walked in while I was phoning.'

'When did you leave the second message?' he said.

'Saturday, about five-thirty.'

'So either your girl, or whoever broke in, erased the earlier message.'

'Hardly *my girl*,' I said. 'And the message was only to say I'd arrived.'

'Thoughtful of you.'

I let that one ride.

'Why would a burglar be interested in my messages?'

'You say you left the second one about five-thirty on Saturday?'

'Around then.'

'So, assuming the doxy didn't erase the message—'

'Her name's *Daryna*,' I said, 'and there's no reason she should. She never liked to answer my phone.'

'Rules of the game,' he said. 'They learn early.'

'For Christ's sake, Charlie!'

He shrugged.

'Then whoever broke in erased it,' he went on, 'which means it was prior to five-thirty on Saturday.'

'Yes,' I said, calming down.

'Early for burglary,' Charlie commented. 'But it would have been dark by four-thirty. Perhaps he wanted to get a job in before dinner.'

'Don't be facetious,' I said. 'Anyway, *common* thieves as you call them are generally having dinner and watching the football results at five.'

'Now who's being facetious? And I said the burglary was common, not the thief. Anyway, what's that, statistical fact or class prejudice?'

'Not prejudice,' I said. 'Just observation. What were you doing at five on Saturday.'

'Having dinner and watching the results.' He grinned. 'Of course, it could have happened Friday night.'

'Daryna was here then,' I said, bringing me back full circle.

'Got anything to drink?' he asked.

'Put the kettle on,' I said, 'unless you want something stronger.'

'Why don't we put the kettle on *and* have something stronger?' He turned into the kitchen, calling over his shoulder, 'Okay, so either there's more to your girl than meets the eye or—'

'There's more to my burglar than meets the eye.'

I finished tidying the table in the dining room. It was then that I noticed that the translations of my father's letters, which Daryna had made, were not among the papers. I sorted through everything again, looked under the table, and tried to remember if I had put them anywhere else. I looked in the wastepaper basket but I'd emptied that before I'd left. We had actually finished transcribing the letters months before but, in my usual manner, I had left them where I had last read them rather than putting them away. Since I rarely used the table for eating — preferring the kitchen or in front of the television — it habitually attracted whatever it was I happened to be working on. In this case most of the material was connected to the Ukraine.

Charlie came back with two mugs of coffee, a bottle of Scotch and two glasses. He put them on the coffee table at the lounge end of the room and dropped into an armchair.

'The translations of those letters I told you about are missing,' I said.

His nose wrinkled. 'Are you sure? You've not just misplaced them?'

'Of course I'm sure. I retired because of my back, not because my brain was addled.'

'Point taken, old man,' he said easily, pouring two generous measures of whisky. 'But that's interesting. What about the originals?'

I went into the kitchen. After giving Standing the rest of the contents of the biscuit tin in which they'd lain for years, I had meant to throw the old tin out but — again as usual — found I couldn't quite bring myself to do it, given its history. Instead, I'd put the letters back in it and left it in the kitchen. The tin was on the worktop in full view where I had left it. The letters were no longer inside.

'They've gone,' I said, bringing the empty tin back.

'Why would he want them?' Charlie asked. 'What was in them?'

'Nothing,' I said. 'Nothing of interest at all. To anyone else, I mean.' I sat down and drank my coffee, then turned to the Scotch.

I looked at Charlie. He was holding his mug of coffee between his two hands, tapping thoughtfully with a finger against the rim. He glanced at me, seeming to know instinctively there was something I wanted to say.

'I'm worried about Daryna,' I finally admitted. 'If she only stayed Friday night like she said she was going to, I would have thought she'd have left a note of some sort.'

'Are you sure she didn't?' Charlie asked, casting a critical eye over the untidy room. He must have heard my sigh of exasperation because he put his hand up in acknowledgement. 'All right, no note. Perhaps your burglar took that too.'

'I don't like it.' I said.

'Tell me what you know about her and I'll see what else I can find out,' he suggested. 'And before you say it, I'll be discreet and try not to bring immigration down on her.'

'I would have thought,' I said, 'that your Sonja would know more about her than I do.'

'Sonja?'

'East European desk? The girl that found her?'

'Right,' Charlie said. 'Humour me, anyway.'

So I humoured him. It didn't take long and, when I'd finished, I realized how little I really knew about Daryna Marianenko.

Charlie made a couple of notes as I poured out another scotch.

'Was there something else in particular?' I asked.

He looked at me blankly.

'When you rang earlier.'

'Oh yes,' he said. 'Your burglary put it out of my head. You heard they've arrested someone over Standing's death, I suppose?'

'A vagrant, they said on the news. Now why am I not surprised?'

Charlie gave me a sardonic look. 'Because you're a cynic, Alex. They found the guy in a squat a few streets away. Apparently he had Standing's wallet on him and got him on CCTV trying to use one of his cards.'

'Not very bright.'

'I thought we'd established that,' he said. 'He's one of the kind that always has a dog in tow and has had the same pitch so long everyone knows not to trip over him.'

'Busking?'

'Not that industrious.'

'So, how does it go, then? Whoever killed Standing took his wallet and dropped it in the vagrant's cap to establish robbery as the motive?'

'How did you guess?' Charlie asked. 'He says a man walked by and dropped him the wallet.'

'That's what *I'd* say if I were him. But I'm guessing there's no CCTV to back up his story.'

'No. Blind spot. That's why he chose the pitch. They're hoping to find forensic on him.'

'Have they run the tests yet?'

'Not that I know, but it stands to reason the killer had blood on him. The man's clothes were clean when they picked him up, apparently. Well,' he added, 'as clean as you're going to get on a vagrant.'

'He got rid of the bloody clothes and put something else on.'

'That's the line they're taking but we're not talking about a man with an extensive wardrobe. He lived in a squat half a mile from his pitch. He's dressed in the same clothes for as long as anyone can remember. And he only owns one pair of shoes. *And* there were shoeprints in the kitchen, remember?'

'What are you trying to tell me, Charlie, that the police are getting fussy all of a sudden? There was a time when they'd sweat him long enough to get a confession.'

Charlie looked aggrieved. 'Times have changed, believe it or not. Too many dodgy convictions. And, since they had to release the man they put away for the last high-profile TV personality killing, they're not jumping on the first misfit they can find.'

'Isn't that just what they've done?'

'Don't forget the wallet.'

'And here's me beginning to think that Justice was starting to rear her ugly head.'

'You know it's always self-preservation first,' Charlie said.

'I thought that was women and children.'

'That's just at sea.'

'Why are you making it sound as if I shouldn't be reassured, Charlie?'

'I only wanted to warn you that you'll get another visit from Bedford and that they'll want a DNA swab.' He offered what I supposed was meant to be a reassuring shrug. 'It's not just you. They'll be taking swabs from everyone connected.'

'I'm hardly connected.'

He just looked at me askance.

'So they don't baulk at fitting someone up,' I said, 'it's just they're getting sophisticated and think a vagrant might be too obvious.'

'I'm just saying be prepared — as they say in the Scouts.'

'How would you know? They'd never have had you in the Scouts.'

'The vetting's too rigorous,' Charlie said. 'That's why I joined SIS. They've always been more relaxed about that sort of thing.'

'Where's the DNA,' I asked. 'The wine glass?'

'That's right,' he said looking at me suspiciously. 'How did you know?'

'It's in the file you gave me. Don't you remember?'

'I just took notes,' he said, 'doing a mate a favour. I don't have to remember the stuff.'

'Where did you get the idea that Standing's wife might not have been alone, then? There was nothing in what you gave me to suggest it. Or was it just that you couldn't resist the pun?'

He gave me a *who me?* look as if I'd cut him to the quick.

'Gossip,' he said.

'What kind of gossip?'

'The kind you get with the kind of people Standing mixed with.'

'Academics?'

'Television.'

'So, people expect him to be playing around but really it's her.'

'Something like that.'

'Any evidence?'

'Why are you asking me?'

'You seem to have your finger on the pulse.'

'If you had yours on it instead of where I think you had it,' he said, 'maybe you wouldn't be in this mess.'

'What mess? Am I in a mess?'

He looked over his shoulder at the dining room.

'Oh, that mess,' I said. 'But what makes you think it's got anything to do with Standing?'

'Because that's what you're thinking, isn't it?'

'All right,' I admitted, 'but was there anyone in particular?'

'With Standing's wife? There was talk about a man named Maseryk,' he said. 'A fellow historian.'

'Standing was a bit antagonistic when I saw them together back in the summer.'

'Maseryk was on that last programme that Standing made. And they had an argument,' Charlie added pointedly.

'About Stalin,' I said. 'Hardly a motive for bludgeoning a colleague.'

'Unless he was screwing his wife as well as questioning his historical interpretation. A man can only take so much.'

'When I saw them in Cambridge Standing did make some sort of crack about Maseryk being a ladies' man.'

'*Ladies' man?*' Charlie repeated. 'Who writes your dialogue? Besides, who said Julia Standing was a lady? What did you think of her?'

'Me? What gave you the idea I'd met her?'

'My mistake,' he said. 'I just assumed that as you knew Standing you'd have met her as well.'

'Well I haven't,' I said. 'The damned police seem to have the idea that I know her as well. The closest I got was that seminar in Cambridge. Standing was expecting her to join him but we left before she arrived.'

'Otherwise engaged?' Charlie suggested.

'Perhaps she was,' I said, 'but it wasn't with Maseryk because he was at the seminar.'

And as I said it I suddenly remembered how Standing had seemed on edge while waiting for his wife. Having wondered at the time why he had invited me, I had an odd thought then dismissed it immediately. Yet he had certainly seemed distracted, repeatedly looking out for his wife at the hotel. What had it been, concern or suspicion? Then, thinking about that lunch reminded me of something else.

'What?' Charlie said, as if he were reading my mind again.

'The bottle of wine at Standing's house,' I said.

'What about it?'

'I had lunch with Standing twice. Each time he ordered wine, good bottles too. He knew his stuff and seemed particular about what he drank. Particular enough to pay restaurant prices for what he wanted.'

'So?'

'So a man who does that doesn't buy cheap wine for home consumption.'

'I suppose not,' he agreed. 'What was the bottle in his kitchen? Anything special?'

'No,' I said, 'and that's precisely the point. Nothing special at all. But it just happens to be something I drink.'

14

I sat with the bottle of Scotch longer than I should have after Charlie left. I tried Daryna's mobile again just for the pleasure of being told that the number I had dialled was unobtainable, then looked at the evening out of the window and the pale glow of the streetlight and the occasional car that passed. The business with Standing and his wife was normal life for some people; the cheap wine in his kitchen could have been what she cooked with for all I knew; Daryna might have stayed the one night and left as she had said she would; she had changed her phone to avoid her pig of a boyfriend; burglaries happen. That was all well and good and I could have accepted every piece of it if it hadn't been for the missing letters. That piece was a senselessness act that made sense out of the other random events.

The one fact that still didn't make any sense, though, was that there had been nothing in the letters to interest anyone, not even Michael Standing. The only thing of note about them, *in fact*, was that they were my father's, the only fact of note about *him* being his odd parentage.

Standing didn't add much to what I knew about *them* that day in Cambridge. He had been on the verge of telling me something over lunch but, just as he might, Daryna had butted in with some remark or other and he had taken the opportunity to evade my question. For some reason it seemed as if he could never bring himself back to mention it. Whenever I tried to bring up the matter, he always found something else to say. In the end, what I chiefly remembered about that afternoon was Standing's enthusiasm for his subject. Like a toy with a tightly wound spring, it seemed the merest touch was likely send him into his clockwork dance.

For anyone with no interest perhaps he was a bore. Perhaps he had no other conversation. Perhaps the gossips were right and his wife had tired of his lectures on the failures of Marxism and had looked elsewhere for her amusements. If that was the case, I don't suppose Standing would have had to look too far to fill the void had he been inclined to do so. Olena had thought he did and, like a good little student, she would have put her hand up in his class anytime. Daryna, too, had found him attractive. I could tell, there at the lunch table, by the way she acted with him, eyes fixed on his face and leaning her body earnestly towards him as if she might miss one of the golden words. Serious at the best of times, it didn't take much for her to appear realistic in a display of interest in his subject and I could see by the way her tongue worked along her lower lip that she was concentrating on formulating intelligent questions to ask him.

But perhaps I am doing her a disservice. After all, it was *her* history and, unlike Standing who was merely a student of the subject, her family had presumably lived the reality just as she had been raised in its aftermath.

He had been asking her what she had been taught in school about the famine and then pointing out where Western research differed from her education. He was obviously enjoying sorting the facts from the propaganda.

'By nineteen-thirty-two,' he told her, 'the first five-year plan had ground to a halt. Grain received from the *Kolkhozes* — that's the Collective farms,' he explained for my benefit, 'had nowhere near matched predictions. And this wasn't just from the Ukraine. The black earth region of the northern Caucasus hadn't reached their quota either.'

'I've read they had a bad harvest that year,' I said, remembering that the afternoon I'd first met him he had told me the figures were still in dispute.

Perhaps it was Daryna's attitude or just his propensity for lecturing instead of holding a normal conversation that made me play the devil's advocate, even at the risk of defending the indefensible.

'Well,' he admitted, 'you can read just about any statistic you choose to back up your prejudice if you've a mind to. All writers on the subject have some sort of axe to grind. Those with a political agenda are just about the worst. From the work done by those trying to maintain an objective standpoint — that is, an academic one — I think it's generally accepted that while the harvest that year was not a great one, neither was it the disaster that the apologists would have us believe.'

Standing's bottle of Pinot Noir had arrived just prior to our lunch and was opened. I declined a glass reluctantly as I was driving although Daryna seemed happy to accept in my stead. Standing filled her glass before resuming.

'The main reason for the failure to reach the set quotas was, of course, the opposition of the peasants. You might have thought that common sense would have warned the Bolsheviks what would happen, but no one to my knowledge has ever accused a politician of any persuasion of suffering from an excess of that characteristic.'

His mouth flickered with a half-smile, almost an apology, perhaps remembering then that my brother-in-law was an MP.

He played at the edges of his lunch with his fork. 'These weren't your ordinary politicians, of course. The Bolsheviks were messianic in their faith. And that's no idle analogy. Marxist theory was their creed and like true believers they were convinced that all the pieces of the prophesised Marxist utopia would fall into place once they had removed the anachronistic capitalist obstructions and instituted the dictatorship of the proletariat —' he paused and translated the phrase into Ukrainian for Daryna's benefit. She nodded solemnly and I wondered if it was something she might have had to learn by rote in kindergarten.

'Even Lenin admitted that they weren't economists,' he continued after a moment spent chewing rocket leaves. 'They had to learn on the job, although there is a body of opinion that suggests applying economic theory within Marxist principles is like fighting with one hand tied behind your back.'

This allusion made Daryna frown but if he noticed he didn't wait to explain.

'That's when it all went wrong. In the early twenties there were severe shortages and unrest and Lenin reluctantly decided he had to take some account of Market Forces and introduced his New Economic Policy. This was too pragmatic for the more fervent followers and they began to resist some of the reforms he offered the peasants.'

'Pragmatic, please?' Daryna said to me, leaning so close that I could smell her hair.

'Practical,' I said. 'Practical application rather than theory?' I wasn't sure she understood but she nodded anyway.

'As I understand it,' I said to Standing who had waited patiently while we completed our exchange, a small, slightly expectant frown creasing his tanned face, 'by and large the peasants still resisted the reforms.'

'Certainly,' he said. 'Hard-line Bolsheviks aside — and you wouldn't have found many of those to the pound among the peasantry — they weren't interested in farming State land. They'd done with serfdom when Alexander the Second had freed them in eighteen-sixty-one and they had no intention of going back to it, whatever euphemism the Party wanted to wrap it up in. To get their support during the civil war and afterwards when he introduced his New Economic Policy, Lenin promised them land. Nominally this was to be owned by the state, but he was prepared to give them hereditary tenure, which is ownership in all but name. It was, in fact, more or less a return to what Stolypin in his effort to modernize the three-strip agriculture system had offered them under the tsar before the war.' He shrugged, to illustrate the hopelessness of the offer, I assumed. 'This was anathema to the zealots, of course.'

Daryna began to speak but Standing ploughed on regardless:

'As I said this morning, in his bourgeois way Lenin felt nothing but contempt for the peasantry but he was practical enough to know that he couldn't do without their support. After all, it was the peasant who was going to feed the population. It was their grain, once exported, that was going to provide the hard currency to buy the tools and machinery needed to industrialize the country.'

He pushed his salad around without appetite then placed his knife and fork together on the plate beside the bulk of his lunch. He refilled his glass.

'It had always been assumed from Lenin onwards that any coherent opposition to Collectivization was going to organize around the Kulaks.' He turned to Daryna. 'What is your definition of a kulak, Daryna?'

'What does the word mean?' I said, trying to clarify "definition" for her. But she had become touchy about my interventions and glared at me again, not wanting to be treated like a child in front of Standing, I suppose.

'This is *fist*,' she said, and clenched her fist and shook it at me. 'You talk of *fist* this morning,' she said to Standing.

'At least someone was listening,' he observed dryly. 'But what does it *mean* to you?' he asked Daryna again. 'To call someone a Kulak?'

'The meaning is peasant who lends money for big profit,' she said.

'Exorbitant rates,' I couldn't help myself from prompting.

'Yes,' she said curtly, 'for exorbitant rates.' Then she thought for a moment and decided, 'to call a man kulak, this is how you call a colloquialism, I think.'

'Very good,' I said, inevitably sounding like a patronising uncle.

'And it's also a metaphor,' Standing told her, 'because the fist squeezes money out of the peasant.'

'Metaphor,' she repeated, reaching out and tapping out the syllables on the table with her fingers like a Morse signaller.

'Which is why I used the term this morning,' he added. 'The word "Kulak" offers the perfect illustration of semantics at work in the service of politics. What had been a colloquial term used to describe a man who lived parasitically off his fellow peasants, either as a usurer or an oppressive employer, came to mean under the Bolsheviks any peasant they deemed to be a member of a class which they needed to invent to remain within Marxist strictures.' He gave a small philosophical shrug. 'How many in the audience grasped the point is another matter.'

Glancing at Daryna, I suspected the metaphor had been lost on her as well and, although her hand remained on the table, it had stopped its reflexive signalling, perhaps a physical manifestation of Standing's argument having left her behind.

'"*What is a Kulak?*" Stalin asked, he went on rhetorically,' and I suddenly knew we were going to get the rest of the lecture he seemed to have abandoned that morning. He leaned forward and pushed his plate aside. 'It was a question that had been posed before. Bukharin had asked the same thing although, in answering his own question, he had described a much more affluent character. By the time Stalin had proposed the Collectivization of agriculture the Bolsheviks had discovered they needed a specific class to oppose in order to satisfy the Marxist dialectic. It was also a practical matter. What they really feared, you see, was any peasant who had a bit of land, a little money, and enough sense to see what was going to happen to him under their regime. Peasants may have been largely illiterate and lacking in what we regard as learning but what they did possess was an animal cunning which instinctively told them what was in their own best interest. Without it they could never have survived what they had had to endure over the centuries. The Bolsheviks regarded this as just the sort of spark of independence and ambition that had to be expunged since it ran directly counter to what they needed in an agrarian population.

'So, for the Bolsheviks' purposes any man with two cows and a bit of pasture was good enough to be classed as a Kulak — any man, in fact, that they could distinguish as a discrete class, however loosely it was applied. And, as a semantic instrument, what it came to be in the end was a term of abuse.' Standing parted his hands expansively. 'You know the method, it hasn't changed in two thousand years. If there is a strata of society that a regime wishes to dispossess, first isolate them, then demonise, and lastly dehumanise them. After that you can justify just about any barbarous method you chose to dispose of them. So any members of the peasantry who proved to be obstructive were deemed to be Kulaks and were disposed of — deported or just taken away and shot. Liquidated. And anyone else that they deemed needed to be disposed of was included in the class as well; Kulak came to mean whatever the Bolsheviks wanted it to mean.'

He relaxed back into his chair again, his point made.

'Once that had been accomplished there was nothing to impede the introduction of Collectivization. The land of the dispossessed was incorporated into the kolkhozes and the rest of the peasantry were cowed and easier to handle. But that doesn't mean they were *willing*. Agriculture may have been rationalized but production still went down. A coerced population is naturally not as productive as one working on their own account. As supplies dwindled the quotas became more severe and took on an element of punishment for those who failed to meet them. With less grain available even those who ran the kolkhozes became reluctant to leave their reserves short as they were needed to feed the members of the Collective. Hungry workers are less productive. Thus a hungry population became a starving population. It became a vicious circle, not the virtuous circle that the Marxist intellectuals had expected, or that their philosophy had predicted.'

He looked around and signalled for the bill, signing for it and waving away my attempt to pay for Daryna and myself. The bottle of Pinot Noir had been finished, to no visible effect, and he asked for coffee in the lounge, an extension of the existing room under glass, with comfortable sofas and views over a lawn to the stream and a picturesque ruin by a leat which I took to be the original mill. We sat down and were presented with a cafetiére as big as a Russian samovar.

I stole a glance at Daryna to see how she was faring. I had not been adverse to the history lesson he had provided. After all, television companies no doubt paid him a large sum for what we were getting for free. Admittedly, we weren't benefiting from the travelogue scenery, but the lawn and the ruined mill and its leat served just as well. Since Daryna's pout did not look any more pronounced, I assumed she was quite content to bathe in Standing's reflected charisma which, judging from the glances that some of the other diners had given us over lunch, I was sure she had not failed to notice. Added to this, of course, she was picking up all sorts of language she was never going to find a use for in any future I could imagine for her. But it was all grist for the mill, as they say — in even less apt situations. For my part, it made a pleasant change from my cramped dining room table and the arcane mysteries of Daryna's lessons in Ukrainian. But, as ever, I had again begun to wonder just where it was leading. After all, Standing and I barely knew each other and, Daryna's decorative attributes aside, it could hardly be *my* company he craved even if he did seem to be at a loose end whilst waiting for his wife.

But it was becoming obvious that he hadn't finished yet and, while Daryna's initial questions might have prompted the lesson, his lecture had taken on a life of its own.

'Of course,' he said, settling back in his armchair after he had poured the coffee, 'the Bolshevik policies became self-defeating. Wholesale deportation of peasants who still resisted Collectivization meant less hands to work the land. It also meant death to a large percentage of those relocated, but perhaps that was part of the thinking. Many of those still independent of the kolkhozes began hiding grain from the authorities. Not only could they see that winter would bring shortages but they knew also they would need seed grain for the next year's sowing. Of course, the Party bleated about peasants hoarding grain and trying to push up the prices, but that was disingenuous at the very least. By this time there was only one buyer of grain and that was the state and if you had it you sold it at the price you were given.

'There had been hunger before but by the winter of thirty-three it had become a famine. The leaders of the kolkhozes tried to tell the Party bosses what was happening and, to their credit, two or three members of the Ukrainian Soviet wrote to Stalin to warn him how bad things had become and that the situation would only get worse unless they softened their policies. There had already been riots and in some areas law had broken down altogether. Stalin, worried that he might lose the Ukraine completely, resorted, as ever, to his favourite method of dealing with a problem.'

He looked at us over the rim of his coffee cup with a grim smile on his lips.

'Have you heard the story of the barge in Tsaritsyn?'

I shook my head.

He placed his cup on the table. 'Tsaritsyn is on the lower Volga. They changed the name to Volgograd later but you'd know it better as Stalingrad. It was strategically important as it controlled the gateway to the northern Caucasus and the grain and oil of that region. During the Civil War the fighting was almost as bad there as it was twenty years later. In nineteen-eighteen Lenin sent Stalin there to stiffen the Comrades' resistance. It's where he met many of the men who became his inner circle after he took power — men who were still with him at the time of the Ukrainian famine. Characters like Budyonny and Voroshilov. Some, naturally, he disposed of later—' Standing flicked a hand as if troubled by a fly, '— others managed to survive although generally not because they were lucky but because in the main they were equally as ruthless as Stalin. Voroshilov, for instance, is generally credited with liquidating forty thousand of his own officers in the terror purges of the late thirties.

'Anyway,' he said, as if this horror had been a mere sidebar, 'you must be aware that Trotsky was the founder of the Red Army?' He grunted as I nodded. 'At the time of the fighting in Tsaritsyn Trotsky was the darling of the Party. This by itself, you understand, would have been enough to make an ambitious man like Stalin hate him, but it seems he hated Trotsky on a personal level, too. His being Jewish might have had something to do with it, but the main reason Stalin hated him was that Trotsky was a *real* intellectual while Stalin was an also-ran and was probably aware of it. Trotsky was closer to Lenin than Stalin was, too. But if Trotsky was a theoretician, he was also a pragmatist—' he gave Daryna a passing nod in indication of his use of the word *pragmatist* again, '—and in creating the Red Army he gave himself licence to use whoever he considered necessary in order to create the efficient fighting force he needed. He incorporated what he termed "specialists", that is officers who had served in the tsarist army regardless of whether they had any revolutionary leanings or not. Of course, to some these specialists were as much an affront to the purity of Marxist ideology as Lenin's New Economic Policy was to become to the zealots later. Even if these men supported the revolution, the mere fact that they had served in the tsarist army was reason enough in the zealots' eyes to have them shot. They were as narrow minded as religious fundamentalists, you understand. Stalin was one of those who regarded these specialists as renegades. Lenin had originally sent him to Tsaritsyn as a Director of Food Supplies and had told him to be "merciless and ruthless". Once there, though, he decided that if he was going to achieve what Lenin had asked of him he would need military control as well and so he promptly had many of the men on his own side shot — his method of "stiffening" resistance. He also had a lot of Trotsky's specialists arrested. He loaded them onto a barge, floated it out into the Volga and had it sunk. When Trotsky protested, Stalin is reputed to have said: "Death solves all problems. No man, no problem". It was the dictum he followed for the rest of his life.'

I don't remember Standing getting much beyond anecdotes after lunch that afternoon at the Mill House Hotel. Following coffee we took a stroll across the lawn to the ruined mill and its leat. Daryna looked pretty in the rustic setting. She had done what she could with the clothes in which she had turned up at my house the previous day and, although a little shabby from overuse, they looked of good quality and, to my untutored eye, stylish. Standing's wife had still not shown up and he had begun extending an interest in Daryna that I suspected he might have reined-in if his wife had been there. He lit a cigarette and offered her one. She took it, which came as a surprise to me as I had never seen her smoke before.

'You don't mind, do you?' he asked after I had declined one. 'I do like a cigarette after food and the new regulations can be a bit of a bore.' He turned his head slightly and made a point of exhaling to one side even though we were outside. 'Perfectly understandable,' he said. 'Why should anyone breath my smoke? Still a bit of a bore, though.'

Daryna inhaled deeply like an experienced smoker.

'Did you say you had made a start on translating that notebook I gave you?' I asked, deciding to tackle him on the subject again whilst I still had the chance. Daryna looked up from where she had been examining the ruins of the old mill and rejoined us.

'David has had a look at it,' he said, 'but as I say, he hasn't been able to make much of it yet. Hand-written Cyrillic is a bit of a bugger if you weren't born to it and whoever wrote the thing didn't have the neatest hand in the world.'

'I translate letters for Alex,' Daryna piped up and for a second I thought she was going to volunteer her services.

'He'll get there in the end,' Standing assured me.

'But you can't say who wrote it yet?'

Standing became evasive. 'Not until we get a handle on the contents. David said he'd be able to get on better once he's got his eye in. He's a bit caught up in other things at the moment.' He shrugged apologetically. 'We took what photocopies of the Ukrainian State files they allowed us but most of what we've got is necessarily in the form of notes. It takes an age to cross-reference everything, especially with what we already had from the KGB files.'

'You've been through those as well?'

'Well, OGPU, strictly speaking,' he said. 'That's the period we're concerned with at the moment.'

'And that's where you found the name of the man who denounced my grandfather?'

'Not exactly,' he said.

'What then?'

Standing didn't reply. Instead he took one last pull on his cigarette then dropped the butt at his feet. When it seemed as if he was never going to answer I said:

'If you didn't get a name, what did you get? Forgive me, but I'm still unclear about what alerted you to Aleksander Zaretsky in the first place.'

'Oh?' He sounded surprised as he ground the cigarette butt into the grass. 'Didn't I show you that deposition we found that mentions Zaretsky?'

'Yes,' I said, 'but his name must have been one of hundreds you came across.'

'But not in connection with Shostak,' he said.

Daryna coughed smoke into my face. I breathed some in which started me off.

'I am sorry, Alex,' she said, laying a hand on my arm. 'You do not like smoke. I am not polite, I think, to smoke with you.'

'It's okay,' I said, catching my breath.

'I did tell you about Gareth Jones, didn't I?' Standing said. 'The trip he took with Jack Heinz? Heinz wrote a book on the experience taken from Jones' diary. Heinz had kept the original notes for the diary but he didn't speak Ukrainian. Presumably, Jones translated for him as they went. The book was published anonymously although Jones wrote a preface to it.'

'So *they* mentioned Zaretsky?' I asked.

'No, not at all.' He looked perplexed as if he wondered where I had got that notion from. 'At least not in the book or in Jones' diary. They travelled through the countryside talking to the peasants and occasionally staying in their houses. By time the Ukrainian Soviet had been charged with collecting grain that the peasants had not declared, that is the grain they had hidden from the authorities for their own use. What Jones and Heinz saw was the result of that grain having been forcibly seized.'

173

No longer short of breath, I found I was running short of patience. 'But it could hardly have been a secret, surely.'

'At the time, it was,' Standing insisted. 'And it was people like Jones and Malcolm Muggeridge who first alerted the West to what was happening. But that's not the point.'

'What is the point?' I asked.

Standing frowned at me. I realized it was the wrong question to ask. He ran his fingers through his hair. Daryna was still hovering around us looking bored.

'We know from the Kremlin files,' he began again, 'that this was a pivotal time for Stalin. He was in trouble with the programme for Industrialization. Contrary to most assumptions he wasn't dictator at this time. Being General Secretary, he was the leader of the Party, and there was some talk of his also becoming Snarkom leader as well when Rykov was sacked — Premiere, that is. But only Russians had been Snarkom leader up to that point and Stalin was a Georgian, of course.' He waved a hand, batting the point away towards the leat. 'But that's another story. The point is, the way the leadership was organized, he was still in danger of being outvoted by the Politburo. In fact, he could have been voted off altogether. There was strong opposition to his plans because it had become obvious that they weren't working. To maintain his position he had to ensure the success of Collectivization and Industrialization. So, while initially mollifying his critics until such a time as he could deal with them, he ramped up his campaign against the peasants who were withholding their grain so as to squeeze out every last ear of corn he could. It was a case of the usual demonization — depicting them as wreckers ... counter-revolutionaries ... kulaks who had escaped the earlier purges — all the usual excuses. But when it finally became obvious that the Ukrainian Soviet was incapable — or in some cases just plain unwilling — to collect all the grain he sent his own OGPU agents in to make sure his orders were obeyed. There are several letters and notes in his hand exhorting them to be "ruthless and brutal and merciless", all wrapped up in Party rhetoric, of course. He demanded that all the grain had to be taken. All of it, that is, including seed grain. If that resulted in the rural population starving to death, then so be it. In his eyes they were a troublesome nuisance best rid of. Another instance of "Death solves all problems". In fact — in reality — this was the desired outcome because when peasants who were starving at home upped sticks and attempted to relocate, Stalin had them sent back to their villages.' He gave me a grim smile.

'It was a case of what Robert Louis Stevenson once maintained — "The bourgeoisie's weapon is starvation." He was talking about writers and artists, of course, saying that those whose ideas run counter to the narrow notions of the bourgeoisie have their means of subsistence silently withdrawn. For the peasants, of course, the Bolsheviks were the new bourgeoisie.'

'And Zaretsky?'

'GPU men obviously needed local knowledge. They had to be able to move through the country on their grain collecting expeditions so they recruited local men. We know the names of some who were involved. Zaretsky went on at least two of these missions with this man Shostak. The deposition, remember? What we need to do is pin down actual locations and, if possible, discover what the peasants' reactions were to what was happening and how men like Zaretsky felt about doing it.'

'Right,' I said, not sure that it had been an answer to my question but aware that Daryna was fidgeting around us impatiently. 'That's a tall order, but always assuming we've got the right Zaretsky, why on earth did he make arrangements for his wife to leave the Ukraine? Surely he must have been aware of the consequences if they were caught?'

'We've got the right Zaretsky,' he insisted irritably, as if my continual harping upon a putative ancestral connection was obscuring the bigger picture. 'And that's precisely the *thing*. Zaretsky was a Party member. *He* wasn't going to go short of food and neither was his immediate family. Most likely they would have been tucked up safely in Kharkov or Kiev.'

'Then why get her out?' I persisted.

He shifted awkwardly. 'There's always the chance,' he suggested, 'that Zaretsky wasn't the one who arranged for her to leave. After all, you told me that once she had got to England his wife never heard from him again. That's right, isn't it? If he had remained a good Party man, there isn't any reason for his disappearance, sudden death aside.'

'But you said he'd been denounced,' I said.

'Yes...'

'And you said earlier you could tell me more about why.'

'Irregularities over the grain quotas,' he said.

'But you said that was a catchall charge.'

'Did I?'

We stood looking at each other and the sense of something unspoken in the air was palpable.

'Yes, you did,' I said.

An expression of discomfort flitted across his face and he glanced at his watch.

'Is that the time? Look, I've got to run,' he said, and began offering excuses about getting back to the seminar before they started slagging him as an ungracious dog, reading his paper then not having the courtesy to listen to the other contributors. He wondered if we would like to listen to any more of the papers scheduled to be given but Daryna was getting restive and I suspected she had seen as much as she wanted of academic seminars and so I made our excuses, saying we really had only come to hear him. He shrugged modestly but looked suitably gratified. His wife had still not arrived and he seemed suddenly unaccountably apologetic for the fact, then said he was sorry for dragging me all that way for what was, in the end, very little in the way of information. Griffiths would get on with the translation of the notebook just as soon as pressure of work allowed and then I could have my papers back and any further news he had on Zaretsky. We'd go through it all soon, he promised.

He took Daryna's hand and told her what a pleasure it had been to meet her and have the opportunity to talk with her in her own language and said he hoped they might meet again. She got all wide-eyed and breathless but, as far as I was able to tell, he didn't slip her a note of his telephone number. Hers, of course, was usually unobtainable.

I dropped him off at the College and turned the Alvis for home. Daryna was sitting pressed against the passenger door and seemed uncharacteristically quiet. I glanced across at her but she was staring ahead out of the windscreen, a disgruntled expression marring her otherwise pretty face. I left her to it, more concerned with what it was that Standing had been so reluctant to tell me.

It was clear that his interest in my grandfather didn't go much beyond Zaretsky's connection to the shadowy Shostak. Although he had never said as much, it was clear that Standing thought Shostak was English, was connected to the Black Sea Company and somehow by extension to an early incarnation of the Cambridge spy ring. Yet to my mind it might not have been as straightforward as that. I had wanted to say: *Take it from one who knows*, but of course I couldn't. His suspicion that the Black Sea Company might be a cover operation for intelligence gathering on the Bolshevik State was eminently plausible. It would have been ideal cover. All foreign embassies have their intelligence wings, peopled by the SIS and given prosaic job descriptions like "passport officer" to cover their more nefarious activities. And, by and large, everyone knows who they are. It's a chess game that's played out in all the capital cities of the world. Harder to identify, though, are the "illegals" those outside the diplomatic umbrella whose cover is whatever mundane reason they have for being in the country and who, if the worst should ever happen, are "deniable". It was the kind of world I had spent a few years in, probing and pricking at the opposition, always on the lookout for individuals who one might groom to become an agent, an informer, a betrayer ... perhaps even looking for those already playing the game who one might turn into a double-agent, those who were themselves in the market for information for their own masters.

That was the essence of the grey world. It was what gave it its spice. One could never tell *precisely* on whose side anyone really was. Was the man offering genuine information or was it disinformation? Or was it *genuine* information designed to hook the mark in order that later *disinformation* would be swallowed willingly? Was the man a spy or a double agent? Could one trust him or not? It was the thing that had made exposing Kim Philby as a spy so difficult. He had certainly passed information to the Russians, but had he done it to bolster his credentials so that when he had wanted to feed them bad information they would accept it without question? One could never be completely sure until he defected. And even then, could it not be that he had purposely insinuated himself into the heart of the enemy in order to betray them the more completely? How could one ever know? One had to take the word of an honest man. But how do you tell the honest man from the rogue?

I wondered how Standing could hope to identify what kind of man Shostak had been. Perhaps for an historian it was a case of *by his deeds shall we know him...*

Daryna sighed heavily and shifted in her seat. She had something on her mind, obviously, and I think I had proved a disappointment in not asking her what it was. We were about ten miles south of Cambridge before she gave up waiting and decided to broach the subject herself.

177

'This notebook,' she said. 'It is too bad, Alex, that you give it to Professor Standing to translate. I can do this for you. I think you do not trust me.'

I glanced across at her, sitting at the far edge of the Alvis's big leather front seat.

'It's nothing to do with trust,' I said. 'I think you're using the wrong idiom.'

'Always you are correcting me,' she complained. 'What is idiom?'

I began to explain but she cut me off almost as soon as I began.

'No, no! I do not want to know *idiom*. What is in notebook, anyway, that no one can see it?'

I laughed. 'I don't *know* what's in the damn thing,' I said. 'That's the whole point. I didn't even know you when I gave it to Standing. If I'd have known you'd be touting for trade I'd have told him to give it me back.'

She looked at me suspiciously. 'Touting?' she repeated. 'I think this is not a good word you use for me, Alex.'

'I wasn't suggesting—'

'No, it is too bad of you.'

I tried to explain but she would have none of it and sat in a sulky silence until we got inside the M25 where she insisted I drop her at an underground station. She was adamant and I didn't feel like arguing so I pulled off the North Circular near Redbridge station. She climbed out of the Alvis and I watched her disappear down the street.

I drove back to the house, back stiffening from the journey. I took a turn around the park once home and stopped off at the pub on the green to make up for the drink I had missed at lunch. It was still warm and across the road in the park parents were out watching over their children on the swings. The offices were emptying and the pub began to fill with workers looking, no doubt, to take the edge off a rough day. Mine hadn't been that rough but it had turned out sufficiently disagreeable for me to resent having to share my table with the incomers. But my thoughts were still my own and they wandered off spontaneously as they had become prone to do, dragging the rest of me behind like an onerous burden.

I watched the people around me in a glassy, sightless way thinking how far I still was from knowing anything of my father's early life in the Ukraine and not much closer in learning anything about *his* father and the life of unrelenting misery he had perhaps helped create. I wondered if his impulse to get Nastasiya and Petro out had been goaded by conscience or even, as Standing had once suggested, a possible decision to swap sides. What did that make him — hero or turncoat? And now Standing was suggesting that it might not have been Zaretsky who had arranged for them to leave. My father might have been able to tell me what had happened if it hadn't been, as I have said, for his utter reluctance to talk about that period of his life. He would chatter happily for hours about his war service, about flying, and about anything that had happened to him subsequently, but on his life before the war he was stubbornly silent.

Despite the crowd I had a second pint for good measure then walked home in the twilight. I suppose I had expected more from Standing and was now beginning to realize that waiting for crumbs from his table hadn't got me very far. David Griffiths had had the small leather-bound notebook I had given Standing for over four months and I was supposed to believe that he hadn't yet found time to translate it — this a notebook that might well have belonged to a man whose life they had been trying to reconstruct. The delay was beginning to sound like procrastination; Standing's explanations like dissembling. If they took any longer I would have to take it to be deliberate evasion. I decided to give him a few more weeks and if I hadn't heard anything by then I'd ask for the notebook back. I had Daryna, after all. She had managed to translate my father's letters, if unproductively, and I could see she would not be mollified until she did the notebook as well. It might also be instructive, I thought, to compare Griffiths' translation with what she might be able to come up with.

A few more weeks, I decided as I reached my door, then I'd get back in touch with Michael Standing and ask him to return the notebook. I suppose I should have said something to him in Cambridge, been firmer, and resolved that the next time I would.

I had no way of knowing, of course, that that afternoon in Cambridge was the last time I would ever see him.

FOUR

11-8-18

Send to Penza To Comrades Kuraev, Bosh, Minkin and other Penza communists

Comrades! The revolt by the five kulak volost's must be suppressed without mercy. The interest of the entire revolution demands this, because we have now before us our final decisive battle "with the kulaks." We need to set an example.

You need to hang (hang without fail, so that the public sees) at least 100 notorious kulaks, the rich, and the bloodsuckers.

Publish their names.

Take away all of their grain.

Execute the hostages - in accordance with yesterday's telegram.

This needs to be accomplished in such a way, that people for hundreds of miles around will see, tremble, know and scream out: let's choke and strangle those blood-sucking kulaks.

Telegraph us acknowledging receipt and execution of this.

Yours, Lenin

P.S. Use your toughest people for this.

TRANSLATOR'S COMMENTS: Lenin uses the derogative term kulach'e in reference to the class of prosperous peasants. A volost' was a territorial/administrative unit consisting of a few villages and surrounding land.

15

I slept fitfully, images of Daryna being in the house during the break-in running around my head like a train on a circular track. At three o'clock in the morning the brain is rarely rational, acquiring the ability to magnify the smallest of incidents into events of immense significance and the mildest of concerns into the deepest of worries. Knowing this, of course, makes absolutely no difference.

I had trawled systematically through the house again after Charlie left, like an obsessive unable to stop repeating the same meaningless gesture, looking for any kind of evidence that she had been there at all. I stripped the bed we had made up for her, searched the bathroom, combed the kitchen, but I found nothing to suggest she had ever stayed in the house. No hairs lay on the sheets or the pillow; no telltale residue stuck to the soap or clogged in the drain; no crockery or cutlery had been left out of place. I wasn't a man who kept an inventory of his food stocks — she might have eaten a meal but there was no way of telling. No waste lay in the garbage.

If I found no trace of her having been there, though, I found equally no trace of her having suffered violence or forcible removal. There were no bloodstains, no overt signs of the house having been cleaned: my dust still coated the tops of the skirting-boards, my ring still stained the rim of the bath. And yet, that by itself did not preclude the meek acquiescence of a victim with a gun at her head. That's what kept me awake.

Just why anyone would want to point a gun at Daryna's head was another matter; at three o'clock in the morning logic loses its relevance. Near dawn, when I finally did fall properly asleep, it was only to be troubled by dreams of OGPU men menacing peasants who looked remarkably like Daryna, and of a pig — in an embellishment purely my own — feeding off a malnourished corpse.

It was this last image that startled me awake again and banished any further chance of sleep. Dawn was beginning to show through the crack in my curtains and, lying in bed looking at the ceiling, I remembered the pig and thought of how Daryna had described her boyfriend. It was possible, of course, that he had found her and, whilst in the house, had taken the opportunity to rifle the place. That might explain the missing laptop but it was hardly an adequate answer as to why my father's letters had been stolen.

I had been sure that there had been nothing of importance in the letters yet now, no longer having the translations, I couldn't be certain. The idea that there was something I had missed and that they had been stolen because of it became less fanciful the longer I considered it. Disconcertingly, the possibility tied in with the wilder theories of why Michael Standing had been murdered and following that logic led to the peculiar possibility that, somewhere, there might be someone who knew more about my father than I did.

Losing my laptop was irritating. There was nothing on it of a sensitive or confidential nature (those days were over for me) and I was the kind of cautious person who backed-up most things I wouldn't want to lose. But the fact that someone had taken the trouble to steal the machine, no matter how obsolete it was, stuck in my craw. Beyond losing the old emails I had elected to keep, the biggest nuisance was going to be that I would have to buy another machine and I thought the amount I might expect to get on the insurance for the loss of the old one and the repair to the broken door would hardly be worth my making a claim. If I did, of course, I would have to report the break-in to the police and although I might have regarded Charlie as an incurable cynic, I could see his point in *not* reporting the burglary. With the best will in the world they were never going to find who was responsible, assuming they even bothered to look, and drawing attention to myself — and more to the point to Daryna — didn't seem like a good idea. If Charlie was right about the DNA swabs they'd be round to see me soon enough anyway.

I made another pointless call to Daryna's mobile while I chewed on my breakfast toast and drank my tea, then put my coat on ready to visit the nearest computer outlet. It was just after nine and I was halfway out the door when the phone rang. Hoping it might be Daryna I backtracked up the hall.

But it wasn't Daryna.

'Is that Mr Maitland? *Alex* Maitland? Father named Petro Zaretsky?' The voice was male, a low growl that bit off words almost before they had been formed. Behind him on the line I could hear a buzz of conversation and ringing telephones.

'Yes,' I said. 'Who is this?'

I heard him wheeze as he took a breath.

'Fielding,' he snapped. A note of irritation sounded through the growl. 'I've been trying to get you. Don't you pick up your messages?'

'Do I know you?' I snapped back. Peremptory phone calls early in the morning had never been start of choice for my day. Then I remembered the name and the call I'd got just as Nick had arrived to pick me up on Friday. I'd written the number down, contrived to lose the note and had forgotten to call back.

'Didn't Michael Standing mention me to you?' Fielding asked.

'No,' I said.

He grunted with an out-of-sorts pig impersonation.

'Can we meet?'

I had wondered when Fielding had rung the first time if he might be a journalist chasing leads on the Standing murder and now the clatter behind him, sounding to me like a newsroom, reinforced the suspicion. I thought the press must be scraping the bottom of the barrel if they had finally come up with me.

'Why would Michael Standing mention you to me?' I asked.

'Black Sea Company,' he said. 'Ring any bells? David Griffiths gave me your number.'

'I didn't know Griffiths had my number.'

'C'est la vie,' growled Fielding.

'Are you a journalist?'

'That's what it says on my NUJ card,' Fielding said. 'But I'm not the kind you should be worried about.'

'What kind's that?'

'Listen,' he said abruptly, 'I can just walk away from this. Standing's dead and it doesn't look as if I'm going to get paid anyway.' He paused as if a thought had just struck him. 'I don't know who killed him. Maybe it was you.'

That made me laugh. 'Vice versa,' I said.

'All right,' Fielding said. 'Fair enough.'

'Anyway,' I added, 'they've arrested someone for it.'

It was his turn to laugh.

'Okay,' I said, 'I'll bite. What's the Black Sea Company?'

'I was hoping you'd tell me that.'

'You rang Friday.'

'And Saturday,' he said.

'Tell me again what it is you want.'

'I thought we might be able to help each other.'

I didn't know what help I needed and, even if I did, I didn't know what Fielding thought he could do for me. But he suggested we meet at noon, gave me directions and said that he'd be wearing a striped scarf, yellow and black.

Like a wasp, I thought. I put the phone down, wondering if there would be a sting in the tail.

Fielding's directions led to a bar in docklands. I got there twenty minutes early. The weather had turned colder and there was a sharp east wind blowing up the river, chivvying litter along the road and dumping it in sodden piles in the gutters. Waiting in a doorway across the road from the pub I got cold while I watched people coming and going. At that time of day it was mostly coming. Up the street was the London HQ of one of the news agencies and it wasn't much of a walk further on to Canary Warf and the big trading houses.

It was five minutes to midday before Fielding showed up. He was a large man wrapped in a larger overcoat and he stopped outside the pub and pulled a yellow and black scarf out of his coat and left it hanging ostentatiously around his neck. Before going in through the door his last act was to drop a half-smoked cigarette onto the pavement and grind it out with the toe of his shoe. I was across the road before the smoke had cleared from the butt.

He was ordering a pint of bitter at the bar when I moved in beside him.

'Make that two,' I said to the barman.

Closer to, I saw he was more than half a head taller than me and as bulky as his first impression had suggested. Whatever journalists are supposed to look like, I didn't think he numbered among them.

'Nice scarf,' I said as he looked down at me.

'Maitland?'

That over, the barman came back with our drinks. Fielding put a five-pound note on the bar. 'That's for mine,' he said.

I paid for my own drink and thanked the barman so he'd know that all his customers weren't as surly as Fielding.

The pub was already half-full with office workers. A pervading smell of chilli and baked potatoes filled the room. I assumed the big money lunched elsewhere. We threaded our way to the far corner and took a vacant table.

Fielding took off his overcoat and sat heavily. He looked to be in his thirties and was big enough to have played in the second row of a scrum although judging from the folds of skin that had gathered around his chin like a badly stuffed cushion what had once been muscle had now begun to slip into fat. He might have been fit once but it was only a memory now. Just getting out of his topcoat had started him breathing hard. He hunched over his beer as I sat down, neck pulled into his shoulders as if poised to heave into the backsides of the front-row ahead of him. His face was fleshy with thick, almost sensual lips and half-hooded eyes that stared back at me as I looked at him. His fair hair was thinning and had already receded from his forehead. What was left he wore close-cropped. It looked as if at some point his nose had been broken although not badly. No cauliflower ears. I tried weighing him up but all I could tell for sure was that he was out of condition.

'Standing never told you anything about me?' he finally asked.

'All I got from Standing was history lessons,' I told him. 'You didn't say what kind of journalist you are.'

'Freelance,' he said.

I sipped at my pint. 'That covers a wide area of interest.'

'Investigative,' he said. 'Financial, mostly, but it depends where things lead.'

'Where did you phone me from?'

He frowned, eyes almost disappearing beneath their hoods.

'The wire service up the street. I used to work there.'

'So what was it you were helping Standing with?'

'He was trying to dig up information on a company that traded before the war. The Black Sea Company. He thought you might know something about them.'

'I never heard of the company until Standing asked me about it,' I said, 'so why he'd tell you that, I don't know.'

He had mentioned it to me that first afternoon we'd met, and again in Cambridge when we'd talked about the spy ring. I remembered that he had suggested the company might have been a conduit for intelligence.

'Why was he interested?' I asked Fielding.

His face remained impassive. 'He never told me. What he wanted was any documentary evidence on the company I could find.'

'Would that have been difficult?'

'They ceased trading when the war broke out. Went into voluntary liquidation. Standing asked me to dig up anything on Black Sea I could ... names on the Board, executive directors ... employees. He was interested in the company's annual accounts and who their auditors were. Anything I could find, in fact.'

'Why did he need you?' I asked. 'Historians live on old records. And he had Griffiths.'

That seemed to amuse him. 'It's a different kind of research,' he wheezed. 'It takes a specialist to work through company records and financial reports. The chances are, any company of any age will have gone through several incarnations — take-overs ... mergers and acquisitions... They might become a holding company or a shell. And that's just the run of the mill stuff. If there's deliberate obfuscation, anyone not used to that kind of maze hasn't got a chance.'

'Okay,' I said, 'but you just said they'd gone into liquidation.'

'Yeah. That's what I found out.'

'What kind of business had it been?'

'Import-export,' Fielding said.

'That covers a wide area of interest, too,' I said.

'They were commodity brokers. Mostly around the Near and Middle East. They had offices in Cairo and Istanbul, trading through Turkey and what was Persia.'

That's what Standing had told me. 'Russia or the Ukraine?' I asked.

Fielding shook his head. 'Local agents. That's what Standing was after.'

'Did they trade grain?'

'Some. Egyptian cotton, spices, rugs. They had a lot of interests.'

'What was yours?'

Fielding blinked at me. I drank some more beer. He hadn't touched his and I wondered if he had just bought it as a prop or whether the first of the day opened the gates.

'Money, of course. He was paying me for what I could turn up. He also told me that there might be a story in it.'

'What kind of story?'

'Wouldn't say. All he told me was that he had come across the name of Black Sea in the Ukrainian political police files.'

'Would that be unusual?' I said. 'If the company was trading out of Black Sea ports OGPU would be bound to have kept an eye on them.'

He shrugged his meaty shoulders. 'Not my field.'

'But you know who OGPU were, I assume.'

Fielding began nodding his heavy head. I was put in mind of an American bison. He picked up his pint then put it down again.

'You're not the only one Standing gave history lessons to,' he said.

'So what else did you find out about the company apart from the fact that they'd gone into liquidation?'

'That's the thing,' he said. He held my gaze. 'I had to pass everything I found through David Griffiths. When Standing was murdered I contacted Griffiths to find out what I was supposed to do and he told me to keep digging. I asked him about the financial arrangements and he gave me your name and number.'

'Me?'

'Are you connected to *George* Maitland?'

'Loosely,' I said.

He grunted again as if loose was good enough and picked up his pint. He drank two-thirds of it without pausing then banged the glass back on the table.

'Nothing,' he said.

'What nothing?'

'That's what I found. Well, next to nothing.' He eyed me oddly and I assumed I was supposed to infer something suspicious from this. 'If I didn't know better,' he said, 'I'd say the records have been deliberately cleaned.'

We were back on the Black Sea Company and he seemed to imagine that my connection to George guaranteed his eventual remuneration. Just where he'd got that idea from I couldn't say. I decided not to disabuse him of the notion.

'And do you?' I asked. 'Know better, I mean.'

Fielding grimaced. It wasn't a pretty sight.

'I'm not sure that I do,' he said.

'What does that mean?'

'When I said next to nothing, I meant next to nothing of any use. There are some incomplete company reports, trading statements and auditors' report for several years... Only fragments but even so, everything you'd expect from a bona fide company. But—' He stopped, as if he'd just dropped the ball.

'But what?'

'But none of it leads anywhere. Okay, accept that a lot of paper was lost in the war ... that's what you'd expect. But what's left... For instance, the accountants who audited their books have gone out of business.'

'Hardly surprising after seventy years,' I said.

'But the office they worked out of no longer exists and I can find no trace of their ever having worked for anyone else.'

'Okay,' I said. 'Still not *that* surprising. Sometimes accountants only have one client, don't they? And then, as you say, there was the war... A lot of premises were lost and their records no longer exist.'

'But the same goes for the directors of the company,' he said. 'All I could find was a list for nineteen-thirty-two, but they're just names. Not only do the Black Sea offices no longer exist but neither do the home addresses of the Board.'

'Coincidence?'

'Perhaps,' Fielding said.

'What about the electoral register?'

'The directors?' Fielding said, 'I thought of that. The names and corresponding addresses do check out except one, a chap named Robinson. But, as I say, the people are dead and the buildings destroyed in the Blitz.'

'There you are then,' I said.

'No, I mean the *people* all died in the Blitz.'

'It happens,' I said, thinking of Nastasiya.

'So I checked the census records,' Fielding said.

'But they're only released after a hundred years.'

'Nineteen-o-one, right. But I thought there might still be a chance that one of the names might match up. A young man starting work in nineteen-o-one would only be in his fifties thirty years later.'

'Maybe,' I said, 'but still at the same address...? Any luck?'

'No.'

'There you are then,' I said again.

'But the occupations given for those who were living at those addresses at the time were interesting.'

'Oh?'

'Working class. Billingsgate porter, docker, bricklayer... Not what you'd expect. All except one.'

'It depends upon what you expected,' I said.

'I expected middle-class occupations,' he said. 'The exception was a bank clerk. Yet thirty years later the Black Sea records maintain that the company officers were living at those addresses.'

I shrugged but I knew what he meant. There was something all too familiar about it. Only I couldn't tell him that.

'Areas get gentrified,' I said, but it sounded weak even to me.

Fielding finished his pint at his second attempt.

'On the face of it,' I went on, 'the fact that they went out of business seems reasonable. A company might well cease to trade on the outbreak of war if all their trading links and transport was closed

188

to them. Then perhaps their offices are bombed and all the staff are killed ... and they have to go into liquidation.'

Saying it made it sound all the more reasonable. Then why didn't I believe it?

'What made you think I can help you?'

'I didn't know where to go next,' he said. 'What I have got is no good to me without more information and after Standing was murdered it didn't look as if I was going to get any. He didn't give me any details on why he was interested in Black Sea in the first place so when Griffiths told me Standing was working with you on that angle I thought you'd be my best bet.'

'Griffiths said that?'

Fielding looked across the table at me morosely.

'Standing didn't tell you any more than he told me, did he?'

'Not about the Black Sea Company,' I said.

'Something's not right,' he said. 'I can smell it. Suppose he was killed because of this. There'd be a big story in that.'

'I imagine there would,' I said. 'But is it likely?'

'What have you got?'

I told him how Griffiths had first contacted me and why and that I'd met Standing three times.'

When I mentioned Frederick's name Fielding cocked his big head to one side like a St Bernard who'd been offered a walk in the snow, but all he said was, 'The Ukrainian famine.'

'For a new television series,' I said. Then added, 'Perhaps.'

'And he never told you what he'd found out about this grandfather of yours, Zaretsky?'

'If it was him, no, not a lot. I thought he was being evasive. I always got the impression he knew more than he said.'

'Right. Secretive bugger for someone who liked to talk, wasn't he?'

'I suppose he was.'

'So, what do you think we should do now?'

'Griffiths told you to keep digging?'

'Yeah.'

'He must know everything Standing did,' I said. 'He's still got my papers, so why don't I see what he's got to say?'

'All right,' he said, then began rummaging in the inside pocket of his overcoat. He pulled out a manila envelope. 'Here. It's copies of everything I've got on Black Sea to date. There's not much but there might be something in it you recognize.' He took a card out of the top pocket of his jacket and slid it across the table next to the manila envelope. 'Call me, if you find anything. There's still one or two things I want to check out.'

I picked up the card and the envelope and tucked them into my inside pocket. I stood up.

'You haven't finished your beer,' he said.

'It's a bit early for me,' I admitted. 'I'll call you after I've spoken to Griffiths.'

At the door, I glanced back to the table. Fielding had swapped glasses and was sitting hunched over what was left of my pint.

I took a walk along the river and stopped in a pub for lunch then spent the rest of the afternoon at a computer store listening to a sales assistant outlining the pros and cons of the bells and whistles attached to the different models on offer. Finding the language only slightly less foreign than Daryna's Ukrainian, I tossed a mental coin and made a choice and paid not too much more than I'd intended to anyway. I bullied the assistant until I was sure I was going to have no more than the usual amount of trouble getting on-line, then saw it was gone five. The offices were beginning to empty. I called Charlie and arranged to meet in the usual pub.

He was already there when I arrived sitting in a corner like part of the woodwork, so completely playing the chameleon that I almost missed him. I had been tempted on occasion to watch him unobserved to see just how it was he managed to melt into his background so perfectly, and to assure myself that he didn't have the kind of tongue capable of flicking out in a blur to scoop up some unsuspecting morsel.

'Heard from your girl yet?' he asked as I sat down and slid a scotch towards him.

'No. Have you got anything?'

'I've put out the feelers,' he said, 'but if I've got to be discreet I can't go charging in like a bull.'

'If I didn't think I'd get her into trouble,' I said, 'I'd call the police.'

'And report the break in? A bit late in the day for that, isn't it? You'll just make them suspicious.'

'It was your idea not to call them,' I said. 'Anyway, suspicious of what? *I* haven't done anything.'

'Since when has *that* got anything to do with it?' he said. 'Anyway, you know as well as I do they wouldn't be able to do anything. There's no evidence that anything's happened to her. The chances are she left the house sometime Saturday before our boy arrived. Isn't that what she said? She only wanted to stay one night?'

'Yes.'

'Then leave it to me, will you?'

I raised my glass to him. 'Sure, Charlie. You know I'm grateful for whatever you can do.'

'Good. Mine's a Bells,' he said, tossing off the first scotch. 'I take it you haven't seen Bedford yet?'

'No, but I haven't been home much today.' I told him about Fielding.

'It could be just chance,' he said.

'That's what I told him.' I got up to go back to the bar. 'And I didn't believe it then.'

When I came back with two more drinks Charlie was wearing his non-committal face, as bland as a processed cheese.

'Come on,' I said. 'It's got departmental fingerprints all over it. Have you ever heard of the Black Sea Company?'

'Hudson Bay Company,' he said, 'and East India... What about South Sea, or was that a bubble? History was never my strong point.'

'This isn't history, Charlie. This is the twenties and thirties, just before the war.'

'How old do you think I am?' Then he shrugged. 'You might be able to make out some sort of case — Soviets all round the Black Sea ... Persian oilfields ... Attaturk an unknown quantity and the Balkans swinging Hitler's way...'

'No,' I said sarcastically, 'history was never your strong point.' I clinked glasses and drank my scotch. 'But it's obvious, isn't it? Why would anyone *not* want to know what was going on in the region? And some sort of trading company with links in all the countries around there would be ideal cover—'

'Employing agents to keep their eyes open?'

'Why not?'

'Spooks?'

'Exactly.'

'A ghoul in every port?' He was grinning again.

'I'm trying to be serious,' I said. 'They didn't give up on Soviet Russia just because we withdrew from Baku.'

'Now that *is* before my time. So, what are you saying — your Zaretsky grandfather was a British agent?' He snorted scornfully.

'What's that then, something in the DNA? Evolution has predisposed you for spying?'

'Maybe not the DNA,' I said, 'but it might be in Registry.'

He gave me a sideways glance. 'You could always try the Freedom of Information Act.'

'As if that ever applied to MI5 files.'

He pulled out a handkerchief and wiped his nose. 'What have you got exactly?'

'Nothing,' I said. 'Fielding's come up with names and addresses that are dead ends and he says he can't find much on the financial side either. That would make sense if it was nothing more than cover for an operation, but if it really existed something somewhere must have survived. Either way, if it was SIS business MI5 should have picked up some sort of trace on it.'

'So what is it you want me to do?' he complained. 'You know damn well how touchy they are about us looking through their files. Besides, anything going back that far will be buried in records so deep I'll need an aqualung. Never mind the dust. What's that going to do for my asthma?'

'You don't get asthma, Charlie. Besides...' I added, deciding it was time to enlist the old soldier, 'if I hadn't been forced to retire...'

'Your choice,' he said callously. 'You could still have your feet up behind a comfortable desk if you wanted.'

'Like you? You know I've got no talent for management.'

'No, just emotional blackmail, it seems. I'm going to need a damn good excuse to go poking around in records that old. Assuming first, that there is anything to find; second that it wasn't destroyed with all the other pre-war records when the Scrubs was bombed in the war, and lastly that, if there is anything to find, it wont be above my clearance grade!'

I raised my empty glass to him. 'Now if you find *that's* the case,' I said, 'you'll know you're on to something.'

16

I have to admit to letting things slide after seeing Standing in Cambridge. I have already said that discovering what kind of man my grandfather had been had lessened my enthusiasm for learning more. Although seeing Standing again had piqued my curiosity to a certain extent, I wasn't sure I wanted to know any further details of Zaretsky's life. It was probable that a creature much like himself had denounced him and unearthing facts like that seemed to me akin to turning over a compost heap. Besides, there were a lot of excuses to do nothing to hand: the garden had run riot, there was my tax return to complete, my roof tank sprang a leak and while I had the plumber on hand I decided to replace my old boiler. I daresay if I had sat down and given it much thought I could probably have come up with a few more reasons for not following up on what I had learned from Standing — or not learned, to be more accurate. But excuses were all they were. To be honest, the steam had gone out of my curiosity. If human boilers could be renewed with the ease of their mechanical counterparts the operating theatres would be full of people on the wrong side of middle age looking for another twenty years of optimum performance. As it was I was feeling distinctly in need of refurbishment.

Standing, I realized, would have seen my interest in my father's family as just one small part of his research. He probably had several other leads to Shostak to follow up and no doubt even this man was little more than another small part of his research. My frustration at his apparent lack of progress seemed hardly fair on the man. As we all tend to do when ensnared by some fixation or other I was looking at things from my standpoint only. So instead of chivvying him along as I had resolved to do, I just put things off, confident that when he was ready he would get back to me.

The fact that I saw next to nothing of Daryna over the next few weeks helped relegate my interest in the Ukraine to the back burner. I wondered at first whether I had mortally offended her and kept replaying our last conversation over in my head. But I could remember nothing specific beyond her touchiness over my continual correction of her English. I thought that had been part of our arrangement and was surprised at what I regarded as her lack of maturity. I missed her company, I admit, and phoned her now and again, even managing to get connected on those occasions when I assumed she had enough spare cash to keep her phone active. The few times we did meet, she seemed distracted as though her mind was elsewhere. She would ask how my studies were going and I'd say, fine, knowing that she wasn't really interested enough to challenge me on the subject. She usually wanted to know if I'd been in contact with Standing again or had got the notebook back so that she might translate it, all of which made me think she was still touting for business although I was always careful not to suggest it again.

Also while the weather was good I took the opportunity to spend time at the chalet out on the Essex marshes. There was always work to be done on the place if it was to be kept water-tight and habitable and a good spell in September gave me the opportunity to paint the outside and keep on top of the endless task of replacing wood that didn't look as if it would take another winter. I didn't mind the isolation. I had a clockwork radio and my mobile and it wasn't much more than an hour's drive back to the house if I needed to pick up my mail or email. There was a large shed behind the chalet that I had helped my father build, full of drums of paraffin, timber and paint tins. There was room to keep the Alvis inside away from the salt air and also space for the dinghy my parents had sailed whenever they found the opportunity. She had got a little dilapidated over the years but whenever I had had the time, I put a few hours in on her restoration and had got her back in the water. My enthusiasm outstripped my expertise when it came to sailing, but I was good enough to sail the creeks and channels and even happy to make my way down the estuary and out to sea on a calm day if I could keep the land in sight.

I preferred to stay over — days at a time — mostly because it allowed me to get up early and watch the dawn come up over the marshes from the estuary to the east. The mornings were already beginning to get heavy with dew. The mist and the smell of the sea and the pungent aroma of mud on the air with those first rays of light were always enough to get me out of bed to tramp the creeks for an hour or two before breakfast. There was a boatyard on one of the wider channels a mile or so upriver where I could buy any timber and paint for my repairs that I didn't have to hand and there was a pub beyond the yard on the edge of the village, if I ever fancied a drink and an hour or two of conversation. Most of the time, though, I kept myself to myself and was content to do so.

The weather changed with the coming of October. After what looked to be the last decent weekend I could expect, I renewed the store of essentials I always kept to hand so that there would be no need to shop as soon I was next there and took one last walk around the place to make sure the chalet was watertight for the coming winter. Satisfied everything was in order, I locked up. It would be Spring, I assumed, before I returned.

It was almost lunchtime by the time I'd finally stowed away all my gear in the boot of the Alvis and a few miles down the road I stopped off at a pub where the food was good and the prices still reasonable.

I had just walked in, ordered a pint and picked up a menu when someone shrieked and grabbed my arm. Startled, I turned and for one head-spinning moment thought it was Jennifer beside me, the years somehow stripped away. But the hair was a mass of blonde curls, the clothes contemporary, and I belatedly realized it was Georgia, her daughter who was looking up at me.

'Alex!' she cried, 'what are *you* doing here?'

'Hello, Kat,' I said.

Another woman stood at her shoulder, slightly older than Georgia and in her mid-thirties perhaps, but dressed like Georgia in tight jeans and designer boots and a sweater with a heavy roll at the neck, as if they had spoken to one another before going out and co-ordinated their clothes.

'This is Charlotte,' she said, stepping aside slightly so that her friend could take a pace forward and offer her hand. 'Alex Maitland, my...'

She hesitated and I said, 'Cousin.'

'I was going to say sister-in-law's brother,' Georgia finished with a laugh.

'Now expired,' I said to Charlotte. 'Not me, you understand, the marriage.' I took her hand and held it a moment. 'Pleased to meet you.'

She was dark with bright eyes, vivacious rather than pretty with a wide mouth that had begun to play with a smile.

'I thought I knew the family,' Charlotte said, 'but Georgie's never mentioned you, Alex.'

'I'm the one they don't talk about,' I whispered to her theatrically.

'Alex!' Georgia said again and gave me a playful nudge on the arm. 'Are you stopping for lunch?'

I said I was and when they invited me to join them told them to find a table while I bought the drinks. They took one on the other side of the room by a large window that overlooked the creek.

It had been some while since I had seen Georgia, around the time of Olena's divorce, I suppose, and recalled she had been engaged herself then. There had been no marriage — at least, not one to which I had been invited — and I wondered whether I ought to bring the subject up. She was very like Jennifer, I realized, unnervingly so, and I wondered why I had never noticed the fact before. She was the youngest of the three children and was usually known as Kat, a childhood nickname. She was now thirty-one, or two — keeping up with family birthdays had never been my strong suit. When she was a little younger Georgia had always had a penchant for the wilder end of contemporary fashion which contrasted heavily with the simple clothes that Jennifer had always favoured. Now, dressed as Jennifer might have done at her age, I saw that the resemblance was uncanny.

I took our drinks over to the table, almost colliding with a waiter who had turned up. He glanced at me, dressed as I was in creased trousers and thick check shirt and rumpled jacket, assuming I was not one of their party. After an exchange of apologies he took our lunch order.

Georgia gaped at me as I sat down. 'You look...' Words failed her.

'Windblown?' Charlotte suggested.

I glanced down. There were splashes of creosote and paint on my clothes.

'Tanned and healthy, I was going to say,' Georgia decided.

I beamed at them. 'I've been doing a bit of sailing,' I explained. 'But what are you doing here, Kat? It's a little bit out of your orbit, isn't it?'

They exchanged a meaningful look and she said, 'We've been to see a property we're thinking of buying a couple of miles away.'

I must have looked askance at them because they glanced at each other again and burst out laughing.

'Really, Mr Maitland!' Charlotte said with mock affront. 'What *are* you thinking?'

I joined in the laughter. 'Absolutely nothing,' I assured her. 'My mind runs along far more sedate lines these days.'

'There's a big old house up for auction next week,' Georgia said, 'just ripe for redevelopment. We're going after it.'

'Redevelopment? Has George got his fingers in another pie now?'

'No,' she said. 'For us. We've just finished our first development and we're looking for another.'

'Property development? I thought you were in company law?'

She pulled a face. 'I couldn't stand it any longer, Alex. When Charlie suggested we try something different —'

'Charlie?'

Charlotte's eyes glittered. 'Me,' she said.

'I met Charlie through Jeremy,' Georgia said.

'Isn't he your—'

'*Was*n't he my fiancé,' she amended.

That solved that problem, I thought. She told me how she had woken up one morning and suddenly decided that she couldn't face finding Jeremy there everyday of the rest of her life and broke off the engagement. It had been a long-term relationship but within three months, she said, he had married someone else. Her mother had confessed to being relieved. A narrow escape from another unwanted in-law, I thought. Then we chatted about George and his recent move and Nick's prospects in the next election until our food arrived. I kept catching Charlotte's eye, as if she were watching me while I talked to Georgia. She contributed a remark now and then although, more often or not, there was a barbed edge to it as if her default response was to tease. They told me about the house in north London they had developed together, and the mistakes and near disasters and how despite it they looked to be coming out with a small profit. They were hoping the next project would be a step up, a large waterfront property that needed completely gutting. It crossed my mind that George might be putting the money up — he had always been indulgent where his children were concerned — and I would have liked to ask but could find no way of framing the question without it sounding crass. We had almost finished eating when Georgia asked after Olena.

'I haven't seen a lot of her,' I admitted. 'We speak on the phone now and again.'

'Tell her to phone me, Alex, please. I know it's awkward but I still want us to be friends.'

'I'm sure Olena does, too,' I said, wondering why it might be awkward since the divorce had been amicable as far as I was aware. 'As a matter of fact,' I told her, 'I had lunch with her back in the summer and Nick was there. It was as if nothing had happened.'

Charlotte laughed as if what I had said had been funny but when I turned to her to see if she was going to share the joke she merely looked at me squarely and raised her eyebrows. I had no idea what that was supposed to imply but it prompted me to ask Georgia:

'Is he seeing anyone at the moment, do you know?'

Her eyes darted at Charlotte and I thought she was going to evade my question, but she gave a small shrug and said, 'A friend saw him with someone a week or so ago. They were in some out-of-the-way place as if they didn't want to be seen. He told me he went up to say hello and apparently thought they were both a bit put out.'

'You know what politicians are like,' I said, making a joke out of it, although Charlotte didn't seem to find this as funny and I wondered if there might have once been something between her and Nick. She just stared back at me, a little vacuously I thought.

'I wondered if she might be married,' Georgia said. 'Has Olena said anything?'

'No, nothing.'

We ordered coffee and, as casually as I could, I asked Georgia if she remembered much about her grandfather.

'Granddad Frederick, you mean?' she asked, a little startled. 'Yes of course I do.'

'Who's this?' Charlotte asked.

'Dad's father. Fredrick Maitland.'

Charlotte turned to me questioningly. 'Wasn't he your grandfather, too?'

'No.' I explained how Georgia's father and my father were half-brothers. 'I never actually met him.'

'Didn't you? Georgia said, obviously surprised. 'How odd.'

'There'd been some sort of rift between him and my father,' I explained. 'They never spoke after the war.'

'I knew uncle Peter never came to family gatherings but I thought that was because of Grandma Elizabeth.'

'Why was that?'

'I understood that your dad had objected to Frederick marrying again after his mother was killed.'

'Who did you hear that from?'

She looked from Charlotte to me, wide-eyed. 'I've no idea,' she said.

'George or Jennifer?'

'I don't think so. Perhaps it was Grandma herself. Why don't you ask Dad?'

'Olena told me she didn't like Frederick,' I said.

'He always smelt of tobacco,' Georgia said, as if that might have been grounds for dislike.

'You never found him repulsive, though?'

'Repulsive?' she repeated and laughed. There seemed something forced about it. I felt she was suddenly uncomfortable.

'That's what Olena said.'

'Well,' she said, 'you know your sister.'

'He was just Granddad, then,' I said.

'I wasn't very old,' Georgia reminded me. 'He would make me sit on his knee which I didn't like much, I admit. It was Granddad who started calling me Kat.'

'Was it? I always thought it was some baby name George came up with.'

She pulled a face at *baby name*. 'It's Russian,' she said. 'Kartli... something. *Kakheti*, something like that. The old Russian name for Georgia, apparently.'

'Where did Frederick get that from?'

She shrugged. 'He often used to talk to me in Russian,' she said. 'Pretending he couldn't understand me just to tease.'

'He spoke Russian?'

'I thought you knew. He'd been there before the war, or something.' She began looking around the room in a distracted fashion.

I was surprised that nobody had ever mentioned this before and it must have showed in my face because Charlotte said:

'Family secrets?'

Georgia turned to her sharply. 'Don't be ridiculous, Charlie!'

Charlotte looked stung and to cover the awkward moment I said:

'Nick told me he didn't care much for him, either.'

'Oh?' She was now obviously uncomfortable with the whole subject and shrugged it off with a slight movement of her body as if she regarded that as Nick's problem. 'I was a girl. Perhaps he treated me differently.'

'If he was anything like the rest of the male members of your family then he definitely preferred girls,' Charlotte put in having recovered her equilibrium.

I half-expected Georgia to round on her again but she seemed relaxed about this comment and merely said, 'You're just thinking of Ollie and Nick,' although I couldn't help feeling that the retort was not without some point.

I knew that her brother Oliver had acquired a reputation as something of a womaniser but I hadn't known Nick was regarded in the same fashion. I wondered if I'd been kept in the dark because he had been my sister's husband.

'And certainly not Dad,' Georgia made clear.

This time I couldn't mistake the meaningful look I got from Charlotte. It plainly said I must know different. I was taken aback. I had never heard that sort of rumour concerning George before and was sure that if there had been any I would have been first on Olena's list of recipients for the gossip.

'What about you, Alex?' Charlotte asked pointedly, catching me on the back foot. 'Do you come with a reputation? Should a girl be worried?'

But before I could reply, Georgia laughed and said:

'I don't think you have to worry about Alex on that score. Steady as a rock is how Daddy always describes him.'

'Is it?' I said, somehow not particularly flattered.

'So steady you've never even managed to find a wife,' she added.

As soon as it was said it crossed my mind that Georgia might be aware of how I had felt about her mother and I listened to catch a trace of any contempt that might be in her voice. But I didn't find one and put the statement down as nothing more than an unthinking cruelty on her part. It was the kind of thing her brother, Oliver, was often guilty of.

'I find that hard to believe,' Charlotte said coquettishly. 'Perhaps you haven't been trying, Alex.'

'Perhaps,' I said, not wanting to encourage this turn in the conversation.

'Time's running out, Alex,' Georgia chimed in, teasing.

'Rubbish,' Charlotte insisted. 'He looks to be in his prime.'

It was the sort of remark that would once have embarrassed me. Now I just found it tedious.

'That's just the wind-blown effect,' I told her.

I felt an obligation to offer to pay the bill and we argued over it briefly. As soon as Charlotte conceded the point Georgia gave in too. While I settled up they went off to the ladies. I was still thinking about Frederick being able to speak Russian and the possibility that he might have been there between the wars when they came back. I stood up, smiling as they approached. Charlotte's eyes caught mine for the briefest of moments before she quickly looked away and began fussing with her handbag. Outside, I gave Georgia a peck on the cheek and said how nice it had been to see her again, then held out my hand to Charlotte. She took it and gave me an automatic smile and said, 'Nice to meet you.' She turned away and I raised my eyebrows and grinned at Georgia.

''bye, Kat,' I said.

Flustered, Georgia waved goodbye and skipped a couple of paces to catch up with Charlotte. I watched them to their car, knowing exactly what had happened. Charlotte had asked about me and Georgia had said that I had no claim on the Maitland money. End of any possible interest. At least, I thought as I walked back to the Alvis, those on the outside always knew where they stood.

~

The fact that Frederick might have been in Russia before the war threatened to shed a whole new light on what I thought I had known. If he had been in Russia, I thought, why not "Little Russia" — the Ukraine?

I got home, unloaded the Alvis then garaged it in the lock-up I rented up the road. I stuffed the washing I had accumulated on this last trip to the chalet in the machine, turned it on then booted up the laptop.

I had never Googled the Maitland name; after all, why bother? I thought I had known all there was to know about my family. In fact there was more information than I could have imagined. Once I had sorted out the extraneous Maitlands from those to whom I was connected, I discovered that Georgia and her friend, Charlotte, had a website devoted to their property development business. Nick, too, had his own site, promoting his image as an MP and the work he maintained he was doing on behalf of his constituents. Even Olena had a couple of pages on social networking sites, revealing a computer literacy I had never suspected. The only Maitland absent was myself. And I was not even conspicuous by my absence. But then secrecy had become endemic, my refuge of first resort without even having to think about it.

It was George, though, and his business interests that figured most prominently. But cutting through the various sites and pages of company PR to factual history left me with slimmer pickings. There was an entry on Wikipedia that lacked citations and I was mildly surprised that no one among George or Oliver's PR team had thought it worth their while to employ a biographer for them. I did find a brief biographical sketch of George that mentioned Frederick in passing — how he had founded the family firm before the war without going into any detail — but nothing of any real note. In fact, chasing down Frederick in particular brought forth nothing except the endowment of his Cambridge scholarship and then, beyond mentioning him as the benefactor by name, dealt only with the bursary itself and how to apply. I tried a few other avenues but, after an hour, I decided the Internet didn't hold what I wanted. I went back to the sites dealing with George's companies and, taking the names of the firms they had subsumed, worked backwards to the original companies and particular commercial interests they held. There were phone numbers listed for various offices and I began ringing them in an attempt to blag my way to some archivist or even a company secretary who might be able to point me in the right direction. My cover was as an undergraduate doing his thesis on the origins of the modern multi-national, but it didn't get me far. Either they were busy, I wasn't persuasive enough, or the age of my voice gave me away. I tried passing myself off as an adult student but I was invariably pointed towards Company House and Registrations. I gave up, feeling deflated.

I listened to the washing machine in the last throes of its cycle and wondered if Michael Standing might be interested in what I had discovered, fragmentary though it was. Then it occurred to me that I had no way of contacting him. He had rung me on each occasion we met and had never given me his number; I had never thought to ask for it. I could have emailed David Griffiths with my suspicions, but that meant booting up my laptop again and, besides, what did I have? My father's stepfather spoke Russian and had probably visited the country. Nothing more. Of course, it might be that he had met Nastasiya in the Ukraine and not after she had got to England as I had always supposed. But there was no way of proving that unless someone knew it to be a fact and the only person who might know would be George. But even if he didn't, I assumed that he'd at least know the date of their marriage. The earlier that had occurred, the more likely it was that they had been acquainted before she left the Ukraine.

I decided to see if I could finally pin George down and take a look at any papers he might have dating back to that time. Although I had given Standing his London number the first time we had met, Standing had never actually said whether or not he had followed up on it. Nick had been vague on the subject and I couldn't remember, when I last saw him back in the early summer, whether or not he had said he had spoken to Standing. So, in the event, I decided not to bother Griffiths until I had more information.

In retrospect it seemed like a mistake. A month later Standing was dead.

17

After having a drink with Charlie I returned to the house and got my new laptop up and running without mishap. I logged on to my email and found a fresh crop of rubbish but nothing new of interest since I had last looked on Friday before my weekend away.

All my old emails had been downloaded from the server and lost with the stolen machine, but the server still had my address book and contacts and since I had replied to Griffiths' original enquiry I was still able to email him:

Dear Mr. Griffiths,
I was shocked to hear of Michael Standing's death and although I only met him on three occasions I had grown to like him. I wasn't going to bother you at present as you must have a lot on your plate but at some point I was hoping I might be able to retrieve the material I gave to Standing concerning my grandmother, Nastasiya Zaretsky. If you are thinking of continuing with the work, however, you must of course keep it as long as it might be useful.

What has prompted this email is that today I was approached by a journalist named Fielding who said you had given him my telephone number. He told me some rather interesting things and I was hoping that it might be possible to talk them over with you. If this is the case, please email or call (you apparently have my number) and perhaps we can arrange to meet.

What also may or may not be relevant is that my house was broken into over the weekend. My laptop was stolen as well as some letters my father wrote his mother as a boy and the translation from the Ukrainian I have since made of these. Standing saw them when he visited me and decided they were of no relevance to your research although, as they were hand-written in Ukrainian Cyrillic, he wasn't actually able to read them thoroughly. After seeing him I employed someone to translate them for me although in the event they proved to be nothing more than one might expect of letters from a schoolboy to his mother. I have no idea why anyone would want to steal them but thought it might be worth mentioning.

Regards, Alex Maitland.

I read it over, found it a little long-winded but sent it anyway.

It then occurred to me that before translating the letters, Daryna had first copied them out in Ukrainian to make the job easier. The copies, written on sheets of A4, had been sculling around on my tabletop for months until a fit of conscience the previous week over my lax housekeeping had prompted me to dump anything I no longer needed in a bin I kept in the shed for recycled paper. The household collection wasn't due until the next day and while the intruder had apparently made a thorough search of the house I knew he hadn't bothered to investigate the garden shed. I had found the padlock on the door intact when I had fetched the boards to repair my French windows. I left the laptop running, put my coat on and picked up a torch and trudged down the garden to the shed. The night was cold, the sky having cleared although no stars were visible above the city's light haze. In the shed I rooted through the bin and found the crumpled copies of the letters that Daryna had made.

Back inside I examined the strange script, now able to make out the odd word. Not enough to make any sense of the whole but perhaps a place to make a start. I pencilled in the English for the words I understood, struck how the lines of Cyrillic flowed so neatly in Daryna's hand and how it reminded me of that rapt expression she had worn, concentrating on her task with her tongue licking at her lips as she had tried to decipher my father's handwriting. I felt a sudden pang, a mixture of guilt and affection and what I hoped wasn't loss.

Back at my new laptop, I found a reply from Griffiths already waiting:

Alex,

I had planned to get in touch. Mike's death was an appalling shock. Everything is on hold at the moment. TV series is in the balance until decision about new presenter is made. Maseryk's name has been mentioned, although he will have his own ideas and research material and won't need me. My thinking is they'll cancel altogether. Have all the material that Mike and I gathered and I can give you your papers back as soon as you like. Had difficulty with some of it and not too sure of relevance though Mike thought it good. If you've no objections I'll keep copies along with all other research as I may decide to use it at some future date. Can't bear the thought of all that work wasted! If you're free this Wednesday 9th could meet at your convenience. You heard I suppose they arrested some homeless man for killing Mike? I had the police round today again after a DNA swab so there seems some doubt still.

Sorry to hear about your break-in. You don't think it has anything to do with Mike's death, do you? — David.

It was interesting to see that a television series had been on the cards and that Griffiths wasn't as evasive as Standing had been about the fact. But then, Griffiths wasn't expected to front it.

He had included his phone number so I emailed back straight away to say I could drive up to Cambridge on Wednesday morning and give him a call when I arrived. I had no sooner sent this, though, than he replied again, giving me his address and some directions on getting there. Anytime Wednesday morning would be fine with him, he said.

I replied a second time to confirm and had just turned off the machine when the doorbell rang. It was gone nine and I wasn't expecting anyone. Except perhaps Daryna. I peeked through the gap in the curtains in my bay window to see who was on the doorstep. The light from the street lamp across the road gave an unhealthy orange cast like a cheap bottle tan to DI Bedford and DS Graham as they waited.

'DNA swabs,' I said, letting them in.

Graham eyed me suspiciously, assuming, I supposed, that I must be guilty of something even if he couldn't quite decide what it was. Then he said:

'Have you had an accident, Mr Maitland?'

'I'm sorry? Oh, the plaster... I banged my head on the weekend. A few stitches, that's all. As a matter of fact,' I explained, 'I've just exchanged emails with David Griffiths. He said you'd taken a swab from him so I assumed you'd be after me for one as well.'

'That's exactly what we'd like,' Bedford said. 'If you've no objections.'

'None at all,' I said breezily.

'We came round earlier,' Bedford said as Graham took the kit out of the bag he was carrying and laid it out on the dining room table. I had a sudden urge to tell them about the break-in, but even if I kept Daryna out of it I couldn't think of any reasonable explanation for waiting a full day before reporting the crime. Fortunately I had drawn the drapes across the broken French windows because Bedford's gaze wandered around the room while Graham prepared the swab. Then, as if he had learned his conversational timing from a dentist, as soon as Graham had inserted the swab into my mouth he asked:

'Would you mind telling me why Mr Griffiths has been in contact with you, Mr Maitland?'

I gurgled at him until Graham had finished.

'Actually,' I said, wiping a dribble of saliva off my chin, 'I was the one who contacted him.'

Graham bagged the swab and put his kit away.

'I asked him if I could have the papers I'd given Standing back now that...' I dried up, not wanting to finish that particular sentence. 'He says the production company may cancel the project without Standing, although there's some talk of Edward Maseryk taking over.'

Bedford raised his eyebrows like a policeman who'd just tripped over a motive.

'Anyway,' I said, 'I'm driving up to Cambridge to see Griffiths tomorrow. You've no objection, I suppose?'

His sallow features hardened perceptibly. 'Why would I object?'

'Collusion of suspects?' I suggested. It was meant to be a light-hearted riposte but, once said, the remark gained weight and promptly fell flat on its face.

'While we're here, Mr Maitland,' Graham said, filling what Bedford had turned into an ominous silence, 'could we just clear up exactly when and where it was that you and Mr Standing met?'

I went through it again for them, beginning with Griffiths' original email and almost making the mistake of offering to show it to them before I remembered it was gone along with my old laptop. Bedford might have caught a note of hesitation in my voice because he said:

'I'd be interested to see that.'

'Sorry,' I said, 'but it was on my old machine and - '

'Yes,' he said, 'I noticed you'd got a new laptop.'

His eyes were suddenly boring holes in mine and it was all I could do to hold his gaze.

'It was time for an update,' I said as levelly as I could manage.

'What did you do with your old machine?'

'It was pretty obsolete,' I said, 'so I junked it.'

'Pity.' Then he gave me the briefest of smiles, moving the corners of his mouth a millimetre or two. 'They recondition old machines for African schools. Did you know that?'

'No,' I said. 'I could have donated it.'

He didn't say anything more so I went back to describing Standing's initial visit, realizing as I did so that the first time they'd interviewed me I hadn't told them in any detail about our lunch in the early summer or about the seminar I had attended in Cambridge. But then, they hadn't asked. Now I went through it all with them giving as much detail as I could remember. Graham tried to keep up with his notes and skewered me now and then with his pale blue eyes before asking for some corroboration, like the name of the hotel in Cambridge and the time of day. As Daryna had been with us at the Mill House Hotel, I tried to concentrate on the restaurant where Standing and I had first lunched together. I suggested that the maître d' might recall me as he had undoubtedly known Standing and had taken the trouble to show me to my seat.

Graham smiled although, as only his mouth seemed really engaged in the expression, for one disconcerting minute he suddenly resembled a ventriloquist's dummy.

'Perhaps not,' he said. 'It was one of Mr Standing's favourite haunts and he often ate there with guests, apparently.'

I glanced at Bedford, hoping to catch his lips moving, and thinking, *why ask?* But he was trying to unsettle me, of course - the first rule of interrogation.

'And you maintain you have never met Mrs Standing,' Graham went on.

'It's hardly a matter of having to *maintain* it,' I replied frostily, giving way to irritation over the manner in which he had phrased the question and beginning to get just as unsettled as I suppose they wanted. But the implication had been that my having met her was still open to question. 'I have never met Julia Standing in my life,' I said. 'As it happens, Standing was expecting her at the hotel in Cambridge where he was staying while speaking at the seminar although she never turned up. Not while I was with him anyway.' I returned Graham's dummy's smile. 'Perhaps I passed her on the motorway and caught a glimpse of her without realizing it.'

But that was just so much water off Graham's back. 'Just double-checking our notes,' he said amiably.

'What about the vagrant?' I asked. 'I thought you'd arrested somebody?'

'We're holding a man but still continuing our enquiries.'

Bedford stepped towards my mantelpiece and peered at the photographs that Graham had examined on their first visit.

'Wasn't he caught using Standing's credit cards?' I persisted.

'How did you know that?' he asked.

Charlie had told me.

'It was in one of the newspapers, I think,' I said evenly. Then felt guilty about trying to implicate the tramp.

Bedford picked up the photo of Olena. 'Had your sister ever met Mr Standing to your knowledge?'

'No,' I said, wondering what he was getting at now. I thought about adding that her ex-husband had been at university with him then kept my mouth shut. There was no point in dragging Nick into it. It would only sound as if I was desperate to shift suspicion in any direction I could — first a tramp, then an MP.

'When Mr Standing called you to make the appointment the day before he died...' Graham persisted.

'Four days before he died,' I said, getting tired of repeating myself. 'And as I told you, it wasn't Standing. It was a woman. His secretary, I assumed.'

'Mr Standing didn't employ a secretary.'

'Oh?' I replied testily. 'You didn't tell me that the last time you were here. It was a woman's voice and not being privy to his clerical arrangements I assumed it was his secretary. Perhaps it was his wife. Have you asked her?'

'She says not,' Bedford said, 'but we're checking the phone records.'

'You did tell me that.'

They exchanged glances as if my being rattled was of some significance.

'Do you recall the time of day you received the call?' Bedford asked.

'No.'

'Well, easy enough to check if it was made from Standing's house,' he said. 'You're retired, aren't you Mr Maitland?'

'That's right.'

His face softened although the expression didn't fit well on features as lean as his. It just made him look ill.

'If you don't mind my saying so,' he said, 'you don't look old enough to have reached retirement age.'

'I don't mind you saying so in the least, Inspector,' I told him. 'The fact is I took early retirement on medical grounds.'

He turned to Graham again and I expected some double-act repartee on how healthy I looked. Instead they performed a variation on the routine of the absent-minded policeman. 'Did we ask Mr Maitland what it was he did for a living, Sergeant?'

'I don't believe we did, sir' Graham replied, making a play of going back through his notes.

'I was a civil servant,' I told them, not wanting to miss my cue.

'May I ask in what capacity?'

'Trade and Industry,' I said, just to ring the changes. 'I was abroad a lot. My office was charged with trying to drum up overseas business.'

'Interesting work?'

'It kept me busy.'

They were going to look into my background, of course, if they hadn't already done so. I supposed it would be a bellwether on how interested in me they were, whether what they found would be taken at face value or whether it would make them even more suspicious. And of course, the more suspicious they became, the less they'd be able to find out. Sooner or later they'd come up against the need for security clearance. It was the kind of vicious circle that only total frankness could breach, and frankness of that calibre was something with which I was out of practise.

'This famine you mentioned,' Graham asked unexpectedly. 'When we were here before, if you recall, sir. Was there a connection with your father that particularly interested Mr Standing?'

The way Bedford turned to his partner suggested that he had found the question as unexpected as I had.

'He was more interested in documentation,' I told him. 'Anything relating to that time that I might have. There were a few papers that my grandmother had brought with her in nineteen-thirty-two when she and my father came to England. Nothing of value, just personal items. But that was his style, you see.'

'His style?'

'Yes, not so much in his books, I think, but in his television programmes.'

Graham looked perplexed.

I attempted to explain, and not for the first time, I recalled.

'Standing liked to illustrate historical events by using incidents in the lives of real people. It made his work more accessible. At least, I suppose he thought it did.'

'More marketable,' Graham said.

'Less dry,' I compromised.

'Was he going to use the story of your grandmother and father?' Graham asked.

'I've no idea. He never said. He was certainly interested in my grandfather, so he might have given them a mention to illustrate how desperate people were. How willing to leave their homes if the alternative was to stay and starve, that is.'

I looked from one to the other to see if they had understood, wondering if they could tell that personally I didn't believe a word of it. Staying and starving apparently hadn't been the case with my grandparents. As the family of a Party member, Nastasiya and my father would not have gone hungry. Besides, there were countless other stories Standing could have used to illustrate the starvation of the population — many of them well documented. His interest in my family had stemmed from some motivation other than that of peasants fleeing the starvation.

Tweedledum and Tweedledee looked back at me as if they were expecting more. But at that moment I didn't have any more so I changed the subject.

'Any new leads?' I asked.

'There are one or two matters we're looking into,' Bedford replied unhelpfully.

'What about his movements after he left the television studio? Have you managed to find out where he was? What was it, about ninety minutes, you said?'

'Yes,' Bedford confirmed. 'You've a good memory for details, Mr Maitland.'

'It was my work,' I said. 'Always a lot of facts to assimilate. I expect you find the same thing.'

'That's why Sergeant Graham takes notes, isn't it Graham?'

'Yes sir,' Graham replied tonelessly.

It was a joke of sorts but not much better than any of mine had been. They exchanged one more glance then turned back to me.

'Thank you for your co-operation, sir,' Bedford said.

'Not a problem,' I assured him, though I wasn't sure any of us believed it. 'If there's anything else I can do?'

'I'll be in touch if we think of anything.'

I stood on the step and watched as they walked to their car. They had just opened the doors when Daryna turned the corner and passed under a streetlight heading towards the house. She saw Bedford and Graham, took in me at the door, then put her head down and continued past, picking up her pace as if suddenly remembering she was late for an appointment. Graham had climbed behind the wheel of the car but Bedford stood, looking back over the roof at Daryna's receding figure as she hurried down the street. He threw a speculative glance at me again before ducking into the car.

I would have called out to her but they hadn't started the car and was afraid that they might hear. I stood a moment longer until Daryna had turned the next corner and Graham had finally started the engine. He turned on the lights and swung out into the street.

I waited at the door for a minute or two, half-expecting her to circle the block and come back. Then I thought that Bedford might just do the same. For no good reason, I found myself inventing excuses for her being there — *she comes in to do my cleaning, Inspector ... she's a distant cousin visiting from the Ukraine ... Actually I'm interviewing for a secretary* — but none seemed any more plausible than the truth which, predictably, I didn't even consider. Then I wondered what reason there could be why a young woman shouldn't be able to call on me at ten o'clock in the evening without arousing suspicion? But I didn't really have to pose the question: some circumstances naturally invite an inference and the epithet *old goat* sprang unpleasantly to mind.

I was still indulging in mental self-flagellation when the phone rang behind me. I shut the door and picked it up.

'Alex,' she said. 'It is me, Daryna.'

'I know it's you,' I said. 'I saw you. Where the hell have you been?'

'Those men by the car—'

'That was the police. Don't worry; they're not looking for you. It was about Michael Standing again. They wanted to ask me some more questions.'

'Did they come for break-in?'

'No, I haven't reported it.' There was a pause so I went on, 'They've gone now so you can come back. But wait ten minutes, to be on the safe side.'

'Which is safe side?' she asked.

'Just wait ten minutes and come back,' I said. 'I'll leave the door unlatched.'

211

'This is not necessary,' she said. 'I have key.'

She looked wan and although it had only been four days since I had seen her last, somehow thinner. Dark arcs had settled beneath her eyes and her hair appeared dull and uncombed. She was dressed in jeans, sweater and a jacket, and was carrying a handbag. There was grime smeared on the jeans and the jacket was creased and threadbare at the elbows.

'You look as if you've been sleeping rough,' I said.

'From where comes "rough"?' she asked, ever the etymologist.

I had taken off my sticking plaster, tired of alarming people, but the stitched skin didn't look very pretty either. If Daryna noticed it though, she didn't mention it.

'You were here when they broke into the house?' I asked.

'No.'

'But you knew I'd had a break-in,' I said.

She blinked at me hesitantly.

'Saturday I go out,' she explained. 'In afternoon I go to visit a friend.' She darted a wary glance at me and added quickly, 'Not pig of boyfriend. Girl I know. I am coming back maybe nine o'clock. I am walking up road and I see a man letting himself out of your door.'

'Did you see his face?'

'No. Too dark and he wear a...' she waggled her fingers by the side of her head, 'wool hat ... like ski hat.'

'A ski mask?'

She scowled at me impatiently. 'No, not mask. *Hat*. I say hat. It covers much of his face and is too dark.'

'Was he young? Old? A beard—'

'No, no hair. Young. My age but not pretty.'

I smiled at her presumption.

'You think this is matter to laugh over?'

'Sorry,' I said. 'He was ugly, then. Did he get into a car?'

'No, he walk towards me.' She became animated. 'I feel I should run but I know this will make him chase me. I walk past like I am ... a person walking out in evening.'

'What did he do?'

'He look at me as we pass. I carry on to corner, then I wait.'

'And you didn't get a good look at him as you passed?' I said.

'I told you. I didn't look. No contact with eyes.'

'What did you do then?'

'When I am sure he is gone I go back to this house and let myself in with key. Back door is broken with glass on floor. Upstairs, your room is searched. *My* bag is searched. Everything has been pulled onto bed. So, I think maybe police will come or maybe ugly man comes back. So I put things in bag and leave quickly.'

'You should have come to me as soon as I got back on Sunday,' I said. 'I've been worried about you.'

'Who is ugly man, Alex? Why does he break into door and search your house?'

'I wish I knew,' I said.

We had moved to the kitchen and Daryna was sitting at the table while I made a pot of tea. She had her elbows on the table and held her head in her hands as if the weight of it was too much for her to carry any longer. She looked exhausted and as if she might fall asleep at any minute. I poured the tea and sat opposite her.

'Where have you been sleeping? At your friend's? Where's your suitcase?'

'In locker at coach station. I sleep on seats and in cinema.'

'Are you hungry?'

'No. I eat in café.'

'Drink your tea and go bed,' I said. 'We can pick up your suitcase in the morning after you've had a good rest. I've got some clean clothes you can wear if you need them.'

She gave me an odd look over the top of her mug as if wondering why I would have clean women's clothes in the house. But she didn't seem to have the energy to ask. She'd find out soon enough anyway that they weren't women's clothes.

She finished her tea, picked up her handbag and pulled herself up the stairs. I heard her in the bathroom for a few minutes before the door to her bedroom closed. I poured what was left in the teapot into my mug and wondered why a man who broke in through the French windows would let himself out through the front door. Then I tried to think of all the ugly men of Daryna's age I knew. Only one name kept springing to mind and I didn't exactly know him so wasn't in any position to judge how ugly he might be. If he resembled his father, though, George's man Patterson, he wasn't going to be any oil painting

~

She slept late and it was almost eleven before I heard her moving around in the bathroom. I made some tea and was pouring it when she walked into the kitchen draped only in a large bath towel. I gripped the pot tighter and only splashed a little tea over the tabletop.

'You have clothes?' she asked.

She had washed her hair and it hung in wet rattails around her head. It was the first time I had seen her without makeup and she looked oddly naked — bath towel aside — and somehow younger than I had expected. She stopped in front of me, barefoot and with her right hand clasping the towel at her breast.

'I've made some tea,' I said, stating the obvious. The only other thing in my head at that moment was better left unsaid.

'I wash my clothes,' she announced. 'They are dirty. Now I have nothing.'

'So I see. I'll see what I can find.'

I edged past her like someone trying to avoid a contagion and climbed the stairs. She followed a moment later carrying her mug of tea. I began sorting through clothes that I no longer wore and which by some sort of centripetal force had left my orbit and migrated to the cupboard on the landing. Through the open bathroom door I saw the clothes Daryna had been wearing the previous evening hanging on a line and dripping water into the tub, a blouse and jeans and her underwear.

'You could have used the washing machine,' I said, pulling out a shirt and a pair of Levis I had stopped wearing when I'd turned fifty. I passed them to her and she let go of the towel for a second before grabbing it again quickly as it began to slip.

'I'll leave you to it,' I suggested. 'Use anything you want. I'll make a start on breakfast. There's an ironing board in the spare room if you need it.' I left her on the landing, the shirt and Levis a crumpled heap by her bare feet.

Half an hour later she came down again. Her hair had dried and she had put on a little makeup. She was wearing one of my white shirts, belted at her waist over a pair of pinstripe suit trousers I hadn't worn since I had given up going to the office. The long shirttails hung down to her thighs disguising the bagginess in the seat of the pants. She had ironed a sharp crease into them and even found some pins to turn the cuffs up so that they didn't drag on the floor. Needless to say, she looked better in the clothes than I ever had.

She held her arms out from her side and looked down at herself and then at me.

'You look wonderful,' I said.

She smiled in that way of hers that never quite managed to banish her sullen pout.

'You are very nice man, Alex.'

'Eat your breakfast before it gets cold,' I said.

I called Charlie Hewson to let him know that Daryna had turned up unharmed. He didn't sound surprised.

'Do you believe her story?' he asked.

'Of course. She was scared half to death.'

'They give awards for that sort of thing.'

'You're a cynic, Charlie. How many people have we debriefed together? Don't you think I know when someone's lying to me?'

'As I recall,' he said, 'not too many of them had a pretty pout.'

'You think?' I said. 'Water off a duck's back to me.'

'Ever thought that all that water's made you rusty?'

I had, but that wasn't the time to tell him.

'Come and talk to her yourself if you like.'

'You know how I always scare children,' he said.

'She's not *that* young.'

'Relative to what?'

I told him that Bedford and Graham had been back and taken a DNA sample.

'I wish you hadn't got mixed up in all this.'

'Me too,' I said. 'But what can you do? Anything on the Black Sea Company?'

There was a pause. 'Not yet. Things have been a bit hectic around here so I haven't had the chance to go snooping through all our yesterdays.'

'When you can, Charlie.'

'Meaning ASAP.'

'Never put off ... as they say.'

He rang off with an expletive and I saw Daryna watching from the doorway into the kitchen.

'You smile again,' she said as if it were a crime. 'What is funny?'

'A friend,' I said. 'He's looking into something for me.'

'About man who breaks in?'

215

'In a roundabout way,' I said. 'He stole my laptop and the letters you translated. When you saw him leaving the house, do you remember if he was carrying anything?'

She froze in contemplation, a picture of concentration, the fingers of one hand caught in the act of combing through her hair. She held her head on one side, a frown creasing her brow.

'Yes, he was carrying something under his arm. Something black.'

'Like a laptop computer,' I said.

'Sorry, Alex. I do not remember before when I tell you. I look very quickly at him. No more.'

'It doesn't matter,' I assured her. 'You couldn't do anything about it.'

'But he stole your father's letters? This is too much, Alex.'

'True,' I said, 'but it means I'll need you to translate them again, I'm afraid.'

'You still have?' she asked in surprise.

'I've got the pages on which you copied the Ukrainian out. It won't take as long this time.'

'I thought you had thrown away.'

'Only into the shed. Just as well, otherwise he might have taken them, too.'

'But why he take them? They are only letters of boy at school to his mother.'

I gave her the benefit of a fatherly smile.

'That's what I'm going to find out,' I said.

18

Standing had never told me where he lived. Although the general area, even the name of the street, had been all over the media for days, they had been meticulous about not identifying the house itself. But it would have been difficult to miss the large number *thirty-four* on the portico above the front door from the numerous photographs splashed across the newspapers. I might have considered telephoning his wife before I arrived, except for the fact that I didn't have her number and that she wasn't going to want to talk to me anyway. I didn't want to give her any excuse to be out when I called. There was no guarantee, of course, that she would either be in when I did or, if she was, that she wouldn't slam the door in my face. But that was a chance I had to take.

I had told Daryna not to answer the door if anyone called. I wasn't worried about a second break-in and I doubted that Bedford would be back until after they had got the results of their DNA tests but one can never be sure about the police. I told her that I was going to do some shopping, stocking up on supplies if she was going to be staying. That was all she really needed to know.

I found Standing's house easily enough. It was only a few streets from where Nick and Olena had lived — where Olena still lived — and although there wasn't much to choose between the two houses from the outside, Standing's place didn't quite smell of the same amounts of money that Olena was currently wallowing in. That wasn't to say he hadn't done very nicely for himself. It wasn't a bad house for someone on an academic's salary although I assumed his books and television work had taken up the slack in his income. Walking up the few steps from the street to his front door, it made me wonder how hard financially his demise was going to hit his wife. Perhaps she was already comfortable and it wouldn't matter; if what Charlie had hinted at were true, she had already been stoking other fires before her main boiler had been extinguished.

I rang the bell and waited, assuming my most trustworthy look and taking a step back so I was foursquare at eye-level in front of the spy-hole in the door. I was aiming for a vague incarnation of my military policeman persona, although without the incipient threat of looking as if I was about to crack any recalcitrant skulls. I thought it might get me in the door providing my stitched forehead didn't alarm her. At least I'd never be taken for a journalist.

I didn't hear anything from the other side of the door — they were solidly built — but a tingling sensation between my shoulder blades told me I was being scrutinized. Then I heard a lock, or perhaps two, being disengaged and the door opened on a security chain. It crossed my mind that that particular horse had already bolted. Half a face peeped around the edge and looked at me warily.

Even half a face was enough for me to recognize Julia Standing. I had never seen her in the flesh before — despite the notion that had lodged somewhere in DS Graham's head — but I had seen her featured in enough press photos recently for her face to be instantly recognisable. It happened to be the kind of face that took a striking photograph although it wasn't quite so obvious why.

'Yes?,' she asked, peering at me suspiciously. 'What is it you want?'

'To talk to you for a few minutes, if I may,' I said. Adding, 'I'm not from the press. I knew your husband.'

She squared up in the gap between the door and the frame and looked me in the eye.

'I don't know you, do I?'

'I believe we may have spoken on the telephone once,' I said. 'My name is Alex Maitland.'

I thought I caught a widening of the one eye I could see but she closed the door before I was sure. I heard the rattle of the security chain being unlatched, then the door opened all the way.

Standing as I was on a step below her, our eyes met on the same level. Hers were blue, deeper than her husband's had been yet were curiously empty of expression. I could see what Olena had meant about her Englishness. Dressed in a simple shift dress and sweater with the sleeves pulled up to reveal a soft down of pale hair on her forearms, there was something quintessentially middle class about her somehow. Her skin looked translucent, like fine china, which hinted at having been crafted. Her hair was fair, not quite blonde, and almost reached her shoulders. It was tangled as if, after pulling on the sweater, she had not bothered to brush it. In much the same way as it was difficult — given her looks — to define why her photographs should have been so striking, she seemed to exude an allure that wasn't easy to pin down either. It certainly wasn't any overt sexual glamour, but I could sense some quality that almost approached magnetism. An air of fragility, Olena had called it, and I was disturbed to realize that it engendered an impulse to grab hold of her and treat her roughly. It was disconcerting and attracting at the same moment. Despite myself, I recognized it as an aura that certain men crave, the vulnerability of the ready-made — and somehow willing — victim.

'Alex Maitland?' she said, as she turned that empty gaze on me. 'I believe Michael mentioned you.'

'We met several times this last year. I wouldn't trouble you at this time under normal circumstances...'

'You'd better come in,' she said, standing aside.

I stepped in and experienced one of those sudden flickers of memory, almost *déjà vu*, as if I had been there before. Yet it wasn't that. It was some other sense. Then, before I could grasp it the moment was gone.

I followed her down a wide hallway, trying not to stare at her body in the shift in front of me. Forcing myself to look around, I saw the walls were hung with contemporary artwork. Most of it was the kind that doesn't need paint and I read some of the signatures without recognizing any. But if they weren't Hurst or Emin or Anish Kapoor, I wouldn't have and, anyway, I didn't suppose Standing's finances had run to that end of the market. At the end of the hall she turned into a room that looked onto a garden of bare-stemmed shrubs and empty borders. An ornamental birch was still dropping leaves on a patch of dull wet lawn, the leaves yellowing and curled like pages discarded from a notebook. It was only just past midday but a December gloom had already begun to descend and Julia Standing turned on the lamps from a switch on the wall. There was more artwork hanging on the walls and in one corner stood what I supposed was an installation piece but looked to me more like a variation of one of those old tickertape machines investors once used to keep abreast of the stock-market prices.

'Would you sit down, Mr Maitland?'

I thanked her and looked around for a chair. The furniture was low, angular and minimalist and there wasn't much of it. Comfort hadn't featured on her designer's drawing board. I found one that looked as if it might take my weight and sat down gingerly, beginning the rehearsed statement of condolence that I had been practising on the journey over. She waved it away with a quick 'Thank you' and sat in a twin of my chair a few feet from me across a pale blue Chinese rug. Almost Cambridge blue, I noticed, and a match for her husband's eyes. She crossed her legs as she sat and angled them at forty-five degrees beneath her. I couldn't help looking and she pulled at the hem of the shift in what seemed a deliberately modest gesture. She regarded me with those vacant eyes.

'What was it you wanted to talk to me about? If it was to offer your condolences on Michael's death, a card would have sufficed.'

I hadn't sent a card, of course. I hadn't considered it. It had been Standing I had known, not his wife.

'I was supposed to lunch with your husband the day before he was … before he died.' I paused having sidestepped the word although it hung, unsaid, in the air between us. 'I waited at the restaurant,' I finally went on, 'but he never arrived.'

Something flickered behind her eyes and she regarded me coldly, as if my sole reason for being there was to register a complaint.

'I'm sorry you were inconvenienced,' she said.

I grew conscious that something darker than just the gloom of the afternoon had seeped into the room. I glanced through the window at the bare trees and empty sky.

'The appointment,' I persisted, 'was made by phone. I told the police that it had been made by your husband's secretary...'

'My husband didn't employ a secretary,' Julia Standing said.

'So the police informed me.'

'Then you were mistaken.'

'Not about the call,' I said. 'I wondered if it might have been you who telephoned me.'

This time her eyes narrowed. 'I have never spoken to you before today,' she said.

'The police told me that, too.'

'Then I fail to see why you are here, Mr Maitland. Am I to understand that you don't believe me?'

She lifted her chin and looked at me challengingly, as if I had accused her of doing something indiscreet and daring me to repeat it. I felt momentarily pinned like an entomological specimen in that uncomfortable chair.

I asked if it were possibly that it was someone at the university or perhaps the television studio who had phoned me on her husband's behalf.

'Possibly,' she said without any emphasis. 'I wouldn't know.' She went on in that same monotone, 'Michael liked to make his own arrangements. He found people were flattered that he had taken the trouble to do it in person.'

'That's what I was wondering,' I said. 'When we met before he had always phoned me himself. Can you remember if there was any reason he might not have on this occasion? Was he particularly busy that day?'

For the first time she betrayed a sign of emotion as a slight sigh of exasperation escaped her lips. She shifted her gaze to the fireplace. The surround was marble and a vase of dried flowers sat in the blackened grate. It seemed an oddly quaint touch in such a modernist room.

'When was this arrangement made?' she asked.

Something in her manner managed to convey the impression that, along with the police, she didn't entirely believe in it either.

'It was Wednesday, late in the afternoon.'

'The Wednesday before he was murdered,' she said.

Not so fragile that she had to sidestep the word, I thought. And it seemed there was something almost provocative in her use of it.

'Michael was in Bath. He took an early train and spent the night there. He returned midday on Thursday.'

'Do you know why he went to Bath?'

'Of course I know,' she said, frowning slightly as if the idea of her not knowing was unthinkable. 'It was a research matter. His research assistant David Griffiths went with him.' She held my eyes with hers and I sensed she was challenging me again. 'Are you trying to suggest that my husband had some other woman with him in order to make this phone call?'

I cleared my throat. 'I'm not suggesting anything of the sort,' I said. In fact it was something I hadn't even considered. Until that moment, I hadn't known that Standing had not been in London when the call was made.

'I'm seeing Mr Griffiths tomorrow,' I said. 'Perhaps he can clear the point up.'

'Perhaps he can,' she said. She stood up. 'Was there anything else?'

I climbed awkwardly out of the low chair, riding a spasm in my back.

'No,' I managed without grunting. 'Thank you for taking the trouble to see me, Mrs Standing.'

The pain made me grimace and for a second she subjected me for the first time to a look of interest, the kind she might have reserved for some odd new piece of art that she didn't quite understand. Then the interest waned and she waited until I was on my feet and led me back down the hall towards the door. I took another look over the work that decorated her walls as we passed but it hadn't grown on me. She stopped at the door before opening it.

'Would you mind telling me just why it matters who telephoned you to make the lunch appointment with Michael, Mr Maitland?'

'Because he never kept the appointment for one thing,' I said.

'And is there another thing?'

'Only that I don't think the police entirely believed me when I told them it was a woman who made the appointment. They also wanted to know how well I knew you.'

'But you don't know me at all,' she said.

'No, that's what I told them and I'm afraid they didn't believe that, either.'

I detected a hairline crack run across the china of her forehead, the faintest of frowns.

She opened the door. On the step I turned back.

'The police told me they were checking your husband's phone records. If they find there was a call on Wednesday afternoon from this house to mine, they're going to know that one of us is lying to them.'

I saw then, for the first time, something flicker behind the vacancy of her eyes and she compressed her lips as if not trusting herself to reply. I was still looking at her when she shut the door in my face.

Riding home on the tube, I thought about Julia Standing's apparent antipathy to my visit and that odd allure I had experienced and whether either had been real of merely my imagination. Yet there had been a certain coldness about her I didn't think could be put down solely to the circumstances. But, if that was the case, why her dislike of me? She surely couldn't suspect that I was responsible for her husband's death? And even if she did and was still reckless enough to let me in, on what grounds did she hold her suspicion? We had never met and I had never been to the house before, although I couldn't help remembering that feeling I had as I stepped through the door. I had experienced some vague sense of familiarity that didn't make sense.

Considering how flatly she had denied ringing me to make the lunch appointment, the almost unspoken notion that Standing could have been in Bath with some other woman now came back to me. I hadn't realized that he had been away from home and that fact added another dimension to the puzzle; I could just picture Olena's face if she was proved right about him after all. David Griffiths would be able to tell me, I presumed: if he had been with him in Bath, he would be able either to confirm or deny that Standing had been with another woman. If he hadn't been in Bath with him, then Standing had lied to his wife about going with Griffiths which more or less suggested the same thing. Having a woman phone me from

Bath didn't mean he was having an affair, of course, he might just have got a receptionist or someone's assistant to make the call on his behalf because he was busy. I didn't mind which. His affairs — or lack of them — were no concern of mine. All I wanted was confirmation that the appointment had been made, if only for the satisfaction of having Bedford and Graham accept the fact.

Walking from the underground station, I was just approaching my road when I heard the siren of an emergency vehicle behind me. I stopped to watch as the ambulance passed and take the corner ahead of me at speed, the cacophonous wail cut to silence some way down the road. I quickened my pace and as I turned the same corner saw the ambulance parked a hundred yards further on, between my house and me. They had turned off the siren although the emergency lights were still pulsing rapidly enough to induce an epileptic fit in anyone susceptible. A small knot of people had gathered around the rear of the ambulance and appeared to be looking at something on the ground. A police car was stationed on the other side of the road and a constable had stepped into the middle of the street to direct any passing cars. I walked up and joined the crowd on the pavement.

A body was lying, half-on, half-off the pavement, spread-eagled but at an odd and barely possible angle. Someone had thrown a coat over it.

I glanced at the man next to me. 'What happened? Did someone get knocked down?'

The man's eyes were fixed on the body.

'I saw it happen,' he said. 'Poor bugger was about to cross the road when this car comes haring out of nowhere. He jumped back but the car mounted the pavement and hit him.'

'Trying to avoid him?' I asked.

He shrugged. 'I suppose so. He wouldn't want to hit him deliberately, would he?'

I looked around. 'Where's the driver?'

'He didn't stop. He knew he'd hit him, though. Poor bugger went right up over the bonnet.' He pointed to glass on the road. 'Smashed the windscreen.'

The medics had got the body on to the trolley and were lifting it into the back of the ambulance. It was a bit of a struggle for them because the man's yellow and black scarf had somehow managed to wind itself around the trolley wheels, hampering their efforts to roll it into the vehicle.

Besides, Fielding had been a bulky man.

~

I waited until they had loaded Fielding into the ambulance and had sped away, then spent a minute or two looking at the spill of blood on the road. The police had started taking statements. I told them I hadn't seen anything and slipped passed them into the house.

I found Daryna curled up on the sofa. Her earlier Cyrillic copy of my father's letters still lay on the table. I noticed that she had looked at them because the pages were slightly out of the alignment in which I had left them relative to a tablemat. She looked as if the sound of the sirens had woken her.

'I have headache,' she said from the sofa.

'Have you eaten anything?' I asked.

'No.'

'I'll make us some soup. Then I think you ought to go back to bed.'

'I am a lot of trouble for you, I think, Alex.'

'Don't worry about it,' I told her.

If there was any trouble, I was beginning to realize it was all of my own making. I put a pan of soup on the stove to heat and went upstairs and found a rug to put over her. Then I fetched her a couple of aspirins and a glass of water.

'I do not like pills,' she said, looking up at me weakly.

'Better than headaches,' I suggested.

She took them reluctantly and drank them down, pulling a face.

I cut some bread and we ate it with our soup, Daryna tucked up in the blanket and sitting up on the sofa. When she had finished, she folded the blanket neatly, laid it on the arm of the chair and went back up to bed. I turned on my laptop and brought up a map of Cambridge to find Griffiths' address. I printed out a copy then emailed him.

David,

Fielding was knocked over and killed by a car near my house about an hour ago. Maybe it's just paranoia but this and the break-in following Standing's death seems a coincidence too far. I'll see you in the morning. Until then please be cautious.

Alex.

He must have been working on-line because a few minutes later I received a reply.

Alex,
Sorry about Fielding. He was an odd chap but he knew his business. Point taken about caution, paranoia or not. On another note book that lecture we talked about concerning the medieval monk, why don't you? It's all incomprehensible to me, those Pages dressed up in leather. Very suspicious! As far as I'm concerned it's time they came out of the closet! Talk to you tomorrow.
David.

I stared at the screen wondering what on earth he was talking about. No one had ever suggested attending a lecture on any medieval monk and my first thought was that he must have confused me with some other correspondent. I was about to reply to point out the error when I stopped myself. He had mentioned Fielding by name so he must have known he was emailing me. Also, I had just warned him to be cautious. It occurred to me that, if he had deliberately written so cryptically, he wouldn't thank me for asking him to explain himself in any clearer language. I scratched absently at my head and read the email again.

His remark about Fielding was plain enough. On the other hand, his next sentence had an awkward construction: *On another note book that lecture we talked about concerning the medieval monk, why don't you?* Why hadn't he written: On another note, *why don't you* book that lecture we talked about concerning the medieval monk? Perhaps only if he hadn't wanted to split the words *note* and *book*? Notebook. I read the rest. *Pages dressed up in leather* rather than meaning a servant wearing a jerkin could refer to the leather notebook I had given Standing and the medieval monk would be Cyril who had given his name to the Cyrillic script. He seemed to be telling me, apparently, that he didn't understand what was written in it. The penultimate sentence presumably meant that the notebook was kept in a closet.

Taking my own advice to be cautious I couldn't help thinking that, in the minute or so he had had between receiving my email and sending his, he had been remarkably quick-witted. I sent a reply:

David,
Will get tickets for lecture as advised. Studying the monk together might make things clearer.
Alex.

I wondered if it was the news of Fielding's death that had suddenly made him cautious or if he already had suspicions of his own. Thinking that one's emails might be monitored could indeed be thought of as a symptom of paranoia but, given the fact of violent death not a hundred yards from my front door, displaying any amount of caution seemed reasonable in my book. Perhaps Griffiths was taking the Sunday paper allegations of KGB dirty tricks seriously. I wasn't aware of any suggestion that Michael Standing's computer records had been accessed but *my* laptop had been stolen and whatever information had been in Fielding's head had now been pretty thoroughly deleted. It might have been that Griffiths was just taking precautions against anyone getting their hands on Standing's research. That made me start wondering about the material I had gathered.

Upstairs, I looked in on Daryna. She was under the duvet and asleep. In my bedroom I took the papers Fielding had given me the previous day out of the safe where I had put them after Bedford and Graham had left. I had had little opportunity to examine them since Fielding had given me the envelope; from meeting him in the pub in docklands, I had spent the afternoon looking at laptops then had met Charlie for a few drinks and ended up in an Indian restaurant. By the time I had got back home I had only had chance to get the machine up and running and email Griffiths before the police had arrived. Now, I sat on the sofa — still indented from Daryna's prone body — and pulled the papers out.

Each of the pages was a photocopy of an original that betrayed their age and the quality of some pre-war printing. Riffling through them, I saw that Fielding had been right when he had said he had not managed to find much on the Black Sea Company. There were a few financial statements dating from the thirties, mostly the usual audited profit and loss accounts outlining income from various trading ventures. The amounts might have been respectable in their day but they seemed very small beer by modern standards. It probably wasn't more than the sort of money that George spent on his office cleaning. According to the accounts Fielding had found, by

1939, when the company was wound up, it had declared an operating debt that almost equalled the previous two years' profit. I ran my eye up and down the columns of figures but I was far from proficient in reading balance sheets and was unlikely to pick up on any discrepancy that Fielding might have missed. He had circled the odd figure on various pages and put a question mark against others, but hadn't elucidated as to why. There appeared nothing about them that struck me as significant. On another page there was a list of the directors of the company, the company secretary and some other officers, and their addresses. On the top of this Fielding had scrawled 1932. He had also managed to track down the names of a few overseas agents who had dealt with Black Sea, listing their registered offices in a variety of foreign cities: Cairo, Istanbul, Damascus, as well as agents centred on the Black Sea itself, Sevastopol, Odessa, Yuzhny, Novorossiysk... In the margins, he had scribbled a few symbols that resembled shorthand, which I supposed had meant something to him but meant nothing to me. I went through everything twice without finding anything that might possibly have been a link to the events Standing had been researching. I could understand his having an interest in a company trading in commodities in the region of the Black Sea in that they may have had a connection with the grain sales made by the Bolsheviks during the famine, but there was nothing in what I had read that suggested the remotest connection — or, come to that, to the gathering or the dissemination of intelligence. It was far-fetched. Grain seized from a starving Ukraine and used by Stalin to raise foreign exchange to finance his programme of Industrialization was one thing — it was reasonable to suppose that the Bolsheviks would need a western company willing to buy their product — but some fancied connection to what might have been an embryonic Cambridge spy ring was quite another. What Standing had been looking for, I suppose, was something to link his Shostak to the company — although as far as I could remember he had never told me what it had been that had aroused his suspicions about Shostak in the first place. Anyway, even if it was true that this Black Sea Company *had* been buying shipments of grain taken from the mouths of starving peasants for sale overseas, what difference did it make after all this time? The company no longer existed; it had gone out of business at the start of the war and even if any of those who had colluded with the Bolsheviks were still alive they would be very old men. Embarrassment over financial dealings dating back seventy-five years hardly seemed a likely motive for murder. An intelligence connection, if there was one, might still cause some embarrassment, another opportunity to drag Philby, Burgess and Maclean out of the Cold War closet and heap more opprobrium on the head of SIS, but after all this time it was hardly a disclosure of the calibre likely to get one killed. Russian politics were as hot today as they had ever been — witness radioactive assassination on the streets of London — but 1930s spy stories were now as cold as an old bowl of *borscht*.

The one argument countering this view, of course, was that ninety minutes earlier I'd been out in the road standing over Fielding's body.

I went back through it all a third time, looking for something I might have missed.

I was examining the addresses of the company officers again when I finally saw something I should have seen the first time. The address of the Company Secretary had been registered as Lavender Gardens, Hackney. I stared at it until I had to force myself to blink.

It was the address my father had written on the one envelope surviving from letters he had sent his mother. It was the address of the house in which Nastasiya had died during the Blitz.

FIVE

Better that ten innocent people should suffer than one spy get away. When you cut down the forest, woodchips fly.

Nikolai Yezhov, NKVD commander

(Roy Medvedev, Let History Judge [Columbia University Press, 1989], p. 603)

19

I once read somewhere that one of the consequences of ageing is the gradual loss of the linkages between brain cells. This affects memory and the ability to reason and, if true, is probably why I sat for so long like some latter-day Neanderthal, while the scattered jigsaw pieces in my head took an age to rattle down alternative neural pathways and middle-aged detours until they finally met and collided and began to make sense.

It hadn't been the content of my father's letters that was the reason for their theft, but the address written on the envelope. And the messages erased from my answer phone had been from Fielding trying to arrange a meeting. He had been researching the Black Sea Company and had a list of addresses. I had an address that took the link a step further.

It might be wondered why I hadn't made these connections before. After all, Frederick Maitland had founded his fortune on international trade, he apparently spoke Russian, which suggested he had spent at least some time there, and he had received his university education at a Cambridge college. These things had registered with me and the suspicion that Frederick might have been the foreigner involved in grain seizures in the Ukraine in 1931 and 1932 had been growing, if unconsciously. But the evidence was still circumstantial. There was no hard documentation that linked Frederick with either the Black Sea Company or with the Ukraine.

And any leads that pointed in that direction had been snuffed out. Evidence in itself, perhaps. But if so the curious thing was: who still cared? Why did it still matter?

I went back to Fielding's papers and the list of Company Directors. The only year he had found addresses for was 1932, well into the famine and a year that would have chimed with Standing, but at this date a man named William Robinson supposedly lived at the Hackney address. I couldn't remember precisely the dates on my father's letters to Nastasiya but I knew that by 1934 he was already at his boarding school in Dorset and writing to that address. It was possible, of course, that I had mistaken the number of the house on the envelope, but I didn't think so; I had seen it a dozen times over the past months and was certain I was right. The one other reasonable explanation for a discrepancy could be simply bad record-keeping on the part of Black Sea's book-keepers, entering a wrong address for one of their employees; but Fielding had said he had checked the names and address against the electoral register and had said that only one had not checked out. I went back through the list. The only one Fielding had circled was that of William Robinson. The electoral register was updated every year as far as I was aware and I wondered if Fielding had checked the names of the occupants for the following years. If he had, he would have found that by 1934 Frederick Maitland was living there. But if Fielding had checked further, why hadn't he said so? He *had* reacted when I had mentioned Frederick's name, I was sure, but if he'd come across Frederick in his research what was it that had kept him silent? Caution? He had said he wanted to double-check something before getting back to me. Was it something about Frederick? If so, perhaps it was getting back to me that had got him killed.

If Fielding's suspicions had been correct about the veracity of those Black Sea records that remained, then a fictitious background had been constructed for the company using addresses that no longer existed and names of people who were already dead. Using Frederick and Nastasiya's address *might* have been coincidence — just sheer chance that whoever it was who had been charged with the fabrication had picked that particular address, but given everything else it seemed unlikely. More probable was that using the name William Robinson for an actual address had been an oversight by whoever had doctored the papers. It had been a moment of carelessness, the easy option to take because the falsifier knew the house had actually been destroyed. Just tack on some dead man's name. It was just the kind of sloppy methodology that bored pen pushers are prone to — *that'll do. Good enough.* What gave it away wasn't whether in 1932 William Robinson had or had not lived there; what betrayed the fabrication was that in 1934 Frederick Maitland *had.*

I had never been to where the house had stood. What had been left of the place had been bulldozed more than ten years before I had been born. My father, to the best of my recollection, had displayed no sentimental attachment to the area. He had moved to Chiswick after the war and I couldn't remember his ever speaking of the house in which his mother had died. All I knew about it was that it was to where Frederick and Nastasiya had moved after their marriage.

It occurred to me that Frederick could well have already owned the house before his marriage and that if Fielding had checked the electoral register or parish records for the years subsequent to 1932 he might have come up with Frederick's name. That he hadn't said anything to me, might simply be that, like Standing, he hadn't wanted to put all his cards on the table at once — another who had liked to play them close to his chest. Fielding had asked if I was related to George Maitland, although at the time I had just assumed it was his way of feeling me out as far as the financial possibilities went rather than any knowledge he had about my family's involvement in whatever it had been that Standing was investigating.

I put Fielding's papers to one side and hunted out my A-to-Z of London to look up Lavender Gardens in Hackney.

It wasn't there.

For a second I thought I must have made a mistake. That all my suppositions were worthless. But Fielding had got the address from the list of company directors and checked it against the 1932 electoral register. So it must have existed then. I found a Lavender Gardens in Battersea, but I knew from my father that the house hadn't been there. The only possible reason for Lavender Gardens in Hackney to disappear in the intervening years was because it had attracted the attentions of Göering's Luftwaffe.

I looked back at the index again. There was a Lavender *Grove* in Hackney, lying to the west of London Fields. It might have been that Lavender Gardens had become Lavender Grove after the bomb damage had been cleared and the area rebuilt, or that Lavender Gardens had been a separate street and had disappeared altogether. I got back on the laptop and began looking for any local history societies in the borough, or anything connected to the war or the Blitz. I already had a working knowledge of organisations dedicated to preserving the history of wartime London, given my interest in my father's RAF service, and I wrote a short email asking for information and sent it to several of the contacts I had made.

I picked up the file I had made up from George's papers and pulled them out to look back over the photographs of Frederick and Nastasiya I had scanned and printed. As I did so the scrap of paper I had scribbled on in George's study fell on to the table: *Frederick — Call Olena.*

I had written the note while looking through the photographs. There was something that had jogged my memory of the lunch I had with her and Nick back in the summer. I had meant the note as an *aide-mémoire* then had promptly forgotten I had written the thing.

It was still early in the evening but I suspected the chance of finding Olena at home was remote. Fortunately, since their invention, she never moved more that a hand's-breadth away from her mobile phone and was one of those people who interrupt whatever they are doing, no matter how important, to take a call. If the day ever dawns when one is able to have mobile communication surgically implanted, Olena will be at the head of the queue.

'Alex?' she said, unable to keep a note of mystification out of her voice. She was usually the one who called me. 'What do you want?'

That she should assume I wanted something was a little hurtful, but tempered in this case by the fact that I did.

'To see you,' I said. 'What are you doing?'

'To see me? What about? What's happened?'

'Nothing's happened, Olena. It's just there's something I want to talk about.'

She sighed ostentatiously. 'I'm at a gallery showing. I don't have the time at the moment.'

'Where is it?'

'New Bond Street. Invitation only, Alex.'

'Talk them into it,' I said.

I got the name of the gallery out of her, called a minicab and left Daryna a note. I looked in on her first but she was still fast asleep. I put my coat on and waited by the door until the cab arrived, then let myself out as quietly as I could.

I could see from the pavement that it was the kind of gallery that specialized in young tyros fresh from Goldsmiths, hopefuls ready to take the modern art market by storm with their off-the-wall creations. As I stepped through the door I wondered idly if an inability to hang that sort of thing on the wall was where the phrase had originated, but that thought was chased out of my head when I saw the crowd in front of me. I hadn't given a second thought to dress, of course, and the designer evening wear and smattering of dinner jackets made me acutely conscious of what I was wearing beneath my overcoat, a garment itself of a vintage that would have looked less out of place in prohibition Chicago than a New Bond Street gallery. Normally that sort of thing doesn't worry me but I didn't want to give Olena any excuse to avoid seeing me. She could be remarkably petty about that sort of thing. The girl on the door was obviously thinking along similar lines because when she asked for my invitation it was in a tone that suggested I couldn't possibly have received one.

'My name is Alex *Maitland*,' I said, perceptibly accentuating the surname. 'I'm looking for my sister, *Olena* Maitland? I believe she is attending this showing.'

'Thank you, Sophie,' Olena said, hobbling purposefully across the crowded room with as much speed as the skin-tight dress and needle-sharp heels she was wearing allowed. 'It's my brother.' The statement seemed to hang in the air between us for a moment, covering any number of my sins and failings. She waved a hand at Sophie to indicate we all knew what brothers were like and that we couldn't expect proper behaviour from any of them. Then she linked an arm through mine and pulled me aside with all the subtlety of a Gestapo thug. 'Alex,' she complained, 'you could have made an effort. Really!'

'Sorry,' I said, pecking her on the cheek. 'I didn't give it any thought.'

She smiled, turning to an elderly couple near us who were peering with some trepidation at an iron and aluminium construction bolted to the wall. The iron had begun to rust, although whether as an integral part of the concept or merely as an unfortunate by-product of ferrous metal wasn't easy to deduce. The couple exchanged a word with Olena but she made no effort to introduce me.

'I could do with a drink,' I said when they'd moved on.

Olena raised an imperious arm at one of the waiters who came over bearing a tray of champagne flutes and glasses of wine, sherry and port.

It hadn't been the kind of drink I'd had in mind and as I grabbed a glass I heard Charlie's voice in my head saying, 'Any port in a storm'.

Olena drew me off to one side where a pillar half-hid me from the other guests.

'You're looking very beautiful this evening,' I told her.

'Alex!'

But she was. The tight dress was silver with some sort of reflective material woven in that caught the gallery lights and made her shimmer even when she wasn't moving. You could catch men's eyes on her without casting bait and I doubted that anyone was going to bother with my inappropriate dress while I was standing next to her.

'What is it you want?' she asked. 'I'm with friends. I can't just desert them to talk to you.'

'Of course you can't, Olena,' I said. I looked at the crowd over her shoulder. They were still coming in through the door and the waiters were having to do the quick-step to keep up with the demand. I supposed there were some art collectors and critics, mixed in with the usual amalgam of society, celebrity, and plain old money. The young artists themselves were easier to spot; by and large they were younger than the rest, more self-conscious and compensating for the fact with flamboyant dress. Given how they looked, I didn't see why anyone should have objected to me.

'I'm surprised that you've never run into Julia Standing at this sort of affair,' I said. 'This is the kind of stuff she's got hanging on her walls.'

'As a matter of fact, I have,' Olena said. 'I told you that I'd met her at a gallery showing. You never listen to a word I say. It was *him* I never met.'

'Didn't he ever come with her?'

'Not whenever I saw her. She was always with someone else.'

'Who?'

'Not the same man every time,' she said, 'if that's what you're thinking.'

It was, but it obviously wasn't going to be that easy.

'Did you know her to speak to, then, if Nick knew Michael?'

'I told you, I was introduced to her. I really don't remember by whom, Alex.'

'Nick wasn't with you then?'

'Oh, Nick hardly ever comes to these things. He's a Constable and Gainsborough man at heart.'

'It's the rural constituency,' I said. 'I'm sure it would be different if he'd stood for Chelsea.'

She threw me a sardonic look. 'If that were the case we'd probably still be married.'

It had been an off-hand remark and I found it difficult to tell whether there was a note of regret in it or not. She had been the one who had wanted the divorce but I had often wondered whether it had been meant as more of a threat than a request, an attempt, perhaps, to get him out of parliament and back in line.

'Nick was never with you when you saw Julia Standing?' I persisted.

She sighed with irritation. 'He might have been. How am I supposed to remember that?'

'I just wondered,' I said. 'Since he had met her at university, I mean.' I was thinking that it might have been an indication that Nick had seen more of Standing than he had admitted to. But then I remembered that Olena had not known that Nick and Julia had been acquainted. Perhaps that's what had occurred to Olena because her eyes narrowed, always a sign that she was thinking. Then she snapped out of it in that manner she had when she decided to deliberately stop thinking about something that troubled her and put it away for another time.

'Anyway,' she said, 'how do you know what Julia Standing has hanging on her walls?'

'I went to see her this afternoon.'

Her eyes widened. 'You didn't! Why?'

'The phone call. The lunch appointment that Standing never kept.' But I couldn't remember whether I had told her about that or not and she didn't seem interested in that anyway.

'Oh,' she said, sounding disappointed as if she'd thought I might have gone to see the widow to check for bloodstains. 'Well,' she suddenly continued briskly, 'that's as may be. I can't stand here with you all evening. What was it you wanted?'

'Of course you can't,' I said to her again. 'Good of you to give me as long as you have.'

She punched me on the arm, her rings looking like an up-market knuckle-duster. I slopped port on the floor narrowly missing her dress.

'You remember when I came over to lunch back in the summer,' I said. 'Nick was there?'

'Of course I remember. What about it?'

'I happened to run into Georgia a couple of weeks ago and I was talking to her about Frederick?'

'Is this about Dad again? Don't you ever give up? You're becoming a bore on the subject, Alex. You know?'

'Probably,' I said. 'Anyway, we were talking about Frederick, remember?'

'I've just said I did, didn't I?'

'Did he ever speak Russian to you?'

'Why on earth would he speak Russian to me, Alex? Talk sense for God's sake. How would I understand if he did? Really!'

'But you knew he spoke Russian?'

'Of course I knew. He was always showing off, reading Tolstoy in the original Russian, that sort of thing. He was a bore, too.'

'Who? Tolstoy?'

'Don't pretend to be stupid, Alex,' she said. 'Frederick was a bore about his Russian. It was usually Tolstoy and that other one...' she fluttered an impatient hand in the air, 'What's his name...'

'Dostoyevsky?' I suggested. 'Turgenev?'

'Yes, but not them. More modern. Oh, what's his *name*?' She stamped a foot in frustration. 'He was always boasting about how he used to know him but really he'd only met him once or twice, that's all.'

'Not Gorky?' I said.

'Yes, that's him. Maxim Gorky.'

I must have looked surprised because Olena said:

'What's the matter now?'

'Nothing,' I said. Then, for some reason added, 'Georgia told me she thought Nick was seeing someone.'

She stiffened. Her face set like stone, as rigid as a piece of sculpture and far more impressive as art than anything else on display in the gallery.

'Who is she?'

'I've no idea,' I said. 'Georgia didn't know. I wondered if you did.' I tried to keep the tone light but Olena's eyes were boring into mine to see if I was hiding anything. I could see I'd ruined her evening but I really didn't know what she expected now they were divorced. Perhaps she had assumed he would still be faithful.

She didn't say anything so I went on, 'I was with him last weekend down at George's new place. He seemed much the same as usual.'

'Really.'

'We dropped by that house he bought down there. Have you ever been there?'

'No, there are too many cows.'

'I just wondered,' I mumbled, nonplussed.

'And how did you find George and Jennifer?' she asked in a tone that suggested she already knew the answer.

'They were well. And I saw Nora. She asked me to send her love when I saw you next.' Her lips tightened momentarily and if I hadn't known her better I would have thought I saw her eyes glisten. 'That son of hers,' I said. 'Does he work for George still, do you know?'

'Hardly,' she said, face hardening again. 'Jennifer wouldn't have him around after the last time.'

'What was that?'

'Didn't you hear? Perhaps it was while you were in hospital. He got five years for grievous bodily harm. Some pub brawl. It was the last straw as far as Jennifer was concerned. I don't blame her. Little prick was always gawping at me.'

'Is he still inside?' I asked.

'How would I know?' she snapped back. 'I suppose so. The best place for him.'

She finished the champagne in her glass and looked around, waving one of the waiters over. 'Is this going to take much longer?'

'Only a second,' I said. 'It's about Frederick.'

'I don't know why you insist on talking about that repulsive old man.'

'That's what you said back in the summer,' I told her. 'You called him repulsive.'

'Well? He was.'

'Yes, but what was it about him you found repulsive?'

'Everything.'

'His manner or what?'

'His drooling mostly,' she said.

'I know, but you didn't like him much before his stroke did you?'

'No I didn't. It was that hand of his. It always gave me the creeps.'

'What about his hand?'

She looked at me as if I was being deliberately obtuse.

'His fingers, of course.'

'What about his fingers?'

She shivered again as she had done that hot May day and I began to feel my own flesh creep.

'You don't know, do you?' she said in surprise.

'For God's sake, Olena! Don't know what?'

'One of his hands,' she said. 'It had six fingers.'

~

Daryna was up when I got back to the house. She was standing in the lounge looking disgruntled.

'You go out, Alex, and do not tell me,' she complained.

'I left you a note,' I said.

My papers were still lying on the sofa where I had left them, the photocopies and the photographs I had got from George and the papers on the Black Sea Company that Fielding had given me. I'd left them lying around in my usual untidy fashion instead of locking them away in the safe.

'I do not understand,' Daryna said.

'You don't understand the note?'

'I do not understand why you go out without telling me.'

I wondered exactly when I had come into custody of a dependent, noticing that she no longer seemed the self-assured creature I had first met in the park.

'You were asleep,' I said. 'I didn't want to wake you.'

'What if ugly man comes back?'

'I don't think that's likely.'

'Where do you go without telling me?'

'I went to see my sister.'

'This is Olena, yes?'

'Yes. I hadn't seen her for a while.'

Her nose had started twitching, like a dog catching a scent, but I didn't know whether it was because of Olena or because of the bag I was holding.

'What is in the bag?' she asked.

I had got the cab to stop at an Indian takeaway on the way home. I was still holding the bag, the oil from the dishes beginning to soak through the brown paper.

'Dinner,' I said. 'Do you like curry?'

'I never have before.'

'You've never liked it before or you've never had it before?'

She was past instruction, though, and already clearing the table so we could eat. She must have been hungry because twenty minutes later nothing was left except silver foil and cardboard and despite Daryna's nose wrinkling at the alien aromas she hadn't turned it up at the meal. I didn't know what the Ukrainian diet consisted of — borscht I imagined — but it looked as if Indian cuisine had yet to make inroads into the country.

'Good?' I asked when she had finished.

'I eat too much,' she complained.

Some people were difficult to please.

I cleared away and left Daryna washing up while I found a magnifying glass and returned to the photographs I had copied of Frederick. They had all been taken at his wedding to Nastasiya and in each except one his left hand had been obscured by that characteristic pose of his. Only in the group photograph where Nastasiya was standing on his left and had her right arm linked through his was his left hand visible. I focused the magnifying glass on it and counted: a thumb and five fingers.

There was nothing about the hand that looked deformed, the extra finger being quite unobtrusive. I imagined that even when seeing the hand clearly one might not notice the supernumerary unless one was already aware of it. After that, of course, one wouldn't be able to look at anything else. Georgia would have known all about it yet never mentioned the fact when I told her of Olena's dislike of Frederick. Had she been evasive on the subject? I couldn't recall although I did remember that Nick had interrupted Olena when we were talking about Frederick over lunch.

Olena said she had found him "repulsive", but she had always been squeamish about any physical abnormality and had been predisposed to dislike Frederick anyway. No doubt our father's antipathy to the man had laid the groundwork and the fact that Frederick, too, had opposed her marrying Nick had finished the job. But if Olena's dislike was understandable, it didn't explain my father's; he wasn't the kind of man who'd let the little matter of an extra digit dictate how he felt about someone. Besides, if his letters were anything to go by, as a boy he had not disliked Frederick at all. It was something that had happened later that made my father turn against him. What the photograph did do, though, almost beyond doubt, was to show that Frederick Maitland and Standing's Shostak were the same man.

I was still considering the matter, holding the magnifying glass over the photograph when my eye fell on the man standing to Frederick's right. I had experienced a feeling of familiarity when I had first seen his face in George's study and now I felt it again.

The quality of the photograph was not good and to compound the problem he had turned away as the photograph was taken as if his attention had been caught by something off-camera. I played the magnifying glass over the face and was convinced that there was something both familiar and unfamiliar about it. On joining the Service I had been indoctrinated into the art of surveillance and identification and had spent hours memorizing books of diplomatic photographs and clandestinely shot snaps of hundreds of faces of people of interest. This man was not one of them, I was sure — he would have been far too old to be of interest to the Service by the time I joined — but the face was familiar nevertheless. I tried imagining lines of age and grey hair and for an instant felt a stab of recognition that almost formed itself into a name. Then it was gone, skittering away to fall, no doubt, into some middle-aged chasm in my memory left by a burnt out neural pathway. I looked at the face for a while longer then turned on my scanner, plugged in the laptop and scanned the photo into the computer. I cropped the man's head, enlarged it as much as I could without losing his features completely, then printed out the result.

I put the photo on the table, wandered into the kitchen and took a beer from the fridge. Daryna was still at the sink.

'Would you like a beer?' I asked.

She looked over her shoulder. 'No, thank you. You have fruit?'

'Apples in the bowl,' I said.

She dried her hands and took a small knife off the drainer. She always peeled apples, I had noticed, and would never eat the skin.

'That's not very sharp,' I said, gesturing at the knife. 'There's a better one in the drawer.'

'Not sharp?' she repeated.

'It's blunt,' I explained.

She said something but I'd stopped listening. I rushed back to the table, picking up the photo again. I had only ever seen pictures of him as an old man, those taken when his name had been splashed across the front pages back in 1979. He'd been a broken man then, thin and gaunt and looking older than his seventy years. But it was the same face. Even as a young man he had that expression of haughtiness, of superiority, that he customarily wore, that he never lost even as his world fell apart.

For once I knew what I was doing, even if the risk was ill-defined. For a moment I felt again like that reckless young boy I had once been, poking at a wasps' nest with a stick.

If I had recalled the face, I knew it would ring a whole peal of bells in Charlie Hewson's compendious ragbag of a head. I emailed him and attached the photo I had scanned as a jpeg file:

Charlie,
Take a look at the photo attached. Comments on a postcard.
Alex.

Someone was going to get stung now.

I logged off and collected all the papers together. I sorted out those I was going to take to David Griffiths in the morning and locked the rest away in the safe. Daryna came back into the room, munching on her apple.

'What do you do now?' she demanded.

'Sorting out some stuff,' I said. 'I'm going back to Cambridge tomorrow to see a friend of Michael Standing's. He's got some papers belonging to me.'

'What about me?' she said.

'Haven't you got any English lessons?'

It had long been understood between us that there was no language school for her to attend and 'learning English' meant picking it up wherever she could. She pouted as if I were mistreating her.

'You leave me here again?'

'You can come if you want,' I said. 'I thought you might have something better to do than spend all your time with me, that's all.'

'I like being with you, Alex,' she said.

Which wasn't quite how it sounded, of course.

We picked up her suitcase at the coach station then, since she had spent most of the day sleeping and wasn't tired, we had to sit up half the night playing Scrabble. I'd found that with Daryna the game was more of a compulsion than an entertainment and her

241

competitive instinct drove her to remember each unfamiliar word I ever proposed — once she had satisfied herself of their veracity by looking them up in the dictionary. She hadn't managed to beat me yet but I could see the day coming.

Still, I was beginning to feel that to see any new day dawn was something of a bonus.

20

Back in the long vac when we had driven through looking for the venue of Standing's seminar, Cambridge had still been heaving with people. The missing undergraduates had been replaced threefold with foreign exchange students on summer courses and hordes of tourists from America and Germany and Japan and just about anywhere else you could name; you could hardly hear yourself speak for the deafening click of camera shutters. There had been Chinese, too, I had noticed and it had made me wonder if some Russian entrepreneur had ever thought to organize tours for old Communist hard-liners who might be nostalgic to visit scenes of former triumph. Now, though, in the days before Christmas, there was a pervading sense of emptiness, as if everyone else knew something that you didn't and had packed up and left.

Griffiths, it turned out, lived a mile or two from the colleges in an area that seemed devoted to student lodging. I suddenly remembered I had told Griffiths I would ring him first although now, so close, there didn't seem any point. His address was one of a terrace of small Edwardian cottages. I drove past the house and found somewhere to park further along the street. Daryna and I got out and walked back. The house was redbrick, narrow and deep and constructed like an old weaver's cottage. One end of a pair of terraces, it was separated from the others by an alley that gave access to the rear. I knocked on the door and exchanged a meaningless glance with Daryna while we waited.

'He is out,' she announced with her usual certainty after a minute or so without a response.

'He said he'd be in all morning,' I told her. 'He's expecting me.'

I walked around the house down the alley on to a path that ran along the rear of the terrace alongside a small ditch that in wet years might even have passed for a stream. Daryna trailed behind me. The gate to Griffiths' back garden was open, giving onto a muddy tangle of rank grass and overgrown shrubs. I picked my way past old arcing brambles to the back door and knocked again. It swung open under the pressure. I exchanged another glance with Daryna, this one full of meaning. As she tried to unhook a bramble that had snagged her skirt, the heels of her shoes sank into the muddy grass.

I stepped into a rear lean-to extension cluttered with a washing machine, a pale blue plastic laundry basket and a clothes dryer that was dropping small shards of cracked plastic onto the vinyl floor. A mop and a bucket leaned against the wall and some garden tools, rusting from disuse, lay in a trug.

'I don't like, Alex,' Daryna said, having finally freed herself from the clutches of the bramble and joined me. 'We should not walk into other man's house.'

I called out. There was no reply, only the sound of music coming from somewhere inside. I went in.

The lean-to gave on to a small kitchen just large enough for the usual worktop and cupboards and a small table. A radio stood on the worktop tuned to a local station, the presenter giving the station identification before announcing the next track. It was Marvin Gaye's *I heard it on the Grapevine* and the pounding intro lent a sense of menace to the otherwise silent house. I looked around. The previous evening's washing-up lay in the sink — plate, cutlery, and saucepans. On the table stood a half-eaten breakfast, a knife and fork resting on the plate like the hands of a clock at twenty-past-eight as if just left for a moment. Beside it was an open newspaper and a half-drunk mug of tea.

Marvin was asking if we wondered how he knew. I knew because the hairs on the back of my neck had begun to bristle.

I reached over and touched the back of my hand to the mug of tea. It was cold. Moving past the table, I leaned my head through the doorway into a hall. Daryna had her hands on my shoulders, as close to me as she could get without climbing on my back.

The front door lay at the end of the hall and David Griffiths lay on the floor about four feet from it. He was by the foot of the stairs and lay on his back, his head towards me, with his eyes open. From where I stood I could see the neat red hole in his forehead above the bridge of his nose.

I stepped down the hall then over him towards his feet. Behind me I heard Daryna give a small, strangled cry. Griffiths was dead although, had I touched him, I knew he wouldn't be as cold as his tea. There was a look of astonishment on his face, which I don't suppose is particularly remarkable in one who had not expected death to come calling so early in the morning. The bullet hole in his forehead seemed to accentuate the fact, giving his face a third — albeit bloodshot — eye to open in surprise. It was a pity, I thought, remembering my email to him that paranoia wasn't an infectious disease. If it had been he might have taken more care in answering his door. Then he probably thought it was me and that I had arrived early. He was dressed in jeans, a sweatshirt and trainers and looked to have reached somewhere in his mid-twenties before someone had stopped him growing any older.

'He is dead,' Daryna said flatly, her tone not quite a question yet still managing to hold a suggestion of curiosity.

'Very,' I said. 'Stay where you are and don't touch anything.'

Two other doors gave off the hall. I stepped into the first, the front room, crowded with an oversize television set, sofa and armchair. A few books stood on shelves built into the recesses either side of the chimneybreast. Yesterday's newspaper, *The Guardian*, lay on a small coffee table. A three-quarter-length quilted coat was draped over the back of the armchair. The room did not look particularly tidy but nothing seemed obviously out of place. I went back into the hall, over Griffiths and into the room beyond.

He had used this as his study and even someone as apparently unfussy about orderliness as Griffiths would not have left any room in this state. Bookshelves lined the walls although most of the books had been pulled down and lay in a jumble on the floor. There were two desks. On one papers had been gathered in a heap as if his killer had been thinking of having a bonfire. On the other stood a computer, the screen dark. The lights on the tower were flickering, though, and I reached over and tapped the 'enter' key on the keyboard with my knuckle. The screen flickered briefly and a box came up that said, 'Formatting Drive C...' I reached quickly for the plug, then stopped myself. I couldn't take the computer with me and to switch off the power was going to betray the fact that someone else had been there. I looked through a few of the papers on the other desk but knew that anything of relevance must have already gone.

I turned around and bumped into Daryna.

'I thought I told you to stay where you were,' I said.

'He is dead,' she repeated unnecessarily. 'Will you call police?'

'*The* police,' I said without thinking. Then, 'Not yet.'

I stepped around her and went upstairs. Daryna followed. There were two bedrooms and a bathroom and it looked as if whoever had killed Griffiths had been through them. I didn't suppose that it had ever crossed Griffiths' mind to hide his research. Why should it? Standing's death had been just one of those things — a tragedy, admittedly, but tragedies happen. Yet when I had emailed him to say that Fielding had been killed he had at least been cautious enough to send me a cryptic reply.

Daryna was standing behind me in the doorway. The room I was in looked to have been the one Griffiths slept in himself. Against the far wall was one of those old heavy wardrobes that had gone out of fashion once built-in closets had become the thing. The doors were open and Griffiths' clothes had been pulled aside.

'Take a look in the other rooms,' I said to Daryna, 'but don't leave fingerprints.'

'What do I look for?'

'Anything whoever searched the place might have missed,' I said.

She looked at me questioningly and I didn't blame her. I spoke the language and what I'd just said didn't even make sense to me. It got her out of the room, though, and I crossed to the wardrobe and looked through it. There was a shelf above the hanging rail with a few sweaters and shirts but nothing else. I felt through the pockets of the jackets hanging on the rail but they were empty, Griffiths' killer no doubt having already done the same. The base of the wardrobe was a piece of plywood that raised it a few inches above the bedroom floor. I tried to prise it up but could get no purchase. Then, with my head inside the wardrobe, I saw a line of scratches on the interior side of the front lip below the door where the plywood had rubbed against it. I leaned further in, placed my hands against the plywood base at the back and put all my weight against it. The back collapsed downwards, raising the front. I squeezed my hand through the gap and felt around with my fingers. I touched something and I pulled it out: the leather-bound notebook my father had retrieved from the house where Nastasiya had died; the notebook I had given to Standing. There were some loose papers folded inside it but I could hear Daryna muttering to herself in the other room and so quickly slipped it into my coat pocket without examining them. I felt around for anything else and touched an envelope. It was A5 size and thick and I tore the side of it as I pulled it back through the narrow gap. I had just replaced the plywood base and wiped away my prints when I heard Daryna behind me.

'I find nothing,' she said with a note of reproach in her voice. 'What are you doing there?'

I got back on my feet.

'Just looking through the wardrobe,' I said. 'Whatever he was looking for he must have found.'

'What are we to do now?'

'Get out of here,' I said.

We backtracked through the house. Before leaving I glanced again through the lounge, study and kitchen, looking for the obvious, I suppose — a wine glass, a bottle of Chilean red, a second cup — some casually dropped item that could be traced back to me. But there was nothing that blatant. Maybe there didn't have to be. I had already told Bedford and Graham that I would be visiting Griffiths that morning.

We left through the garden but, instead of retracing our steps along the ally, I grabbed Daryna's hand and took the rear path at the back of the terrace to where a small plank bridge spanned the ditch. We crossed it to a patch of waste ground which, judging by the shit, was a favourite of dog walkers. A track led through a scrub of flattened grass and heaps of dumped rubbish.

Daryna stumbled on the uneven path as she tried to keep up with me. She was wearing heels and an expression of indignation.

'Where are we going?'

'Back to the car,' I said.

Beyond the waste ground the path gave onto a road that led towards a junction. Here a corner grocery store, a newsagent and a hairdressers flanked a pub. A public telephone box stood in front of the newsagent.

I squeezed into the box, dialled 999 and gave Griffiths' address, telling them I had heard a disturbance an hour or so earlier and that Mr Griffiths was not answering his door. I left no name. Pulling Daryna after me again I circled around, coming into the road where we had parked. I sat in the Alvis for a minute or two, mostly telling Daryna to be quiet as I looked down the street. Then I drove back to the pub. We spent half an hour over a coffee then I bought another for her and told her to wait until I came back.

'Where you go?'

'Back to the house. The police should be there by now.'

'Why can't I come?'

'Because the police will want your details if they see you with me. I won't be long.'

'What will you tell them?'

'I'll think of something,' I said.

By the time I drove back to Griffiths' house there was a police car parked outside. As I got out of the Alvis a second drew up, its lights flashing.

I walked hesitantly up to the uniformed officer standing by Griffiths' door.

'Hello,' I said. 'Is there a problem here?'

He tried to move me on until I told him I had come to see Griffiths, then he called inside for the detective who had just walked past us into the house. The detective said he wanted to get back to the body and told the constable to get my details.

I explained how I had emailed Griffiths yesterday and arranged to meet him that morning. Not at any particular time, I made clear, just in the morning, glad now I had not rung Griffiths first. I had got lost, I told the uniform, and had arrived later than I had expected. He asked some questions about Griffiths and about why I was meeting him and it was then that I threw in Michael Standing's name which seemed to excite him. The detective was called out a second time and I went through it all once more as the SOCO team arrived kitted out as if expecting to find something contagious. It struck me that as it was the third death they weren't far wrong. I showed the detective some ID and told him that DI Bedford who was investigating Standing's death could vouch for me. He kept me hanging about until he had reached Bedford on his mobile, keeping his eyes on me while listening to what he was told. After a few minutes he rang off and I gave him my address and phone number again. He said I could go but that Bedford would want to talk to me. I could only imagine how much. As I walked back to the Alvis I noticed the uniform making a note of the registration number.

Daryna had fallen into a mood for having been left so long on her own in the pub and was subdued on the drive back to London. Finding a body, you'd think, would prompt a host of questions, but these things take different people in different ways. It was a relief in some respect. It gave me time to think.

We were a mile or so from home when Daryna suddenly remembered she had promised to do something for a friend. I wondered if it was always the same friend that she was habitually forgetting appointments with or whether she had a string of them she could never remember. I dropped her by the underground station. I said I'd see her later as she climbed out of the Alvis.

She stopped halfway out and gave me an intent look and for a moment I thought she might have something to tell me. I waited expectantly but she thought better of it. I watched her cross the pavement to the entrance to the tube station. She looked back in my direction once before descending, then disappeared from view. I drove back to the house.

Cars were parked the length of the road and I drove past slowly. They were all empty, though, and I continued on, turning the next two corners and circling around before I parked.

The phone started ringing just as I opened my door. I went in and closed it behind me, stepping down the hall towards the phone. A pace away, I stopped. The bolt on the cupboard door under the stairs was undone. It had one of those plastic button latches that had worn smooth over the years and had an irritating habit of springing open. Rather than replace it, I had fixed a small barrel bolt on the outside of the top of the door to keep it closed. The door was closed now but the bolt was not fastened. The telephone stood on a low table to one side of the door and was still ringing. I reached over and silently slid the bolt back into place then I lifted the telephone receiver and laid it carefully on the table.

'Yes?' I said into thin air, 'Alex Maitland speaking.'

He pushed against the inside of cupboard door but the bolt held. On the second attempt he used too much force and the bolt gave way and the door flew open, catapulting him into the hall. He stumbled onto his knees and I dropped on top of him, ramming my right elbow into his windpipe with as much force as I could. He went down on his side, grunting as my weight knocked the air out of him. The gun was in his right hand, an unwieldy revolver, and I grabbed for it, reversing my grip to lever it upwards. He began pulling at my wrist with his free hand trying to twist the barrel towards me. I leaned heavily on his windpipe again and he let go of my wrist and reached up for my eyes with his fingers. I twisted the gun as hard as I could as his free hand clawed across my face. He grunted, his finger tightening on the trigger as I forced his wrist around until I heard the bone snap. His yelp of pain was drowned by a deafening shot. I raised my elbow and dropped it into his throat again for good measure. I needn't have bothered. He had gone limp. I got to my feet and looked down at him. His face was turned up to me but where his right eye should have been was a blackened hole.

I took the gun out of his lax hand and stood up. It was an old Enfield MkII, an odd choice of weapon for an assassin. The entrance wound had left a blackened hole instead of an eye and now looked like a miniature volcano crater. A little smoke still issued from it until it was extinguished by blood welling like lava. The exiting shell had taken half the back of his head with it. Blood, brain and bone had spattered across the floor and walls of my hall. Looking it over I wondered irrationally how the hell I was ever going to clean it up. I glanced at him again with distaste and saw that his jacket had ridden up where we had struggled and the butt of another gun protruded from a shoulder holster. I reached down and pulled it out. It was an automatic, a Glock 33 .357 SIG, a subcompact variant of the 27 and the favourite of the military and law enforcement. I wondered why the hell he had tried to shoot me with an antiquated revolver when he was carrying a gun as handy as the Glock. I pulled the magazine out of the grip. There were the standard 9 rounds and I squeezed one out. It was anything but standard. Hollow-point, it was the same kind I suspected had killed Griffiths. I looked at him and wondered if it had felt any different for him than it had for Griffiths. The hollow point bullet that had killed Griffiths would have hit bone and disintegrated into shrapnel, like particles in an accelerator, each tracing a path of its own through his brain. I pushed the bullet back into its clip and saw that my hand was shaking. I took a couple of deep breaths. I was out of condition and twice his age — heavier, yes, but mostly all in the wrong places. What had saved me was falling on top of him. I'd taken the wind out of him and he hadn't been able to reach the Glock.

But why had he waited in the cupboard? He had killed Griffiths was soon as he had answered the door, probably thinking it was me keeping our appointment. Why hadn't I been treated to a similar reception? The killer could have simply hid in the kitchen or the lounge and stepped out... He might have been warned that I was a bigger man than Griffiths and that I'd been trained, but I must have been nearly thirty years older than him and not exactly in prime condition. It didn't seem a reasonable explanation. It occurred to me that perhaps he had needed to get close and that was why he had waited in the cupboard, until I answered the phone so that he could step out as my back was to him.

I picked up the receiver and listened. The connection had been broken. I dialled 1471.

'*The number you have requested has been withheld...*'

I dropped the receiver back on its cradle. It began ringing again immediately. I ignored it and went upstairs.

I had learned the art of travelling light a long time ago. First rule of espionage: a*lways have a bag packed and a back door handy. Take nothing you can't collect in five minutes.* I was a little rusty, perhaps, because it took me seven minutes to empty the safe, pick up the bag I always kept packed at the foot of the cupboard and get back downstairs. I was stuffing papers into the bag and picking up the laptop when I heard a key turn in the front door.

I put the laptop back down softly on the table and pulled the Glock out of my waistband. I'd put the magazine back, a clip of those pitiless soft-nosed shells that had killed Griffiths. I had always hated them; if they didn't kill instantly they maimed, the victim usually bleeding to death from the internal wounds made by the sharp shards slicing indiscriminately through the body. I had never had to use one in anger nor wanted to start now; I hoped the look of the thing would be sufficient. It was ugly enough, small and open-mouthed like death itself.

In the hall I heard a faint exclamation and the sound of the door closing silently behind it. I waited a moment screened by the open dining room door and listened as footsteps moved down the hall. Then I stepped out.

Daryna was kneeling over the body with her fingers at the man's neck feeling for a pulse. I was quite taken by the professionalism she was showing, even if, with half his head missing, he'd have needed to be an android to survive that wound.

'He's dead,' I said.

She jumped in surprise and almost fell across him. The blood drained from her face quicker than from a stuck pig.

'Alex!,' she cried, recovering with commendable speed. 'I thought it was you!' She even crossed herself in good Orthodox fashion before she saw the gun in my hand. Doubt began to flicker in her face and her eyes stayed fixed on the short barrel as if its angle in respect to her was going to dictate her next move.

I lowered it but didn't put it back in my waistband. Her relief was almost palpable. You could practically see the way she was thinking — no articles, definite or indefinite, just quick bursts of thought that took her from one situation to the next.

'Who is he?'

She looked back down at the man, crammed awkwardly sideways on the floor in the narrow hall with the smell of blood hanging over him like a miasma. I took another quick look but I hadn't known him. He had had a pinched, sharp-featured face with a fashionable fuzz of beard and probably hadn't looked any more prepossessing in life than he did in death.

'He was waiting for me.' I said. 'He killed Griffiths, then came here to wait for me. Lucky you weren't with me,' I added.

She smiled at me nervously, unsure about the irony in my voice. Oddly enough I had used the word 'irony' the previous evening playing scrabble and she had looked it up, not trusting me. I might have pointed out the irony in irony but I supposed the time for English lessons had passed.

'Did you come back for your case?' I asked. 'Best not leave it here. Best not *be* here.' I beckoned her towards me and nodded up the stairs. 'We'll get it now, shall we?'

Her eyes flickered towards the gun again and she didn't try to argue. I let her go up ahead of me, keeping several steps below her. She had never struck me as the athletic type but it is always a mistake to rely on appearances. I don't suppose I've ever looked the athletic type either.

Her case was in the room she had used and all her clothes were already packed. She hadn't meant to visit for long. I didn't know what the arrangements had been and I was pretty sure I didn't have the time to ask. She could have told me some of it but probably not all and taking her with me just to satisfy my curiosity wasn't covered in the first rules of espionage as far as I was aware. I carried the suitcase downstairs, Daryna going first, then stopped at the door.

'Have you called police?' she asked. I was beginning to lose count of how many times she had asked me that question.

'No police,' I said. 'Give me your mobile and the door key.'

A frown creased her forehead for a second and I thought she was going to employ the pout but, to her credit, she knew that that wasn't going to work this time. She opened her handbag and put both items in my outstretched left hand. The right was still gripping the Glock. I put the phone and the key in my pocket. The man lying dead on the floor behind me had not broken in and I wondered if he had a copy of the key or had merely slipped the latch.

Daryna looked at me seriously, mouth turned down at the corners as was her way, and for a second I saw her lower lip quiver.

'Where you go, Alex?'

'You know better than ask that,' I said.

She took a step towards me, slowly so as not to surprise the Glock, then she saw the look in my eyes and knew that that wasn't going to work either. She stopped and smiled in a way I had not seen before.

'I wish you luck,' she said, and I was just pleased she still had her heavy accent.

I reached out my left hand, holding her throat between my thumb and fingers. She didn't struggle or try to say anything. I pulled her towards me, the Glock hard against that flat stomach of hers. I felt her body shake.

My face was close to hers. 'You should have told me,' I said quietly. 'Now, take some advice. Leave and keep going. They don't like complications and you're beginning to look like one. It's no life, Daryna. Take it from one who knows.'

Then I kissed her lightly on the forehead and let her go.

I bundled her and that awkward case through the door and walked her round the street until we reached the Alvis.

'Remember what I said,' I told her, climbing in. Then I left her there on the pavement watching me as I drove away.

~

Passing through Basildon I stopped at a shop that sold mobile phones and bought a cheap model and some air time and a dongle for the laptop to a network I could rely on. At a supermarket I stocked up on some extra food and batteries and bottled water. Back at the car I transferred all my contacts to the new phone. Then I dialled Charlie's number.

'Hello? This is Hewson.'

He hadn't recognised the number and there was a distant, professional edge to his voice that I hadn't heard for some while.

'Who's calling?'

'It's me, Charlie,' I said. 'Alex.'

There was a heartbeat's pause.

'You've got a new number,' he said.

'The old phone's dead,' I replied. 'So is David Griffiths.'

'David Griffiths?' he repeated evenly, as if the name were unfamiliar.

'Standing's research assistant. You remember. I just found him in his house with a point three five seven size hole in his head.'

'Jesus, Alex! What have you got yourself into?

'Oh, you know. The same old trouble.'

'Where are you?'

'I thought I'd take a few days away,' I said. 'Things being what they are.'

'Come in, Alex,' Charlie said reasonably. 'Let's straighten this thing out now. We'll have a drink and talk it over.'

'It's a bit late for that,' I told him. 'Oh, and Charlie, there's a bit of a mess at my place. You'll need to get the cleaners in … if you know what I mean.'

'Alex—'

'I'll be in touch, Charlie.'

21

Leaving London to the north-east it always seems to me that there is a line of demarcation that one comes upon so unexpectedly that it sometimes appears as if one has stumbled over the edge of civilization. This abandoned debris of industry, like atrophied tentacles of the city, has left an almost apocalyptic landscape, a mix of the crumbling remains of modern industry with detritus of an earlier age. Beyond, on its outer fringes on the marshes, one finds the rotting hulks of barges, derelict boats hauled up on to the mudflats and left to decay over the slow years until their timbers have become almost indistinguishable from the mud in which they lie. For me, marshes have always been a mystical landscape. It is that commingling of land and sea and sky that keeps one permanently wrong-footed, pervaded as it is with a sense of alienation. For some reason I have always felt it spark an affinity within me. A psychiatrist might make something of it but I've always been too practical a man for that. Perhaps what is at its root is that, when nearing the marshes, I have always become aware that I am entering another land where different rules apply, where different endings are possible.

And I was a man who needed a different ending.

It was getting dark by the time I neared the estuary. To the north the yellowing lights of Foulness swirled in the mist. Fog hung thickly in the hollows and the lights of the Alvis cut murky cones between the mud banks and the flats, momentarily clearing here and there to give a view over the fields. Cold had seeped into the car defeating the groaning heater. I leaned forward, peering through the windscreen searching for the turning. In the fog after dark even a familiar landscape assumes an alien aspect.

There were no lights in the rear-view mirror. No one had followed me. I had holed up in a multi-storey car park for an hour, scrambling under and around the Alvis for possible tracking devices. The fact I found none gave me little comfort; paranoia is a profligate dispenser of fear. Sitting back behind the wheel I considered the sobering possibility that the absence of a device might mean that they knew where I was headed. Yet I doubted it. Over the years I had remained particularly tight-lipped about still having the chalet on the marshes — had taken pleasure in the very secrecy of hiding the fact from everyone — and I was confident that the old place had been forgotten. It was true that a few weeks earlier I had run into Georgia no more than ten miles away, but I didn't think she ever gave much thought to her old cousin Alex and, with luck, she would have quickly forgotten our meeting. By the time she had been born George and Jennifer no longer spent weekends with my parents there and the chances were she had never heard of the place. Worryingly, George had asked about it the previous weekend but we had been looking at old photographs and he had seemed satisfied with my casual reply about my father having sold the chalet.

The boatyard loomed up out of the fog with a suddenness that had me pulling on the wheel. Then I was past it and saw the turning ahead. I swung the Alvis onto the muddy track and a mile further on made out the outline of the chalet in the dark. I slowed, pulled off the rutted track and stopped behind the shed. I climbed out of the car, pushed open the shed doors and inched the Alvis inside. Switching off the engine I reached for the flashlight and the gun. Everything else could wait until I was sure I was alone.

In October when I had last been there, some residual warmth from summer was still lingering over the marshes and the chalet had felt like my familiar retreat. Now, in the first week of December, the bleakness of winter had closed its icy hand over the estuaries and the creeks and it made me feel like an unwelcome intruder. Outside the car I became aware of the faintest of breezes swirling the fog in eddies in the hollows. The air had the keenness of a razor's edge freezing in the lungs and numbing the flesh. I picked my way in the lee of the shed to where the chalet sat silent and dark, looming like a giant ox on the tundra.

The padlock I had left on the back door still held, icy to the touch and beaded with moisture. I slipped the key into it and turned it slowly. I unhitched it from its latch and opened the door. It creaked on rusting hinges. I let out the breath I had been holding and turned on the flashlight, walking through the chalet and arcing the beam over the interior. Everything inside was just how I had left it. Back then Standing had still been alive, I was learning Ukrainian from Daryna and I still had a family of sorts.

I drew the curtains and lit the oil lamp on the table. I had left the wood stove laid, ready for my return as I always did. The paper beneath the kindling felt dry and I put a match to it, watching as it caught. The tongues of flame licked at the wood, charring and burning as they grew. I went through the cupboards, double-checked the paraffin then went back out to the shed.

I had an extra drum of paraffin stored next to a pile of firewood, stacked and dry. In a corner stood a spare bottle of gas. I carried my bag and the few supplies I had bought back inside then went out again, shut the shed doors on the Alvis and locked them. To continue using a car as distinctive as mine would be too risky.

The stove had begun to warm the chalet and I lit a second lamp and checked over the interior. Over the years I had repaired the rotten wood and reversed the slide into dereliction that my father's later apathy had ignored. I had insulated the place and installed bottled-gas and a heater for hot water and showers. As a teenager with my parents, and Olena as a toddler, we had swum in the creeks and doused ourselves with cold water afterwards to get clean. But they had been summer days when everyday had seemed sunny and a child's energy and enthusiasm provides its own heat. Now I was no longer a boy and had lost my enthusiasm along with my youth.

I put a kettle on to boil and wound up the clockwork radio and tuned it to Radio 4 to catch the news. I had my laptop but there was no electricity, leaving me dependent on battery power and the need to recharge and I was going to have to use it sparingly. As far as I was aware, no one had yet invented the clockwork television.

I drank a mug of tea while I waited for a can of soup to heat listening to the seven o'clock news bulletin. Earlier in the day they had briefly reported Griffiths' death but the link to Standing had yet to be established and the news had slipped out of the headlines. No one was talking about finding a body in Alex Maitland's house. I turned off the radio and ate my soup, deciding what to do next. It would have been easier had I known what to expect — countering gambits within a restricted range of probabilities was no more than a game, a dance with rehearsed moves, but this game, unlike chess, had no fixed moves. The opposition had already stepped so far out of what I might have expected them to do that I realized I must still be missing some of the pieces. That made it difficult to put myself in their shoes and to imagine what I would do if I were them. But that, of course, would be dependent on what *they* expected *me* to do. Over that, at least, I had some control. It was a strategy of inner spiralling circles that, inevitably, could only end at a vanishing point. But there was nothing to be gained by thinking about that. I finished my soup and fetched the bottle of scotch I kept in the kitchen cupboard. Pouring a shot, I wondered just how many Charlie had had by now.

I considered how much time I might have. With luck it might be as much as a week's grace, or perhaps even enough to see me to Christmas. That would depend on whether or not the police had started looking for me. I knew several people in the area although few knew me by name. I was known at the boatyard and by sight in the nearest pub and the local shop, but unless the police released my details to the press I doubted they would give much thought to my being there. The locals were used to my making sporadic appearances. No one else lived close enough to wonder what I might be up to. There had once been two other chalets nearby when my father had first bought this one, holiday retreats which, as the fifties had moved into the more prosperous sixties, had become used only intermittently and had fallen into disrepair. By the time my parents had stopped using the place the other chalets had reached a point of no return. Now one was little more than a few rotting stumps of timber and the other merely a discoloured outline in the salt grass.

I washed up my glass, soup bowl and the pan, my slovenly habits for some odd reason never having extended to the time I spent in the chalet. That done I put away the few spare clothes I had bought with me then sorted through the contents of my safe that I had hastily jammed into my bag. I had no safe at the chalet. Instead, I had constructed a box that hung beneath a loose floorboard in the bedroom. It would never have survived a thorough search but it was discrete enough to elude the casual thief. I packed everything in sealable polythene bags to keep out the damp, put them in the box, then placed the Enfield revolver, wrapped in cloth, on top. The lighter Glock I had slipped into a jar to keep handy in the kitchen. When I finished I carried the oil lamp back to the kitchen table and took the leather-bound notebook and the envelope I had retrieved from Griffiths' wardrobe out of my pocket.

That morning in Cambridge seemed a long time ago at that moment. A kitchen clock told me that it was almost nine and the events of the day had begun to catch up with me. I felt drained and in need of sleep. But there were still things I did not understand and I hadn't yet had the opportunity to examine the papers Griffiths had hidden in his wardrobe. I took out the wad he had slipped inside the cover of the notebook first, then pulled the contents of the envelope out and spread them on the table. Much of it was in the Cyrillic script and the pages swam in front of my eyes as I looked it over. I rubbed my eyes and poured myself another scotch and forced myself to concentrate. I had hoped that Griffiths had left some sort of note explaining exactly what the papers related to, and I noticed there were many hand-written comments in the margins of the papers, but at first glance there appeared to be no comprehensive explanation as to what he had left. The pages inserted into the notebook, I saw, were all hand-written, scribbled in a disjointed, sloping script that I assumed belonged to Griffiths; the papers I had taken from the envelope were a mixture of both printed and photocopied material, most stapled to other sheets with appended comments and notes, part hand-written, part typewritten. The top sheets of each group appeared to be copies of official documents which, judging from the marks had once been stapled to other papers, the photocopier faithfully reproducing every old crease and mark and even the outline of the original staples that had once connected them. The top photocopies were in either Ukrainian or Russian — I still couldn't tell the difference — and many held some kind of official stamp designating successive bureaucratic departments of the Cheka, GPU, NKVD ... the mundane paraphernalia of the police state. An English translation, often printed but with many pencilled emendations was stapled to each. The hand-written pages, which had been folded into the notebook, were all in English, although here and there a Cyrillic word remained un-translated, some with queries pencilled-in beside them.

I looked down on the papers spread across the table lit by the gloomy light of my oil lamp and wondered if I would ever make any sense of it. Hadn't that been what Griffiths had emailed me: *It is all incomprehensible to me, those Pages dressed up in leather...?* Perhaps Griffiths had not understood what he'd found in the notebook either. I picked it up and flicked through the pages. It was familiar to me only in the sense that I had looked through it a dozen times since I had found it in my father's house; its true meaning remained impenetrable as ever. I read through what Griffiths had translated and found it consisted of groups of unfamiliar names listed beside dates so old that only an historian like Standing could have found them of interest. On another page I found several scrawled descriptions of people, like character sketches for a story. Here and there was the occasional recognizable place name. Beside these were more dates and a grid references noted obsessively in minutes and seconds of latitude and longitude. Further lists of names corresponded to addresses, some even in towns I recognized — Odessa, Kharkov, Kiev, Sevastopol ... others I did not know. I went back to the notebook again, running my finger down the lines to see where the entries matched Griffiths' translation. Where the place names corresponded to an address, I found they were written in English; where they had been inscribed in Cyrillic they corresponded to the grid reference. I looked at the place names written in English again and noticed now that the handwriting was vaguely familiar, a fact I had never registered before. One of the reasons I had always doubted that the notebook had belonged to my father was that the Cyrillic script had never corresponded to the handwriting in the letters he had written to Nastasiya; even the entries in English had seemed unlike his usual familiar scrawl. But I had never been sure; people's handwriting can change as they get older. Now, though, I knew I had seen the handwriting before: the loop and swirl of the small 'k' in *Kharkov* was quite distinctive; the final 'v' in Kharkov and Kiev finished with an upward stroke that left it hanging high above the rest of the word. I reached for the file of papers I had gathered at George's house and rummaged through until I found the letters that Frederick had written to Nastasiya while he was overseas. There weren't many K's and V's but those I found were identical. The six-fingered Frederick had been Shostak and the notebook had been his.

I poured another glass of scotch and picked up the nearest sheets of papers. They consisted of just two pieces stapled together, the top a photocopy of an official form in Russian with a stamp in one corner, a few typewritten lines and a signature at the bottom. I turned the page. Griffiths had not attempted to translate or reproduce the form. Instead, he had simply written in pencil: *Arrest warrant for Aleksander Zaretsky signed by Kosior, 21/03/1932.*

I reached for another. Below the top sheet in Russian was a printed translation. At the top of the page was the reference:

ST 10-U-1 followed by: Deposition of Mikhail Gerasimov 02/03/32
When the Red Army arrived from Kharkov in December nineteen-seventeen the Bolshevik administration set up the Soviet Congress and began collecting grain from the local area. We were told that Comrade Lenin required the grain for the war effort and to stop it falling into German hands. Anyone who refused to co-operate was regarded as a German agent or a Ukrainian nationalist. Many were necessarily shot. The Cheka leader in Kiev, Comrade Lācis, organised the shipment of grain. The seizures were made by groups of Chekists, local men and Russians. I knew one of these men. He was Comrade Aleksander Zaretsky and I knew him because he came from Kiev. He told us he was a fellow Ukrainian and that it was in our own interests to do as the Bolsheviks said, otherwise the Germans would shoot us. This was all very well but we knew his grandfather had come from Russia to work in a local factory and that he was a member of the Ukrainian Bolshevik Communist Party. Later I was told he had married a girl from one of the villages where her family had a little land. Rich peasants, I heard. He knew which side his bread was buttered.

The next paper was dated October 1939 and appeared to be an extract of an interview or interrogation. The reference was ST 09-R-2 and beneath this Griffiths had scribbled: *Ministry of Justice.*

Witness: Lev Kiminski, Ukrainian Jew of Kiev region.
Present: Comrade Officers Gamenev and Golitsyn.

Interrogator: *Do you recall when the puppet Ukrainian government in Kiev left when the Red Army arrived from Kharkov?*

Witness: Yes. It was December Nineteen-seventeen.

Interrogator: *Is that when you first met Aleksander Zaretsky?*

Witness: Yes. I was with a unit of the Red Guard. We were known as the Black Shooters. We had a reputation as loyal men. Many of us were Party members. We —

Interrogator: *Get on with it.*

Witness: Yes, your Honour. Sorry, your Honour. We found the man Zaretsky wandering the streets and detained him for questioning. You understand that many counter-revolutionary elements had stayed behind to disrupt our government of the city.

Interrogator: *Perfectly well. Did you establish that Zaretsky was not a member of these counter-revolutionaries?*

Witness: Yes. He showed us his Party card and gave us the names of prominent Cheka men who could vouch for him. He told us he was from Kiev himself and was looking for members of his own family. He thought the Rada puppet government might have shot them.

Interrogator: *He was looking for his wife?*

Witness: No. A brother and sister and his elderly mother, he told us.

Interrogator: *Did he find them?*

Witness: No.

Interrogator: *When did you next see Comrade Zaretsky?*

Witness: It must have been three or four years later. Shortly after this time my unit was transferred to the front and we spent the next years in the struggle against the Whites and the Greens. When I returned to Kiev I found that Zaretsky was on Comrade Lācis's staff and —

Interrogator: *You are aware that the man Lācis has been executed for counter-revolutionary activities and is no longer to be referred to as "Comrade"?*

Witness: Yes, your Honour. I am sorry. I meant to say Zaretsky was on the staff of the man Lācis. This was before knowledge of this man's treachery was known, of course.

Interrogator: *And what was his function?*

Witness: Zaretsky?

Interrogator: *Yes, Zaretsky. That is why we are here.*

Witness: *Yes, your Honour. His function was to collect grain from the peasants under the directive issued by the Central Committee.*

Interrogator: *And you learned something of his personal life did you not?*

Witness: *Yes. I learned that he had married a girl from my village. Ivan Kirov's eldest daughter, Nastasiya. Kirov was a peasant with two hectares of land at this time.*

Interrogator: *Kirov was a Kulak?*

Witness: *Not at this time, your Honour, no.*

Interrogator: *Were you aware that Ivan Kirov was later re-classified as a Kulak?*

Witness: *Yes. Under the New Policy brought in by Comrade Lenin, Kirov was able to rent more land and grow more wheat. He was a good farmer. Prices were high and he prospered. By the time he was decreed as a class enemy he owned fifteen hectares and two cows and a horse.*

Interrogator: *And he exploited the labour of other peasants?*

Witness: *He employed a man, yes.*

Interrogator: *You do not think that profiting from the labour of others is exploitation?*

Witness: *Yes sir. The man Kirov exploited other peasants.*

Interrogator: *Was he denounced?*

Witness: *By the man he employed, your Honour.*

Interrogator: *And who arrested him?*

Witness: *Zaretsky. He took the whole family.*

Interrogator: *Even though he was related by marriage?*

Witness: *(inaudible).*

Interrogator: *Speak up.*

Witness: *He was a good Party man, your Honour.*

Interrogator: *Was there opposition to Kirov's arrest?*

Witness: *(hesitant) Some, your Honour.*

Interrogator: *And Zaretsky's wife? Was she arrested also?*

Witness: *As the wife of a Party member it was decided that she could not be classed as a Kulak.*

Interrogator: *How do you know this?*

Witness: *The matter of Kirov and his family was debated in village council.*

Interrogator: *How did you vote?*

Witness: *I do not recall.*

Interrogator: *Comrade Zaretsky decided the matter himself?*

Witness: No, your Honour. The matter was put before the Troika.

Interrogator: Wasn't Comrade Zaretsky the head of the Troika?

Witness: Yes, your Honour. He voted for deportation.

22

I woke with a start, disorientated. Then the smell of the chalet came to me in the darkness and memory seeped back carrying images of the dead man in my house, of Griffiths' body and of Daryna shaking as I held her by the throat with the Glock pressed against her stomach.

I rolled over and reached for the clock, peering at the hands until I made out it was 6.15. I climbed out of the bed and dressed and grabbed the Glock from beneath the pillow. Leaving some water on to boil, I took a flashlight and slipped out into the cold morning. There was no sound except for the gentle lapping of water in the creek where the tide was in. I waited until my eyes adjusted to the darkness then moved slowly in a perimeter sweep, a middle-aged fool playing soldiers. After ten minutes, convinced I was on my own, I went back inside and lit an oil lamp. The papers still lay on the table where I had left them the night before.

I stared down at them, mulling over the conclusions that had formed in my brain while I slept — such sleep as I had had. The thing about jigsaw puzzles is that, once finished, one has two choices: one either leaves the thing complete, always there, in your way, something forever to work around, or one pulls it to bits, puts away the pieces and dismisses the picture and gets on with life. It was true I still didn't have the full picture, but from the pieces that Standing and Griffiths had managed to dig out of the old KGB files, an outline had begun to emerge. The gaps that remained would have to have been filled by logical assumption and leaps of faith. The one thing I had learned, though, was that my jigsaw was going to form no pretty picture. There were no rose-decked peasant cottages, no happy families at the gate. The picture my jigsaw painted was one of brutal realities, of a choice of either conforming to a heartless ideology or of starving and dying. Perhaps I could have stopped there, pulled the pieces I did have apart and got on with my life — after all I did have other worries to claim my attention — but I knew the bits would never stay in the box, that the picture would never go away.

I had long suspected that Michael Standing had discovered more than he was ever willing to tell me and from those few morsels of information he did let drop at our first meeting back in February it was obvious now that he already had some of the pieces. He had told me then about grain seizures conducted under Martin Lācis during the war and how Aleksander Zaretsky had assisted him. Later, when I had seen him in the summer, he told me he had been back to Kiev and collected more information. In the restaurant he had shown me the deposition made in 1932 detailing how Zaretsky, a decade later, had conducted more grain seizures in the company of a man known as Shostak. I wondered how long Standing had known my grandmother's family name and the fact that Zaretsky had had them all arrested as Kulaks. Had he known when we had talked in Cambridge when he had explained how the Bolsheviks had come to liquidate the Kulaks? If he had, when was he planning to tell me? Griffiths had suggested in one of his emails that Standing hadn't wanted to shock me with unpleasant revelations, and I remembered how he had seemed on the verge of telling me something after lunch when we had walked down to the leat behind the hotel. But how much of his reluctance was a natural secretiveness, less to do with my sensibilities than with an historian's miserliness with uncovered facts? He was dead and perhaps I should have been magnanimous and accepted the fact that Standing was trying to spare my feelings. Yet, if that *was* the case, when was I to find out the truth — sitting in the comfort of my own home while watching Standing's latest documentary series on the television? No, a concern for my sensibilities did not fit with the facts. There was more to it than that. I believe he had first latched on to Zaretsky's name because he had discovered his involvement with the character, Shostak, a foreigner whose identity was obviously sensitive and who was involved with the export and sale of seized grain to raise money for Stalin's programme of Industrialization. At some point, somewhere in the files he and Griffiths were researching, they had turned up information that Shostak was more than just a facilitator of grain shipments. Whether it was only the insistence on the use of a pseudonym when referring to the foreigner, or some harder piece of evidence he had found, it was something that had prompted him to dig deeper to see what else he might find. He must have thought he had struck a rich seam when his enquiries about Aleksander Zaretsky had turned up surviving family members. It was odd how it had brought him to me. I don't suppose for a minute he would have imagined that the trail would lead back to the man who had sponsored his own scholarship to Cambridge.

Thinking about the university sent me back to the photographs I had copied in George's study, the one of Frederick and Nastasiya's wedding and the gaunt young man whose face I had recognized, the photograph I had cropped and enlarged and had emailed to Charlie. I took it out of the file again and studied it. It wasn't easy to see the old man's face in the young one. Those last years of disgrace had been written in every line. He had been stripped of his knighthood and his Honorary Fellowship of Trinity College; he had been made aware of the strength of public feeling against him; his long-term partner had tried to commit suicide by throwing himself from a sixth-floor balcony... A few years later he was dead himself, victim of a heart attack.

Anthony Blunt had confessed to spying for the Soviet Union in 1964 after Kim Philby had defected. By then he had risen to the post of Keeper of the Queen's Pictures and had been knighted for his services to the Crown. It had proved a bone of contention with many people that his services *against* the Crown had been less easy to reward. An American named Straight had alleged that Blunt had attempted to recruit him as a Soviet agent in the 1930s. Confronted with the accusation, Blunt had admitted his guilt. He became the fourth man in the Cambridge spy ring. During the war he had joined MI5, passing information to the Soviet Union. He had left the Service after the war to pursue other interests. He had been interrogated without success after Burgess and Maclean had defected but, following his confession, he was interrogated again and offered immunity from prosecution in return for what he could reveal. I had never met him, of course; his treachery had finally been made public fifteen years later when an investigative journalist exposed him — albeit anonymously, although with enough pertinence that the government had felt compelled to make a statement to the House on the matter. I had joined the service a couple of years later but I still remembered being made acutely aware of how the press revelations had stirred up the old scandals concerning SIS penetration again.

Standing couldn't have known about Blunt and Frederick — he was dead by the time I had found the photograph — but I think he had come to suspect that Frederick had been involved in the Cambridge spy ring nevertheless. If so, perhaps I *was* doing Standing an injustice. I suppose one can hardly blame him for not wanting to tell a man that not only was his grandfather, in his capacity as a member of Stalin's secret police, responsible for his own wife's family's arrest and almost certain death, but also that his step-grandfather might have been a traitor to his country.

Reading how Zaretsky had denounced his wife's family had sobered me and I had remained at the table, examining the papers long into the night. There was more to it than that, of course, undocumented but plain between the lines, and I wondered if Standing had ever found confirmation of what I suspected; and whether he had told Griffiths to keep it from me if I ever asked. Still not quite wanting to accept what I had come to believe, I had gone back through all the papers again hoping for another explanation. The references, I had finally come to realize, denoted the successive visits Standing and Griffiths had made to the Russian and Ukrainian archives, being further subdivided depending upon subject and content. I had even found my own classification: *Alexander Maitland Ref: ST-UK-26/02/10*. Knowing this I had begun to assemble an overview of what I had. Griffiths, I supposed, had already done much the same. He would have had subjects other than Aleksander Zaretsky, I assumed, dozens of them perhaps on his computer. They were deleted now, any copies taken by his killer. All I was really interested in, though, was material that could lead back to Frederick Maitland. The man I'd left in my hall had had nothing on him when I'd searched his body, no memory sticks or discs, but then perhaps he had left a car nearby or had even already delivered what he had found to his masters. It hardly mattered now. Even my own attempt at an overview got no further than a few lines:

Aleksander Zaretsky, b. (?) Pre-revolutionary political activity (Ref.) Native of Kiev (Ref.) Selected to join Martin Lācis in weeding out undesirable elements in Cheka (Ref. & Ref.) concerned with grain collection. Married Nastasiya Kirova (Ref.) daughter of middle-peasant family from Kharkov...

At that point I had given up. One might have thought that the fact of my grandfather and Frederick Maitland being complicit in murder and the deliberate starvation of a national population would have weighed heavily with me — sitting like an incubus in the night, one might say — but the mundane truth is I barely acknowledged the fact. I felt numbed. The other revelation, unstated but obvious, was bad but just another blow on senseless flesh. In truth, Aleksander Zaretsky had never been anything more than a name to me. Now, it was just one that I would prefer to forget.

~

Some time in the small hours I had finally fallen into bed. It all still careered through my head but the rest of me had reached the end of its tether. Perhaps this had been what my father had discovered about Frederick and what had caused the breach. Lying in the dark I realized that if I found the facts distasteful after a full seventy-five years without ever having known the principal characters, how much more deeply must he have felt the sense of betrayal? To find that his real father, whom he must still have remembered, had been one of Stalin's thugs and had been responsible for the arrest and death of his mother's family (did he remember them?) must have been devastating. How much else he knew there was no way of knowing for sure. There was nothing to help me in the notebook, for instance, as far as I could tell, beyond an arcane melange of intangible facts. Yet he had kept it. Perhaps *he* had understood it. And, of course, there might have been more pulled from the rubble of the Hackney house that I hadn't seen, other documents which had not survived my father's possession. It might even have been that Frederick had told him the story. With Nastasiya dead he might have decided that she was beyond being hurt any further, or that my father was simply owed the truth. Either way, I realized I was never going to find out now.

Had my father been less of a tight-lipped man he might have been able to share the knowledge with his family. But knowing Zaretsky as a father, perhaps, keeping the memory of him alive for almost a decade after leaving the Ukraine, only to discover that this memory was a false one, might have persuaded him that the first twenty years of his own life had been founded on a lie. I wondered if he had ever told my mother. If he had, she had kept it from me and — I was equally certain — from Olena. And he hadn't allowed what he knew of his parents' background to destroy his own family life.

266

Yet it had still left a shadow of melancholy over that life, a fact I was only now coming to recognize. It had made him cut all the ties he had had with his boyhood — with his memories of his father, of the Ukraine, of even the memory of his own mother and lastly with Frederick himself. Only George had somehow remained unscathed, spared from being written out of my father's own history because he was just an innocent child. But as a man? Time changes everything. Lying sleeplessly in my bed I had to consider that. How much did George know of his own father's past? Was he an innocent still?

Perhaps.

Dawn was creeping up over the estuary by the time I began clearing the tangle from my head. I had only slept for a few fitful hours but there was no time for more.

Leaning across the table, I extinguished the oil lamp, sorted out the few papers I was taking with me and pushed the rest into my makeshift safe — out of sight if not out of mind. There was no point now in picking the bones out of old betrayals, I decided. There were the consequences of newer ones to deal with.

I wound up the clockwork radio and listened to the news while I ate breakfast. At the end of the bulletin it was announced that the man held for questioning in connection with the death of Michael Standing had hung himself in his cell. There were no further details. I booted up the laptop and searched for more information but the news had been fresh and the on-line networks hadn't yet caught up. There were no other revelations and if the police were looking for me they had not made the fact public. Who else might be on my tail was another matter altogether. I put on my coat and boots, stuck the Glock in my waistband and buttoned my coat. I slipped Frederick's notebook into the pocket and went back outside, trying not to think of the vagrant.

A grey light was drifting up river, carrying tongues of mist that had followed the incoming tide. Mud sucked at my boots as I tramped along the track then crossed a marshy field towards a low, salt-blown stand of stunted trees.

I knew now that they had wanted me dead, but not like Griffiths. His death would fit a pattern of conspiracy that explained Standing's murder, however unreal and tenuous it might seem; mine might have looked like a murder too far. Besides, I was connected to the Maitland family and it seemed no breath of scandal could be allowed to touch them. It would have had to look like suicide and that is why he had waited in the under-stairs cupboard, to be sure he was close enough when he shot me. There had to be powder burns on my temple, an Enfield revolver in my hand. It was an old Service pistol, the kind my father would have been issued during the war, or something an ex-soldier like myself might have kept as a souvenir. That was the kind of touch they liked. I couldn't help thinking that there might have been a better way to approach the problem but there are no guarantees that the type of psychopath employed for this kind of work thinks too deeply of the contingencies of the business.

You get what you pay for in death as in life, I suppose, and we've all been made aware that these are straightened times.

I wouldn't have rated an obituary, of course, but the rationalizations would have come to lips readily enough.

Poor Alex. The injury he sustained in Africa gave him constant pain. And he had had to retire from his job and had little else. Bit of an aimless life and plagued by insomnia... He had *been depressed lately. I suppose it had all become too much. Hardly surprising that in the end he had taken the easy way out.*

Well, I wasn't going to make it that easy.

Skirting the trees I picked up another track and came into the village from the north. There was an early bus into Southend and I waited at the stop with a teenager, half-asleep between his headphones. We yawned in unison and exchanged a surly nod in greeting, then ignored one another until the bus arrived. It was early and I found the garage I knew that rented cars still closed. I bought a couple of newspapers and sat reading them over a mug of tea in a café, scanning the inside pages for anything about bodies discovered in houses and men the police wanted for questioning. The front pages were more concerned with the murder of David Griffiths now the link to Michael Standing had been established and had begun following the Sunday papers' leads by speculating about the involvement of foreign intelligence services. The news of the suicide of the man the police had been holding for Standing's murder had come in too late for the morning editions. I supposed that, my having also turned up at the house in Cambridge shortly after the murder, would mean Bedford and Graham would be wanting to talk to me just as the detective had said. It might be that they had already tried and not found me at home. Still, the fact that my address hadn't featured in the news suggested that, either Charlie had sent the cleaners in, or the police were keeping what they knew to themselves. Either way, I suspected I probably had less time than I had hoped.

I finished my tea and walked back to the garage.

No news isn't necessarily good news.

23

Most people were surprised when Bill Vickery retired to the backwoods of Sussex. Not many would have suspected his fondness for animals and, if asked, might have presumed his interests lay in collecting. Anyone who considered the two would, perhaps, have suggested lepidoptery — the trapping and classifying, the pinning and displaying of trophies so that their true colours and markings might be examined. But that would have been to suppose that Bill had taken his working life into retirement. He hadn't. He had walked away from the secret life with not so much as a glance back over his shoulder. I know this because I was one of the few people who had kept up with him after he had left the Service. We had always met occasionally for a drink when I had been home on leave. I had visited him once in Sussex after I got out of hospital and had been fit enough to drive. We still exchanged Christmas cards.

For a December day it wasn't bad and once south of London and away from the worst of the traffic a milky sun began to push its way through the cloud and give me cause for optimism. It wasn't a sentiment I had been much burdened with of late and I felt a definite lift of the spirit once I hit those narrow country lanes tucked between their tall banks under the bare winter trees.

Had I been inclined to analyse it, I would have realized that my lighter mood probably had more to do with the prospect of seeing Bill again than any newfound confidence in my immediate prospects. He had been my mentor when I'd first joined SIS, was one of the instructors in the various courses my intake had undergone, and had also taken a personal interest in me. His background was necessarily vague — in a way we were all born-again entering the Service — and I soon learned that a stoic tight-lippedness about our respective pasts was what was expected. Bill and I had become friends, though, perhaps because I was older than most of my brother recruits and closer to Bill's age. He would have been in his forties then, a tough man with a wiry frame who carried no unnecessary weight. He'd come through the police, into Special Branch and then MI5. That much I knew. He'd joined SIS to impart his skills in surveillance and interrogation during those early days of rapprochement between the MI5 and SIS that had followed the nearly fifty years of distrust and mutual hostility that had begun before the war. It was a new approach to co-operation and he taught us what he knew, not so that we might emulate his skills in watching and questioning but so that we could personally avoid being the subject of both.

The smallholding he had bought in retirement lay a few miles to the southeast of Midhurst. I'd found it with difficulty on my previous visit, nestling as it did at the far end of a long farm track tucked beneath a fold in the hills on the northern edge of the South Downs. It was now later in the year than the time of my last visit and there was more mud than I'd expected. I felt the wheels of the small Honda I'd hired slip and slither beneath me as I made my way along the track. I had used false identification at the garage and had paid cash and now began to wish I'd rented something with a bit more grunt. I dropped a gear and slowed and hoped I wasn't going to get stuck.

I hadn't phoned ahead to let Bill know I was coming. He had been retired for fifteen years but, despite appearances, in that line of business it always paid to assume that links are never entirely broken. I hadn't seen him, in fact, since the funeral of his wife, Pat, a couple of years earlier. I hadn't known her well but Bill had attended the funerals of both my mother and my father although I don't recall he had ever met either of them. It was a matter of decency, I suppose.

I caught sight of him as I approached the house, an odd tumbledown affair with a variety of gables that angled this way and that as if they had never really decided on which way they ought to run. An agglomeration of outhouses, lean-tos, additions and extensions added to the effect. Bill was standing in the doorway, a bucket in one hand and the other closed over a walking stick on which he leaned heavily. He was nearing eighty now and I realized with something of a shock that he was looking it. His always-spare frame seemed even thinner and his skin had taken on that detached look the elderly often have as if the muscles and ligaments had grown weary of grasping the bone beneath. In my head I always thought of him as the tough, sardonic instructor I had first met; now his weather-beaten face seemed crumpled, like a sheet of paper that had been screwed up and flattened out again.

There didn't seem much wrong with his eyesight, though.

'Alex?'

I picked up the file I had brought with me and climbed awkwardly out of the Honda, my boots sinking into an inch of mud.

'What's prompted this?' Bill asked. 'You should have phoned. If I'd known you were coming I'd have cleaned myself up and had a shave.'

He stroked the beard he'd grown when he'd left the job and through it I saw his mouth was curled in a surprised smile. At the same time, I couldn't help noticing a certain wariness in his deep-set eyes.

'Just passing, were you?'

'It's been a while, Bill,' I said.

It wasn't an answer but he nodded and didn't press the point.

'I was about to feed the chickens.' He rattled the bucket at me. It was half-full of malodorous pellets. 'Go inside. I'll only be a few minutes. You remember where the galley is.'

'I'll tag along,' I said, 'as long as I'm not going to frighten your birds.'

He gave a hoarse grunt, shutting the front door behind him. 'Soon as they see the bucket they won't have eyes for anything else.'

I followed Bill around the back and through a muddy yard. The chicken house stood behind a run of rusting wire, their shed a jumble of sagging, weathered timber that didn't look as if it would survive the next strong blow. Bill unhitched the wood and wire door, pushing it open against the mud. A motley flock of squawking birds ran towards us, getting underfoot. Bill scooped up a handful of pellets and scattered them around. The squawking stopped, replaced with clucks of satisfaction. Bill ducked into the shed and picked up eggs from the nest boxes, placing them in the bucket. I waited at the door, the warm odours of manure and damp straw drifting out towards me.

'Lunch,' he said, lifting the bucket as he emerged.

We crossed the backyard to the house and I stopped at the door to unlace my muddy boots. Bill waved a dismissive hand at them and tramped past me in his Wellingtons into the kitchen.

'After years of Pat's nagging about muddy boots,' he said, 'it gives me a great deal of satisfaction to do just as I please.' He gave me a challenging look as if expecting me to argue the point and I could see he hadn't meant it. Then he shrugged. 'I swab it out once a week.'

I took him at his word but it didn't look as if he wasted much time swabbing. I had never been a careful housekeeper but Bill was downright negligent. He'd let the place go. Washing-up lay in a pile in the sink. Half a loaf of greening bread and its attendant crumbs stood on the table next to a brimming ashtray, old newspapers and the other detritus of past breakfasts. The wooden work surfaces looked as if they would have benefited from a good scrub and the number of empty spirit bottles lying around betrayed who kept him company in the evenings.

I asked how he was getting on.

'Pretty good,' he said. 'Yourself?'

'Can't complain.'

Mutual untruths over, I sat at the table while Bill made a pot of tea from the kettle sitting on the top of his old and greasy range. He cast around for clean mugs and settled on two fresh from the dusty shelf of the Welsh dresser. He had the decency to rinse them under the tap.

'Touring holiday?' he asked, glancing back at me sardonically.

'I am away for a while,' I admitted, trying to determine from his demeanour whether or not he had heard anything about me in the last couple of days. His expression gave little away, however, and nothing that he wouldn't have wanted to give.

His eyes slid down to the file I had placed on the table.

'Taking your work with you?'

'Actually, there was something I wanted to ask you about,' I said.

He nodded, displaying no curiosity. He emptied the hot water from the pot into the mugs, dropped a couple of tea bags in and refilled it from the kettle boiling on the range. That done he set it on the table between us, sipping a tea cosy over the top. He sat down and reached for his cigarettes.

'How's your sister? Olena, isn't it? I heard she divorced that husband of hers.'

'She's well, thanks. Couldn't see herself as a politician's wife. Olena's never been one to shrink meekly into the background.'

Bill blew smoke into the air and coughed. 'No, that's what I thought when I heard her husband had gone into politics. Television might have suited her better.'

For a moment I wondered if there was more to the remark than there seemed, but then he said:

'Still that's where a lot of them end up these days, isn't it? A failed political career must look good on a TV hopeful's CV.'

'Nick's still a way from failure,' I said.

Bill nodded sagely and poured the tea. He pushed a sugar bowl towards me then got up and fetched a bottle of milk from the fridge. I was relieved to see it looked reasonably fresh. I remembered that he had kept a couple of cows for their milk and had had no need of delivery. As ever, he could tell what I was thinking and said:

'Got rid of the cows. Pigs, too. Getting too much for me. Just got the chickens and a couple of goats, now.'

'Rebecca?' I asked.

His eyes clouded for a moment.

'She died back in the summer, poor old girl. She'd had a good run, though.'

Rebecca was a donkey Bill and Pat had inherited on buying the smallholding. She hadn't been young then but had taken the change of ownership with equanimity and the couple had grown fond of her.

'I'm sorry,' I said.

He shrugged again. 'We all go sooner or later. I rent out my bit of land for pasture now.' He drew on his cigarette, watched me for a moment then dropped his eyes to the file that lay on the table. 'So,' he said, 'what's the problem, Alex? They don't want you back, do they?'

Quite the contrary, I thought, but I hadn't made up my mind how much I could tell him. Instead of answering I opened the file, took out the two photographs I had brought and laid them in front of him. He glanced across at me then picked up a pair of spectacles and turned his attention to them. He left the enlarged shot of Anthony Blunt on the table and held up the wedding photo of Frederick and Nastasiya I had cropped it from.

'I've not seen this before,' he said.

'I thought not. Did you know he was best man at my grandmother's wedding?'

Bill shook his head absently and peered at the photograph.

'Pretty woman. Died in the Blitz, didn't she?'

'Nineteen-forty.'

'Still,' he said, dropping the photograph back on the table, 'you didn't come here to show me the family album.'

'I wanted to ask you about Blunt. You interrogated him, didn't you?'

His gaze shifted to some point over my shoulder, to a glimpse of his younger self in a different world, perhaps.

'I interviewed him,' he said. 'I certainly wouldn't call it an interrogation. He'd gone through all that after he confessed in nineteen-sixty-four, although in retrospect I'm not sure it ever did us much good. When it became common knowledge he'd worked for the Russians it was thought it might be a good idea to take another crack at him. He was at a pretty low ebb just then.'

'Was there anything left to learn?'

Bill stroked a thumb and forefinger down the length of his beard. 'Loose ends,' he said.

He stared at me and I found myself shifting awkwardly in my chair. He wasn't going to make it easy for me.

'What I'm interested in,' I began, 'is anything you might have learned about Fredrick Maitland.'

'He was the man your grandmother married, wasn't he?'

I stared back across the table at him. I felt suddenly irritated. He knew full well who Frederick was and I wondered how old a man had to be before he began to consider how much secrecy still mattered anymore. Bill had been out of it for fifteen years; the events I was interested in had happened sixty years before that. Everyone concerned was long dead; the world had moved on.

He knew what I was thinking — mind-reading was one of the turns he had kept in his magician's box of tricks. He tapped his hands on the table top before suggesting we go for a walk.

'Put those away,' he said, nodding down at the photographs. 'You'll stay for lunch, won't you Alex? I don't get many visitors and I've never liked eating alone. Keep me company.' He walked to the back door and peered up at the sky. 'Do you think we'll get any rain?'

We crossed the yard once more, skirted his chicken run and passed through a gate into a field, making sure it was shut behind us. A small herd of cows was grazing on the far side. One or two looked up at us curiously, wondering I suppose if it was worth the effort of their sauntering over before going back to cropping grass. I followed Bill along a muddy track beside the hedgerow to a stile. He had brought his stick although I couldn't help noticing he was walking perfectly easily without its aid. He clambered over the stile nimbly.

'When I saw you with the walking stick at the door,' I said, once on the other side of the stile, 'I thought your legs might be giving trouble.'

'What? Oh, the stick.' He grinned at me and waved it in the air like a rapier. 'I don't get many visitors out here. Picked it up when I heard the car. Suspicious nature, I suppose. Been conditioned by the work.' He poked the end of the stick at a few bloodied pigeon feathers under the hedge. 'Fox. Buggers will have my chickens if they could.'

'I wondered,' I began again, 'if Frederick Maitland's name had ever come up while you were talking to Blunt.'

He turned to me innocently. 'Any reason you thought it might have?'

'Several,' I said. 'The main one is I believe Michael Standing and David Griffiths were trying to connect him to the Cambridge spies.'

That stopped him in his tracks. For the first time it looked as if I had his full attention. I didn't doubt that I always did have, but it was part of Bill's technique never to let it show.

I told him about Standing and Griffiths and Fielding and threw in the Black Sea Company for good measure. I didn't tell him that they'd tried to kill me as well or that the police might be looking for me. *Need to know*: first rule of espionage. There was a possibility that he might already have known although, if he did, he gave no visible sign. We reached another gate and turned onto a gravelled path that angled slightly uphill. Bill bent his slight frame and wheezed a little at the extra effort. The sun briefly broke through the thin cloud, throwing faint shadows from the trees. Brown leaves rotted underfoot adding a smell of decay to the air.

'I've seen it in the papers, of course,' he said, 'but I just thought the story was journalistic hyperbole. They never said how Griffiths was killed.'

'Between the eyes,' I said. 'A Glock.' For dramatic effect I unbuttoned my coat and showed him the butt of the gun in my waistband. 'But not me, of course.'

'Put it away, Alex,' he said mildly. 'You need a licence for those these days.'

Across the fields I could see a collection of farm buildings, barns and a hay store. A tractor was moving away, carrying hay bales on its front lift. The growl of its engine carried faintly on the air towards us. In the trees above rooks put up a raucous cawing.

'I'm beginning to think Standing might have been right,' I said. 'Although that doesn't tell me why they wanted him dead.'

'Who?'

'That's the question, isn't it?'

He looked at me warily. 'Is this on the books or are you freelancing?'

'It's personal,' I said.

He thought about that for a moment.

'Then you're wondering about our old friends,' he said. 'But that's out of order, surely.'

'That's the worrying aspect,' I admitted.

We left the gravel path, taking another stile and skirted a wood.

'I'll tell you what I can,' he offered. 'I don't know how much it will help.'

'Whatever you can,' I said.

He pursed his lips. 'Well,' he began, 'when I said we were tying up loose ends that's exactly what I meant. To be honest, the bad days were behind us, but you know what Registry are like — if anyone on file so much as stubs a toe they wanted chapter and verse on the incident. It was thought that since Blunt's life was more or less in tatters he might be a little more forthcoming on his past associates. He had been somewhat reticent back in the sixties when it came to any of them who were still around.' He swung his stick at a clump of weeds beneath the wire fence. 'We didn't get much, in truth. There was a little more detail here and there about what we already knew but nothing you could put your finger on, nothing to make you say, *this is interesting, what could that mean?*'

'Had he ever said anything about Frederick Maitland?'

'You're assuming he was asked.'

'All right, Bill,' I said, 'was he asked?'

'Yes. He admitted that he had known Frederick at Cambridge in twenty-eight but we knew that already. Frederick was one of the people Arthur Martin had wanted to talk to in the sixties when Blunt confessed. They had drawn up a list of all his possible associates going back years. There was a hundred or more to begin with but after whittling them down to those who were in a position to know anything or, to be more exact, knew enough to be able to do anything with it, they were left with perhaps a dozen names. Frederick's was one.'

'They interviewed him, then.'

276

'No. His was one of the names permission was refused for interview.'

'This was when Hollis was head of SIS? He refused?'

'Yes, but don't jump to conclusions. There *were* good reasons why he should have been excluded.'

'Such as?'

Bill shrugged. 'He had left the Service after the war ... he was a City businessman with a lot of influence... We had a Labour government back then. Don't forget there were a lot of economic problems. Any breath of MI5 interest in a prominent financier would have scared the City shitless. Besides, they were still focussing on the Cambridge ring, Burgess, Maclean and Philby. Frederick had left Cambridge before any of the others went up. In his day it wasn't the hotbed of political extremism that it became later.'

I recalled that Michael Standing had told me much the same thing, although I remembered that he had had his reservations.

'Unlike Frederick, Blunt had stayed on as a Fellow. It's probable that he was the one who recruited Burgess, possibly Maclean and Philby as well, although we were never able to pin that down.'

'But who recruited *him*?'

'That's the question. He always maintained he was approached in thirty-three but to me that never had the ring of truth. You know, of course, there were those who thought that Hollis himself was the fifth man and that he was being deliberately obstructive in not allowing certain individuals to be interviewed. Frederick was one of them but no one at the time thought he was a serious risk, only that he might have known something useful. In the end his name was traded off for some Cambridge don that they were more interested in.'

'You said Frederick left the Service after the war.'

'Did I?' Bill said.

'You're confirming he worked for British Intelligence.'

He looked at me sideways. 'I thought you'd established that.'

'Circumstantially,' I said. 'I've no actual proof.'

He stopped abruptly, turned and stood in front of me. 'If it's proof you want, we might as well shut up shop now. I've none to give you.'

I looked down at him, old yes, but no longer the frail stick of skin and bone I'd seen by the door to his house. Recalling the work had somehow breathed life back into him.

'I'll settle for suspicion,' I said.

Bill smiled, 'Then we can do business.'

'So Frederick did work for SIS between the wars.' I repeated.

'And during it. After Cambridge he was sent to Turkey. His job was to set up a network of agents in the southern Soviet territories.'

'Through the Black Sea Company?'

'I've never heard that name.'

'He was an illegal, then?'

'Yes. He had no diplomatic cover at all. Relations between the Bolshevik government and the Western Powers were not particularly cordial, you might recall.'

'The Bolsheviks gave him a code name,' I said. 'That can only have been to conceal his identity.'

'That's an assumption,' Bill said.

'A reasonable one. They called him Shostak, because of his hand.'

'His six fingers?'

'You don't recognize the name?'

'No.'

'All right,' I said, 'you knew he was inside the Soviet Union in the late twenties and early thirties but despite this he wasn't interviewed.'

'It was apparently decided it wasn't relevant to the investigation,' Bill said evenly.

I kicked out at a stone on the path. 'Hollis decided and the others fell in line. Why would that have been? Because he was regarded as "one of us"?' I tapped him on the shoulder. 'Suppose they were right and he really was "one of *us*" and they were protecting him because of that?'

Bill shook his head. 'Too much has been made of that sort of attitude in my opinion,' he said, as reasonable as ever. 'Particularly by outsiders who don't understand the subtleties of the game.'

I had to laugh. I hadn't been an outsider and I still didn't understand the *subtleties*, as he called them.

'You believe Hollis was protecting people because he was a Soviet mole,' he said, 'yet there wasn't a scrap of evidence against him.'

'Because he was in a position to manage the evidence,' I insisted.

'You're making another assumption,' Bill replied.

'For God's sake!' I said, 'there are times when you *have* to make assumptions. Then prove them true or false on the evidence.'

'Fair enough,' he conceded. 'Why did suspicion fall on Hollis?'

'Several reasons,' I told him, my jaw tightening. I had come expecting to ask questions not answer them.

'Number them.'

'All right.' I thought about it a moment. 'Information from sources abroad,' I began, 'suggested that a high-placed man in MI5 was working for the Soviets. In at least two cases, once their suspicions reached London, the informant didn't survive. Then, right from the early fifties, a series of counter-intelligence operations against Soviet targets went wrong for no good reason, which suggested that they were being betrayed by someone inside. Also there must have been someone in the know who was able to tip-off the Cambridge spies when suspicion fell on Maclean. When they analysed who had access to what radio intercepts — who knew what and when they knew it — they were able to narrow the suspects down to Hollis and his deputy.' I shrugged. 'They decided it was Hollis. And he didn't exactly help his case by being obstructive during the investigation.'

'Good points,' Bill said, 'but all circumstantial. There was no hard evidence.'

'Nothing concrete, no,' I admitted.

'Right. Let me deal with these points in reverse order. Hollis's obstruction could be read as attempts to contain the damage of a witch-hunt he saw as potentially destroying the Service. Remember the context. America was deep in the throes of McCarthyism. They thought there were Reds under every bed.'

'With justification in some cases,' I interrupted.

'*Some* cases. But in our business suspicion is the default position. If there is something we don't understand our first reaction is to expect deception. Mutual suspicion is a cancer that destroys from within.'

I was about to argue but Bill raised a hand to stop me.

'As for warning Maclean, it was Philby who was ideally placed. He warned Burgess who passed the message to Maclean. In Philby's own case, he was canny enough to know when he'd reached the end of his own rope. And the fact that so many operations went pear-shaped could be put down to slack procedure and bad practice. It's widely accepted that all our best men left the Service after the war. We had to make do with what was left. Lastly,' he said, 'and this is the nub of the matter, accusations of high-placed spies in MI5 *could* be interpreted as deliberate misinformation. In fact one source was definitely later discounted as a plant.'

'I know this, Bill,' I said. 'Isn't that why nothing was ever proved?'

'Look at it from their point of view. How do you assess whether an agent is a double or not? You have a man in foreign territory, he is looking to compromise a known enemy agent to perhaps turn him to work for us. One accepted way is to feed him information that is genuine in order to gain his trust. You keep giving him good stuff so that you are seen as a good source. Your position is ambiguous. Slowly you introduce tainted information. This can work two ways — either your misinformation is swallowed whole and you've managed to corrupt their system, or the man you are passing the information through becomes suspect in his own masters' eyes. Having managed to sow the seeds of doubt, you begin to look like his only way out and you have a prospective defector.'

'Your saying that information we were given saying there was a high-placed mole in MI5 was fed to us to corrupt our system.'

'It always has to be considered. It's a game of bluff and counter-bluff. A snapshot taken of our agent passing information to the enemy isn't necessarily black and white. Is he betraying secrets or is he tempting a defector? Has he been spying on his fellow countrymen or has he been feeding the opposition misinformation?'

'But how can you ever know?'

'You can't, not at any given point during the game. You have to take his word. *He* is the only one who truly knows. That is why those who ran the Services always recruited people like themselves, people they knew, people whose word they could trust. They were all "one of us".'

'Proper vetting would have helped.'

'Certainly,' Bill conceded. 'SIS was the worst offender. If they'd taken a proper look at Philby's background they would have discovered his communist sympathies. But he was St. John Philby's son and that was good enough. His days in Vienna alone should have ruled him out. It was hardly a secret, after all. The problem was that a lot of the bright young men in the thirties had strong left-wing views. Twenty years later most of them weren't so keen on having their youthful idealism exposed. By then they were in positions of power and trust. Many had known Burgess, and given his particular and wide-ranging sexual proclivities they were none too keen on their past association being raked over after his defection.' Bill gave me a knowing look. 'One can hardly blame them.'

I knew the arguments; I had heard them put before. It was a murky world, as George had said. Bill was right in maintaining that the default position of those who inhabit it is one of distrust and that nothing is rarely as it looks, or even that evidence is what it seems. In a country where deception is the currency, one necessarily has to take payment on trust.

Back at his house Bill surprised me by proving an adept cook. While I ensured we ate off clean china by washing up for him, he turned his fresh eggs into an omelette, sautéed some sliced potatoes and garnished the result with chopped mushrooms. As I served he produced a bottle of Chablis that had been chilling in his fridge.

He lifted his glass. 'It really is good to see you, Alex,' he insisted. He tasted the wine, murmured appreciatively, then went on in an off-hand way, 'Anthony wasn't Frederick's best man, by the way. That was a chap named Forsythe. He was in SOE during the war. The Gestapo got hold of him in Holland. They shot him when they'd finished with him.'

I had paused, a forkful of omelette halfway to my mouth.

'How did you know that?'

'Frederick told me when I interviewed him.'

I put the fork down. 'I thought you said Frederick wasn't interviewed?'

'No, Alex, you jumped to that conclusion.' He smiled, enjoying playing his game with me. 'I said Hollis refused permission to interview him after Blunt confessed. I talked to him years later. It must have been sometime around nineteen-eighty, some while after the shit had hit the fan and the press had trashed Blunt.' His gaze wandered over my shoulder to his past again. 'Thirty years,' he said. 'Who would believe it?' Then he re-focussed on me. 'The Thatcher government had come in for some stick and was trying to cover its backside, looking as if they were doing something. I talked to Blunt. As I said, tying up loose ends. When I saw that Frederick hadn't been interviewed back in the sixties I asked him if he'd be willing to talk to me.'

'And?' I asked.

Bill's eyes twinkled. 'He said he'd be delighted.'

'So, what did you think of him?'

The eyes lost their twinkle. 'I thought he was sly, evasive, manipulative... What was the term current then ... economical with the truth? No,' he decided, 'that was used later, wasn't it? When they tried to suppress Wright's book, *Spycatcher.*'

'He lied to you,' I said.

'He didn't tell me the whole truth.'

'Did he tell you what he did in the Ukraine?'

'Only in the most general of terms. Nothing self-deprecating, of course. Certainly nothing incriminating.'

'But he admitted knowing Blunt?'

'Certainly. Philby, too. But then they all worked for the same organization in the war. It would have been more interesting if he had denied it.'

'I know Frederick had been a commando. Was he in SOE, too?'

Bill smiled knowingly. 'You know what SIS thought of them. They decided a man on the inside might be useful.'

'Do you think he worked for the Russians, as well?'

'He worked for the Bolsheviks,' Bill replied, more accurately. 'He was quite up front about the fact, said that that was his brief. He was there to buy their grain and set up his networks. *He* maintained he had to play the double in order to do it.'

'But was he *our* man or was he *theirs*?' I insisted. 'At bottom, I mean.'

Bill opened his hands wide, a slice of potato slipping unnoticed from his fork onto the floor.

'He was one of us,' Bill said teasingly. 'Either you took him on trust or...'

24

It was dark by the time I got off the bus in the village and began walking along the track to the chalet. Driving back to Southend I thought about what Bill had said and even more about what he hadn't said. I had always intended to show him the leather-bound notebook that had belonged to Frederick but, at the last moment, had left it in my pocket. I still wasn't entirely sure why. Something had stayed my hand, some notion that had begun to form in my head but which hadn't yet assumed any recognizable shape.

As I stood with him at the door, his last words to me were:

'I don't have any contact with them any more.'

I still wasn't quite sure what he had meant. Had it been a statement of regret on the passing of his working life and aimed at himself, or had it been a statement of assurance, aimed at me?

~

In the morning I spent a couple of hours going back through Griffiths' papers until, feeling the need to do something physical, I went into the shed and chocked up the Alvis, raising the tyres off the concrete floor. I disconnected the battery then tied a tarpaulin over her in the hope it might keep the worst of the salt air off the bodywork. I thought about draining the sump and emptying the petrol tank but, if I was going to be away *that* long, the Alvis was going to be the least of my worries.

It was almost dark by the time I finished and, cautious as ever, before going back inside I took my customary turn around the grounds like a country squire on his uppers, reduced to a few square yards of marsh. In the fading light I watched the mist creeping up the creeks, rising like a noxious cloud out of the grey water. Back across the fields of winter stubble I heard the call of tawny owls and the rattle of pigeon going up to roost. I listened to them for a few minutes then went inside.

It was later, after nine, when I heard the sound of the car engine.

I turned out the lamp, picked up the Glock and parted the curtains. Somewhere, out towards the boatyard, I saw a momentary flash of light diffused by the miasma drifting over the marsh. A moment later I saw it again on the track. It only led to the chalet; there was nowhere else to go.

I shrugged on my jacket and slipped out of the back door, circling around the shed and keeping flat against the back wall. The engine was loud now, tinny in the silence, over-revving in a low gear as it slid along the muddy track. Nearer the chalet it slowed and stopped. The lights were cut but the engine remained on as if the driver were waiting for something. Then the engine died, too. A door opened and a moment later slammed shut. Just the one. I crept to the corner of the shed and peered around. The moon had risen casting a pearly light through the patchy fog. I made out the shape of a small car and the silhouette of a figure standing beside it. The figure wasn't moving, but standing as if listening for something. Then it moved towards the chalet, playing a flashlight beam on the ground in front of them. I waited. The figure reached the corner of the chalet and stepped up onto the timbered veranda. Silently I ran the few yards between and made the veranda as the figure reached the door. He turned the handle and stepped inside.

In three strides I reached him. I wrapped my left arm around his throat, pulling back hard as I stepped back. I jabbed the barrel of the Glock into the side of his neck.

He gave a high-pitched cry, scrambling with his legs for purchase, feet skidding on the floor. He was short and I leaned back, lifting his feet into the air. The flashlight fell and skittered onto the chalet floor.

'Don't move a muscle,' I hissed in his ear. 'There's a gun in your neck. I'll lose your body in the mud. No one is ever going to find you.'

I tightened my arm around his neck but something felt wrong. He still struggled, pulling at my arm, but he was small and light, weak, and I suddenly became aware of a familiar scent in my nostrils. I had been tensed, waiting for an elbow in the ribs, fingers reaching for my eyes, a stamp on my foot, any one of the usual counter-moves. But there were none. Just an ineffectual struggling and a perfume I recognized. I loosened my grip.

'Alex!'

I froze as she bent double, gasping for air.

I reached down and picked up the flashlight, shining the beam into her face.

'Christ, Jennifer. I nearly...' I left the sentence unfinished. She didn't need to know what I had nearly done.

She rubbed her throat, squinting against the light.

I shut the door and dropped the gun on the table. I lit the lamp again and turned it up. Jennifer hadn't moved. She held a hand to her throat and she was still gasping for air.

'Who did you think I was?' she finally croaked at me. 'Was that a gun?'

There was a mark, livid against the skin of her neck where I had jammed the barrel of the Glock. Where the coarse canvas of my jacket had rasped against her chin a graze had begun to seep blood, stark against her ashen face.

'You're the last person I was expecting,' I said inadequately.

I dampened some kitchen towel and dabbed ineffectually at the graze. She jerked away and scowled at me. I gave her the towel and fetched the bottle of scotch from the kitchen cupboard. I poured two large glasses and handed one to her.

'Drink it,' I said. 'It's good for shock.'

She pulled out one of the kitchen chairs and sat heavily as if our struggle had sapped all her strength.

'That's sweet tea,' she said, her expression suggesting I couldn't get anything right.

I saw my hand was shaking and drank my scotch, putting the glass on the table.

'That perfume you're wearing,' I asked. 'What is it?'

She looked up at me as if I had lost my mind.

'What?'

'Your perfume.'

'Ralph Lauren,' she said. She looked distastefully at the scotch in her hand and drank some down with a shudder.

'What are you doing here?'

'Looking for you, of course.' She was still staring at her glass. She drank a little more.

'Did you come alone?' I asked. 'I mean did you tell anyone you were coming?'

'Like who?'

'Like George. Or Nick.'

'No.'

I poured myself another drink and sat opposite her.

'I'm sorry,' I said. 'I wasn't expecting a woman.'

'I should hope not if that's the kind of reception you give them,' she said.

'Has anyone been looking for me?'

'Olena told Nick that a friend of yours from work was asking about you.'

'Charlie Hewson?'

'Yes, that was his name. Nick said he was worried about you.'

'I bet he was,' I said.

'Nick asked me if I knew where you were.'

'Why would he think you'd know?'

'I did, didn't I?' She finished her scotch and held out the glass. I poured a little more into it. 'Why did you ask about my perfume?'

'It reminded me of something,' I said. 'I thought I caught a trace of it at Nick's house last weekend when he stopped off to pick up some papers, that's all.'

It had been the most vague of bouquets yet enough to make me wonder if he had had a woman there. I had forgotten about it. Struggling with Jennifer had triggered the memory.

'You couldn't have,' she said. 'I never go to his constituency house.' She laughed mirthlessly. 'It gives the voters the wrong impression to see their MP's mother fussing around him. Besides, I've not worn it before. I'm only wearing it now because I had lunch with Nick today. He gave it to me for my birthday yesterday.'

She looked at me pointedly and I realized I had forgotten her birthday. I had always relied on Olena to remind me of family birthdays and anniversaries. Since the divorce she had stopped doing it.

Jennifer finished the little scotch I had splashed into her glass and held it out for a refill.

'Sorry,' I said, ignoring her glass. 'I forget.'

She waved the glass at me. 'Give me another drink.'

Reluctantly I topped up our glasses again.

'I don't drink scotch,' she said taking another swallow.

'I've never seen you drink much of anything.'

'Perhaps it's time I started.'

'What's that supposed to mean?'

When she didn't reply I put my glass on the table in the hope that if I didn't drink she might slow down.

'How did you know I was here?' I asked.

She shrugged. 'I didn't. I came out here four or five years ago... After your father — after Peter — died. His dying brought back a lot of memories. I wanted to see the place again. I knew he hadn't been here for a long time and I expected to see it run down.' She smiled. 'It was always pretty bad when he came here with Geraldine. When I saw that someone had done the place up I stopped at the boatyard and asked about it.' She looked up at me. 'One of the old men there remembered me, believe it or not. He told me you'd bought it but that it had been a secret. You hadn't wanted your father to know.'

'He needed the money,' I said. 'He regarded any offer of help as charity.'

'Peter would.'

'That would have been Jack Pinter you spoke to at the boatyard. I got him to make Dad an offer. I knew he'd sell it to Jack but I thought if anyone else knew I was buying it, it might get back to him so I kept it to myself. Dad told Olena he'd sold it but she was never interested in the place, anyway. No one ever asked about it after he died so I never said anything. I suppose I should have known better than to try and keep it a secret.'

'Jack heard your father had died so I suppose he thought it didn't matter anymore.'

'Did you happen to tell George I still had it?' I asked.

She shook her head, keeping her eyes on me. They had become a little unfocussed and I could see the scotch was already getting to her.

'Everyone's got secrets,' she said.

She emptied her glass and held it out again. I made to take it from her but she said:

'Another one. Before I change my mind.' Her voice was beginning to slur.

'You need to go steady,' I warned. 'You're not used to it.'

She stared at me. 'Suppose I'm tired of going steady?'

I shrugged and poured a little more into her waiting glass.

'So you never even told Olena you bought the place from Peter,' she said. 'You're worse than the rest of us, Alex. Always so secretive. When Nick said no one knew where you were, I tried to think where you might go. I thought you might come here.'

'Clever little Jennifer,' I said. 'So what happens now you found me?'

She waggled her glass in front of my face. 'Depends on how much of this I have.' She tried to smile playfully but the alcohol had already slackened her muscles and she almost had to squint to keep me in focus.

'Does George know you've come looking for me?'

'George, George, George,' she said. 'Don't tell George everything.'

She looked at me slyly and drank some more scotch. She had dispensed with the shudder a couple of glasses ago and, as a small rivulet of whisky escaped the corner of her mouth, she raised her hand and smeared it across her chin with her knuckles. Her hair had come untied during our struggle and stray wisps hung, dishevelled against her cheek.

'Do you know what's going on, Jennifer?' I asked.

'I know somethin's goin' on,' she said.

'Doesn't George tell you?'

She gave a derisory laugh. 'George only tells me what he thinks I need to know.'

She lifted her glass unsteadily to her mouth. She was drunk. Far too drunk to drive.

'Where are you staying? In town? You can't drive back yourself.'

'Don't intend to,' she said.

'I'll take you back.'

'Don't wanna go.'

She blinked several times but her eyes weren't focussing on anything anymore. She laid her glass heavily on the table and let go of it. Her hand slid off and fell to her side. A moment later her head hit the table and she passed out.

'You're really not used to it, are you?' I said to myself.

I went into my bedroom and pulled the duvet off the bed. Back in the kitchen, I lifted her gently and carried her to the bed, straightening out her legs and taking off her shoes. I pulled the duvet back over her and closed the door behind me.

I went outside again. The fog had thickened, drifting up from the marshes where it lay in dense pockets. The air tasted sharp with the cold. The car was a Ford Ka. Her handbag was on the passenger seat. The keys were in the ignition, the fob advertising a rental company in Kensington. I squeezed behind the wheel and moved the Ka behind the shed. Back inside I found Jennifer was fast asleep. Her breathing was laboured and a dribble of saliva had run out the corner of her mouth onto the pillow. I doubted she'd had enough to make her sick although what she had drunk had seemed to hit her like a baseball bat. She was going to have a thick head in the morning. I made sure she was breathing easily then took a couple of blankets and a spare duvet out of the cupboard and took them back to the kitchen to air them over the stove.

I sat in the armchair finishing my drink, conscious of her lying on my bed just a few feet away. I thought of the perfume she was wearing and how it had kicked at my memory and how for an instant a piece of the puzzle had almost fallen into place. But more pressing at that moment was the fact that the police were not looking for me. If they were, Jennifer would have known and have told me. If the police weren't looking for me, though, it probably meant that someone else still was. And if Jennifer had thought to look for me here it wouldn't be too long before someone else might. Sooner or later someone would remember the chalet out on the

Essex marshes and then they'd be down here, cornering me like a water rat against the mudflats.

The blankets had aired and I was making up the bed in the other room when I heard Jennifer stirring. I knocked softly on the bedroom door and pushed it open. Light filtered in from the lamp in the kitchen. Jennifer stood unsteadily beside the bed taking off her clothes.

'Sorry,' I said.

She looked at me dully and carried on undressing.

'Are you all right?' I asked. 'I can drive you home if you want.'

'I want to stay here,' she mumbled.

'Get back in bed then and I'll bring you some water.'

I took a bottle from the kitchen cupboard and poured a glass. I carried them into the bedroom. She had crawled back in bed, her clothes an untidy heap on the floor. I put the glass and the bottle on the bedside table, picked up her clothes and folded them over the arm of a chair.

'Sorry, Alex,' she muttered from the bed. 'Didn't mean to get like this.'

'It happens to us all sometimes,' I said, standing over her. Then on impulse I leaned over and kissed her on the forehead. 'Try and sleep,' I told her.

As I straightened, my head full of that perfume again, memory swept over me like floodwater. I had stepped into Michael Standing's house, following behind his wife, Julia, that same scent hanging like a suggestion in the air.

~

I can't say I slept. My back spent most of the night registering complaints about the strange bed while on the occasions I did manage to drop off my head was filled with a battalion of elderly soldiers carrying antiquated revolvers creeping towards the chalet through spinneys of giant saltgrass. Awake, I listened for them, holding my breath at every creak from the old wood of the chalet. Now and then I could hear a restless mutter from the other side of the wall where Jennifer was sleeping and sometime in the night heard her fumbling for the water. Then she seemed to sleep easier and was out cold when I finally gave up the unequal struggle, got up and went outside.

It was still dark. I could hear the hoot of owls from the trees and the stirrings of whatever else was awake at that ungodly hour. The water in the creeks was in some stasis between tides and still except for the occasional plop of an insomniac fish. I walked along the track as far as the boatyard, unlit flashlight in one hand, Glock in the other. Everything was quiet. I was the only fool who wasn't in bed.

Back in the chalet I stowed the Glock away in the jar, put some coffee on the stove, undressed and showered. By the time I came out, wrapped only in a robe, the coffee was spitting impatiently and Jennifer was sitting back at the table, half-hidden under the folds of an old dressing gown.

'You're up,' I said redundantly.

Her hair was in a tangle and her eyes puffy in the first dawn light leaching in through the window. 'Would you have an aspirin?'

I found her a couple and a glass of water. She took them and drank them down.

'I must look a fright,' she said.

'You always look nineteen to me, Jennifer,' I said. 'You know that.'

She looked at me and smiled. 'I wish I could see through your eyes.'

I poured two mugs of coffee and put one in front of her, fetching the milk from the little wire-framed alcove that served as a larder. I sat down across the table from her.

She looked at me with embarrassment. 'I'm sorry about last night.'

'I'm not,' I said. 'Except for grabbing you like that, I mean.'

'Who on earth did you think I was?'

I thought about telling her that someone had tried to kill me but it would all sound too melodramatic and I was afraid she might think I was fantasizing.

'It's connected to Michael Standing,' I said, 'and that research assistant of his, David Griffiths.'

'It was on the news,' she said. 'He was shot. They're talking about some Russian connection. I thought you'd retired.'

'Did everyone know what I did?' I laughed, only half-joking. 'So much for a secret service. George, I suppose.'

'No, it was something Geraldine once told me.'

'Mum?' I said, surprised. I had never talked to my parents about my work, beyond telling them that I couldn't talk about it which, I suppose, speaks volumes of itself. 'What did she say?'

'I can't really remember. It was something about your work that worried your father.'

'He was a born worrier. What I did wasn't usually very dangerous.'

'I don't think it was you she meant he was worried about.'

'I'm sorry?' I said, not understanding. But it was Jennifer that was looking worried now.

'What's it got to do with you? Are you involved somehow? What about the people you worked with? What about the police? Can't you go to them?'

'Too late for that, I think,' I said lightly, trying to make a joke of it.

An expression of sadness washed across her face and I thought that now she must suppose I really was in trouble. And the truly stupid thing about it, although it seems ridiculous to admit, was that I realized almost for the first time that I was.

'What are you going to do?'

'Go abroad,' I said truthfully. I gave her an optimistic smile. 'Things might blow over.'

She got up and came around the table, putting her arms around my head and drawing me to her. Hardly knowing what was happening I raised my arm and encircled her waist.

'There's just a couple more things I have to do first,' I mumbled, my face pressed into the folds of that musty old dressing gown.

SIX

By destroying the peasant economy and driving the peasant from the country to the town, the famine creates a proletariat... Furthermore the famine can and should be a progressive factor not only economically. It will force the peasant to reflect on the bases of the capitalist system, demolish faith in the tsar and tsarism, and consequently in due course make the victory of the revolution easier... Psychologically all this talk about feeding the starving and so on essentially reflects the usual sugary sentimentality of our intelligentsia.

V. I. Lenin

(Michael Ellman, "The Role of Leadership Perceptions and of Intent in the Soviet Famine of 1931-1934," Europe-Asia Studies, September 2005, p. 823)

25

I still had one of the spare keys to Charlie's flat. I might have put my negligence in failing to return it to him when I vacated the place down to one of those intermittent losses of memory I had suffered. Then perhaps not. The key was one of those items that had been filed under the *You never know when you may need it...* category of life's little collectibles. It had been in my safe beside the ragbag collection of false passports and driving licences that I had had occasion to use professionally and had not only neglected to destroy but had actively kept current. They were all part of the 'back door' that the First Rule dictated one had to keep on hand, like a Euro account and cash in Sterling and US dollars ... an assortment of credit cards in various names... None of it amounted to much and whether I had ever seriously entertained the notion that I would one day need them was debatable, but they were a marker of what I had once been, a crutch that, if need be, I could fall back upon and use to limp away. Some people have religion, others alcohol; I found early on that I always needed a contingency. I put it down to a reluctance to relinquish the world I had once inhabited and which, bar sharing the odd glass and conversation with Charlie, I found was lost to me for good the day I had regained consciousness in hospital. As I always say, old habits die hard.

It was six-thirty and there were no lights showing at the windows of Charlie's flat. Ostensibly he lived alone, yet despite our long association I had never really known the extent of his personal arrangements — certainly not his vices — and I wouldn't have wanted to walk in on some domestic situation that might prove a surprise for all involved. The code on the entrance to the block had not changed and the door clicked open as I keyed the number into the pad. Lights on the stairs sprang on automatically as I climbed to the second floor, then flicked off economically as I passed. The hallways were empty and quiet except for the muffled sound of a television somewhere in one of the flats. I paused at Charlie's door and listened but there was no sound that I could hear within. I slipped the key in the lock and turned it.

Charlie had never bothered with alarms. For a man who worked in security and intelligence his private life seemed to be devoid of the first and wilt under a lack of application of the second. I closed the door behind me and leaned back against it, listening to those small noises that inhabit empty rooms: the gurgle of radiators as central heating circulates water, the purr of the boiler in the kitchen, the creak of timber somewhere as it reluctantly adapts to warming air... My eyes became accustomed to the dark and I began to make out the familiar hallway — the table near the door and the chair that stood beside it; the long-case clock that never worked but stood silently observing whoever passed with its one giant eye; the two large GWR posters on the wall advertising the colourful pleasures of 1930s' west-country resorts. They were not originals, only modern reprints. Charlie was not a collector.

I walked around the flat and found it much the same as I remembered. Neat and tidy in a Spartan way, everything there possessing an air of utility rather than a sense of having been purchased for its aesthetic value. The one exception was the grandfather clock with its Orwellian eye; maybe that was what Charlie liked about it. The flat, though, was where Charlie lived; it wasn't *quite* his home. There had been a wife once of whom he never talked. The most I ever learned was that she had left. Tired, I wouldn't have been surprised, from the effort of trying to leave some sort of impression on the rock face of Charlie's self-contained and imperturbable life. But I was in no position to throw stones. There was no one waiting for me at my house — at least, no one I'd want to see — no one to kiss me on the cheek and ask me if I had had a hard day. And Charlie had the advantage of being at work, reaping the benefits, such as they were, of an — almost — normal life. He wasn't sitting in the dark in someone else's flat, nursing a gun and waiting for their return. I was beginning to wonder if twenty-four hours earlier, given the choice, I would have stepped into his shoes; a day later and I was no longer so sure.

~

Jennifer and I had gone back to bed. To the same bed. Together. I make the point because I still couldn't quite believe that it had happened. We had stayed as we were for several minutes, Jennifer standing by the kitchen table, holding my head to her body, then she had reached for my hand and led me back into the bedroom. We hadn't said anything — there seemed no need to speak — and all that followed seemed so natural one might have thought we had spent a lifetime together. It was only later, when reality began to intrude and I remembered George and Nick and the others that that particular lifetime, for me at least, was beginning to resemble a wasteland.

She was pale and shaky from the whisky and slept some more while I made us breakfast. I took it in to her on a tray and made her eat. Her hair was tangled and her face puffy from sleep and too much scotch and she hid herself in her hands.

'God! I'm sorry, Alex,' she said.

I took her hands from her face. The fine porcelain features were lined now, tired.

'I'm not,' I said.

I sat on the bed with her, sharing the breakfast. Her hands shook as she lifted the mug of tea to her mouth.

'You need some air,' I said.

She put on her clothes and an old coat and a pair of boots that had been at the chalet for as long as I could remember and were probably my mother's. We tramped across a muddy field towards a spinney, putting up pigeons and rooks that flapped away indignant at being disturbed. The eastern sky was a milky grey. A ground mist clung to the scrubby grass and around the few wind-blown bushes that clutched the muddy inlets of the estuary. The sodden ground squelched beneath our feet sucking at our boots as if it were trying to pull us into mud and make us part of that wilderness.

We walked to where we could see the ramshackle Ministry of Defence buildings across the water on Foulness Island. Some colour had come back to Jennifer's face and the lines of apprehension I had seen earlier began to fade. She turned her head up to the sky as a sleety rain began to fall, dampening her unkempt hair.

'Hadn't you better call home?' I said tentatively.

'Why?'

'Won't George be worrying?'

'Fuck George,' she said.

I stopped in surprise. I don't think I had ever heard her swear. I laughed and she turned and looked at me.

'I mean it, Alex,' she said. 'It's not just you. It's been building a long time.'

'How long?' I asked.

She looked straight ahead.

'Oh, a long time,' she said again. 'I knew George was a mistake within the first couple of years.'

'You never gave any sign,' I said. 'Why didn't you leave him?'

'Nick was a baby. I wouldn't have been able to stand losing him. Coming here helped. Peter and your mother made it bearable. Then Oliver came along and Georgia, and almost before I knew it everything had changed, me included.'

'I had no idea.'

She turned and smiled at me. 'You were one person I couldn't tell.'

'You knew I always loved you, didn't you?'

'You weren't very good at hiding your feelings, Alex. Not back then. But you were just a child.'

That stung. 'You weren't much older yourself,' I said.

'Four years is a lot at that age. Besides, I don't think I ever saw you clearly until you came out of the army. It was too late then, of course. You were very self-assured and self-contained. Then there were the children. Life gets on top of you and after a while you're frightened to change it.'

'I didn't know.'

'I could hardly tell you, could I?'

'So you just stayed faithful to George,' I said.

Her hand tightened in mine slightly, an unconscious reflex. Her step faltered.

'So there's been someone else?' I asked, surprised by her again.

'Lovers, you mean? One or two.' She looked at me coyly. 'Nothing really serious. I could never let it go that far.'

'Did George know?'

'He might. He never said. I was always very discreet.'

'No,' I said, 'you never gave any indication.'

'Certainly not to you,' she said. 'But then, I've not seen a lot of you the past few years, have I?'

'I never felt really welcome.'

She stopped and stepped towards me so that I could smell that perfume again and the musky scent of her hair. 'No, it's true. I've never encouraged you. I've always thought you'd be like the whisky, Alex. I could never trust myself to take just one drink. Can you imagine what would have happened if we had had an affair? I thought it best to keep you at arm's length.'

I started to say something but she put her fingers against my lips.

'Don't talk about it,' she said. 'Don't spoil it by analysing it to death. Let's just enjoy what time we have.'

I put my arms around her and kissed her, holding her tighter than I can remember holding anyone before. Then those irrational thoughts started worming their way into my brain again, like Poe's *Imp of the Perverse*, and I thought, *why now, why after all this time?* And I couldn't help remembering what Bill Vickery had said about a snapshot of time and how things were never black and white and how you could never trust what you thought you saw. It was as if, now I finally had what I'd always wanted, I couldn't help looking for the catch, for the ulterior motive, for what I'd come to convince myself must always be present.

~

It was almost eight o'clock before I heard a key turn in Charlie's lock. A moment later the light down the corridor went on and a briefcase was laid on the hall table. The door closed and then a match flared. It would be the second cigarette he had had since leaving the tube station. A moment later steps muffled by the carpet came down the hall towards me and I saw the glow of his cigarette and his silhouetted figure in the doorway, reaching for the light switch.

'Leave it off, Charlie,' I said. 'Come in and sit down.'

He may have stiffened with surprise; it was too dark to tell. To give him his due, though, he barely hesitated a second.

'Alex,' he said. 'I was wondering when I'd hear from you again.'

'You're not carrying a gun are you Charlie?'

He laughed easily, walked into the dark room and sat down in the chair I had placed opposite me.

'Not at my pay grade, Alex. I'm expected to be above that sort of behaviour now. I told you that you should have stayed in.'

'I don't think I would have found the company as congenial.'

'Oh, you get used to it,' he said. 'And you have to move on. I was hoping you'd realize that by now, Alex.'

'Maybe I've always been a slow learner.'

'Don't underestimate yourself,' Charlie said. 'I never have.'

His eyes had become accustomed to the dark because they seemed to have fixed themselves on the gun I was holding.

'You're not going to shoot me are you Alex?'

'Can you think of any good reason why I shouldn't?'

He was silent for a moment.

'Friendship?'

'I rather think that boat's sailed.'

He grunted. 'Pity. But you know how these things work. Never as one would like.' He sighed. 'I'm afraid it was out of my hands.'

There wasn't enough light to make out his expression but I didn't need to see it. I knew it well enough. There would be a half-smile on his lips and a trace of regret in his eyes.

'How much do you know?' he asked.

I suddenly felt irritated beyond reason. 'There you go, Charlie!' I exploded. 'You don't even bloody know, do you? You've got no idea what I know and what I don't know. I might just be some poor sodding innocent stumbling around wondering what the fuck's going on, but that doesn't matter. As far as you and the rest of them are concerned I'm a piece that's become unpredictable so it's best removed from the board. That's it, isn't it? Didn't it occur to anyone just to talk to me?'

'Not my call, old man,' he replied far too reasonably. 'You know if it had been up to me I'd have laid all our cards on the table. The truth is, by the time I was briefed things had gone too far.'

'Bullshit'

He chuckled in the dark. 'No more than pretending you're a stumbling innocent wondering what the fuck's going on,' he said. 'If that was the case, why are you sitting in my flat holding a gun on me? What is that, by the way? It looks from here like an old Enfield revolver. Are you sure it still works?'

'It still works,' I assured him. 'Makes quite a mess of a man's head as a matter of fact.'

'That wasn't my idea,' he said.

'I didn't think for one moment it was, Charlie. You've never been as crude as that.' I waved the barrel of the Enfield at him anyway, just for effect. 'But while you're deciding whether or not you want to find out if it still works, why don't you fill in some of the gaps for me?'

'How much don't you know?' he asked.

'No jokes, Charlie, please.'

He raised a hand. 'You're the boss,' he said. 'Just like the old days.'

'Seems to me there's been some changes made.'

'How about a little light?' he suggested. 'Anyone watching might think it suspicious I've come home and not turned the lights on.'

'Is there anyone watching?'

'Isn't there always?' he said.

He got out of his chair slowly and turned a standard lamp on.

'I'll close the curtains if it's all the same to you.' He walked to the window and pulled the drapes together. He made no hurried movements, didn't peer down into the street, gave no hand signals. What he did do was turn and smile amiably.

'What about a drink?'

'Good idea,' I said.

He poured two tumblers of scotch from the decanter on the sideboard and brought them over.

'Sit down first then hand it to me,' I instructed.

Charlie shrugged. 'You're being very cautious.'

'I'm beginning to think I've not been cautious enough.'

'Fair's fair, Alex,' he said, handing me the glass. 'I tried to warn you. I distinctly remember suggesting you drop it more than once. I even recommended that we should tell you what it was about.' He raised his eyebrows regretfully. 'No go there, I'm afraid.'

'You told me it was too late by the time you were briefed,' I reminded him. 'Which is it to be?'

'I rather think that's been the problem,' he said. 'Crossed wires. Two lines of inquiry. You haven't twigged to that, have you?'

'What do you mean?'

'Standing's death wasn't anything to do with it.'

'To do with what?'

'You and your father's history,' he said. 'I was merely told to keep abreast of it, that's all. Nothing overt. Just an occasional chat over a drink. It's what we did anyway. No harm in that, I thought.'

'If it had nothing to do with Standing,' I said, 'why on earth were they interested?'

Charlie cocked his head to one side, like an attentive spaniel.

'I didn't say it had nothing to do with Standing. I said his death had nothing to do with it.'

'I don't understand.'

'Stumbling around wondering what the fuck's going on?' He began chuckling again and I gritted my teeth. He raised a hand and wiped the grin off his face. 'Come on, Alex. You know what they're like. They never tell you more than you need to know. First rule of espionage, remember? All they said to me was that after you'd done that piece on your dad's RAF service you were looking into his time as a kid in the Ukraine.'

'They told *you* that?' I said. 'You didn't tell *them*?'

He shook his head. 'Not me, mate. Innocent on that charge. They already knew about it, apparently.'

A little understanding began to seep into my thick skull.

'Because they were already keeping tabs on Standing and knew when he contacted me?'

Charlie took a sip at his scotch and licked his lips.

'That's what I assumed. They apparently like to keep an interest into who looks at what in the old KGB files in Moscow. I suppose things being what they were over there a few roubles to an archivist or two was enough to keep a line open. They got the nod apparently if anything they regarded as sensitive was requested.' He sniffed dismissively at the thought. 'I daresay the baksheesh has gone up now the country's back on its feet.'

'So you're saying that when someone starts poking around in some particularly murky corner a light goes on somewhere? They're alerted by Standing's research and when he turns up on my doorstep they take an interest in me. And even then, despite my background, no one thought to have a quiet word with me?'

'I know, Alex,' Charlie said sympathetically. 'It doesn't sound logical does it? But what's logic ever had to do with it? The point is, you'd left the firm and you know how they feel about outsiders.'

'Outsiders?'

'I agree,' he said quickly. 'Gratitude, eh? I should think it's enough to make you want to tell them where they can stick their pension.'

'I imagine that's already pretty well stuck,' I said. 'What do you think, Charlie?'

He pulled a face. 'You know what they're like,' he said. 'Left hand not knowing what the right, etcetera... You'll probably still get it for months before anyone thinks to tell Accounts.'

'Will I live to enjoy it, though? That's the question.'

He shrugged eloquently, looked at me, raised his eyebrows and drummed a tattoo on his knee with his free hand, as if that particular piece of business should have already been taken care of.

'But that's not the issue,' I reminded him, turning the Enfield revolver in my hand just to let him know who was making the decisions.

'No,' he accepted, 'I don't suppose it is.'

'So,' I recapped, 'just because I put Zaretsky's name on the Web and Standing turns up on my doorstep, they ask you to find out what I'm up to. Is that how it went?'

'Spot on, old chap. Just bear in mind that they didn't tell me why, will you?'

'And the "sensitive" part in all this, that would be the name of Frederick Maitland, right?'

He didn't reply and we sat looking at each other for a while. Then he said, 'Look, I don't know if it's the tension but I'm getting hungry. Have you eaten?'

'You're not asking me out, are you Charlie?'

'Microwave,' he said.

'I'll pass, but you go ahead.'

I followed him into the kitchen. He took a ready meal out of the freezer and slid it into the microwave, then fetched a tub of margarine spread from the refrigerator and a plate off a rack.

'Mind if I use a knife?' he asked.

I nodded to him. I had had plenty of time to go through the place before he'd got home and had finally found his gun beneath a Hovis Granary loaf in his breadbin. It was nestling in the waistband of my trousers at that moment. As he lifted the lid of the breadbin I pulled aside my jacket so he could see the grip.

'Speaking of waistlines,' he said dropping the lid, 'perhaps I'll forego the bread. What about a glass of wine?'

I waved my scotch at him. He poured himself a glass of white from a bottle chilling in the fridge and we leaned against the kitchen units looking at each other while we waited for the bell on the microwave to chime.

'To be honest,' he finally said, 'I was told they doubted there was much you could turn up, but when you started looking for someone who could translate those letters you had it seemed too good an opportunity to pass up.'

'Daryna.'

'Well it seemed like a gift horse when you asked me if I knew anyone.'

'Right analogy, wrong way round,' I said.

'We muddle through,' he allowed. 'She was only supposed to keep an eye you, let us know what was in the letters ... if you heard from Standing ... anything significant, that sort of thing. Actually, I was quite proud of myself for picking Daryna. I rather thought she was your type, Alex.'

'What type would that be?'

He pursed his lips, giving it a little thought. 'Not too young to be embarrassing; pretty in a sort of unconventional way. Sort of pouty and sullen.'

'Pouty and sullen?' I said.

'Apparently men of your age reached puberty when Bardot was at her peak,' he said. 'An important childhood influence, by all accounts.'

I laughed at him. 'What's that supposed to be, the sexual equivalent of maternal bonding? Are they going in for cod psychology now?'

He looked offended. 'Profiling is all the rage now,' he insisted. 'Current thinking is that adolescent psychology is the key to why we're producing home-grown terrorists.' He regarded me with enough condescension to make me suspect he believed what he'd just said.

'You're full of shit, Charlie,' I told him.

That made him bite. His eyes narrowed.

'The days are gone when they let dinosaurs like you smack people over the head to find out anything.'

I smiled at him. 'We both know that when push comes to shove it still comes down to a goon with a Glock in his hand. Tell me, did they clear up that little mess they made in my house?'

'They told me you'd never know anyone had been in there.' He frowned and suddenly looked a little guilty. 'You know that wasn't my idea,' he added. 'On my life.'

'Interesting notion,' I agreed. 'Who was he anyway?'

He shook his head. 'Couldn't say. Outside contractor, by all accounts.'

'Perhaps they ought to think about upping the bar for those who apply,' I suggested.

He nodded. 'I'll write a memo to that effect.'

The bell on the microwave pinged and he pulled his dinner out. He peeled off the wrapping and dumped the proceeds unceremoniously on the plate. A smell of fish filled the kitchen. The salmon was neon pink, the beans a livid green. Charlie saw me looking at it.

'Marks and Spencers,' he said. 'They swear it's healthy.'

I shook my head and jerked the barrel of the Enfield at him. 'Not as healthy as talking,' I assured him.

He put his dinner and glass of wine on the small kitchen table and we sat opposite each other. I laid the Enfield next to my hand. Charlie glanced at it now and again as he ate.

'What do you want to talk about?' he asked between mouthfuls.

'Frederick Maitland,' I said. 'That's what it's all about, isn't it?'

26

Charlie cocked his head again. 'When you sent that photograph I assumed you knew.'

'Anthony Blunt?'

'If you knew, Alex, why in God's name didn't you keep the thing to yourself?'

'Actually, I didn't at first,' I admitted. 'He looked so young. All I remembered were those press photographs when he was outed.'

'Seventy-nine?' Charlie said. 'Perhaps he'd have been better off following Burgess and Maclean. But I suppose he didn't fancy the thought of spending the rest of his life in Russia. You can hardly blame him.'

'He didn't do so bad,' I said. 'They never prosecuted him. Or Caincross, or several of the others, come to that. Roger Hollis worked on into a long and respectable retirement.'

'The latest thinking has cleared Hollis,' he countered.

'I saw the book,' I said, nodding backwards towards the lounge and *Defence of the Realm: a History of MI6* on his bookshelf. 'I took a look through while I was waiting.'

'He cleared Hollis. He had access to all of the files,' Charlie said.

'Vetted before publication,' I replied. 'And a Cambridge man, wasn't he?'

'All right,' Charlie conceded, 'let's say the jury's still out on Hollis.'

I shrugged and finished my scotch. I helped myself to his bottle of wine, still cold from the fridge. It was a little sharp but nothing you couldn't get used to.

'So there's Frederick at his wedding with Blunt. I knew it must be relevant but I didn't see how. After all, everyone's lost interest in that by now, haven't they?'

Charlie chased a green bean across his plate and observed me with a jaundiced eye. 'Have they? I doubt we'd be sitting here if that was the case.'

'The Cold War's over,' I said. 'For God's sake! There's nothing left except embarrassment over that fiasco, surely?'

Charlie grimaced. 'Bad enough. From what I've heard about some of the old bastards who worked through it, you'd be forgiven for believing that half the service was being paid by the other side. And even then you wouldn't know if you could trust the word of the other half while they were telling you.'

I remembered Standing and what he had once said about Chesterton's book, *The Man Who Was Thursday*, a story in which everyone turned out to be a double-agent.

'I know Frederick was recruited at Cambridge,' I said.

'Cambridge on Don?' Charlie said, heavy on the irony. 'Where else? But by which side, that's the question. We know he knew Maurice Dobbs — the Marxist economist.' He looked at me speculatively. 'If that's not a contradiction in terms. He might have been the man who recruited Philby. Or maybe that was Blunt. Who the hell knows? From what I can gather, Frederick was pretty much ideal material for the other side, young, intelligent, upper-middle-class. He looked as if he was going places. He was reading economics under Dobbs and the thinking is — such as it is — that Dobbs took the opportunity to inculcate him with Marxist philosophy before sticking him under the noses of the British Secret Service scouts. But we don't know for sure. We suspect that Frederick managed to fool them all.' He looked up from what was left of his dinner. 'Or maybe you've managed to turn up something that everyone else missed?'

I thought of the mess that had been made of David Griffiths' files and his formatted hard drive, then the little leather notebook that still didn't make any sense.

'Not much,' I said. 'At least nothing that you won't already know. Frederick seems to have been a hard man to pin anything on.'

'I'm told most of what Registry had on him was weeded a few years ago when they decided to do a little tidying up. To save future embarrassment, you understand.' He regarded the last piece of fluorescent salmon, gave it a prod with his fork then dropped the cutlery onto his plate with a clatter. 'Not one of their brighter ideas.'

'I know he was in Russia and the Ukraine in nineteen-thirty, thirty-one,' I told him. 'Went under the name of Shostak, worked with my grandfather, Aleksander Zaretsky, seizing grain out of peasants' mouths and selling it abroad for hard currency.'

'I didn't know anything about your grandfather,' Charlie said, topping up his wine, 'and I've not heard the name "Shostak" before, either.'

'No? It's a Ukrainian name for someone with six fingers.'

'That's rum. Did he?'

'Did he what?'

'Have six fingers?'

'On his left hand.'

Charlie blanched. 'Creepy,' he said, as if he had been exchanging notes with Olena. 'Still, as I say, they weeded the files when—' He looked across the table at me and stopped. 'Well,' he said, giving me a tight smile, 'it takes all sorts.'

I waited for more but he just kept his eyes on me while he drank his wine.

'Tell me about the Black Sea Company,' I said.

'Ah.' He ran a finger down the long length of his nose, glancing evasively to the other side of the kitchen. 'I never got back to you on that, did I? Not part of the brief. Still, I did ask. Not for public consumption, I was told.'

'As Fielding found out,' I observed.

'Well,' he said, 'rules are made for breaking, I suppose.' He looked down at the Enfield again and took a deep breath before continuing. 'The company was set up in the twenties, apparently. They'd stopped trying to bring down the Bolsheviks by then and were more or less content just to watch and learn. By all accounts Lenin's NEP had settled things down sufficiently to encourage a little trade in and out of the Black Sea ports and someone thought it might be a good idea to start up a concern with local offices and agents to take advantage of the fact. Ideal cover for gathering information.'

'And Frederick joined the company?'

He was sent out under the cover of a commodity broker with the real job of building a network through the southern Ukraine. There was a lot of opposition to the Bolsheviks there at the time and I suppose they thought they could capitalize on it. He appears to have done as he was told although it looks as if he used his network as a two-way street. He certainly carried some of our stuff to the Bolsheviks. His reasoning was that it reassured the Bolshies and ensured that he stayed active. It also encouraged them to give Black Sea favourable trading terms. At the same time he fed London just enough to keep them happy.' Charlie shrugged his bony shoulders. 'When it came down to it, though, no one was sure that what we got wasn't only what the Bolsheviks wanted us to get.'

'And vice versa?' I said.

'That's how it looks,' he admitted. 'Fair enough, their product was seasoned with the odd titbit to make it look good, but on reflection they could afford to give us the odd Marxist union man or journalist couldn't they? It's not as though they were short of them and loyalty and compassion wasn't exactly their strong suit.'

'So, he was playing both ends against the middle—'

'—and making a decent free-market profit in the process,' Charlie finished for me. He waved the bottle at me, topped up our glasses and killed it. Almost like old times.

'Not that I knew any of this till about two weeks ago,' he added quickly. 'All I was concerned with was Daryna.'

'Me too,' I pointed out, 'and they tried to kill *me*. I'd start watching my back if I were you, Charlie.'

He shifted uncomfortably in his chair.

'You should never have mentioned her pout,' I reminded him. 'You weren't supposed to have met her.'

'I knew as soon as I said it,' he said.

'So what happened with Frederick? Why up and leave the Ukraine with my grandmother?'

Charlie opened his palms. 'Everything appears to have been going swimmingly for him. We suspect he had well-placed chums who were feeding him our secrets to pass to the Bolshies in return for chicken feed—'

'Or vice versa,' I repeated.

Charlie nodded, accepting the qualification.

'And he was making a nice profit on the grain exports. Oh,' he said, pointing at me with one of the fingers around his glass, 'and it appears he was embezzling Black Sea funds into the bargain. Mustn't forget that important point.'

That was a new one on me but hardly out of character for Frederick.

'Maybe his Bolshie friends tumbled to what he was up to, or maybe something else happened... Anyway, the next thing London knows is that he's cabled that his cover's blown and he's back home with a Ukrainian woman and her son in tow.'

'What about her husband?' I asked.

'Sorry, nothing recorded. At least, if there was, nothing has survived. You didn't find anything, I suppose, given that's what you were looking for?'

I had, but I wasn't going to give him the satisfaction of knowing what kind of a man I was descended from. Daryna had doubtless passed on what was in the letters and would certainly have mentioned the leather-bound notebook; she had been so eager to see it, I recalled, that it had made me suspicious.

'No,' I said. 'Standing found his name in the police files but nothing detailed. He was purged in thirty-two, apparently.'

'Shot?'

'Most likely,' I said. 'Or died in the camps.'

'I'm sorry,' he said unexpectedly as if he thought I had felt the bereavement.

But Zaretsky had too much blood on his hands for me to mourn him and I was about to say you choose your friends, not your family, until I found I couldn't trust myself to keep the irony out of my voice.

Then Charlie asked casually and almost on cue, 'Daryna mentioned a notebook you gave to Standing? She said you thought it might have been your grandmother's?'

'Conscientious little thing, wasn't she? On your books, is she?'

'A couple of years,' he said. 'They'll send her home, no doubt. A lot going on there and she shows promise.'

'Her trade-craft needs a little polishing.'

He gave me an apologetic half-smile. 'We all had rough edges when we started, Alex.' He began playing with the stem of his wine-glass, wondering, no doubt, how to get the conversation back to the notebook. In the end he just came straight out with it. 'Did you ever get a translation of the notebook?'

No doubt that was what Daryna had been looking for when she had faked the burglary. Charlie would have told her to take the letters and envelopes bearing the Hackney address that had been carelessly left in the public files and that Fielding had found. And he'd wanted to make sure I hadn't got the notebook back from Standing. Perhaps they were getting concerned that I was beginning to suspect Daryna and that they didn't know how much time she would have left.

'Didn't she say?' I asked innocently.

He'd give her a grilling now for sloppiness provided I didn't put a bullet in him, and she'd have the opportunity for honing her sincerity skills trying to get him to believe I'd lied. It was pleasing to find that there were still some small satisfactions to be taken from the situation.

'Standing said it turned out to be a diary my father had kept at his first boarding school,' I said. 'He told me he was disappointed. But then you could never quite take what Standing said at face value. Never did get it back,' I added. 'No chance now, I suppose?'

'Someone else was running that end,' Charlie said quickly, washing Griffiths' blood off his hands with an alacrity that might have embarrassed Pontius Pilate.

'But you have been looking for something, haven't you?' I said. 'Something in particular.'

His mouth closed as his jaw tightened. I let my fingers stray idly towards the Enfield and I watched him reconsider.

'When Frederick got back from the Ukraine,' Charlie said with a sigh, 'he stayed in SIS. They had no idea then that he had been working for both sides...' he inclined his head, '...if he had. Black Sea continued to trade up until the war but whether he was still channelling stuff to the Russians via other agents isn't clear. They were told he was in bad odour with the Bolsheviks although that might have been disinformation, of course. If there was still money in dealing with them, he probably was still in contact. It looks as if he didn't mind who he betrayed as long as there was a profit in it.'

I felt a sudden pang of sympathy for my father. His real father had turned out to be a Chekist who had betrayed his own wife's family for the cause; his stepfather, a man willing to betray anyone if the price was right.

'When the war came,' Charlie went on, 'Black Sea ceased trading and he joined up. With his background he was soon recruited into SOE although it's not clear whether or not he actually left SIS. Don't ask me what he did because no one seems to know. Given that the two concerns weren't in the habit of exchanging information, it might be that he was spying on SOE for SIS.'

Charlie looked at me, expecting, I suppose, to find I was amused by the irony of the situation. I didn't give him the satisfaction.

He shrugged and went on, 'After the war, of course, he went into business for himself. Legitimately this time, I mean.'

'It must have been a world of opportunity for a man with his talents,' I said.

'It always has been,' Charlie agreed.

'You were going to tell me what it was you were looking for,' I reminded him.

'I'm coming to it.'

I glanced at my watch. 'Just so it doesn't slip your mind,' I said.

'Why, have you got an appointment?'

'I'm assuming,' I said, ignoring him, 'that when they got on to Maclean he thought the shit might hit the fan.'

'So it should have. That's when he first came under suspicion, even if it was no more than a suspicion of guilt through association. They think whoever tipped them off tipped the wink to Frederick, too.'

'He obviously didn't fancy spending the rest of his life in the workers' paradise, then.'

'It would have made things clearer if he had,' Charlie said. 'If he'd shafted the Russians as we suspect, it wouldn't have been a very long life. No one's ever suggested he was stupid enough even to consider defecting, though. In fact he was smart enough to realize that not everyone was going to be unmasked. Philby managed to keep one jump ahead of them and even Caincross and Blunt traded what they knew to escape prosecution. Not to mention Roger Hollis...'

'We've cleared him, remember?'

'So we have,' Charlie said. 'Remiss of me to forget. Some of the smaller fry came out in dribs and drabs. Goronwy Rees and his ilk... There was even talk of Guy Liddell and Victor Rothschild...'

'"Naïve in their friendships", was the general verdict,' I said.

'Well,' he allowed, 'you're obviously better read in these matters than I am, Alex.'

'But Frederick's name never came out,' I said. 'What did he do, spill his guts like Caincross and Blunt to keep his good name?'

'Far from it,' Charlie said. 'He was probably the one man who did know the extent of the pre-war Soviet British network. After all, he'd been in since the beginning. You can imagine how desperate London was to know it all. But they didn't want to find out about it through the front pages of the national press, naturally. I'm sure you remember how touchy everyone is about that sort of thing. Look at the lengths the Thatcher government went to try to silence Peter Wright.'

'They didn't send a goon with a Glock after him, as I recall.'

'If it's any consolation,' Charlie assured me, 'heads are going to roll over that.'

'As long as mine isn't one of them,' I countered. I waited to be reassured but he didn't answer. 'Fair enough,' I finally said, 'but it couldn't have been that easy, surely? Frederick just sat tight because they had no evidence against him?'

'They were scared of him,' Charlie said. 'They thought he had chapter and verse on Soviet infiltration of the London Service and the Americans would have loved to get their hands on that. They'd had their fill of us after Burgess and Maclean, and letting Philby through the net put the tin hat on it. And their press isn't as well-behaved as ours when it comes to that sort of thing. They suspected Frederick had some kind of insurance and the one thing London didn't want was the Yanks finding out the full extent of how compromised the Service had become.'

'In what form did Frederick keep this so-called insurance?'

Charlie shrugged. 'No one knew.'

'It's never been found?'

'No. And not for the want of looking, apparently. They had a few nervous months after he died, by all accounts. They trawled through all the papers he left but nothing surfaced. After a while they convinced themselves that it had all been a bluff.'

'Forgive me if I seem obtuse,' I said, 'but what did it matter then? Dead and forgotten. Why not let it lie?'

'It was and they were letting it lie,' Charlie said. 'Until Standing began poking around in the Ukrainian files. And don't imagine we were the only nervous ones. Remember, the Russians were none too happy when the Ukrainians opened up their police files and started raking up all the old dirt.'

'But Standing had been going through files all his life,' I protested. 'He made a career out of it. What was different this time?'

'I told you they had an alarm system if particular files were requested. Once Standing had looked at them his name was flagged up and it would have been routine for him to be checked out.'

'So what? He was an historian.'

'The files he looked at contained information on the Black Sea Company.'

'But you said the information here had been weeded. What makes you think he could have learned anything new?'

Charlie looked at me with the expression I imagine teachers use when approaching the class idiot.

'Because he made contact with you!'

I felt my stomach lurch.

'I came and told you that he'd been to see me,' I said.

'Now you're getting there,' Charlie said sarcastically. 'If you hadn't come to me I doubt anyone would have been the wiser. But Standing's name had been flagged so I wrote a memorandum saying he'd contacted you. I didn't know any better. All I had was his bloody name on a list. Someone else put the pieces together: Standing, Black Sea, *you*, a Maitland, QED — Frederick Maitland!'

'Even though it was Zaretsky he was interested in.'

'Who the fuck's Aleksander Zaretsky? The name meant nothing to us.'

I ran my fingers through my hair, resisting melodramatic gestures like putting the Enfield revolver to my head. If I hadn't mentioned in the piece on my father's RAF service that his original name had been Zaretsky, Standing would never have found me and Zaretsky was his only link to Shostak-Frederick.

'Even then,' Charlie continued, 'it didn't mean he was on to Frederick. We sent a man over to check the files Standing and Griffiths had requested and found there was nothing in them that mentioned Frederick by name. Though by contacting you the assumption was that he had somehow made the connection, although why he approached you and not George was something of a puzzler for them at the beginning.'

'He did eventually, didn't he?' I said. 'Leastwise, I put him on to George.'

'Yes, but by that time we'd forewarned George.'

'He knows all about his father, then.'

Charlie grimaced. 'I wouldn't go that far. He knows what he needs to know.'

'Enough not to let *me* know too much,' I said. 'Except someone left that bloody photo of Blunt there.'

Charlie shrugged as if saying, what can you expect?

'Even then no one was particularly worried,' he said. 'It was just a matter of keeping tabs on what Standing was doing, and what you were doing, too, for that matter. That's why we took the opportunity to put Daryna on you when you started looking for a translator.'

'Thanks, Charlie.'

'Well what do you expect,' he said angrily. 'I told you to keep your fucking nose out of it.'

I just stared at him.

'In so many words, anyway. The trouble was, when you started to show an interest, it was thought that maybe Frederick's insurance might have come to you through your father. Daryna couldn't find anything that you hadn't given to Standing, though.'

'Not for the want of trying, it seems,' I said.

'And anyway, everyone we contacted said they'd been estranged for years.'

That gave me pause for a moment. I had never really found out for sure why my father and Frederick had fallen out and I began to wonder if perhaps it had not been an arranged estrangement to distance my father and anything he might have been given in trust by Frederick. I rubbed my aching eyes, laying a hand on the revolver for insurance while they were closed. When I opened them, though, I found that Charlie hadn't moved. He was still sitting across the table from me, his eyebrows raised in an expression of slight enquiry as if mutely asking what else did I want to know.

Quite a lot, as it happened.

'If they had it all covered,' I insisted, 'and they doubted that Standing could get much on Black Sea or Frederick, then why kill him, for God's sake?'

He looked at me pityingly. 'For fuck's sake! Haven't you got it yet, Alex? *We* didn't kill him. His wife did!'

'His *wife*?'

'Yes! It had nothing to do with police files and spy rings and your bloody grandfather. He came home and caught her upstairs fucking her boyfriend.'

27

The silence in the flat should have been filled with the ticking of that bloody grandfather clock but it wasn't. Charlie was too cheap to get it fixed. All I had to make do with was the sound of our breathing, mine mostly as I opened and closed my mouth without managing to say anything.

Charlie lit another cigarette.

'Didn't I more or less tell you as much,' he said. 'That evening in the pub when you first came looking for information?'

'Then why get it for me?' was all I could think to say.

He laughed without humour. 'Because as far as I knew the cause of his death was as simple as they were saying it was on the news — he'd come home and disturbed a burglar and got his head caved in for his trouble. *I* didn't know any better. I keep telling you, I was out of the loop. I'm just a bloody infantryman like you were. All I get told is what I need to know. When I told you Julia Standing might not have been alone I was just repeating what I heard from the man who pulled the details for me. For some reason he was up to speed on some of it and assumed I was, as well. Even if I was, he still should have kept his mouth shut.'

He sucked on his cigarette and glanced at the dead bottle.

'He's on his way to Diego Garcia now,' he added almost conversationally. 'There's been a vacancy since the Deputy Administrator went on sick leave with stress. The arsehole will be dealing with all those islanders who want to go home. It'll keep him busy for years.' He grinned at me. 'Careless talk Mal-dives.'

But I'd grown tired of his jokes. 'Not good enough,' I said. 'You know it's pronounced Mal*deeves*, and anyway Diego Garcia is well to the south of them, closer to the Chagos Archipelago.'

Charlie smiled at me sourly, equally tired, I suppose, of my pedantry. 'Who gives a fuck where it is, Alex? How many tropical sunsets can you look at before you start thinking about blowing your brains out? Is that what you've got to look forward to?'

'From where I'm sitting,' I said, 'it beats having someone do it for me.' I looked at my watch again. It was ten minutes past nine.

'Are you sure you haven't got an appointment?' he said again.

'Not just yet,' I said.

'So, where do we go from here?'

I was beginning to think I knew and I didn't like it one little bit.

'So why did *she* kill him?' I asked. 'Besides the fact she's upstairs screwing a third party. I thought they handled that sort of thing with more aplomb in Chelsea these days.'

'Why don't we go back in the lounge?' he suggested, as if he thought I might need a more comfortable chair to hear the rest.

I followed him out of the kitchen. In the lounge he stopped by the scotch bottle.

'You want another or are you driving?' he asked.

I couldn't help smiling. Despite it all he was still trying.

'I'll take another,' I said. 'Give me a fresh glass would you?'

He poured two more drinks, frowning over the bottle. 'Fresh glass? Does that mean you don't mind me having to do more washing-up, or does that mean it doesn't matter how much there is since I won't be around to do it?'

'Never mind the logistics,' I told him. 'Just get back to the story.'

He handed me my glass and we sat down in the armchairs again. I nursed the Enfield against my thigh.

'That television programme he was on was originally scheduled to go out live that night.' He sipped at his drink and savoured the taste. Perhaps he was thinking it might be his last. 'Then, a few days before he was to appear, Maseryk found he had to take an early flight the following morning and so, to accommodate him, they decided to record the thing a few hours beforehand but still show it at the scheduled time. Standing neglected to tell his wife about the change.'

'So she thought he was going to be late.'

'Exactly.'

'But he wasn't.'

'Her story was he came home unexpectedly and caught her at it with the boyfriend. There was an argument and he hit her. She pushed him and he slipped and hit his head on the worktop. He didn't get up.'

'None of that accords with what the police said they found,' I said, remembering what Graham had said about Standing having been hit several times and that there had been a lot of blood.

Charlie went through the teacher and idiot child routine again. 'Nor with the post mortem results. That maintains he was hit repeatedly by something heavy and hard. Actually, it was a meat tenderiser, and a big bastard too. Luckily either she had the foresight to hit him with the back of it or that's the way she just happened to pick the thing up. Otherwise he would have had all those little dimple shapes on his skull. Bit of a give-away, that.'

'And Nick was upstairs while all this was happening?' I asked casually.

Charlie scratched at the stubble beginning to shadow his chin. He said ruefully, 'I should have known you would have worked that out. Pity, though. How long have you known?'

'For sure? Only a day or so. All the signs were there. I was just too damn thickheaded to see them. I had no idea he was there when Standing died, though.'

'Standing suspected something, didn't he?' Charlie asked. 'That's why he didn't tell her he'd be back early. Wanted to catch the trollop at it.'

Ever one for empathy was Charlie.

'I've got an idea he thought it might be me,' I told him, 'unlikely as that may seem. I don't mean that night but earlier, back in the summer. It only occurred to me later but I think he suspected she'd been playing around for some time. I think that's why he invited me to that seminar in Cambridge. She was due to join him and I've got an idea he wanted to put us together. Only he had the wrong Maitland. I turned up with Daryna and his wife didn't show at all.'

Charlie looked at me pityingly. 'Dream on, Alex. Standing didn't think it was you. He knew it was Nick. That's why he wanted to have lunch with him on that Saturday before he died. Man to man, that sort of thing, I suppose. All very civilized. She wasn't having that, though, so when he asked her to phone "Maitland" to make the appointment, she deliberately misunderstood and phoned you. I daresay he found out and that's why he never turned up.' I suppose I looked crestfallen because he chuckled. 'Never mind, Alex. Perhaps he just liked your company, that's why he invited you up to Cambridge.'

A sympathetic ear, more like, I thought. Standing had always liked someone to talk at.

'While you were with him at Cambridge she was probably with Nick.'

'Apparently they'd known each other since university,' I said.

'Actually,' he said, 'they were in the Footlights together, or whatever Cambridge call their drama society. She had aspirations to be an actress until she met Standing. Who knows, perhaps she was jealous of his television appearances?'

'Yes,' I said sarcastically, 'motive always works out neatly like that.'

'Well, whatever. They seem to have rekindled some old spark. Standing had only ever known Nick at Cambridge as a passing acquaintance of Julia's.'

I had a sour taste in my mouth. It had been me who had given Standing Nick's number and suggested he contact him. It was obvious now why Nick had been evasive whenever I had asked if he'd been in touch.

'What did Nick think he was doing?' I asked. 'trying to protect her? How did he imagine he'd get away with it?'

Charlie tried to say something but I wasn't listening.

'Even if they managed to convince the police it was an intruder, the press would have made mincemeat of him if they ever got hold of the fact he was there or having an affair with Julia. Or was he trying to pretend he wasn't...?' Then another thought occurred to me. 'And what if the papers found out about what Standing was looking into, got a whiff of Black Sea and Frederick? But who the hell cares now? They're all dead. So it comes out that Frederick Maitland might have been a Soviet agent and that his business empire is founded on the blood of Ukrainian peasants and their seized grain...? What happens? George's stock falls for a day or two and he suffers some embarrassment. There goes his peerage, perhaps. Nick can kiss goodbye to any designs on the leadership, of course, even if he manages to keep his seat. After all, the Party isn't going to be too happy with the grandson of a Soviet spy leading it, are they? Or would it matter? After all, they've coped with worse, come to think of it. John Amery was hung for treason after the war but it didn't stop his father and brother holding cabinet posts.'

'A little different,' Charlie managed to put in. 'He was a ne'er-do-well. They could discount him as an aberration. Frederick was different. He founded the family fortune.'

I swatted that one aside. 'Nick could have crossed the House,' I said, not altogether seriously. 'I daresay there's still the odd Labour Member who thinks that sort of lineage gives a man kudos. Don't tell me George takes it all *that* seriously. He's made his money for God's sake. And in the end no one really cares where it comes from.'

I suppose I was ranting. Charlie said nothing. He was waiting until I had played myself out. And I nearly had. I think I even laughed. The penny hadn't quite dropped.

'After all,' I was saying, 'he had to get rid of the tenderiser and take Standing's wallet, wipe off *his* prints but not too many of *hers* or it would have looked suspicious ... then there were those bloody shoe prints... You'd be forgiven for thinking it was a professional—'

And that's when it dropped and I finally stopped talking and started thinking, thinking as clearly as I realized Nick must have done that evening.

Charlie was looking at me as if he had begun wondering how I had ever managed to hold down a reputable job.

'You're right,' he said quietly. 'Wiping everything clean wouldn't have exactly accorded with an interrupted burglary. It would have looked a bit too premeditated for a spur of the moment killing. Or maybe that should be post-meditated, what do you think?'

'I'm thinking, *who do you call when you're in that sort of jam?*'

'Who did *you* call when you had an awkward body in your place, Alex?'

'Nick's one of us,' I said flatly.

He continued to look at me steadily but somewhere in his eyes I now caught a trace of pity, not regret but pity.

'One of us?' he repeated. 'How should I take that, Alex? The point is, old son, you no longer are.'

It was a bit like wringing the neck of a chicken, or using a gun on an old pet rather than calling the vet; it was the doctor's frank prognosis given to the patient who can "take it". It was brutal but it was to the point. No shilly-shallying around for Charlie. They had spied on me, they had even tried to kill me, but until it had actually been put into words it apparently hadn't penetrated that thick skull of mine. I had always accused Olena of character flaws; I seemed to have cornered the market in displaying a wilful ignorance of what was staring me in the face. *Once you were out it was over.* You weren't just beneath consideration, you were totally beyond it.

'They tidied up a bit,' Charlie said. 'Got Nick out of there and left a few bloody footprints to the door for the plods to worry over. There was absolutely no point in trying to get the body away. He'd be missed soon enough and planting the body somewhere else would have let in too many imponderables.'

'Keep it simple,' I said almost to myself. 'First rule of espionage.'

'All she had to say was that she had heard a noise, come downstairs and found him. It was easy to remember and that explained the blood on her. Fortunately he'd used the tube to get home so there were no taxi drivers to muddy up the time of his arrival. She just insisted it was later than it actually was.'

'And the wine bottle,' I asked.

'You know how they like to cover all bases. That was just insurance. They knew what you drank so one of the boys nipped out and bought a bottle. They got one of your wine glasses later with DNA so they could swap it if you proved a problem.'

'Daryna?'

'Don't look at me like that, Alex. It wasn't my idea. At least I try to be logical. You just can't get the staff,' he said.

'And what about the vagrant?'

'That's the police for you,' he said with a shrug. 'Grab the first half-wit you come across.' His mouth twisted in a sardonic smile. 'But you can't interfere with an active investigation. It might have looked like a neat solution altogether now the idiot's hung himself. Griffiths complicated things.'

I considered shooting him there and then. It was only the impulse to keep my hands cleaner than theirs that stopped me. And even then I couldn't help reminding myself that it was already far too late.

'Needless to say Nick's controller was none to happy with his behaviour.' He tipped his glass at me. 'You were right about Standing contacting him after he'd first seen you. Nick was asked to stay close and to see if he could find out how much Standing was learning but he couldn't keep his zip closed and stayed close to the wrong Standing.' He smiled again. 'Everyone's allowed a little bit on the side but you would have hoped Nick knew enough to steer clear of psychopaths. That's what she is. Sees something she wants and takes it. Sees no reason why she shouldn't. She was always the same, apparently. Not that they can risk letting her near a psychiatrist.'

I remembered how she had been when I visited her and wondered if I would have spotted anything on closer acquaintance.

'Still,' Charlie said, brightening, 'every cloud has a silver lining, as they say. One more hook in him to keep him on the straight and narrow.'

'They assume he's going all the way, then?' I said.

'That was always the plan. And why not? He's been a long-term investment but not an expensive one. George has paid most of the bills and he only expects a peerage in return. Nick's not the only iron in the fire, of course. It's always been policy to have a few useful politicians on the books. They're just a bit more ambitious these days, looking to fill the top jobs.'

'What is this,' I said, hardly believing what he was suggesting, 'some sort of right-wing coup?'

He looked genuinely surprised. 'Coup? We live in a democracy. It's a way of ensuring that things stay that way.'

'By manipulating the government?'

'By ensuring that the government recognises the need for strong security and intelligence networks. There's a war on out there, Alex, and our enemies aren't sitting behind an iron curtain anymore. They're in the mosques in Bradford and Leeds. They're making bombs on London council estates.'

'You're mad,' I said.

'And you're shutting your eyes to reality.'

'So what were Fielding and Griffiths?' I asked. 'Just collateral damage?'

I could see in his face that he was looking for my understanding.

'I'm just a foot soldier,' he said again. 'You know I don't make decisions. Some people have gone too far. There were better ways of handling Fielding and Griffiths, we know that now. And they should never have sent anyone after you. That was just plain stupid. But the last thing we need now is for the Service to be discredited, to be shown in a bad light.'

I laughed aloud.

'They couldn't risk washing any dirty linen in public just at this time, Alex. There'll be an election within the next year and they've put a lot of time in on Nick. All skeletons are to be firmly locked in their cupboards. Once you've set your foot on a particular path there's no alternative but to keep going to the end. Fielding was digging into Black Sea and Griffiths knew everything that Standing did. Yes, it could have been handled differently and, as I said, heads will roll, but you have to put your mistakes behind you.'

'And I was to be a suicide, I suppose?'

He adopted a pained expression. 'Mud sticks especially when there's blood in the mix. Murder would have been a bit too close to home, being Nick's cousin and brother-in-law. And they really didn't want to risk the press finding out you'd known Standing.'

'And that's why I wasn't framed for Standing's murder.'

'I just said it was an option, but no one considered it seriously. Far too close to home for that. Graham liked you for it but he's been shown the error of his ways. After all, suicide has that hint of nobility about it. You know, Roman senators and all that sort of rubbish. A little judicious leaking of your background and record... Nick would probably have got a decent sound-bite out of it. Picked up a few more votes, who knows?' He smiled reassuringly as if I ought to have been pleased. 'Olena would have looked good in black, something simple...' He almost laughed. 'Your death would not have been in vain.' I was beginning to think he was mad but I could see he now knew that that plan was out of the window. 'That was how it was supposed to go, anyway,' he added with a shrug. 'The good news is that the police aren't looking for you for Standing and Griffiths' murders. We're playing up the Russian angle since the press seem to like it.'

'Shame about the vagrant,' I said.

'You have to be adaptable.'

'And me?' I asked. 'You're not suggesting they'd like me back in, are you?'

He shook his head regretfully. 'I'm afraid it's a little too late for that now, old mate. Given what's happened.'

I let the notion pass. 'I'm going to have to make my own way then,' I said.

I looked at the clock on Charlie's mantelpiece and got up out of the chair. My back went into spasm and closed like the jaws of a mantrap. Charlie saw the look on my face and made a move towards me. It just might have been concern for my well-being but I raised the Enfield anyway and he sank bank into his chair again.

'Time I was leaving, Charlie,' I said, standing over him.

A slight look of unease crossed his face for the first time and I wondered if he was beginning to consider that I might actually kill him.

'We've been through a lot together, Alex,' he began, but I shook my head at him and he didn't finish.

'You know better than that, Charlie. Once you start having to ask it's already too late.'

'If you're worrying about my calling them, don't. I'll give you a head start...'

He rose out of his chair and I clipped him sharply above the ear with the butt of the revolver. He fell back in a heap. A little blood welled through his hair and began trickling down the length of his sideburn. I watched it for a moment then walked down the hall to the door. Charlie's briefcase stood where he had left it on the hall table and out of an old habit I opened it and rummaged through the contents. There were some loose papers, his empty lunchbox and two files. I leafed through the contents of the thicker of the two but they were mostly concerned with activities of some British-born Pakistanis in Leeds. The second file held a few papers but I didn't bother to examine them. Instead, I tucked the file under my arm. The name *Maitland* had been written on the front.

Naughty boy, I thought, bringing confidential work home. They weren't going to be happy with Charlie taking the file out of the office and then losing it. Be it on his own head, though; he should have considered being straight with me.

I went back into the lounge. Charlie was slumped in the chair where he had fallen. I knew he was still alive because the trickle of blood kept coming, the heart still pumping. But that's all his heart ever did.

Pump.

28

The Ka was parked in the street behind Charlie's block of flats where we had arranged. I peered into the shadows as I walked towards the Ford, half-expecting a figure to emerge as the old paranoia surfaced again. The vice in my back ratcheted up with every step. There was sweat on my forehead.

'You look awful,' Jennifer said as I lowered myself in beside her.

I dropped the file on to the back seat. No one. I managed a twisted smile, almost convinced. 'I've just lost a friend,' I said.

We drove east, lost in the night traffic. Lights reflected through a falling drizzle, neon smearing gaudily across wet roads and shining off cars. The streets were crowded with people filing into clubs and bars, stepping out of restaurants. I watched as we passed, looking through the glass at them in their self-contained worlds. I felt as if they were drifting by in a ceaseless stream, a current I couldn't feel.

I had taken a chance leaving Jennifer alone with time enough to contact anyone she might. It had been a calculated gamble, I had told myself, but it had been a chance all the same. I had to trust someone, though. Everyone needs someone to trust. I wondered whom Frederick had trusted. Nastasiya or my father? Or had he trusted no one, playing one side off against the other? I thought about what Charlie had told me and compared it with what Bill Vickery had said. There were some discrepancies, such as when Frederick was first suspected or why Bill maintained he hadn't heard of Black Sea while Charlie acted as if it had been common knowledge. But I was aware that Bill hadn't told me everything he knew and that Charlie was in deeper than he had admitted.

'Did you find out what you wanted?' Jennifer asked suddenly, taking her eyes off the road and turning to me.

It seemed to me that I had found what I wanted and didn't like it one little bit. I could hardly tell Jennifer, though. I couldn't say it was all straightened out and, by the way, your son was in Michael Standing's house the night his wife murdered him.

'Yes,' I said. But I had left it a moment too long in answering and she turned to me again.

'Does that mean you can go home?'

'No, not for a while,' I said. 'It's better if I go away for a bit.'

'You really are in trouble, aren't you?'

'Not with the police it seems.'

'Who then?'

She was paying more attention to me than to the road and had to break suddenly to avoid a car stopped at traffic lights.

'I'll be all right,' I assured her. 'It's just best if I disappear for a while.'

She reached across for my hand. 'May I ask where?'

'I'm not sure where,' I said. 'I'll let you know.'

She put both hands back on the wheel, concentrating on the road now and I glanced across at her, the lights from the street flickering over her face as we drove. I reached across and squeezed her arm. She smiled hesitantly, eyes still on the road ahead.

We lapsed into silence. Past the ceaseless intersections, the neon gave way to the orange fluorescence of streetlights, sprouting like pale unearthly blooms on towering industrial stems. London began slipping by in a succession of boroughs, blighted streets of rundown housing, dilapidated warehouses and factories all looking depressingly similar. We passed hoardings that trumpeted merchandise and services that seemed now increasingly redundant, boards advertising lifestyles that were progressively meaningless. Further out the city gave way to abandoned industrial units and empty car lots. Brown field, it was called, but now perversely beginning to green again as tongues of wildness licked up from the upper reaches of the estuary, scrub and weed in the vanguard of tufted grass and trees. The streetlights had fallen behind us, melding into a livid orange glow pulsing off the city like radioactive decay.

Some of the smaller pieces had fallen into place: Nick had heard the message Fielding had left on my answer phone the evening he had picked me up and at some time over the weekend had stolen the note I had made of Fielding's number to remind me to call him back. Daryna had erased Fielding's messages; Julia Standing had rung me to make the lunch appointment for her husband, wilfully misunderstanding so that her husband wouldn't see Nick. Perhaps she had disguised her voice — just a small walk-on part for the once aspiring actress — I couldn't remember. Perhaps, if he had actually met Nick over lunch, if they had managed to straighten out the affair with Julia, he might still be alive today. But that was just wishful thinking, fantasizing about fate while chance slammed the door shut behind you and made you follow a path you would really rather have not.

The country gave way abruptly to banked dark fields. Beyond the banks, mudflats reared up suddenly in the car's headlights.

'Drop me at the boatyard,' I said. 'I can walk from there.'

She reached for my hand again. 'Let me stay, Alex.'

'Are you sure you know what you're doing?'

'As sure as you are,' she said.

I had no answer to that and said nothing until we had bounced along the rutted track to where the chalet loomed up at us out of the darkness.

'Park behind the shed,' I told her. 'Turn off the lights but not the engine and lock the doors after me. If you hear anything just drive away. I should be back in a moment.'

She didn't argue. She parked and killed the lights. I slipped out the door. I was halfway to the chalet, at the trot and crouched as low as my damn back would allow when I suddenly thought: *how melodramatic is this*? And straightened up and walked the rest of the way. Jennifer would be watching me and I knew we had reached the acid test. If she had told them where I was, this would be where they'd wait. I didn't bother checking the padlock on the back door, or the windows. All I could hear was the chug of the Ford by the shed as I climbed up onto the veranda. Charlie wouldn't have been out that long. Despite everything, I had found I hadn't the heart to hit him very hard. He would have a headache when he woke up, and serve the bastard right, but nothing so serious it would to stop him doing what he had to do. I wondered if he had noticed the mud on my shoes and, like some seedy Sherlock Holmes, had worked out where I had picked it up. Sooner or later a light would go on in his head and he'd work out where I was. I'd told him about my boyhood holidays on the Essex marshes often enough during those interminably tedious hours we had spent time and again waiting for ... waiting for what? Now I could hardly remember.

I turned on the flashlight. I had stretched a hair across the door and frame. It was an old trick but then I was an old agent. The hair was still in place but of course that didn't mean anything. *What did mean anything?* A sort of nihilism had descended upon me, or perhaps I mean fatalism. I was wondering what the point of it all was. The perverseness made me want to laugh. I had Jennifer with me at last but now didn't seem to give a damn. I turned the key in the lock and pushed the door open.

I stood in the doorway for what seemed a lifetime. Perhaps I was waiting for some manifestation of that old saw about a drowning man's life playing over at the moment of his death. Oddly for me, all that came to mind was one of those dictums of quantum theory played out, as if for the mentally short-sighted, on the macro scale. It was Schrodinger's thought experiment meant to describe the Uncertainty Principle, the one they always demonstrate by stuffing some poor cat into a box. It was one of the Copenhagen Interpretations of quantum theory that proposes that no outcome is finally determined until an onlooker actually observers the event. In my case, though, the interpretation was spiced with a kind of Russian roulette. I was leaving it all to chance, you see — live or die.

I waited in the doorway, willing my past up before me but only getting excerpts, trailers for a main feature I'd already missed. I had a brief glimpse of me and my father when I was a boy and of other member of the Maitland family, all like snaps in a photograph album ... a recruit opting for an army career through default ... a remembrance of Charlie and a sudden distastefulness for the work we had undertaken together ... Olena and Nick on their wedding day ... Jennifer as I had first known her, then a picture of her back at the car waiting for me to return — too late now to do either of us any good. Added together, it seemed the scenes were the sum of all my parts and totalled up to so very little...

There was no shot from a handgun or rattle of automatic fire, (how melodramatic would *that* have been?) And if there had been I, of course, would probably never have heard it; I had always trusted to the fact that those employed at the more brutal end of the business knew their business — although that was yet another long-held belief overdue for reassessment. I played the flashlight over the interior of the room and saw it was all just as I had left it that morning. I almost felt a sense of disappointment. But perhaps I mean disenchantment, for now I would have to plod on through each coming day because no one was going to give me an easy way out.

I went through the chalet just for form's sake, but no one had been there. I lit the oil lamp and rekindled the ashes in the stove and put a kettle on to boil. Then I remembered Jennifer still waiting in the Ford and went out to fetch her. The car made a dark silhouette beyond the shed, like a giant tortoise sleeping till dawn. She had turned the engine off and was leaning against the door with the folder I had taken from Charlie's briefcase under her arm.

She seemed a little impatient, tapping her fingers against the file. 'Can you tell me what's going on now, Alex?' she asked as we walked back to the chalet.

I closed the door behind me, wondering how much I *could* tell her.

'The people I used to work for,' I began, 'they had an ... interest in George's father.'

'Frederick?'

She dropped the file on the kitchen table and pulled out a chair. The kettle was getting hot and I rinsed out two mugs and warmed the pot. The milk in my larder wasn't much more than a degree or two above freezing. The kitchen began to warm, condensation clinging to the walls. The kettle started boiling, pushing out steam.

Jennifer's fingers played with the edges of the file, waiting for me to explain. I poured out the tea.

'When Frederick died,' I asked, 'did George or Nick ever mention anyone going through his papers?'

'George? No. That's not the sort of thing George talks to me about.'

'It's not important,' I said. Upon reflection, it wasn't the kind of thing George would have talked to *anyone* about.

'Elizabeth did, though,' Jennifer said.

'His wife?'

Jennifer nodded. 'Yes. You didn't know her, did you? She died not long after Frederick.' She cupped the mug of tea, a cloud of steam rising and reddening her face. 'A day or two after he died, before the funeral anyway, Elizabeth told me two men turned up. George was there and was apparently expecting them. They locked themselves away in Frederick's study and went through all his papers.'

'Did she say if they took anything?'

'No. She said she thought them very brusque, though, given the circumstances. Her having been recently widowed, I mean.'

'I can imagine,' I said. Sympathy was never high on the list of attributes expected of those working in the intelligence services. It was the sort of thing that wouldn't occur to them to be of any use.

'Not that Elizabeth minded being a widow,' Jennifer said. 'Frederick wasn't an easy man.'

'Did George tell her what they were doing?'

'He told her it was something to do with a sensitive government contract. Ministry of Defence. She told me she knew that was rubbish because Frederick wasn't in the sort of business that involved the MOD.'

'No,' I said, 'not the MOD. He used to work for the same people I did.'

She stared at me. 'Is that why you joined?'

It was a pertinent question, if phrased wrongly. It wasn't *why* I had joined but it may have been why I was invited. It was something I had been thinking about a lot over the past twenty-four hours.

'Not entirely,' I said.

The day was beginning to catch up with me and I suddenly felt exhausted. My confrontation with Charlie had taken more out of me than I had realized. I took what was left of the bottle of scotch down from the cupboard and looked questioningly at Jennifer. She gave me a weary smile and shook her head. I poured myself a shot and drank it in one.

'Elizabeth told me something else once,' she said watching me. 'She said that Frederick used to sleep with a gun by the bed. For burglars, he always told her, although she said she never believed that.'

'Did she tell you anything else about him?' I asked. 'About his time in Russia?'

'No. Only that he was a secretive man.'

'I bet,' I said.

'Is that where he met your grandmother,' she said. 'In Russia?'

'The Ukraine, yes.'

'Was he involved in something dishonest?'

'In that business,' I told her, 'very little turns out to be honest.'

'But you did it,' she said. 'I'm not sure I believe you would ever do anything dishonest.'

I smiled, touched by her faith. I nodded at the file on the table.

'I stole that,' I said.

She suggested she make some sandwiches. I said I'd take a shower. In the bedroom I stripped off my clothes, pungent with the sweat of tension, and stepped under the water. I stood there for ten minutes trying to wash away the day.

The sound of the water must have covered the noise of the car.

~

I had pulled on the last of my clean clothes. When I walked into the kitchen it was empty. Two sandwiches lay on a plate on the table next to the file. I looked in the lounge and then in the bedroom. Jennifer wasn't in either. I called her name into the silence and only heard it ringing in my ears in reply.

I pulled on my boots and ran outside. I called out again but another fog had rolled in and my voice, muffled, carried nowhere. I walked around to the side of the shed to where she had parked the Ford but it wasn't there. I listened, straining my ears in the silence for the sound of a car engine that wasn't there either.

Back in the chalet I picked up the flashlight and the revolver. Outside I shone the flashlight beam over the banks of mud and scrub grass, suddenly afraid that someone had been there after all, playing a waiting game until I was in the shower then had gone for Jennifer and stolen the Ford. I ran through the creeks and gullies, up to my ankles in mud, scared of finding her body. When I finally stopped, drenched in a cold sweat again, I realized how stupid that idea was. They wanted Frederick's treachery hidden and Nick protected, not some squalid family scandal involving his mother. My death was sufficient for their needs, preferably by suicide; there was no need to involve Jennifer.

Unless, I thought, whoever had been there hadn't known who she was.

I took the path to the boatyard, stumbling as I hurried, feet sliding in the mud with the ragged sound of my own breathing punctuated by the sucking of my boots in the mire. Hulls of boats loomed suddenly above me, the usual rattling of the stays against masts silenced by the breathless night. I called her name again, a faint echo reverberating around the yard. The village lay a half a mile further on but there were no lights showing now. The pub was closed, the winter residents already snug in bed. I turned around and trudged disconsolately back to the chalet.

On the stove the kettle was boiling dry. She must have put it on again after I had got into the shower. I put the gun down and wrapped a tea towel around my hand and refilled the kettle while it hissed and spat steam at me. I dropped into a chair, the plate of untouched sandwiches beside me. The old Enfield revolver lay on Charlie's file. If someone had wanted to kill her, not knowing who she was, and put the blame on me, her body would be lying there on the floor this minute. But then, why not step into the shower and do me at the same time? A murder and a suicide would have made a far neater package. And why would they steal her car? They would have arrived in one of their own. It didn't make sense. But I wasn't thinking straight; I wasn't thinking at all. No one had harmed Jennifer; no one had taken her. The simplest answer was that she had left of her own accord.

It was then that I noticed the end of an envelope protruding from the file I had taken from Charlie's briefcase. That wasn't how it had been while were drinking tea. I put the Enfield to one side, opened the file and took out the envelope. I hadn't bothered to examine it after I left Charlie's flat. But Jennifer had. It was a large A4 envelope and it had been opened. The edges of three photographs poked out of the top as if they had been hurriedly replaced. They were glossy, six by eight blow-ups, in black and white. They were taken by a camera secreted somewhere high on a wall of a bedroom and showed Nick and Julia Standing in bed together. It occurred to me that the central heating must have been on and the room warm because they were both naked and the bed quilt had slipped onto the floor.

A date-stamp in the corner of each photograph showed that they had been taken a few minutes after ten o'clock on the night Michael Standing had died.

327

29

I slept in the chair somehow, not meaning to. When I woke it was three in the morning and cold. The stove had died of neglect and one of the oil lamps had burned down. I went outside again as if, having given circumstance time to change, I might find things to be different. They weren't, of course. The only difference was that the fog had thickened and seemed full of crystallised ice leaving the air gritty like contaminated ice-cream. I went back inside and climbed under the duvet fully clothed. Within two hours I was asleep.

Dawn woke me again although it wasn't early. Not quite 8am. by my watch. Still far too early for Olena. She let the phone ring for an interminable time but I knew, if it woke her, she would be physically incapable of not answering. When she finally did, though, she didn't sound pleased.

'For God's sake, Alex! Where have you been? Do you know what time it is?'

I wondered idly how many people, untimely disturbed, began their sentences that way.

'Some people are already at work,' I said.

'I don't have to be and you haven't got a job anymore,' she replied, ever the tactful one. 'What the fuck do you want?'

Foul language was *de rigueur* with some of her circle but I doubted that on the phone first thing in the morning was one of the times they used it. This time it was from the heart.

'I need you to do something for me,' I told her.

'Why can't it wait until after noon?'

'It can't,' I said, 'that's all. I want you to ring Nick and tell him you have to see him today. Lunchtime, if possible. Tell him you can't explain over the phone—'

'Why not?' she interrupted.

'Because you're not meeting him, Olena. I am.'

'Why don't you call him, then?'

'Because he wouldn't see me.'

'Alex—'

'Don't interrupt. Just listen. I need you to do this. A pub or restaurant, anywhere. But not your house or his, understand?'

She began to argue again and I told her to ring him now, while she could still get hold of him. When I had finally got her to agree, I told her to ring me back on the number I gave her. I said it three times, just to make sure she had it.

'I'm not stupid,' she insisted. 'And what if he wants to know what it's about?'

'Lie to him, sweetie,' I said. 'You can manage that, can't you?'

A long fifteen minutes later she rang back. If she was going to talk to a man she would first have to brush her hair and put on some makeup, the fact that the conversation was over the phone was immaterial. I'd factored this in but it hadn't made the time go any quicker.

'*Le Coq qui Chante*,' she said. 'Twelve sharp.'

'The *what*?' I said. 'What is that?'

'*Le Coq qui Chante*,' she repeated with deliberate patience, the kind that generally demonstrates a lack of it. 'It's a bistro in Kensington. We used to go there before ... well, you know...'

Judging by the English translation I rather thought I did.

'Are you sure it's open at lunchtime?' I asked. 'Not just evenings?'

'It's a fucking crowing cock,' she snapped back. 'When do cocks usually crow? Of *course* I'm sure or I wouldn't have suggested it. What's this all about?'

'How did he sound?'

'How do you think?' She sighed extravagantly. 'Like he always sounds.'

'Did he mention his mother?'

'Why would he mention Jennifer?'

'You haven't heard from her, I suppose?'

'Now that's hardly likely, is it Alex! Honestly, I don't know what's got into you these days. I'll never get to sleep again now. What am I going to do until lunch?'

'First you're going to ring The Crowing Cock and make a reservation,' I said. 'I assume it's the kind of place where you need one. After that I'm sure you'll think of something else to do. Just don't get the idea of meeting us there, that's all.'

'I have no intention of meeting you anywhere at the moment,' she said and rang off.

~

The time was ten minutes before noon when I reached *Le Coq qui Chante*. The doors were opening and the staff were still tweaking front of house, smoothing tablecloths and straightening cutlery. The restaurant was on a side road just off the High Street with a furled awning they couldn't have used since summer and a tin French cockerel bolted to the wall and crowing as if its team had just won the Six Nations championship.

A couple of taxis were disgorging some lunchers but Nick wasn't among them. I went inside. Meat was roasting on a spit in a half-domed brick oven on one side of the room while a Gallic-looking chef poked at the glowing coals. The heat from the fire and the smell of the food filled the room. No place for vegetarians.

I gave them Olena's name. They looked mildly surprised as if I wasn't her type and showed me to a table. I said I preferred one towards the back and pointed to a table that looked as if it took a lot of traffic from the kitchen. This time the waiter looked astonished. But it wasn't him, but Nick I wanted to surprise. Walking in he wouldn't see me until he was almost at the table.

As soon as it had been fully light I had spent an hour tramping over the marshy ground, trying to lodge the fact in my recalcitrant head — like a slow learner being taught through constant repetition — that I was not going to find Jennifer's body. Wisps of fog hung in the hollows like a sliding miasma of poisoned air. I still held images in my head of Jennifer sprawled in a muddy heap down the bank of a stream somewhere but it was only undisciplined imagination. Nevertheless, I told myself that looking was the professional thing to do.

Curiosity, I suppose, had got the better of her. It had been my own stupid fault for leaving the thing in front of her. After all, the file on the table had been marked 'Maitland' and I can hardly blame her for taking a look. What she saw was her son with the wife of a man who was about to be murdered.

It would have been too much to hope that she hadn't recognized Julia Standing. Her face had featured too often in the press and on television lately for anyone to be ignorant of what she looked like. And the photographs had been good quality, no smudged and grainy honey-traps, these. The modern digital imaging had left little to an innocent imagination never mind a prurient one and, even if Jennifer had been innocent, she was not so stupid as to have overlooked the date and time stamped on the bottom of each photo, no more than an hour before the pathologist had estimated the time of Standing's death.

So I quartered the ground thinking that, however it turned out, not much good of any sort was going to come out of this situation. Back at the chalet, I cleaned up, ate a little and threw out whatever fresh food was left for whatever scavengers could get to it first. Then I cleaned out my makeshift safe beneath the floorboards and packed whatever I was going to need into a shoulder bag. Once done, I phoned for a cab to pick me up in the village, made sure the chalet and shed were secure and tried not to think if I was ever going to see the place again. Then I walked up the track without looking back.

~

Nick arrived ten minutes late and looking as if he had all the time in the world. I caught a brief flicker of concern when he found me sitting at Olena's table but he hid it well.

'Alex?' he said. 'Olena never said you'd be here. We've been worried about you.'

He hardly broke his stride and sat down without reluctance except for a dissatisfied glance in the direction of the kitchen doors. The place had begun to fill up. A pretty young girl sat at the table nearest to us with a man who might have been taken for her father if he hadn't been pawing at her like an over-exited Labrador.

'No,' I said, 'I asked her not to. I'd rather she didn't know what I wanted to see you about.'

'Mysterious,' he said jokingly, but I noticed he couldn't help shifting uncomfortably in his seat. He looked at the glass of beer I was drinking and asked for two more from a waiter who was still hovering a few feet from the table.

When he left I slid the envelope with the photographs across the table to Nick. He glanced at me apprehensively and opened the envelope. He pulled one of the photographs out, his face blanching whiter than the veal on the menu.

Nick stuffed the photos back in the envelope, casting a guilty look around the room before looking back at me.

'What is this, Alex?' he hissed across the table.

'I think we both know what it is, Nick. More to the point is what you want do about it.'

'Is this blackmail, or something?'

'I should imagine it is,' I said, 'but not on my part. I expect you can guess who took them.'

His eyes were boring into mine. Colour had come back to his face with a vengeance. I recalled Charlie's off-hand remark that Nick being in the house was one more hook they had in him; it seemed from the photographs that they had already been familiar with the bait and had let Nick go swimming with the line before netting him.

'This is outrageous,' he began to bluster. 'Spying on me! You put a camera in the house? I'd thought you'd retired.'

'So I have,' I assured him. 'I knew nothing about any of this until very recently. They're your associates now, not mine. I think you know that, Nick. I took the photographs out of Charlie Hewson's briefcase last night. You remember Charlie, don't you?'

He looked genuinely perplexed and, unless he'd started taking night classes at RADA, I was ready to give him the benefit of the doubt.

'Who you used to work with?'

'That's him,' I said. 'Have you got your mobile with you?'

The frown deepened.

'Ring your mother,' I said.

'What?'

'Ring Jennifer,' I repeated. 'Please just do it, Nick.'

'Do you expect me to tell her about the photographs?'

I was about to tell him that she already knew, but that would only complicate a situation I thought was complicated enough already.

Nick took his mobile out of his jacket pocket, thumbed the buttons and held it to his ear, his eyes fixed on mine. I couldn't hear it ringing the other end but it seemed an interminable time before he finally said:

'Hello Mum? It's Nick.'

For a second I thought he was talking to an answering service and found I was holding my breath. Then his eyes dropped to the envelope on the table and he said:

'No, I'm calling because Alex asked me to. Yes, I'm sitting with him now.' He stiffened slightly and looked back at me, holding out the phone. 'She wants to speak with you.'

The waiter turned up with our drinks, put them on the table and asked if we'd like to order.

'Give us five minutes,' I said, taking Nick's phone. Then to Jennifer:

'Are you all right?'

'Yes.'

'You left so suddenly,' I said.

Nick was staring at me and I looked past him to the pretty girl at the next table. The man had taken his hands off her long enough to stoke up on food. Needed the calories, I imagined.

'I saw those photographs you had,' Jennifer said down the line.

'I thought that was it.'

'Have you shown them to Nick.'

'That's what we're doing now.'

'What do you want, Alex?'

'Not what you're thinking.'

'Does he know I've seen them?'

'No.'

'Please don't tell him.'

'Of course not.'

'Will you give them to him.'

'Yes,' I said, 'but—'

'You don't know if there are others.'

'That's right.'

'If there are, could you get them?'

'That's doubtful.'

'Could Nick?'

'Possibly.'

'Thank you, Alex,' she said. 'Will you put Nick on again, please?'

I handed the phone across the table. They talked for a moment or two then he said goodbye and broke the connection, slowly replacing the mobile in his pocket as he watched me.

'What was that all about?' he asked.

'I saw her yesterday,' I said. 'She wasn't ... feeling well. I wanted to make sure she got back home all right.'

I wasn't sure he believed me but I didn't think what his mother and I had been up to was uppermost in his mind at that moment. He gestured towards the envelope.

'Does she know anything about...?'

'No,' I said. 'Nothing. Had you any idea they were watching you?'

'None.'

'Who's your control?'

Nick glared at me and lowered his voice. 'I have contacts with them,' he said through his teeth. 'I don't work for them. I don't have a *control*.'

I tapped the envelope. 'I think they'd beg to differ.' I said.

'They said I was to let them know if you contacted me,' he said, as if hoping this might give him some sort of levererage.

'So they've approached you since.' He looked at me uncertainly and I added, 'Since Standing died.'

'Keep your voice down for Christ's sake, Alex!'

'Well, have they?'

He hesitated. 'They suggested ... advised me to ... *disentangle* myself.'

'I bet. And can you? Will the lady go quietly?'

There was a pained expression on his face.

'There might be a problem,' he said. He didn't elaborate.

He laid a proprietorial hand on the envelope. 'Are you giving me these?'

'Yes. But you have to realize there might be others. Charlie had them in his briefcase. I don't know why.' I might have suggested to him that they were there to add colour to Charlie's otherwise monochromatic life but the notion seemed in bad taste just at that moment.

'He gave them to you?'

'Not willingly.'

'Then he's not someone I could...'

'Trust?' I suggested when he didn't seem able to lay his tongue on the right word. 'No, he's not.'

I thought he might say something, ask me some questions, but perhaps he already had the answers. I remembered how he had phoned me the morning after Standing's murder, half-jokingly offering to alibi me. What he had been doing, of course, was looking to provide himself with one. But at least that suggested he had been unaware that they had considered framing me for the murder.

'Something else,' I said. 'Frederick.'

'How much do I know, you mean?'

'Yes.'

'Not much. Dad handled all that. When he died some people went to the house and took away all his papers. If anyone asked, I was told to say someone wanted material for a biography.'

It occurred to me that they couldn't even get their stories straight. 'Did anyone?'

'What?'

'Ask.'

Nick shook his head. 'No. We were told to forget about it and if anyone asked about Frederick just stick to the business.'

'Nothing about his early life?'

'No. Not that we knew much anyway.'

'And neither you nor George were curious?'

'That was part of the deal,' he said. 'That we helped each other. Now and later,' he added in case I hadn't understood.'

'Would you like some advice?' I asked.

He looked at me oddly, a half-smile coming to his lips as if he thought I was hardly in a position to dispense advice. I gave it to him anyway.

'Get out if you can, Nick. Show them you're not a horse to back. They've got others. They'll let you go if you don't make waves.'

His smile didn't waver and I knew then he wasn't going to take any advice from me. He'd already put his career in the balance but thought he could handle the weights. I guess hubris is the same the world over; the photographs had given him a nasty turn but I could see he thought he could still control the situation.

'Anyway,' I finished, 'whatever you decide, you'd be advised to keep away from the lady.'

He was about to say something when the waiter came back. It was opportune; I didn't want to hear what it was.

'We're not eating after all,' I told the waiter, getting up. I looked back at Nick as I turned to leave. 'Don't forget your envelope,' I said.

~

I bought a fresh change of clothes then caught a train at Olympia and rode to Hackney Central. I had only one thing left to do. I was too early for my appointment at the Civic Offices so I filled the time by writing to Olena. I asked for her to arrange for someone to drop by my house, keep it clean and pick up the post. I asked her to pay my bills until I got back; Father's scruples or not, it gave me a certain satisfaction to know that Maitland money would help finance my absence. I told her where my will was if she didn't hear from me within a year. I dropped the letter in the post. It was better than phoning; Olena couldn't argue with a letter.

The one thing that had been missing from the papers David Griffiths had left for me was the name of the person who had denounced my grandfather to the OGPU. It was the one revelation that Michael Standing had danced around, never quite bringing himself to voice. I knew why, of course. The name wasn't there but it had been plain enough nonetheless.

Nastasiya had denounced him.

The village Troika under Zaretsky had discussed the classification of Nastasiya's family as Kulaks. It would have been impossible for her not to know. The fact that she and my father and Frederick had left the Ukraine at the same time was evidence enough. Frederick had been in a position to provide any evidence that Zaretsky had profited personally from the grain seizures. After all, he had been skimming the payments himself and falsifying the evidence would not have been a problem. Perhaps that is what the rail movement orders had been. But whether it had been a fabricated charge hardly mattered. Innocent of the charge of profiteering or not, he was guilty of so much else it was impossible to sympathize. I searched myself for a sense of satisfaction in the knowledge that his own wife had betrayed him to his own Party — in revenge for what he had done to her family — but I found none. But neither could I condemn her.

Ms Fairchild was custodian of the borough records and I had rung while waiting for the cab into town and had arranged to meet at two. I had been told that she was a local historian and had studied and written on the area.

She was sitting at her desk in her office with a map already spread across the desktop and a smile softening her rather long and otherwise severe face. Behind her spectacles there was a glint of expectation animating her eyes, as if she were counting on my turning up to be a possible outpost of interest in an otherwise quotidian day.

We shook hands across the desk.

'I've pulled a few things together,' she said, inviting me to sit. 'If I'd had more time...'

I apologised for the short notice I had given her. 'I'm passing through London,' I explained. 'It was a spur of the moment thing.'

She gave a small grunt as if impulses were a species of beast with which she was unfamiliar.

'Well, let's see what we can do, shall we? What exactly was it you were looking for?'

I told her what I knew — repeating what I'd said over the phone — and wondered if it might still be possible to pinpoint the site of the house.

'Certainly, to within a few yards anyway,' she said. 'Although you won't find it looks much like it did before the war. The whole area was bulldozed, the damage being what it was. It was redeveloped as soon as building restrictions were lifted. The main problem then, of course, was the scarcity of building materials.'

'I'm aware of that,' I said. 'What I really wanted to do was just take a look.'

She stood up, peered down at the map a moment before twisting it in my direction. She ran a finger along a street to the east of London Fields.

'Here. This was number forty-seven.'

I looked at the small rectangle on the map, one of dozens.

'Now here,' she said, pulling up a second map printed on clear plastic and over-laying it on the first, 'is the modern street plan of the same area. You see the street is no longer extant. It was shortened by this new intersection. What used to be the road now stops a hundred yards to the south. What was Lavender Gardens was incorporated into the surrounding streets once the old terrace was demolished. Forty-seven would have been at this point here.'

She rested her finger on the spot where Nastasiya had died.

'And are there any council records to show who was living here before the war? Besides the census records, I mean. Or can you access those?'

'Sorry,' she said,' they're kept confidential for a hundred years. They're only made available for authorized projects. But there are the usual rateable assessments.' She brightened. 'Utility records and such although we did lose an awful lot of records during the war, you understand. I did a little research before you arrived and fortunately what hasn't been computerized is stored here.'

'Yes?' I prompted.

'The dwelling was registered to a Frederick Maitland as an owner-occupier and his wife, Nesta—

'Nastasiya,' I said.

'Nastasiya. The last records we have show there were two children, Peter and George.'

'Peter was my father,' I said.

'Oh?' She looked at me uncertainly for a second, not knowing perhaps, given that the house had been destroyed by a bomb, whether to offer her congratulations or her condolences.

'Were there were no other occupants?' I asked to relieve her of her dilemma. 'I've got the name William Robinson...' But I already knew the answer — William Robinson may have died in the war but not at Nastasiya's house.

'No,' Ms Fairchild continued. 'I checked back to when Frederick Maitland bought the property in nineteen-thirty-three. The previous owner was one Reginald Barker. He had owned it since nineteen-nineteen.'

'I see.'

'What I have been able to do, though, is to find some details of the raid in which the house was destroyed.' She smiled hesitantly, almost by way of apology as if in her enthusiasm she had exceeded her brief.

'The raid took place on December twenty-ninth, nineteen-forty,' she said. 'It was a landmark raid as it was the biggest the Luftwaffe had launched against London up to that date. It lasted more than six hours and consisted of a huge amount of incendiary devices. The object was to start a firestorm and destroy the heart of the capital. It was touch-and-go for a while whether they'd succeed. Much of the City was destroyed although, rather miraculously, St Paul's survived with relatively little damage.'

'I think I've seen a documentary on it,' I said, remembering it with surprise. It had been screened on television quite recently with a sort of re-enactment with testimonies from those involved. They had given a few personal stories to give the whole thing the human touch — much in the way Standing might have done. I had had no idea that that had been the night Nastasiya had died. Finding out now, I experienced a retroactive shiver.

'Of course,' she said, 'the damage here was peripheral to the main raid... Stray bombs mostly, but nonetheless lethal for that.'

'No,' I said, 'I suppose not.'

'I don't know if you'd be interested,' she said, rummaging around on the desk, 'but there is a man who worked in the Auxiliary Fire Service at the time. That particular night, in fact. His name's Billy Sampson. He's getting on a bit now, of course, but he's always glad of the opportunity to talk about those days. I know him quite well. If you have the time and would like to talk to him, Mr

Maitland, I could give him a ring and see if he'd be willing to see you?

The small front gardens to either side of Billy Sampson's terraced house had been given over to concrete and parked cars. Only Billy's remained intact, a low redbrick wall and single wrought-iron gate making a neat bastion against late twentieth-century incursion. A flagstone path led to the porch and front door and in the garden itself a variety of containers sat among pea-shingle, empty now with autumn's remnants of dried stems and bare-fingered shrubs, all that was left of the season.

I rang the bell and waited, expecting, I suppose, an old man to make his weary way to the door, stooped by the years and his memories. I was wrong, though. Old he might have been but there was no stoop and seemed to be no trace of weariness in his demeanour.

'I was seventeen,' he said over the tea he had already prepared for my visit.

We were sitting in his front room, snug and warm with the gas fire glowing beneath a mantle crammed with pictures that appeared to span the years since the war. Billy sat in a chair that looked to have spent a lifetime moulding itself to his body. That was one of wire and gristle, small-boned with a pugnacious face that led, chin first. He had shaved that morning although, judging by the odd sprout of missed hair, hadn't wasted too much time over the chore.

'I was waiting to go into the army,' he said, 'just as soon as I was old enough. While I was waiting I joined the Auxiliary Fire Service. There were never enough 'ands after the Blitz started.'

He poured the tea and pushed a plate of biscuits in my direction, digestives that looked as if they were more accustomed to the damper atmosphere of his kitchen. I picked one up and lost half before it reached my mouth.

'We were taking a pasting every night back then,' he went on. 'When I got my call-up papers and went for the medical they said I was unfit and told me to stay where I was. Deaf in my right ear. My old man was pleased 'cause 'e never wanted me to go in the army, anyway. My brother had joined up, see, and was killed at Dunkirk right off the bat. The old man and mum didn't want to see me to go the same way.'

'You must have been disappointed,' I suggested.

'I was well out of it,' he replied flatly. 'Not that it felt like it while we was catching it from Jerry, of course.' He topped up his mug from the pot. 'Funny thing was the old man 'ad been the one who'd turned me deaf. Heavy-handed. Gave me a clout when I was a nipper and perforated the eardrum, 'im a copper, too.'

'Your father was a policeman?'

'Yeah. They wouldn't look twice at the likes of 'im now. Be out on 'is ear now the way 'e carried on. Law unto 'imself. Could do with a few more like 'im if you ask me. Give the tearaways round 'ere summat to think twice about.'

'Did Ms Fairchild tell you what I'm looking for?'

Billy looked momentarily perplexed as if I had suddenly started speaking in another language. Then he laughed.

'Oh, you mean Fanny,'

'Fanny?'

'Fanny Fairchild. Her name's Frances but I calls 'er Fanny.' His eyes gleamed and I thought that Fanny probably had to keep on her toes as far as Billy Sampson was concerned.

'Lavender Gardens, wasn't it?' he asked. 'What number again?'

'Forty-seven.'

He scratched at his head. 'Numbers don't mean much now. Street names I can remember and some of the people. Still live here, some of 'em. Those that ain't dead. Fanny said it was your father's house.'

'My father lived there as a boy. Until they were bombed out. He'd already joined the RAF by then, though.'

'Drink up,' he said, 'and we'll 'ave a walk round and take a look. It's the only way I can remember these days.'

'It's not far?'

'Nah. 'alf a mile. If you're up to it, that is.'

Billy led me along the pavement at a rate I had difficulty in matching. 'I remember the first big raid,' he said. 'September, nineteen-forty. Till then they'd concentrated on the airfields and the docks. It was September seventh. They came over just before five o'clock in the afternoon and started pasting the East End. It went on for twelve hours. There must 'ave been 'undreds of the buggers. Terrible it was. Not that we wasn't expecting it, just that when it finally 'appened it was a shock.'

'My father was a fighter pilot,' I said. 'Hurricanes. He told me a bit about the early days.'

'Bloody marvellous, they were,' Billy said. 'Weren't for them Jerry would've been all over us.' We turned a corner. 'Just up 'ere,' he said.

I suppose I had been expecting a sudden rush of realization as to where I was. But it was just an ordinary London street, nothing like the vista of bombed carnage I had always pictured.

He led me past two blocks of 1950s redbrick flats, boxy and flat-roofed with rows of uniform windows, like a giant Lego construction left by the roadside.

'All them are new,' Billy said, flinging an arm at the flats, eighty years of life giving him a relative perspective on modernity. 'The 'ouses that stood there all copped it 'round Christmas time as far as I recall. Forty-seven, you said?'

I looked at the numbers and saw that all the odd numbers were on the other side of the road. They'd changed, of course, with the coming of flats and now ran out at an intersection before number forty-seven. The street beyond had another name.

'You know the date?' Billy asked me, looking around him as if he might spot the wing of a Heinkel bomber or a the casing of an old RC 500 shell he could use as an aide-mémoire. 'Trouble was, they was comin' over every night. They'd switched to night bombin' by then to avoid our fighters.'

'Ms Fairchild — Fanny — said it was likely to be December twenty-ninth, nineteen-forty.'

'I remember that one,' he said. 'That was the night they used incendiaries down the Mile. They came over in waves till the 'ole bloody sky was alight.' He cocked his head at me. 'What about a name?'

'Maitland,' I said. 'He was overseas but his wife was in the house. She was killed.'

'Maitland ... Maitland...' Billy repeated.

I looked over the rebuilt street.

'There was a small child. A boy,' I said. 'He survived.'

He didn't reply and I looked back at him.

Billy Sampson had gone white. He stared at me in horror before quickly looking away. He muttered under his breath but I didn't catch what he said.

'I'm sorry?' I said.

'December the twenty-ninth, nineteen-forty.' he finally said again.

The blood had not returned to his face and I could see a faint tremor in his right hand as he brought it to his chin, wiping at something that wasn't there. 'Number forty-seven.'

'Do you remember it?'

'Little kid,' he said. 'Weren't cryin'. Not a tear. Just kept talkin' to 'er. All the time, talkin'.'

'Do you want to sit down?' I asked. He didn't look well and I was afraid I'd brought back memories he'd rather have forgotten.

'Could do with a drink,' he said. 'An' that's the truth. There's a pub down the road.' He looked up at me wanly and quickly away again. 'It's been so long I didn't think anyone would ever come to ask about it.' He bit his lip and looked at me sideways. 'There's summat I'd better tell you,' he said.

30

The pub stood on the corner of the street, a narrow bar with a handful of tables, a few barstools and a brass rail for those who didn't want to use either. The barman greeted Billy by name as we walked in and reached for a pint glass before being asked. I got the same for myself and, after paying, took a chair opposite Billy where he had gone to sit at a table. He was still looking shaky.

'You remember that night,' I said as I sat down.

Billy took a long pull at his beer and nodded, a little colour coming back to his cheeks.

'We'd missed the worst of it. They'd been after the Mile but we caught a few strays from some stragglers. One was a direct 'it just down the street. Middle of the terrace gone just like that. Number forty-seven must 'ave been across the road. The downstairs front was taken out by the blast. Everythin' on top just came down on it. These weren't incendiaries but there'd been fire, just not so much as you'd expect. Jerry used to carry all sorts so you'd never knew what you were goin' to get from one night to the next. We got in about dawn — light enough to see, anyway. They'd doused the whole place down but it was still smoulderin'. The all-clear sounded and there was always this dead silence after the siren stopped. Like a heartbeat, before you started breathing again and noise started. Eerie, it was. Always 'appened.'

He drank some more beer. 'That was when we 'eard 'im. The kid. Not cryin', like I said, but just sort of chunterin' away to 'isself. We'd been scramblin' about next door so we climbed over the rubble and saw the legs. Just sticking up in the air they was.'

'Legs?'

'Almost comical it would 'ave been if 'e 'adn't been dead.'

'It was a man?'

''e must 'ave been comin' down stairs when the blast hit 'im. Probably fell and the roof sort of caught 'im 'ead first as it came down. I nipped up the stairs while the others were diggin' 'im out.' Billy gave me a quick smile, colour in his face again and beer foam giving him a ghostly moustache. 'I was only a runt of a thing so I was the one to do any climbin' about. Least likely to bring any more rubble down on the others, see. Back of the 'ouse was almost untouched. Funny 'ow a bomb would take a place sometimes.'

'And you found the boy upstairs?'

'Yeah. And a lady. The kid was sittin' on the bed next to 'er, talkin' like I say.'

'That would have been my grandmother,' I said. 'She was dead?'

He gave me another quick, shifty look and drank some more beer. 'Yeah.'

'But you must have seen dead bodies before,' I said. 'I mean, some of the sights must have been... Had she been badly injured?'

'No,' Billy said. 'Not a mark on 'er as far as I could see. She was just lyin' on the bed. The kid was sitting next to 'er, holdin' 'er 'and.'

'What had killed her, then? The blast, I suppose?'

He looked at me once more but this time held my eyes. I could see he was steeling himself not to look away.

'She'd been strangled,' he said.

'*Strangled*?'

I almost yelped it and several of the other drinkers looked round at us curiously.

Billy nodded and lowered his voice. 'There was this coloured scarf pulled tight round her neck. A ligature my old man called it.'

I just stared at him.

'I picked up the kid and took 'im down the stairs,' Billy said. 'I told the other blokes what I'd found. They'd dug the bloke out who'd been buried 'ead first by then and said I'd better fetch my old man. So that's what I did.'

'You called the police?'

'No,' he said. 'I got my old man. The old bugger 'ad been up all night and only just gone to bed and 'e didn't want to get out again. I said I'd go down the station then, so in the end he got up and got dressed again.'

'What was he?' I asked. 'Uniformed?'

'Nah. 'e was plain clothes. A detective-sergeant. They was short-'anded in the war so most likely they would 'ave got 'im out on it anyway.'

He'd finished his beer so I bought him a second, standing at the bar while I waited for it feeling a peculiar sense of guilt in never knowing what had really happened to Nastasiya. I took Billy's pint back and he took a small sip and sat back his the chair.

'I took my old man back to the 'ouse,' he said. 'People was comin' up from the shelters by then goin' 'ome to see if they still 'ad one to go to. There was a few of the neighbours 'round about and my old man asked 'em who lived there. They told 'im the woman's 'usband was overseas. 'e got some of 'em to look at the bloke we'd found on the stairs though I don't s'pose 'is own mother would 'ave recognized 'im the state 'e was in. No one said they knew 'im.'

'Didn't he have any papers on him?'

'Yeah, I'm comin' to that. They was Russian. Least, that's what my old man said. We used to get 'em over in the docks sometimes but they never used to come this far. Weren't in the war, then, neither. Leastways, not on our side.'

'Do you remember his name?'

'Nothing we could make out. All 'is documents were in that funny Russian writin'...'

'Cyrillic,' I said.

'Yeah. That's what it was. Anyway, they'd shored up the landing by then so my old man and one of the others climbed up to take a look at the woman. When they brought 'er down there wasn't no scarf round 'er neck. My old man 'ad taken it off.'

'Should he have done that?'

'Told me 'e'd solved it. Bloke on the stairs 'ad obviously broken in, lookin' for summat to steal, found the woman and strangled 'er. Then, just as 'e's leavin', the 'ouse gets it. Rough justice, my old man said. No point wastin' time lookin' for anyone else. And no point upsettin' 'er poor 'usband who's off fightin' for 'is country. Bad enough that the poor bastard's lost 'is wife.' Billy looked at me apologetically. 'Excuse the language, 'im bein' your granddad an all.'

'Did your father even record that fact there'd been a murder?'

'Told me not to say nothin' about it. Told the others to keep shtum, too.'

'So no one ever said anything?'

'No one ever crossed my old man if 'e could 'elp it,' Billy Sampson said.

'And there was no evidence of there being a crime at all.'

'Only the scarf and the Russian bloke's papers.'

'What happened to them?'

Billy looked at me across the table.

'I've still got 'em,' he said.

He had kept them in a small cardboard box at the bottom of a cupboard. A place where he wasn't likely to come across them, in much the same way, I suppose, as he had secreted them away in his memory; something he did not want to think of too often yet something he could not bring himself to completely forget.

'It was wrong, I know,' he said, handing me the box. 'I found 'em after my old man died. I don't know why he kept 'em. I knew what they was, of course. It should 'ave been looked into properly. It was murder. Even a kid like me could see that.'

'Your father was a detective,' I said. 'I'm sure he did what he thought was best.'

'Best for 'im, perhaps,' Billy said. ''e could be an idle bugger sometimes.'

'It was a busy time for everyone,' I said, wondering why I was trying to defend the man. 'He was probably right. This Russian sailor probably did kill her. Why else would he have been there? And if your father had investigated it, how far would he have got? They were both dead. The house had been bombed...'

'Yeah,' Billy said. 'But it's been on m' conscience all these years. The little kid... And her 'usband not bein' told.'

'Her husband has been dead a long time,' I explained. 'And he married again before the end of the war.'

'What about the boy? What would 'e 'ave been ... your uncle?'

'Yes. My uncle George. Did very well for himself.'

'Good,' Billy said, holding on to that. 'That's summat at least.'

I started to open the box but he put a hand on it.

'Take it,' he said. 'She was your family. Take it with you. It'll be a weight off my mind, I don't mind tellin' you.'

~

It wasn't until I was in the airport bar awaiting my flight that I had the opportunity of examining the contents of Billy Sampson's box. I bought myself a double scotch and found a table well away from the other drinkers and settled myself in the chair before I took the box out of my bag.

The scarf was brightly coloured, a little faded with age or perhaps from washing. It was the kind of head scarf I might have pictured on sturdy peasant women as they trudged out of a village for a day's labour in the fields. Nastasiya's, I assumed. But that had hardly been Nastasiya's life. She had married young to a rising Bolshevik, an agent of the Cheka.

Beneath the scarf lay a few papers, cheap and grey under their fading print, the paper was now brittle and threatening to crack as I turned the pages. They were identity papers, showing a photograph of a man who, at first glance, I could not recognize but with a name in Cyrillic that I could. It was a name I had asked Daryna to write out for me in her own language while we had sat around my table. It had belonged to Aleksander Zaretsky.

There was nothing else much: a few Russian coins he must have had in his pocket, a scrap of paper with the address of Frederick and Nastasiya's house written in English... How he had travelled from Russia I could only imagine. In December 1940 the non-aggression pact Stalin had signed with Hitler was still in force and I assumed Russian ships would not have been welcome in British ports. The files Michael Standing had retrieved from the archives in Moscow and the Ukraine showed that Zaretsky had been purged from the Party and, presumably, had been sent to some God-forsaken labour camp. If there had been any kind of justice he would have been set to work alongside some of the Kulaks he had helped arrest and deport - if any had been lucky enough to survive. "Lucky", of course, was a subjective assessment on my part.

If that had been the case, I could only hope that the irony of the situation had troubled his policeman's mind. Some of the other papers that David Griffiths had secreted with the leather-bound notebook in his wardrobe had suggested that Zaretsky's case had later come up for review. One can only suppose that even within a hierarchy as blinkered by ideology and quasi-religious orthodoxy as the Bolsheviks had been, some must have realized that war was inevitable. Stalin's purges of the army had seriously weakened their capacity for defence and men once purged but who had remained loyal to the Party were rehabilitated. As Michael Standing had once remarked, by then it had been all hands to the pump.

Zaretsky had been given a second chance at some kind of life.

If it wasn't easy to guess how he had managed to get to England, it was easier to surmise why he had come. When pressed by my child's curiosity, my father had always told me that they had expected Aleksander to follow them and that his mother had said that he must have been arrested, shot or sent to a labour camp. But I now knew there had been something of the lie about it, either one that my father had constructed for my benefit or one he was passing on that had been made earlier for his. Nastasiya, it was clear, had known Zaretsky would never follow. She had married again too soon, married, I supposed, because she had assumed him dead. But eight years later he had come to find her. He had used that second chance of life to track down the people who had denounced him — his faithless wife and his one-time comrade Shostak.

I picked up the scarf and held it beneath my nose, burying my face in its soft folds.

Could I detect the faint trace of scent? There was *something* beyond my imagination, somewhere under the musty odours it had acquired after almost three-quarters of a century in a box. Or perhaps it was the tang of sweat on the hands of the man who had tightened it around Nastasiya's throat I could smell. Whichever it was, it was the closest I was ever going to get to her. Or to him.

I remained with the scarf in my hands for a long time. Betrayal as a motive for revenge sat comfortably with me. It was something I could understand, something with which I could even sympathize. I wondered how long Nastasiya had nurtured a hatred for him, how she had planned to exact her revenge. It could not have been easy. To kill him as he slept would have meant forfeiting her own life and she had a young son to consider. The arrival of Shostak must have seemed a godsend to her. Had she set about seducing him, or had they just happened to fall in love? It must have been love, at least on Frederick's part, for he took her home and married her, albeit bigamously on Nastasiya's side. Somehow that fact jarred with everything else I had learned about Frederick's character. It would have been more in tune with the man if he had enjoyed the dalliance and then left her to her fate. I suppose the fact that he didn't spoke volumes for the kind of woman Nastasiya had been.

They must have planned it. Frederick had been benefiting financially from his handling of the grain sales he had helped seize and, no doubt, from his handling of the secret intelligence he was channelling, too. But, when the time came, he had abandoned all that as they had cut the ground from beneath Zaretsky's feet and thrown him to his own OGPU wolves. I had to admit that there was some poetic justice in that: an OGPU man fed to his own. I'm sure she had enjoyed the irony. I knew, because I enjoyed it and it was her blood that ran in my veins. She had avenged the betrayal of her family and must have thought she had got far enough away to escape the consequences. But secret police have long arms. They have even longer memories.

I still couldn't be sure what Frederick had been to her. Perhaps she had loved him. Perhaps in her world he represented something exotic, a foreigner from a land where life was free; perhaps he was just convenient, someone to use to exact her revenge. She *had* married him, but that might only have been part of the convenience. From what I had learned of Frederick I thought of him as a deeply unpleasant man, one who was willing to profit from the misery of others and betray anyone whose trust he shared. He could not have helped but know exactly what he was doing, working as he did with Zaretsky on the grain seizures ... the raids on the peasant villages ... the round-ups ... the interrogations ... the executions...

Eventually I put the scarf and the papers and coins back in Billy's box and wondered just where it all left me. Ultimately I was the product of a political zealot and a peasant girl, both capable of ruthless betrayal. Yet she'd brought Zaretsky's son, my father, out of the Ukraine with her, so she could not have seen the evils of the father when she had looked into the eyes of the boy. He had grown up but she had had another small son. Why they had not taken shelter when the raid began I could only guess. Perhaps she thought they were safe that far north of the City and the docks. Perhaps crowding in the dark with strangers brought back other fears of peasant villages in another war. And even Zaretsky, for his part, on his murderous reappearance out of the dark London streets under the rain of German bombs, had let George live. It might have been that he had seen the boy and couldn't bring himself to kill an innocent. I find it easier to believe that George had been sleeping despite the raid and Zaretsky had had no idea that a child was in the house.

George had been luckier than he knew. He had survived the bomb that had wrecked the house, but only because he had survived Zaretsky first.

31

Charlie had been wrong about tropical sunsets. He'd wondered how many a man could look at before he'd want to blow his brains out. But Charlie had never been one for the tropics. He was a creature of dank streets, of shadow, of black and white.

For me, the sunsets never pall. Each one is different in its own way, so Charlie can keep his dank streets. Sitting on the terrace of a beach restaurant, a bottle of Safari beer in hand and with the spicy smells of your dinner cooking on the open grill is nice work if you can get it — even if you never had a choice.

Now I find I have a lot of time to think. Fine, you might say, except that a lot of what I think about is the same thing. The past should always be behind you, but now and again you do start to wonder whether it's caught you up. Sometimes, when I think I am being followed, I take some circuitous route through the back alleys of Stone Town until I realize my pursuer is nothing more than a man who happens to be going in the same direction. Having taken a sharp turn or two, though, long after I have managed to throw off my imaginary tail, I still find myself taking a roundabout way home. Old habits and paranoia are a volatile mix and one of the resulting intoxicants are hallucinations in which strangers become familiar and the familiar becomes sinister.

And, looking back, I have discovered that, at bottom, we were all boy scouts at heart. I wonder how many of us who found ourselves in intelligence work were there because of what we believed; wasn't it more about what we had always imagined? The games we had played in our heads as children and as adolescents had softened us up for that first approach. In reality the men who had recruited us were preaching to the predisposed. And so we joined the game, the adventure, the lark, and as we grew older we scouted for our replacements, looking for our younger selves in those that came our way, perpetuating the cycle, keeping the well of mistrust brimful for when next we had to refill our pitchers.

~

I finally translated the leather-bound notebook. After all, I had the time and the advantage over Griffiths in that I knew what I was looking for. There were still a few gaps and some of it was guesswork, but they had been educated guesses. It was a case of the jigsaw puzzle again: as more pieces slotted into place I came to realize I recognized the picture. Bill Vickery would have known what it was but it wasn't surprising that Griffiths and Standing had found it incomprehensible. Despite all of their delving into police files and intelligence reports they had never worked at the sharp end. They saw the bureaucracy, not the operation.

The notebook had consisted mainly of names and addresses — mystifying things to translate from an alien script until you realize what they are. Then there were the directions and the landmarks to look for, the bus routes and the train times, all written in such a way as to disguise their meaning. Lastly, and the pieces that finally formed the picture for me, were the detailed descriptions of dead-letter drops and the procedure to be followed when using them. When light at last dawned, I thought I had found the one substantial nail to secure Frederick's coffin. I hadn't, of course. Dead-letter drops are no more than secret post-boxes and Frederick could have used them just as easily for receiving rather than sending information. All that I *could* be sure of was that the procedure was clandestine. I daresay that in writing it in Ukrainian Frederick had thought that it would be safe enough, but to me it seemed like bad tradecraft. He should have committed it to memory, never have written it down.

First rule of espionage. But there are so many first rules one can be forgiven for forgetting some of them.

Why my father had the notebook I didn't know. I had always assumed it had come out of the bombed house in Lavender Gardens even though it showed no signs of the damage I'd found on my father's old letters. Billy Sampson told me that the back of the house had remained reasonably intact and so perhaps it had been found there, my father keeping it as some sort of hold over Frederick.

350

Alternatively, Frederick might have given it to my father to hold in trust for him. It might have been part of what the men who had searched Frederick's papers had been looking for but, if so, it meant nothing now; old addresses, timetables and forgotten dead-letter drops were no sort of evidence. Now it was just a curio, lying in a drawer in the bedside table in my rooms.

It was four months after I left Nick in the restaurant in Kensington that I heard he had been killed. I saw it on the BBC news web page. It was headlined: *Shadow Minister in Fatal Car Crash*. It had happened on the M3. Nick's BMW Roadster had hit the central reservation at speed, somersaulted the barrier and been hit by a lorry approaching on the other carriageway. Both he and his passenger had been killed outright. There weren't many details. He had been travelling back to London from his constituency where he had been spending some time during the Easter recess. Visibility had been good and the weather dry. Traffic was light. A driver who witnessed the crash said the BMW had been travelling too fast. No further explanation could be offered until after the post-mortem and an examination of the vehicle.

The English-language papers available were erratic and always several days out of date and so I spent the next days trawling the on-line editions of the dailies, afraid that Nick's passenger might have been Olena. I phoned her mobile number and, worryingly, there was no reply. Still loath to leave a number where she might contact me that could be traced, I left no message, feeling like a coward who couldn't see any further than the preservation of his own skin. Caught between apprehension for Olena's life and misery over Jennifer's loss, I might have contacted George. But somehow I convinced myself there was nothing I could usefully do. Finally, I ended up doing nothing at all.

Over the following days the papers featured the story, carrying decent obituaries of Nick that covered his political career and his background within the Maitland family. It wasn't until forty-eight hours after the accident that Nick's passenger was finally identified as Julia Standing.

I had half-expected the sky to fall in as soon as it had been made public that Julia Standing had been in Nick's car. But it didn't. Given that he was now dead, I suppose that it was thought there was little point in dragging up all the murky details. After all, they would

351

never make the story run far and it would have only been an exercise in muckraking. Tempting enough, perhaps, but I doubted that any newspaper owner or editor would think the benefits were sufficient to outweigh upsetting George. Or his money.

But then I realized I was looking at it from purely my own perspective. I was the only one who would have found the fact that Julia Standing had been with Nick significant. The papers merely noted that they had been friends since university days and that Nick had been a comfort to Julia Standing since she had suffered her loss — poor tragic Michael always being resurrected and included with the dead couple to make a rather uncomfortable trio. No one apparently found it curious that in all the coverage of Standing's murder the couple's close friendship with Nick had never been mentioned. To give the angle weight, many of Nick's friends were on hand to endorse the fact that he had proved a tower of strength for the unfortunate widow since the events of the previous November. Even the suicide of the prime suspect was brought in to quell any lingering doubts. Russian conspiracies and David Griffiths had been conveniently forgotten. Finally, as if to tie up all loose ends, George issued a statement to the effect that Julia had stayed with them for the few days Nick was down on his constituency work.

Olena, it was reported, was not available for comment.

A week passed before the autopsy findings and a report on the vehicle were released: no alcohol had been found in Nick's system although the car had been seen to be exceeding the speed limit. It was deemed that mechanical failure of the brakes was the probable cause of the accident. Within a day or two the media had moved on to other business.

I wasn't as quick to lose interest. Under other circumstances I would have given Charlie a call and asked him to find out what he could. That option seemed more or less out of court now, though. One or two of the Internet sites that encouraged wilder theories still manfully attempted to link the car accident with Standing and Griffiths' murder by the Russian security services, but I thought the proffered connections seemed too tenuous to swallow even for the kind of audience who were usually quite happy to feed on a diet of faked Moon landings and Palace involvement in the Death of Diana, Princess of Wales. Oddly enough, no one had linked poor wheezing Fielding's death to anything at all. Losers, it seems, continue the habit even in death. Had some imaginative soul ever discovered that he had known both Standing and Griffiths and had died prematurely at the end of *my* road, I suppose even I — and my absence — might have been dragged into the conspiracy, neatly squaring the circle with Nick and Julia and affording me my fifteen minutes of fame. On the whole, though, I was happy to settle for obscurity.

It was just the fact that the brakes of the roadster had been judged to have failed that disturbed. After all, George's man, Patterson, had little else to do these days other than make sure the family's cars were kept in optimum condition. It made me almost wish I'd been present to listen to the conversation over breakfast in George's kitchen when the coroner's report was released. I wondered how much George knew or suspected. There'd be no top job for Nick now and I didn't suppose there'd be much lustre left on the prospect of a peerage for George, either. Not so much a case of the sins on the father, more one of the grandfather.

32

I caught first sight of her as she came walking along the beach. She was wearing a fetching straw hat under which her hair fell loose, blowing in the breeze. Her thin short-sleeved top and white slacks were what one might expect but looked to me to have been carefully selected to draw any eye that happened to be available. She had a commodious designer bag slung over her shoulder and was carrying her sandals in one hand, slightly away from her slacks as if she didn't want to leave any unsightly marks on the pristine cotton. Her bare feet were scuffing through the powdery sand.

I was on the restaurant terrace, beer in hand — hardly surprising as I spent a lot of time there in much the same sort of pose. She was about twenty yards away when she saw me. She stopped abruptly and stared for a moment as if, although she knew it must be me, she couldn't quite believe it. Then she came on again, wearing a frown under the hat.

I jumped down off the terrace onto the hot sand. My feet were bare, too, and I wasn't wearing anything more than a pair of khaki shorts and a safari shirt. These days even *my* hair was long enough to be stirred by a breeze. I'd acquired a tan, although the scar on my forehead where I'd taken out my stitches shortly after I'd arrived always refused to darken. It had left a pale sickle-shaped scar that always reminded me of the mark of Cain.

'You look like an old hippie,' she said, stopping a few feet from me.

I would have laid odds that her first words were some sort of veiled criticism — would have been oddly disappointed if they had not — but she was smiling and the customary edge of frustration that invariably coloured her relations with me was absent.

'And you've lost weight,' she said.

'And you're still the most beautiful woman I know, Olena.'

She closed the few feet between us, kissed me on both cheeks and gave me a hug.

'How you've managed to avoid finding yourself a decent woman when you're capable of saying such nice things is a mystery to me, Alex. I think you've remained single on purpose.'

Perhaps I had. I'd never given it serious thought. It was a notion that spoke volumes — if I had ever been the kind of man who'd take the trouble to listen.

I took her hand and climbed the steps back onto the terrace. 'You're just in time for lunch,' I said.

We ate and drank beer, talking inconsequentialities and skirting the topic that sat at the head of our table like an uninvited guest. Finally, when I could step around the subject no longer I told her how sorry I was to hear about Nick.

She hadn't been able to talk to people for a couple of days after it happened but she had got the message I had finally plucked up the courage to leave. I had spoken to her briefly on the phone and told her that I'd write. I'd met an English couple who were returning to the UK and I had given them a letter to post once they were home. In it I gave Olena a number to call along with the proviso to use someone else's phone when she did. It was hardly foolproof but by then I was beginning to wonder if there was much point in my caution anymore. When she said she wanted to see me I told her to book a safari holiday in Tanzania with an extension to Zanzibar. Once she had reached her hotel on the island I told her to follow a set of instructions which would take her to where we would meet. I had expected some sort of outburst at the intricacies of the arrangements and the fact that she would necessarily be travelling in Africa on her own. To my surprise, though, she made no complaint.

It made me wonder if she had in some way become aware of what had been happening under her nose the previous year.

We spoke of Nick and, as if reading my mind, she said, 'That woman,' and made a sour face that suggested the very thought of Julia Standing left a bad taste in her mouth. 'How *could* he?'

I offered a neutral shrug to indicate that it wasn't anything to which I'd given much thought.

'Well,' I said, 'they'd known each other a long time. After her husband died...' I didn't try to finish, hoping she would recall the line the press had followed. Olena, though, gave me a look that would have made vitriol taste sweet.

'I think it was going on before her husband was murdered,' she said.

'Really?' I said, managing a modicum of surprise.

'Now I think of it, I can see there was someone else. He was always *too* considerate when there was someone else.'

'There were others? This time the surprise was genuine. I knew his brother, Oliver, had a reputation but I'd always thought of Nick as somehow too disinterested to be a womaniser. 'You never said.'

Olena wouldn't meet my eyes and I guessed that the infidelities in their marriage hadn't been confined to Nick's side of the bed.

'Did George and Jennifer know?'

'About the women? George, perhaps. I don't think Jennifer ever did. She wore rose-tinted glasses as far as Nick was concerned.'

'I mean about Julia Standing in particular. In the papers it said he'd taken her down to their place in the country.'

'She never stayed with them,' Olena replied contemptuously. 'They'd been at Nick's house.'

'Didn't George give a statement to the press saying she'd been staying with them before it happened?'

'Only because they pressured him to say so,' Olena said.

'They? Who?'

'How do *I* know?,' she complained. 'The Party, I suppose. Jennifer said they were stuck in George's office for hours the day after it happened.'

'You've seen Jennifer?'

'Don't look so surprised,' she said. 'It was after the funeral.' She looked at me pointedly. 'Your absence was noted, by the way. I had to make excuses for you. As a matter of fact,' she went on, 'Jennifer and I get on better now than we ever did when Nick and I were married.'

'Nick's death must have hit her hard.'

'You know how she felt about him,' Olena said. 'Actually she took it better than George did. It's broken him.'

Somehow that didn't come as a surprise to me.

'Poor George,' I said. 'All those grandiose schemes.'

Olena gave another of her contemptuous laughs and drank some more beer. 'She's left him, you know.'

'Who's left who?'

She looked heavenward with an expression of exasperation.

'*Jennifer*. She's left George.'

'Good Lord,' I said.

'You had a thing for her once, didn't you? When you were young.'

It was my turn to laugh. Even Olena's questions had barbs.

'Mummy told me.'

'Is there anyone who didn't know?' I asked.

'Nick,' she said.

'She's really left him?'

'I thought you'd be pleased.' When I didn't say anything she added, 'If you still feel the same you should come home and do something about it.'

'I don't know if I can,' I said.

'What? Come home or do something about it?'

'Both.'

'That friend of yours, Charlie whatever-his-name-is came round after Nick was killed.'

'To see you?'

'To offer his condolences, he said.'

'And to ask if you'd heard from me, I suppose. Did he ask if you knew where I was?'

'He told me you were in Africa.'

That gave me an uncomfortable moment, but I said, 'It's a big continent.'

'He said the next time we spoke to tell you that he'd sorted out that problem with your pension and that they've resumed payments.'

'He said that?'

'Yes. I checked with your bank account and it's going in every month again. Although how you ever manage to live on *that* I'll never know.'

'I get by,' I said, still assimilating what Charlie's message meant.

'How *are* you managing to live here, anyway?'

'I do a bit of guiding,' I told her. 'My Swahili was always pretty good from my years here so I sometimes pick up a little translation work. I even teach a little English,' thinking even as I said it that my time with Daryna hadn't been entirely wasted. 'It's surprising how cheap you can live when you put your mind to it.'

Olena gave me a look of sheer incomprehension.

'Here,' she said, hauling her bag up on to the table. 'if you need money,' and to my amazement she pulled out Grigori the Cossack doll, our father's old mascot.

'What on earth are you doing with that?'

She sat Grigori on the table. 'I always take him when I go abroad, just like Daddy did.' She smiled affectionately at the doll. 'Do you remember that logbook he used to fill in for him with all the countries he'd taken him to?'

'No.'

'Of course you do, Alex! It was like the flying log he used to keep. So I do the same. Besides, he's where I keep my emergency money.'

'Your what?'

Olena put her fingers on the doll's head and pressed something. The top of Grigori's head beneath his Cossack hat sprung open.

'Good God!' I said. 'I never knew he did that.'

'It was a *secret*.' She looked at me in triumph. 'Daddy said it was just between him and me.' She turned Grigori around so I could see the small compartment in his head and I felt the hairs on the back of my neck bristle. She put her fingers in and pulled out a tightly wound roll of banknotes. 'No one would ever think of stealing Grigori,' she said.

I barely heard her. For just a moment the roll of notes had looked like a roll of photographic film.

'If you need money...' Olena said.

'He took it everywhere?' I whispered.

'Yes, every time he flew to Europe. Even before he left the RAF, Mummy told me.' She looked at me. 'What's the matter, Alex? You look odd.' She ran her fingers around her neck wiping the beds of perspiration on her skin. 'It *is* hot,' she said. 'Where can I freshen up?'

I waved a hand across the restaurant towards the toilets, still thinking about the doll and the hidden cavity, about my father and Frederick's notebook.

I looked out across the sand to the sea and the dhows plying over water that sparkled with jewelled facets where the sun played on the swell.

The picture of my jigsaw was complete but it wasn't as pretty as the one of the dhows on the water. Somehow, I realized, Frederick had involved my father in his treachery. Unwillingly, I hoped, but how could one ever tell? He'd got out, I was sure of that, which was why he would never see Frederick again, but he must have spent his life on a knife-edge. I could only imagine what he had felt when he learned I had joined SIS.

Olena came back, smiling at me, the only member of my family who had turned out to be what she seemed. She picked up Grigori the Cossack.

'Do you need some money?' she asked.

'No,' I said, 'I'm fine.'

'I almost forgot.' She delved into the bag again and brought out a letter. 'From Jennifer,' she said and nodded meaningfully.

I took the letter and looked at the name on the envelope in Jennifer's neat, looping hand: *Alex Maitland*.

'So,' Olena asked, 'when are you coming home?'

I put the letter in the pocket of my safari shirt to read later. I looked across the table at Olena and smiled.

'Soon,' I said.

Printed in Great Britain
by Amazon